Also by DJ Geribo

The House at the Top of the Trees
Eddie Easel and the Case of the Missing Green
The Miracle Dog
Mouse Bound
Seven Storied Houses
Me & Them

All titles are available for purchase directly from BBD Publishing at www.BBDPublishing.com.

Selected titles are also available on Amazon in paperback and Kindle formats.

# The Mart

# The Mart

DJ GERIBO

BBD PUBLISHING ~ ALTON, NH

The Mart is published by:

BBD Publishing
P.O. Box 351
Alton, NH  03809

www.BBDPublishing.com

Book Layout and Editing by James J. Fontaine

Cover Design by Positively Creative Solutions, LLC based upon an original design and visual concepts of the author

Printed in the United States of America

10  9  8  7  6  5  4  3  2  1

Library of Congress Control Number:  2023950101

ISBN 978-0-9883068-7-5

# TABLE OF CONTENTS

## A MADNESS MOST DISCREET - A NOVEL

## FRIENDS, LOVERS, AND OTHER STRANGERS<br>- STORIES

# A Madness Most Discreet

# Chapter 1

Bitsy checked her reflection in the full-length mirror as she dressed for her interview at the A-to-Z Mart. The biggest employer in Campton, she wanted to shine and stand out from all of the other candidates who might be applying for the same job.

She smiled at herself in the mirror. She was confident that the freshly washed and ironed permanent press pale orchid Easter suit she chose to wear for her interview was perfect. A cobalt blue butterfly pin brought out the blue in her eyes. She never liked her eyes and tried every way possible to enlarge them, doing her best to duplicate the instructions found in Glamour magazine. They looked to her like they should belong to someone more petite. Not that 5'7" was unusually tall but her height was above average and in school she towered over many of her 5' tall friends. Her grandpa Gordon on the other hand thought her eyes were beautiful.

"Debbie Reynolds' eyes, that's what you've got, sweetie. You are one lucky gal." He always followed up his compliments with a wink and a smile.

"Who is Debbie Reynolds?" Since Bitsy had never heard of Debbie Reynolds, she wasn't sure if this was a compliment. But then her grandpa followed that with what definitely sounded like a compliment, "Ah, a beauty beyond compare." Another wink and a smile.

Bitsy still wanted her eyes to look larger so she brushed her lashes with mascara and crimped them with an eyelash curler. She covered her slightly turned up lips with Violet Paradise, soft and bright without being too bold. She liked her lips because even when she wasn't smiling, she looked like she was and people would smile back at her. She added a soft pink blush to her cheeks. She had a few freckles on her nose which she tried to downplay - so that she didn't look too kiddish - by adding just a touch of powder to cover them. She wanted to be seen as a professional young woman who could do the job, any job, that she was given. She decided to clip her shoulder-length honey blonde hair back on the sides with white barrettes so that it wouldn't get in her way when she was filling out her job application.

Although she wanted to wear some fancy white pumps with a small heel, she had to walk a little more than half a mile from her home to the bus stop and then back again so she chose to wear her sneakers instead. She thought about carrying the pumps in a paper bag to change into when she got to the A-to-Z Mart, but she decided at the last minute to just go with the sneakers. She polished them with white sneaker polish so that they looked almost brand new, as long as it didn't rain. The last time she had polished them, she wore them to church and when she came out of church, it had started to rain. She and her parents usually went to breakfast at Connie's Diner right after church. Sitting in the booth with her mom and dad and while reading over the menu, Dora the waitress walked up to their table to take their order. Before her parents even got a chance to order their coffee, Dora, who didn't miss a thing, said, "I think your shoes sprung a leak, sweetie." White shoe polish from her wet sneakers was smeared all over the rust-colored tiles under her feet. She knew she might be taking a chance wearing them to her interview, but the weather man had said no rain today.

When Bitsy arrived at the A-to-Z Mart she asked for Mr. Howard. According to the newspaper ad, he was the man who would interview her. They were looking for cashiers. This would be Bitsy's first real job as an adult since she left high school just a year ago. Bitsy had no way of knowing this would be a year of so many other firsts.

Before this job all she had done was babysit; for Mrs. Klyski who had Bobby Jr. and Lisa, and for Mrs. Zimmerman, who had Belle. Belle was her favorite. The Klyski kids were okay, but at seven- and five-years-old, they had a lot of energy that overwhelmed Bitsy sometimes. Belle was three and perfect with curly dark brown hair, eyes that sparkled like glitter had somehow been sprinkled in them, and a pink bow mouth as adorable as if it was taken right off of a prettily-wrapped present. Belle would make pretend tea and they would sit at Belle's table with her dolls occupying the other two chairs and Belle would jabber on about nothing as if in a real conversation. Apparently, she was imitating her mother, Bitsy thought.

The woman at the service desk pointed to the far-right corner of the building.

"See that sign that says Boys. Then right behind that is Men's. And right after that is a door on the right that says Employees Only. You want to go in there and the first door on the left is Mr. Howard's office. He's the Assistant Store Manager. Good luck, hon." The woman, whose badge said Kitty, was rosy cheeked and had a smile that exposed two front teeth that crossed as if preparing for a duel, went back to work. She had a stack of papers in front of her and apparently was counting how many were in the pile. Bitsy wondered if she would like that kind of a job. There was probably a lot more responsibility working at the service desk. She imagined you had to know something about every department in the store to work at the service desk. Right now, working as a cashier sounded like enough of a challenge to Bitsy. Bitsy turned to wave and mouth 'thank-you' to Kitty but now she was on the phone.

Bitsy found the "Employees Only" door and hesitated for just a second before entering. After all, she wasn't an employee. Mr. Howard's door was closed so she knocked lightly. There was no answer. The shyness in her, as usual, directed her behavior. As Bitsy stood outside the door, she remembered how friendly she was when she was a tot and how she had talked to everyone. Too friendly, her mom said. She taught Bitsy how to be shy and withdrawn when she told her "You can't talk to everyone, people don't want you to bother them. Many grown-ups don't care for children. You'll make them angry." Although her mother had meant well just wanting to protect her daughter from all the evil that existed in the world, she couldn't possibly have known how her words would be misinterpreted by the five-year-old Bitsy. Bitsy loved talking to people, sharing stories with them, mostly made up. To her they enjoyed her chatter, even laughing and exclaiming how adorable and intelligent she was for such a young girl. How could she have been so wrong? She thought they liked talking to her but their smiles, she decided, were lies. According to her mom, they were angry. Her mother's words had crushed little Bitsy – she withdrew into herself and decided right then that she would never talk to strangers again. And she kept her word, right into adulthood.

But now, at nineteen, Bitsy decided that since this was a new place and no one knew her here she was ready to be herself, her true self, that little five-year-old who was bold and daring and spoke to strangers. She knocked again, loudly and forcefully. The metal door stung her knuckles a little.

"Come in."

Bitsy turned the doorknob and opened the door to Mr. Howard's office. The office was small and brightly lit overhead with two rows of fluorescent lights. The gray linoleum floor, like the flooring in the store, was scuffed and stained. She wondered if anyone ever mopped it. A scrunched-up piece of paper and a Milky Way candy bar wrapper sat on the floor next to the wastepaper basket. The only furniture in the room, besides Mr. Howard's rolling secretary's chair with arm rests and a hard-backed conference guest chair, was Mr. Howard's gray metal desk, a beige two-drawer filing cabinet, and a 3-shelf black metal bookcase that was piled with binders and an assortment of loose papers. There wasn't room for anything else, or as grandpa Gordon might have said, 'barely enough room to change your mind'.

When Mr. Howard stood up and pointed to the chair for Bitsy to sit, the lights reflecting off the surface of his smooth, shiny head nearly blinded Bitsy for just a second. A short stout man who was apparently wearing a shirt that Bitsy guessed was at least two sizes too small due to the stretch marks around the buttonholes, Mr. Howard looked at Bitsy over the tops of his thick black-framed glasses. His smile was quick and short-lived, impatient almost. Bitsy was glad she had worn her sneakers or she would have towered over him.

"You must be Betsy Gordon. I'm Mr. Howard, Assistant Manager."

"Yes, hi, I'm Bitsy… I'm Betsy Gordon. Hi, Mr. Howard. So nice to meet you." She extended a hand but pulled it back quickly when Mr. Howard sat down and busied himself with papers on his desk. Bitsy continued to stand.

"Have a seat, Miss Gordon."

"Thank you." Bitsy sat in the chair directly across the desk from Mr. Howard. She scanned his desk top that was almost completely covered with various piles of papers and folders filled with more papers. A framed photo on the corner of his desk showed a woman who was nearly bursting out of her dress and a boy and girl, Bitsy guessed around ten and twelve-years-old, likewise pushing at the seams of their too-small clothes. A sign on his desk, right in front of Bitsy, said Edward Howard, Assistant Manager; except it was abbreviated to fit on the sign so it read, Ed Howard and underneath, Asst. Mgr. A phone, a tape dispenser, several pens, a stapler, a day-to-day calendar, and a caddy holding additional pens and pencils added to the chaos on the top of Mr. Howard's desk. Most of the items had the A-to-Z Mart logo on them. Bitsy wondered if Mr. Howard walked through the stationary aisle and pulled boxes of pens, tape, staples, and whatever other supplies he needed if he felt like it. She wondered if he was part owner of the store and so perhaps could take whatever he wanted whenever he wanted.

"Do you have a resume?" Mr. Howard asked.

"Oh, no, sir. You see this would be my first real job. I've only babysat, that's the only other job I've ever had." Mr. Howard looked down at some papers on his desk.

"Besides," Bitsy continued, "the ad didn't say anything about a resume or experience or anything."

"Oh, right, yes, that's fine. It would be to your advantage if we didn't have to train you, that's all. Did you fill out an employment application?"

"No, I did not. I just got here and I asked for you. I called and they said to come at 2."

"Yes, well, why don't you fill this out, Miss Gordon, before we go any further." Mr. Howard handed Bitsy a clipboard with an employment application clipped to it.

Bitsy took the clipboard and started to stand, not sure if she should leave and fill out the paperwork at home or maybe go into the hall outside the office or fill it out right there in Mr. Howard's office.

"Right here, or should I go…" Bitsy pointed to the door, unsure if Mr. Howard wanted her to sit in his office while she filled out the application.

"Oh yes, that's fine, just fill it out right here."

Bitsy searched for the pen in her purse, glad that she had remembered to bring one. The majority of the application was easy enough to fill out and included space for her name, address, and schooling information. She hesitated when she got to 'Previous Experience' and wondered if she should give the names of the two people she babysat for. She decided to ask Mr. Howard, who was now focused on several papers he was reading and writing notes on.

"Excuse me, Mr. Howard, I was wondering, should I put my babysitting jobs here?"

"Oh yeah, sure. We can use them as references for you."

"Oh, okay." Bitsy wrote down the two names and their addresses and tried to recall their phone numbers. She could only remember Mrs. Zimmerman's phone number. She really never called either of them, they called her when they needed her to babysit. She quickly filled out the rest of the form and went back to Mrs. Klyski's information but still could not remember her phone number. She double checked all the information she had written on the form before handing it to Mr. Howard.

"Ahem, Mr. Howard, sir? I finished but I can't remember one phone number so if it's okay, I'll call you when I get home with that number, okay?"

"Sure, no problem." Mr. Howard seemed to be figuring out a problem and Bitsy felt like she was bothering him just being there. His deeply wrinkled forehead looked like it had plump worms spread across the middle. He rubbed at them, forcing them to wriggle across his shiny brow. Bitsy checked her watch to make sure she had come at the right time. If she had arrived too early and he was busy with a project, well, it would make sense that he would be working on it and she was interrupting him while he was trying to work. But it was 2:15 and she was here on the dot at 2pm, the time of her appointment.

Mr. Howard put his head back down and was concentrating on his papers. Bitsy sat quietly and waited. She thought maybe she should get up to leave – maybe he forgot she was there and she could just sneak out without disturbing Mr. Howard. She pushed her chair back and got ready to stand. The metal chair legs screeched on the floor and Mr. Howard was pulled back into the interview with Bitsy.

"Okay then Miss ah… Gordon." He glanced at her application. "We'll call you soon."

"Okay. Oh, and I'll call you like I said with the phone number of Mrs. Klyski, one of the ladies I babysit for, the one whose number I couldn't remember."

"Oh, yeah, right. Just call the service desk and tell them who you are and give them the information. And thank you for coming in today." Mr. Howard half-stood and extended his hand, again briefly looking at her over his glasses.

Bitsy stood up and took Mr. Howard's cool, damp hand, and shook it firmly. Her grandpa Gordon always said a firm handshake was the sign of an honest person. Bitsy wanted Mr. Howard to know that she was honest and trustworthy; two qualities Bitsy felt were important to have if you were a cashier and in charge of some of the store's money.

Mr. Howard sat back down and continued to pore over his papers. Bitsy let herself out of his office.

After exiting through the "Employees Only" door, Bitsy thought that since she was here, perhaps she should buy something because she might be working here and should support her almost employer. She didn't have a lot of money on her so she went up to the cash register to buy some gum or a candy bar. There were two people in line ahead of her. She looked for a Baby Ruth, her favorite, but decided instead on a package of Doublemint gum. She stood in line watching the cashier, thinking maybe she could pick up some tips.

His name tag said Lewis. His thick, wavy, dark brown almost black hair was a few inches past his ears, just touching his shoulders, parted in the middle and pushed behind his ears. He was about three or four inches taller than Bitsy. He kept his head down mostly as he scanned the items on the conveyor belt. His thick, dark mustache covered his mouth so Bitsy couldn't see too much of his lips. She was interested in lips — she didn't care for boys with too-thin lips. She noticed that the bad guys on TV were usually the ones who had thin lips. When she saw a boy who had nice full lips, she would imagine what it might feel like to kiss them. She liked the way Lewis looked so she hoped he had nice lips, too. She was next in line so she put her gum up with the space bar between her order and the person in front of her. When Lewis was finished with them, and Bitsy was next, she stepped up, directly across from him. He looked at her gum, took the space bar away, and lifted his head to look right at Bitsy.

Bitsy felt her cheeks rising in temperature and could almost see her blush reflected in Lewis' black wire-rimmed glasses that had slid forward on his nose so that his eyes were unobstructed. Although she had intended to rate Lewis' lips, she never got that far. She couldn't pull her eyes away from the most beautiful Prussian blue eyes she had ever seen. Or maybe they were peacock blue. She thought about her paint palette and tried to come up with the exact shade of watercolor paint that matched his eyes.

"Is that all?" He whispered so only Bitsy could hear. It was as if he had just whispered sweet nothings in her ear. She closed her eyes for just a second and imagined him kissing the back of her neck. When she opened her eyes, she looked directly at Lewis' mouth and then right back up into those eyes.

"Yes," she whispered back.

"Would you like a bag?" Again, the softness in his voice left Bitsy feeling light-headed, a feeling like nothing she had ever experienced before. She completely forgot what he had asked her as she looked again at the perfectly pouty lips beneath his moustache and back to his dazzling azure eyes. Or maybe they were ultramarine blue.

"Excuse me?" she somehow managed to form the words.

"I said, would you like a bag?" Quietly, intimately, like two lovers who know each other so well, have known each other for so long that they speak as one, he asked and she responded. A smile, a knowing, a secret shared. For her ears only.

"No, thank you." He picked up her gum and put it into her open hand. Their eyes locked and she started to walk away but he wouldn't let her go.

"Wait." Bitsy paused, waiting for the words, those three little words that every woman longs to hear from the man she loves. She held her breath.

"Yes?" She asked, hoping.

"You didn't pay for the gum."

*Dope, what a dope.* Bitsy snapped out of her dream and now the color again flew up to her cheeks.

"I'm sorry, um, how much is it?"

Lewis continued to stare into Bitsy's eyes and seemed as unable to pull himself away from her as she was unable to pull herself away from him. And in his now so familiar soft voice he said, "forty-five cents."

Bitsy opened her coin purse, took out fifty cents, and handed it to Lewis, making a point of touching his hand to see if they were cold and clammy.  They were not.

As Lewis put the fifty cents in his cash drawer and took out the five cents in change, Bitsy found her voice and announced to Lewis, "I might be working here. I just had an interview with Mr. Howard. My name is Bitsy." She wasn't sure why she told him "Bitsy" instead of "Betsy". There was something comfortable and safe about telling Lewis her pet name.

"Good luck, Bitsy." Lewis dropped the five cents into Bitsy's hand, touching his warm fingers to hers.

"Thank you, Lewis." And the lovers parted. Lewis put his head down to scan the next customer's purchases, and Bitsy slowly turned away, walking towards the exit and out the door to catch the bus ride home.

Bitsy barely remembered the bus ride, she was still at the A-to-Z Mart, still with Lewis. He whispered to her, "Do you want a bag?" She closed her eyes and listened to his voice, looking deep into his ultramarine blue eyes.  Or maybe they were cerulean. She imagined how his soft, warm, full lips felt on her neck. She opened her eyes just in time to see the bus approaching her stop. She jumped up, pulled the cord, and ran to the front of the bus. The driver gave her a look that said, "Why don't you wait until the last second?" She smiled and said, "Thank you." in her sweetest possible voice.

The walk home seemed longer than usual. But she was anxious to get home to see if Mr. Howard had called yet. Then she reminded herself that she just left the store. He probably wouldn't have decided to hire her in such a short time. Also, he probably had to talk to someone else about who he was going to hire. Or maybe not. She hoped she had made a good impression on him. She should have asked him when she would know about the job. Maybe she could call the store when she got home and ask the lady at the service desk if she knows when they will decide. Lewis. She couldn't get him out of her mind. She imagined herself working there already and she just got off from work and was on her way home, which she was. But then she would get up in the morning and go back to the A-to-Z Mart where she worked and see Lewis. She had to get the phone number for Mrs. Klyski and when she called with that information she would ask when they would make a decision about hiring her for the job. She should write a list of all her questions so that when she called the A-to-Z Mart she would have them ready. Lewis. What else, what else did she want to know about the job? She knew they were opened late a few nights a week so she hoped she didn't have to work late or she would miss her bus. Maybe her mom could pick her up on those nights if she had to work late. She'll ask that question, too; what are the hours? Lewis. She didn't even know how long lunch was or if she got a lunch break or any other breaks during the day. The ad just said 40 hours a week. And how much did it pay? She couldn't believe she didn't know that, but she figured it paid minimum wage. Still, she should have asked. She supposed those were the most important basic questions that she had and would write them down when she got home. Lewis.

# Chapter 2

Bitsy walked directly to the phone, found a notebook and a pen, and looked through her parents' address book that had phone numbers of all their close friends and relatives. She thought about getting her own address book now since she will probably make some new friends. She'd put that on her list of things to buy when she got her first paycheck. Of course, a car would be on that list but for something that extravagant she would have to pay for it over time.

Bitsy wrote "Questions for Mr. Howard at the A-to-Z Mart" at the top of the paper. She listed, as she remembered them, the questions that she had thought of while walking home. Also, it might be a good idea to carry a small notepad in her purse so that when she had these kinds of thoughts, she could write them down immediately. Question #4 was Mrs. Klyski's phone number. She looked under "K" in the address book, found the number for Klyski and jotted it down. Fortunately, she had written down the number of the A-to-Z Mart; she was sure the newspaper with the ad had been thrown out. Her dad tossed the newspapers as soon as he finished reading them.

She picked up the phone to dial the number but hesitated, suddenly feeling nervous, unsure of what to say. But little Bitsy pushed on and dialed the number, waiting for someone to pick up. Lewis.

"A-to-Z Mart. How can I help you?" The voice was a woman's, loud and forceful. Bitsy pictured Kitty, the woman who gave her directions to Mr. Howard's office.

"Yes, hello, this is, um, Betsy Gordon. I was just there, at your store, for an interview with the Assistant Manager, Mr. Howard, and I forgot to ask him a few questions, and I…"

"Hold on please." Music started to play in Bitsy's ear.

"Hello?" Music continued to play. Then a voice came on the line.

"This is Mr. Howard."

"Oh, hi Mr. Howard. This is Betsy Gordon. I was wondering, I had a few questions that I wanted to ask you, that I forgot to ask in the interview with you just about… um… an hour and a half ago." Bitsy checked her watch so she could be exact on the time.

"Oh yes, I remember you, Miss Gordon. What are your questions?"

"Okay, well, I forgot to ask how much the job pays. Not that it really matters that much, I still want to work there, I just wanted to know, that's all. And I wanted to know…"

"The job pays minimum wage."

"Oh, okay, thank you."

"Is that all Miss Gordon?"

"Um, no, I have another question, questions. How many hours would I be working… and how long for lunch?"

"It is a 40-hour week and you get ½ hour for lunch, 9am to 5:30pm Is that all Miss Gordon?"

"Yes, thank you. Oh, and I have the lady, Mrs. Klyski's, the lady I babysit for, I have her phone number for you." Betsy read carefully from the paper she wrote the number on.

"Okay, fine." Bitsy waited for him to write the number down but she didn't hear any sound so she figured he was done.

"Is that all now, Miss Gordon?"

"Yes, oh no, wait, um… when will you decide about the job?"

"Well, we will probably decide by the end of this week, maybe next."

"So, should I call on this Friday, or next Monday, or will you call me?"

"We'll call you. Okay? Now, you have a good day, Miss Gordon." And Mr. Howard hung up.

Lewis.

Bitsy wondered what she would do with her time waiting to hear back from Mr. Howard at the A-to-Z Mart. She didn't want to get too involved in a project in case Mr. Howard called and then she would have to abandon the project and go to work full-time at the store. She wished that they would call tomorrow. But it was only Monday and she thought she should make the best of the time off. After all, she might be working for the rest of her life now. Suddenly Bitsy thought about all the projects she had wanted to do and thought she should make a list and pick the one that she wanted to do most and that she most likely would finish before she started working at the A-to-Z Mart. She loved painting with watercolors but she would have to start a new painting. She thought about the color of Lewis' eyes.

Her mom, of course, had lots of projects for Bitsy to do, but they mostly involved cleaning around the house; like cleaning out the refrigerator, or cleaning the shelves in the pantry, or cleaning the basement, which was mostly where Bitsy's stuff was, like old toys and things that she didn't use or care about anymore. This applied to the garage, too. But Bitsy wasn't in a cleaning mood; she was in a creating mood. She decided to go to the basement and look around for her sand terrarium tools. She had made a couple of those as Christmas presents years ago and loved how they came out. She always wanted to make one for herself and decided that she would do it now. That project wouldn't take much more than a couple of days. Then she would do her ironing and get ready for her new job. And she would definitely take a little time to clean the refrigerator; that would make her mom happy.

Bitsy found all of her tools for the sand terrarium in the basement. She just had to buy a plant to put in the terrarium. Lewis. Yes, she could go to the A-to-Z Mart to buy the plant. It would be cheaper to go there than to buy it at the local florist shop. Of course, she'd have to pay for the bus fare there and back. But it would be worth it. Plus, she should get to know the layout of the store, in case a customer asked her where a certain department was while she was working. She was just about to run upstairs to her bedroom to get ready to go to the bus stop but glancing at the kitchen clock and seeing that it was 5:15, realized it was too late. She would have to go tomorrow.

The next day Bitsy rose early, barely able to sleep over her excitement about going to the A-to-Z Mart again. Her mom was already showered and dressed and was coming out of her bedroom when Bitsy was walking towards the stairs.

"Well, aren't you up early this morning? What do you have planned, Bitsy?"

"Oh, I'm working on a project today and I have to take a ride back to the A-to-Z Mart to buy something. I won't be long, though, because I want to finish this project before I start my job."

"Did the store call you already?"

"No, but I'm pretty sure I'm gonna get it. I have a feeling about it."

"Well, that's great honey. I hope you do." Her mom worked at Sears in the credit department and Bitsy knew her mom wanted Bitsy to work at the store with her, would even put in a good word for Bitsy, and they could drive in together. But Bitsy needed to find her own thing and she was sure it was at the A-to-Z Mart. She was feeling more independent now that she was out of high school. She was finally allowing her inner Bitsy to come out, all the way out. Her mom had over-protected Bitsy all of her life. It was time for Bitsy to make her own decisions. And once she was working, she would find her own apartment, too.

In the kitchen, her mother put the coffee on while Bitsy took her vitamins and poured a glass of juice.

Bitsy loved her parents and thought they were the best parents anyone could possibly ever want. Bitsy sometimes wondered if she had almost died when she was a baby because her parents were so protective of her and always wanted to keep her close. But Bitsy felt a little too protected, and sometimes even suffocated by their grand love for her. She took a deep breath and coughed.

"Are you coming down with a cold, Sugar?"

"No, just got something stuck in my throat."

"What? Well, let me take a look, let me see, here, let me get you a glass of water, come here, let me see."

"Mom, it's nothing, I took a vitamin, that's all, and I swallowed it wrong."

"Well, drink this water to rinse it down." Her mother handed her a glass of water. But Bitsy was already drinking down her juice.

"See, all better." She opened her mouth and stuck out her tongue so her mother could see the vitamin was gone, just like she used to do when she was a little girl sick with a cold and her mother gave her baby aspirin. She always loved the little paper cups her mother would give her, just big enough for a swallow to rinse her mouth with salt water when she had a sore throat, or get a drink when she woke in the middle of the night. The tiny cups had seven yellow daisies on them, spaced evenly around the middle of the cup.

"You know, Bitsy dear, I'm sure you could work at Sears with me. Even if you didn't want to work in the Credit Department with me, there are always openings in the different departments. And I could drive us in the car, you wouldn't have to take a bus. I don't think you'll like taking the bus every day. It can get crowded and people are always pushing."

Somehow Bitsy didn't believe that. It took her about 15 minutes to walk to the bus stop and then another 20-minute bus ride to get to the A-to-Z Mart and there was never more than about 15 people on the bus, and always plenty of seating. She could get some reading done on the bus ride. Bitsy was looking forward to that. She loved reading and always took out books from the library, as many as was allowed. She was feeling excited thinking about all the new and positive experiences she would have with her first real job. And Lewis.

Her dad walked in just as the coffee pot stopped percolating and her mom was taking two mugs from the cabinet. He poured them each a cup and sat at the table.

"Mornin' Bitsy! How are you doing today?" Her dad had to be the most up-beat positive guy she ever met, which is probably where Bitsy got it from.

"I'm good, daddy. I'm going to the A-to-Z Mart today to buy a few things so I can work on a project."

"Buy some things, eh? That's great, Pumpkin." Bitsy loved it when her dad used his special name for her, as long as no one else was around to hear it.

"I'm making a sand terrarium. And I just need a plant to complete it, and maybe a seahorse, you know, the kind they put in aquariums with fish."

"Why don't you just go to the florist shop in town? It's much closer than going all the way to the A-to-Z Mart. What's the name of that place, uh, Jolly something, or Joelle, something like that?"

"Josephine's Florist. You know, it's your cousin's place, remember, your cousin Josephine?"

Her dad chuckled. "Oh yeah, that's right. Josephine, my cousin. So, why aren't you keeping the money in the family instead of giving it to the big ole' A-to-Z Mart?"

This was a sore spot for her dad because although he could joke about it with Bitsy, he was upset over all the businesses that had closed in town, including his own business, when the A-to-Z Mart came in. Her dad had worked long hours building his business over the years but there just weren't enough local customers to keep it going so he had to close. He got a job at Stop-and-Save, the big supermarket that was three towns away, in Goldeen. He said he liked it there; they were good to him; he managed the meat department. But her mom hinted that he preferred hardware to beef and he would never admit that he was anything but happy at his job. He would never work at the A-to-Z Mart and was a bit bothered by Bitsy's choice to work there. But he also knew she was stubborn, like him, and determined to do her own thing.

"Well, a cousin isn't really our family now is it, dad?" Bitsy smiled and gave her dad a kiss on the top of his head.

"No, I guess you're right there – the money isn't going into our bank account, that's for sure."

Bitsy poured herself some cereal with milk and ate it quickly, hoping her dad wouldn't notice she was eating it in large gulps, nearly choking. She stopped and took a breath. Her mom put a couple of pieces of toast in the toaster-oven.

"Anyone else want toast?"

"None for me, thanks." Her dad usually only ate breakfast on the weekend when they had scrambled eggs or pancakes.

"I have to get going in a few minutes. Can I drop you off at the store, Bitsy?"

She felt a lump form in her throat – she would see Lewis even sooner than she had planned. She kind of wanted the walk and bus ride to think about him and what she might say when she saw him again. Hopefully something more clever and not as goofy as the first time. And she certainly wouldn't forget to pay this time either. She was so embarrassed. She suddenly remembered that and considered forgetting the whole trip. But she had to go.

"Are you sure it isn't out of your way, dad?"

"No problem sweetie, I have time. It isn't that far out of my way."

"Okay, that would be great, dad. I'll be ready in a minute."

"I'm just finishing up my coffee and talking to your mom for a bit and then we can be on our way."

Bitsy ran back upstairs to her bedroom. She had some jeans on this time, a pair that she really liked and that fit her slim body. And she wore a short white top with ruffles. She checked herself in the mirror, brushed a light coating of lilac eye shadow over her lids, just a touch of mascara, and a jazz pink lip gloss. She fluffed her hair with her fingers and dashed out her bedroom door and down the stairs just as her dad was getting up from the table.

When her mom stood up from putting the dishes in the dishwasher, Bitsy gave her a kiss on the cheek.

"I'll see you later, mom. I'm only gonna be a couple hours, I want to finish my terrarium today. And I'll start supper, just let me know what you want to have."

"Okay honey, I'll take out some pork chops and you can make mashed potatoes and frozen peas. I should be home at my regular time today. What about you, Keith, anything going on at work or will you be home by 6?"

"Sure, I'll be home by 6. Why don't I cook the chops on the grill, Vi?" Her dad loved cooking on the grill any time of the year and summer gave him even more opportunities.

"That's fine with me. I'll take them out right now so they'll be defrosted by supper."

Bitsy's dad, who was a bit of a goof, was telling her something funny one of the guys did at work. He worked with two men and two women and they were all full of stories, most of them were about their kids and the funny things they did. Bitsy wasn't really listening, she was too busy recreating her first meeting with Lewis, except this time everything was perfect. She said all the right things, she was dressed in a super-tight dress, her hair was flowing like in a TV commercial where the women are walking around in their underwear and high heels and their hair is blowing around them. She had a red silk boa wrapped around her neck – this was also blowing around her, as if she was riding along in a convertible. She sighed, appearing bored. She looked really cool and sexy. And Lewis, of course, was stunned by her beauty and flowiness. *Flowiness? Is that even a word?*

"Okay, I'm sorry I'm boring you with these stories, sweetie. I'll stop now."

"What? No, it's okay dad, I was just thinking about the job, wondering when I would hear from them."

"Oh, okay, well, you have to give them a little time. I'm sure they need to interview other people for the job, too. And I'm sure they'll call you back and offer you the job. They would be fools not to give it to you. You'll be a real asset to that place."

Bitsy was beaming as her dad sang her praises. He was always her biggest fan.

They were at the A-to-Z Mart before she had time to prepare what she would say to Lewis when she saw him. Her dad dropped her off at the front door.

"Okay, Pumpkin, see you tonight."

"Thanks, dad. She leaned over and gave him a peck on his cheek.

Her stomach did a flip-flop as she walked through the front door. She got a carriage to make herself look more like a regular shopper. She walked with her head down, like she was sneaking into the back door of a movie theater where she hadn't paid for the admission ticket. Then she realized that her behavior was ridiculous since all were welcome to shop at the A-to-Z Mart and she was just another customer. It was early and she was the only customer in the store. She looked around as if trying to find the thing that she had come here to buy while also searching the front registers for Lewis. He wasn't there. She pushed her carriage toward the back of the store where the sand terrarium supplies could be found along with a plant and hopefully also a ceramic seahorse. That would probably be in the department where they sold fish and pet supplies.

She was almost to the back of the store and saw the sign overhead that identified the pet department and, turning her carriage towards it, she nearly collided with a customer.

"Lewis!" She couldn't believe she had nearly run over Lewis with her carriage.

"Hey Bitsy, nice to see you again." His eyes bore a hole through her eyes. She stared back, as if hypnotized, unable to speak.

Bitsy pulled her eyes away from his and felt her whole body, not just her face, heating up, as if she had just walked into a sauna. Her first thought was, he remembered my name.

"Sorry, Lewis. I nearly ran you over." She giggled just a little. Sexy, try to be sexy. She put her hand on her hip and pushed her hip out, at the same time throwing her hair over her shoulder. It fell right back into her face.

"No harm done. What brings you to the Mart today? Are you shopping?"

Cool, Lewis was so cool. He knew just the right thing to say. Her hands were sweating.

"Um, yeah, I have some shopping to do. And what about you?"

"Well, I'm working here today."

*Stupid. Of course, he works here. He probably wouldn't come here on his day off.*

"Oh, right. Ha! I forgot, you, um, work here. Lewis."

"Are you okay, Bitsy? You look a little flushed. Do you need to sit down or maybe you should get a drink of water. The fountain is right back there, where it says Customer Service."

"Oh, no, I'm fine, thanks. But it is warm in here, don't you think?"

Lewis just smiled at Bitsy. He seemed to know the effect he was having on her and he was enjoying it. She felt even more nervous now and knew she should leave and do her shopping; but she didn't want to, she wanted to keep talking to him. She wanted to make plans for dinner, she wanted to ask him what he wanted her to cook and what time he would be home from work, and if they were going to watch a movie tonight. She wanted to have a life with Lewis. She wanted him to belong to her and she wanted to belong to him. But she couldn't move.

"Well, I have to get back to work now. It was nice seeing you again, Bitsy. I hope you get the job."

"Oh, yeah, me too. Thank you, Lewis." And he walked away. She just stood there watching him. He looked back over his shoulder at her, smiled, and she finally snapped out of it, realizing how ridiculous she must look staring after him, like a little school girl with a crush. She hurried away, flustered with herself. So much for flowiness.

Bitsy found her plant, a small cactus, and decided to get another bag of sand. She also found a seahorse to put in the terrarium. Of course, a seahorse really didn't go with a cactus but she didn't care. She liked it so she decided to buy it.

As she walked to the front of the store with her 3 small items in her big carriage, she was trying to decide if she should go to Lewis' register or another one. She finally thought that if she wanted to seem cool at all, she should go to another register. Otherwise, he might think she really came to the store just to see him and she definitely didn't want him to get that impression. Going to another register would be the more mature thing to do, definitely.

She saw Lewis and walked past his register to three registers down from his, even though his line was shorter. She looked at the candy bars and gum, trying to decide which she wanted to buy. Again, she chose gum, spearmint this time and put it in her carriage with her other items. Since all of her items were so small, she had placed them in the top section of the cart with the plastic shelf that came down, where you would usually put a small child. She briefly thought about a baby sitting in there with messy diapers and picked up her gum, holding it in her hand instead.

Her name tag said 'Cindy'. Cindy didn't look at Bitsy. Bitsy was hoping to make small talk so she wouldn't be tempted to look at Lewis. She stole a glance now and then anyway but he appeared to be busy with his customers. Cindy was putting Bitsy's cactus into a bag and the sand and ceramic seahorse into a separate bag.

"Do you want the gum?"

"Oh, yes, thanks." Bitsy took the gum and put it in her purse. At the same time she looked over at Lewis, she saw him look up at her and just as quickly look away, smiling in an almost embarrassed way. Like he should not have been looking at her and she had caught him. She saw his face flushing pink. He busied himself around his register. She gave Lewis a quick smile, not really sure if he saw her, and looked away. She paid for her purchases, thanked Cindy, took her bag with the cactus carefully and the other bag with the sand and ceramic seahorse and walked away, passing Lewis on her way to the exit.

"Have a nice day, Lewis." Cool, very cool, she thought.

"You too, Bitsy. Come again." He never looked up, just kept himself busy and then another customer walked up to his register and he turned to help them.

Well, at least she was making a smooth exit. Bitsy struggled not to turn to see if Lewis was watching her but she knew he wasn't. Anyway, she thought it best to leave it this way. She flipped her hair over her shoulder as she walked through the automatic doors. She hoped he was looking.

# Chapter 3

The week flew by and Bitsy managed to keep herself busy. She made her sand terrarium in two days. She also cleaned out the refrigerator discarding all of the expired salad dressings and other condiments. And she spent a little time in the pantry upstairs as well as the one her dad had built in the basement for when they stocked up on different supplies from the wholesale club. She brought the soups, crackers, and pasta upstairs that were the closest to expiring.  She also spent a lot of time at the library reading every Nancy Drew book that they had, which was a total of eight books. She was a fast reader and mysteries were her favorite. She read all the Miss Marple and Hercule Poirot stories by Agatha Christie and then read the other Agatha Christie books that the library carried. She had already read several of these books so there were only a few that she hadn't yet read. Sometimes she just stayed at the library and would finish a book right where she sat in just a few hours. She only did that once or twice though because even though she could walk to the library, she realized she would get really hungry after four or five hours and so she started bringing a snack. Then she started bringing a travel alarm clock and she would set it for four hours. If she hadn't finished a book in that time she would take the book out, finish it at home, and then bring it back the next day.

Reading was a great way to distract herself from thinking about the A-to-Z Mart. She was so sure she would get that job; she just had to get it. She thought about making another trip back to the store to see Lewis. What if he forgot about her? She decided that she would call the store on Monday and find out if they had made a decision about the cashier position. She wanted to know, but she also didn't want to know if they chose someone else over her for the job.

On Monday she wanted to finish reading a book and get it back to the library. When she got back from the library it was time for dinner and she realized that most likely, everyone in personnel who could tell her if she got the job or not had already left for the day.  On Tuesday she got up with renewed enthusiasm about the job. She felt that today was the day that she would get the phone call she had been waiting for. It was time. She was so sure of it that she brought the phone, that had a long extension cord from her bedroom next door, into the bathroom with her when she took a quick shower, not even washing her hair because it would take too long and then she would have to dry it, too, and she was afraid she wouldn't hear the phone ring over the hairdryer. Right after she dressed and waved good-bye to her mom and dad as they each left for work, she sat down to start another book she had taken out of the library, "A Mind to Murder" by P.D. James, an author she had just started reading. And, that's when the phone rang. It was right beside her and she jumped and lunged at it but quickly composed herself and instead calmly picked it up, her heart beating in her throat. She hoped it wouldn't interfere with her talking.

"Hello, this is Bits… Betsy speaking, who may I ask is calling?" Too formal, way too formal. She made a mock swat at her face pretending to slap herself.

"Yes, Miss Betsy Gordon?" A woman's voice, efficient and confident.

"This is I…um, her…yes, I'm Betsy Gordon."

"Yes, Miss Gordon, I'm calling for Mr. Howard. We are happy to offer you the position as cashier at the A-to-Z Mart. You will start next Monday at 9am. Report to the personnel department to fill out some forms before you are trained in your new position. Congratulations, Miss Gordon, and we'll see you on Monday."

Click.

"Thank you. Hello?" No answer. Yup, she was definitely gone. Well, I guess that's how people are hired. They figure you wouldn't have gone to the trouble of setting up an interview if you didn't want to work there so of course you will take the job. But what if she had another interview someplace else? Bitsy figured she would have to call them back and tell them that. But

since she didn't have another job lined up, she had only
interviewed with the A-to-Z Mart, she was happy to accept their
offer and couldn't wait to tell her parents. And Lewis.

Her parents were thrilled and that night they took Bitsy
out for dinner at their favorite Chinese food restaurant to
celebrate. Her mom took a day off to take Bitsy shopping the
next day to buy a couple of outfits that, as she put it, would
make Bitsy look a little more grown-up. Her mom wanted her
to buy a suit with the reasoning that "everyone needs to have an
interview suit." But Bitsy argued that she just got a new job, she
wasn't thinking about an interview with any place else. Her
Easter suit had worked just fine so she didn't need another suit.
Having persuaded her mom, she instead decided on 3 skirts, 4
sleeveless blouses, and one pair of dark blue slacks, creased
down the front. She had her sneakers, but she wanted a nice
pair of shoes to wear at work as well. She decided on a
comfortable pair of flats, beige with little bows.
Bitsy was happy with all her new clothes and happy to now
be part of the working class. She could mix and match her new
clothes with a few of her school outfits that were fashionable
without looking too much like a high schooler. Bitsy really
didn't have a lot of professional looking summer clothes in her
school wardrobe since she didn't go to school in the summer.
Her summer wear consisted mostly of just shorts, capris, and
jeans and tank tops or t-shirts with a couple of dressier blouses.
That was what she lived in all summer. She didn't think she
could wear jeans at work and wished she had paid attention to
what the other girls were wearing when she had been at the A-
to-Z Mart. But, of course, she had been mostly interested in
Lewis so never even thought to look at what the other
employees were wearing, what they were doing, or even what
the other employees looked like. Bitsy thought she remembered
Lewis wearing, of course, the store's men's smock, and a pair of
dark chinos. She had a hard time looking past his eyes and his
face, which she clearly remembered was quite attractive.

The weekend went by faster than Bitsy expected. She kept busy during the day, and at night, she watched a movie or played a board game with her parents. But when Sunday night finally came, Bitsy couldn't sleep. Every time she looked at the clock only five or ten minutes had passed since the last time she'd looked at it. She tossed and turned. She knew she had to get some sleep because she was starting her new job and she wanted to arrive fresh and alert. Her alarm was set for 6am. Finally, at around 4:30am, she fell asleep. It seemed as if only ten minutes had passed when the alarm went off. She jumped out of bed and went to her bathroom to shower. Her parents had their own bathroom off their bedroom.  This bathroom, down the hall from Bitsy's room, was kind of like Bitsy's own bathroom since they rarely had company stay at their house, except for the few times her aunt Sophia and uncle Dan from California came for a visit. And once her uncle Jeff had visited, but he lived in France and didn't get back to the States that often. He did send postcards from the many countries he traveled to for his job and he always sent presents at Christmas. He had some important high-level position with a national security organization and couldn't talk about what he did. But, other than these few visitors, the bathroom was essentially hers. So, Bitsy had decorated it with all the things she liked to have in her bathroom, including everything in shades of her favorite color, purple.

She showered quickly, washed her hair, and decided to wear her jeans skirt with a white sleeveless top that had fine lace around the collar to give it a more feminine look. Standing in front of her full-length mirror, she approved of her new grown-up look. She also decided to wear her sneakers but brought her new pair of flats to wear at work.

Downstairs her mom had put the coffee on and was making lunches for all of them. Bitsy helped her finish up and put her lunch into a brown paper bag and put ice cubes in a baggie, tying the top so that when the ice melted it wouldn't soak into her sandwich. She also brought a thermos bottle with water; although, they did have the snack bar where she could get a soda or use the public water fountain. She sat down to breakfast and her dad walked in, giving her mom a kiss and leaning over to kiss Bitsy on the top of her head.

"So, how did you sleep? Excited about your new job?" Bitsy's mom rolled her eyes at her dad. She knew Bitsy hadn't slept much.

"No, not really. I mean yes, I'm excited about my job so no, I didn't sleep much. I just couldn't get to sleep. I didn't feel tired at all. I guess I was just too excited. Anyway, I'm sure it's just 'first day on the job' nerves and I'll be fine tomorrow. At least I hope that's all it is. I just want to do a good job, you know. I want to be a good employee. I want them to be happy with me and the work that I do."

"Well, then, sweetie, you have nothing to worry about." Her dad always said the right thing. Her mom smiled and gave Bitsy's shoulder a squeeze.

"Well, I've gotta run. We're having a morning meeting. How about pizza for supper tonight since it's Bitsy's first day on the job?" her mother suggested.

"Sounds great – I'll pick it up from Alberto's, mushroom okay?" Bitsy knew her dad could eat pizza every day and Alberto's, his favorite pizza place, was on his way home.

"You know mushroom is my favorite. Thanks dad. See you tonight, mom."

"Give me a call if you get a chance, okay Vi?" Her dad gave her mom a big kiss and a hug. Bitsy loved that her parents loved each other so much. Her mom almost seemed to melt into her dad's bear hug, closing her eyes and smiling. Bitsy saw the look of contentment and happiness on her mom's face and only one thought crossed her mind. Lewis.

# Chapter 4

Bitsy left soon after her mom with her dad close behind. As she was about to start her walk to the bus stop her dad called to her.

"You don't think I'd let you start your new job on your first day by taking the bus, do you? I'll drop you off right at the door. How's that sound?"

"Are you sure dad, I don't want you to be late."

"Don't worry about me. I'll just tell them I had an important date. And then maybe we can start thinking about a car for you. You do have a license so you might as well use it. I think by winter you're going to want to drive to work and not have to walk to the bus stop. We can start looking around after summer, okay? But you have to help pay and so, now that you are working, you can start saving money for a car and then pay for your own car insurance. We'll find you something dependable that gets good gas mileage. How does that sound?"

"That sounds great! Thanks dad!"

There were times when Bitsy just couldn't believe her good fortune and thought she must have the best parents in the world.

On the drive to the A-to-Z Mart, Bitsy suddenly realized she was very nervous about starting a real job and her stomach started feeling like a dozen butterflies were flitting around in there. She wasn't sure how to calm herself and hoped she wouldn't throw up before she got there, or even worse, wouldn't throw up on the job. She figured someone would have to train her and wondered if it would be Lewis. That made her even more nervous. She didn't want him to see her make a mistake and look stupid – she had already done that, she reminded herself. Of course, that made her feel even more nervous now. Hopefully Lewis didn't remember her first meeting with him. Even though she would love to spend time with Lewis and be that close to him, she thought she would probably just make more errors with him around and started to hope she would have someone else as her trainer. Maybe she would have Cindy. She would be a perfect teacher for Bitsy. She would most likely be as detached teaching Bitsy as Bitsy felt about having her as a teacher, which is exactly what Bitsy needed – no feelings, just learning.

Bitsy realized her dad was talking to her while she was lost in her own thoughts so she stopped him before he went any further.

"Dad, I'm sorry I haven't been listening but I'm starting to feel really nervous. This is my first real job. I hope I do a good job. What if I make a lot of mistakes? What if they don't like me and they fire me, who will hire me then? I'm… I'm feeling kind of scared. I didn't think I would be, but I guess I am. I just want to be good at my job, I want them to like me… I want you and mom to be proud of me, you know?" Bitsy stopped talking then, she thought she might start crying and her mascara would run and wouldn't that be a great way to start her new job with her eye makeup smeared around her eyes. She blinked hard and dotted at her eyes with a Kleenex. She didn't want her dad to know she was just a split second away from a full-blown crying spell.

"Oh sweetie, I'm sorry I was going on like that, I guess I was just talking so you would relax. I thought you might feel a little tense starting a new job and all. But you know, I have complete faith in you and I know you'll be an asset to them and will give them all you've got. So, if they don't appreciate the fabulous person that you are, well then, I guess you should work someplace else where they will appreciate you."

"Oh, thanks dad. That makes me feel better."

Before she knew it, they were at the A-to-Z Mart. Bitsy got out of her dad's car, thanked him for the ride, and watched him drive away. She wished she was driving away with him. She wished she had never gotten out of bed this morning. She wished she had never applied for this job. She felt nauseous again. She counted to ten, took a deep breath, and then walked into the store.

"We aren't open yet, we don't open for another ten minutes, please come back then." The woman at the service desk stared Bitsy down, waiting for her to walk back out the way she had come in.

"Oh, um, I work here now. Today is my first day. My name is Betsy and I'm…"

The woman didn't wait for Bitsy to finish but cut her off mid-sentence.

"Okay, fine." And she went back to the pile of papers on the desk, ignoring Bitsy.

Bitsy walked to the back of the store where the "Employees Only" door was. She walked through the door, past Mr. Howard's office, and the next door said "Accounting Dept." She walked down the hall to the last room just to see what was there. The door was open and the sign on the door said "Employees' Lounge". She walked back to the Accounting Dept. door since she figured that was where she was supposed to go first and they would tell her what to do. She knocked on the door. A small voice said, "Come in."

Bitsy opened the door to a room that was about twice the size of Mr. Howard's office. There were three desks in the office, two filing cabinets, and only one small woman, who looked like a kid pretending to be a grown-up. The desk she was sitting at looked way too big for her. Her straight shoulder-length mousy brown hair and thick round glasses accentuated the look of terror that filled her eyes as if everyone who came through the door was a potential serial killer and she was their next victim. She stared hard at Bitsy, speechless for a second and then she composed herself, her eyes softened and a small but kind smile found her lips.

"Are you Betsy Gordon?" The name plate on her desk said "Barbara Johanna." Bitsy wondered if she was called 'Barbie' in high school. Not exactly the type. She looked more like a Mary who works at the library.

"Yes, ma'am, I am. Nice to meet you, um, Barbara."

"You can call me Barbie. Nice to meet you, too, Betsy. I need you to fill out a W-4 form and a couple of other papers so have a seat here. And then you'll be training with, um, Lewis? No, Anna, Anna Baker. She should be up at the front at her register now. She'll be training you as a cashier. Here you go. Just fill these out and then you can go, okay?

"Okay, thank you, um, Barbie."

Bitsy sat in the chair beside Barbie's desk. She felt like she was applying for a loan at a bank. She filled out all the forms, which didn't really take very long since she didn't have much history about herself to share. When she finished filling everything out, she stood to go and leaned over to shake Barbie's hand.

"Oh, okay, well, good, Miss Gordon. You have a great day now and good luck with your new job."

"Bye!" Bitsy walked out of the Accounting Department office, closing the door behind her. She walked up the hallway, past Mr. Howard's office, and out of the "Employees Only" door, right into Lewis who was reaching for the doorknob.

"Oh, my Lewis! I'm so sorry, I didn't know you were right there."

"Hi Bitsy. That's okay, no problem, I'm fine."

"I think I stepped on your foot. I'm very sorry." Bitsy stopped herself from dropping to her knees and rubbing Lewis' foot.

"It's okay, no harm done. Is today your first day, Bitsy?"

Bitsy loved hearing him say her name. He said it slowly, quietly, as if he cherished the sound of saying it, his mouth smiling when the word left his lips.

"Yes, it is. I'm very nervous, Lewis. I hope I do a good job. I've never been a cashier before and I'm afraid I won't do well."

Lewis smiled, dipping his head and looking at Bitsy over the top of his glasses. Those eyes, those sapphire blue eyes, like beautiful gems that Bitsy would love to wear for earrings, or a ring so she could look at it whenever she wanted. She stopped thinking when Lewis looked at her this way. She couldn't get out of his eyes, she wanted to linger there as long as possible, to float, to do the backstroke, the dog paddle, to dive under and drink the blue out of them and into her. She wanted to drown in his eyes.

"You'll do just fine, Bitsy." The smile, his lips behind the mustache. That's all Bitsy could think about, could focus on. She wanted to kiss those lips. She felt herself move towards Lewis.

"So, who will be training you today?" Bitsy snapped out of it just in time. She couldn't believe she was thinking about kissing Lewis, and had started to move towards him to do just that! She really wanted to but since she had only met him a few times and for just a few minutes and hadn't said more than a couple dozen words to him, kissing him would have been inappropriate. She couldn't believe the spell he had on her. This had never happened to Bitsy before. She felt more than just a little nervous around Lewis whenever she spent more than a few seconds with him. She thought she should leave. But oh, wait, had he just asked her something?

"I'm sorry, what did you say?"

"I said, who will be training you today, Bitsy?"

"Oh, um." Bitsy drew a blank. She couldn't remember who was supposed to train her. She thought about going back to Barbie and turned. Lewis grabbed her arm. A feeling, an energy, went up her arm where Lewis touched her and spread throughout her body. She turned back to Lewis. Again, she had to stop herself from moving into his arms.

"Bitsy, wait. Could it be Anna? Anna is at register 6. She's there now."

"Oh, yes, Anna. Thank you, Lewis. And I'm sorry."

"Why are you sorry?"

"For stepping on your foot."

Lewis smiled, his head lowered, his eyes staring at her. Bitsy felt his hand fall off her arm, slowly, reluctantly. She felt her arm raise towards his hand like iron to a magnet. She didn't want him to let her go. She didn't want to leave, but she had to go to the registers, find Anna, and begin her cashier training.

"I'll see you later, Lewis?"

"Yes." And Lewis disappeared behind the "Employees Only" door.

# Chapter 5

The morning passed quickly. Bitsy found learning to be a cashier an easy job and not the least bit challenging. The most important thing was to make sure she figured out the correct change. Anna warned her that there were people who would ask for change for a $20 and then try to confuse Bitsy so that she would give back more than $20 to them. They would ask for a $10 and two $5's and then decide no, give me 4 $5's, and then 3 $5's and 5 $1's hoping to confuse the cashier. If someone wanted just change, Bitsy should inform them that they must go to the service desk for change. Otherwise, she should pay close attention if someone gave a $20 bill for a pack of gum. That was one lesson Anna relayed to her that Bitsy would not forget. Other than this, there wasn't much that was likely to mess her up. Every item had a bar code and all Bitsy had to do was scan it. Most people paid with cash or they wrote a check. Bitsy decided she would be a great cashier. And to make her job more pleasant, she would engage each and every customer in conversation.

Anna was friendly enough but Bitsy wanted to take it to a new level. She really wanted to connect with the customers. She talked to them about the items that they were buying. If they bought Pepto Bismol or some stomach medication, she was concerned and asked if they were okay. She commented on the clothes they bought, telling them how the colors matched their eyes, or the style was very slimming, or she had a pair of shoes just like the ones they were buying. Sometimes the customers would engage in these conversations and other times she was completely ignored until Bitsy told them their total and asked whether they were paying with cash or check.

Bitsy couldn't believe it when Anna told her to put the closed sign on her register so they could go to lunch; the morning had flown by. Bitsy was really happy with the progress she had made in just one morning on the job and on her first day, too. This is a breeze, she thought. And then she thought maybe she should be asking for an office job, something that took more intelligence; but maybe more education would be needed and Bitsy had only completed high school. So first, she figured, she should prove herself to the bosses, whoever they may be, and become the most proficient cashier they've ever seen. She would do such an amazing job that they would soon know her name and they would be asking her if she wanted a job in the office.

Bitsy looked around to see if Lewis was available. She didn't see him anywhere and decided to just hang out with Anna during lunch. They only had half an hour anyway and you couldn't really go anywhere in that time. Barbie had told her about the refrigerator where employees could put their lunches and she suggested Bitsy put her name on her bag. She had also warned Bitsy that some people just helped themselves to whatever was in the fridge, so she should bring some money with her just in case she had to buy a sandwich. It was a problem and they were trying to do something about it, but it was difficult to know what sandwich belonged to which employee and if someone took a bag out of the fridge whether or not it was their bag or if it belonged to someone else. Bitsy decided she would just keep her lunch in the paper bag with her at her register. That should take care of the stealing problem for her.

Bitsy and Anna walked through the "Employees Only" door, past Mr. Howard's office, past the Accounting Dept., and into the "Employees' Lounge" that Bitsy had peeked in earlier. The name made it sound like there would be reclining chairs and sofas to stretch out on and nap. But there were just three 6-foot metal tables with about 20 or so chairs; some were set up around the tables and others were stacked up, one on top of the other, against a wall. Bitsy figured they expected a big crowd and then she wondered how many people were employed by the A-to-Z Mart.

Bitsy sat down at one of the tables with Anna and they started to eat their lunches. Anna had also brought her lunch in a paper bag; she shared a story with Bitsy about when she started working there, how her lunch had been taken every day for her first week. Nothing was ever done about it so she took matters into her own hands and started bringing her lunch in a paper bag from that time on that she kept with her at the register. Everything Anna said confirmed what Barbie had already told Bitsy.

Bitsy was enjoying her sandwich of tuna salad and romaine lettuce when Lewis walked into the room. She looked up at him and her stomach did one of those flip-flops it always did whenever she saw Lewis. She was pretty sure his cheeks turned a slight pink color as he headed for the refrigerator. There was a sandwich sitting on a shelf in the refrigerator, wrapped in aluminum foil. He took the sandwich out and turned to look at the table where Bitsy and Anna were sitting. Bitsy watched him out of the corner of her eye, pretending like she wasn't waiting and hoping he would sit with them. Then she couldn't wait any longer and decided to invite him.

"Lewis, do you want to sit with me and Anna?"

He made a move toward the table and at that moment the door to the Employees' Lounge opened and three guys, around Lewis' age, walked in, laughing and joking, and one of them punched another in the arm. Bitsy didn't pay any attention to them and continued watching Lewis.

His reaction to the group was a little strange. He seemed to tense up as his eyes moved from Bitsy to the group of guys who had come in. They stopped when they saw Lewis. One of the guys seemed to be the leader of the group. He smirked at Lewis and walked towards him. Lewis turned from them and headed towards the door of the Employees' Lounge, flung the door open and walked out. The three guys laughed and walked over to the refrigerator.

"So, what do we have today?" The apparent leader bent over and started pawing through the sandwiches. Bitsy couldn't believe it; right here in front of her were the sandwich stealers. She had to stop this.

"I don't think it's a good idea to steal someone else's sandwich. You know, they might not have any money to buy something else to eat." Anna gave her a little kick under the table. Bitsy looked quickly at Anna, wondering what that was for and then looked back at the sandwich stealers.

The leader stood up and looked at Bitsy, as if he just realized she and Anna were sitting there.

"A new girl. Well, aren't you all brave and out-spoken. And cute, too. What's your name, honey? Do you have a boyfriend? Although that doesn't really matter to me, I'll make you forget all about him."

Bitsy got a better look at the sandwich stealer and decided he wasn't anyone she would ever be interested in. He was tall, probably over six feet, and had a full head of light brown hair, his bangs swept to the side. He was well-built; Bitsy figured he had muscles under his blue work shirt. He was obviously one of the maintenance workers since he didn't wear a smock like the others in the store who worked in the various departments or as cashiers. His shirt said "Joe" on the pocket. He was good-looking, too, with a little bit of hair above his lip and a triangle of hair under his lip. Just as she was checking him out, he came up to her, squatted down beside her, and gave her a big smile, shaping a kiss with his lips. Bitsy felt her cheeks heating up and swallowed hard. She looked at Anna for help.

"Leave her alone, Joe, today is her first day. Try not to scare the new girl away on her first day, will ya?"

"Betsy, my name is Betsy."

Joe stood up and smiled, extending his hand to Bitsy.

"Well, nice to meet you miss Betsy." She gave him hers which he took in his and bent over to kiss it, looking at Bitsy and winking as he did. Again, her cheeks flushed and she held her breath, pulling her hand back. Joe stood up and turned toward the door.

"Come on, boys, let's go get something to eat from the snack bar." He turned and smiled at Bitsy as the group walked out together.

"He's really okay, just likes to put on a show for his buddies. If you ignore him, he'll leave you alone. But I think he kind of likes you, Betsy."

"Why did Lewis leave? I thought he would sit with us, but when they came in, he walked out. I thought they were going to fight or something."

"Joe is very smooth, Lewis not so much. There was a girl who worked here that Lewis was dating and Joe just swept her off her feet. Lewis didn't have a chance. So, they have this competition thing going on, you know?"

"Lewis doesn't seem like that at all, the competitive type."

"Yeah, he isn't like that. But he and Ginny went out a few times and I think Joe just did it to see if he could, you know, steal her away from Lewis.  So, then Joe asked her out and he's so smooth, Ginny fell for him; and then he dumped her. She ended up quitting. Lewis has never forgiven Joe for that and Joe likes to rub it in. He just has to stand and smile at Lewis - that's all he has to do to set Lewis off."

"Well, that was pretty mean of Joe."

"I guess.  Joe is a flirt, a real ladies' man, too. But he sure is cute. Anyway, Lewis just stays clear of Joe."

"Oh, I see." Bitsy had a whole new image of Lewis. And she saw another side of him, too; a sensitive side, that she really liked.

# Chapter 6

The afternoon went by as quickly as the morning had. Bitsy did not see Lewis again all day. She and Anna took a break sometime after 3 and walked outside for the short fifteen minutes. The day was warm and it felt good on her skin after being in the air conditioning all day. She stretched and twisted her back, bending over to stretch her upper body and touched her toes. She stood back up and walked over to the bench where Anna was sitting.

"How long have you worked here, Anna?"

"Oh, it seems like forever. Right out of high school so, let me see, about ten years now. Yikes, that is a long time. But I was pregnant in my senior year and now I have a second baby, Joy, who is three, and my oldest, Teddy, is nine. But they were great here at the Mart when I had Teddy and let me take some time off and gave me a nice baby shower. Bobby, my boyfriend, is in construction and in the winter, he doesn't have as many jobs so he spends more time with the kids. Then I put in extra time so I can be with my kids more in the summer months when my oldest is home with my little one. Bobby has odd jobs in the winter but just not steady work. He wants to start his own business, building houses. He's really good and did a lot of work on our place. We got it cheap because it needed a ton of work but it's looking good now. Anyway, the Mart lets me be more flexible, you know. They've been real good to me."

"Bobby's your boyfriend? Don't you want to get married?"

"Oh yeah, sure. We will someday. Right now, we're both just so busy. We can't think about a wedding and a honeymoon, all that kind of stuff. We have two kids to feed."

Bitsy noticed how Anna lit up when she talked about Bobby and her kids. That was what Bitsy wanted. A man she was crazy in love with and a couple of kids. It sounded like their life was hard with them both working a lot but when two people work on a common goal, things work out for them. When only one of them is working toward a goal and the other one has a different goal, that is when things fall apart. Bitsy was happy that she met Anna and that she was the one who was training her.  She knew that if Lewis had been training her, she wouldn't remember anything he said and she would probably get everything wrong and would appear stupid, which she definitely wanted to avoid. She knew she was pretty smart but for some reason, around Lewis, she forgot all of her life skills and her brain turned to mush.

They walked back into the store and back to their register where Anna was training Bitsy. The last two hours flew by and they were soon cashing out and bringing their cash drawer to the cashiers' office. Bitsy remembered to put the sign at the end of her conveyor belt that said 'This Register is Closed – Next Register Please'.

"If you have a bus to catch or something, Betsy, I can just run this down to the accounting office. I'll see you in the morning." Betsy was ready to run down to the cashiers' office with her but stopped and watched Anna walk off.

"Okay, thanks, see you tomorrow." Bitsy waved to Anna. Anna gave her a wave over her head and walked off with the cash drawer.

Bitsy gathered up her thermos and her purse and folded up her smock and put it on a shelf under the register where they had worked. She didn't know if she would be back at this same register tomorrow but she figured she might as well leave the smock here. She didn't think she should bring it home with her since it was really the store's property. But maybe it was hers while she worked there and maybe she would need to wash it, too. She would be sure to ask Anna about this tomorrow.

Bitsy walked out the door and the heat of the day hit her. She really wanted something cold to drink and realized her thermos was empty. She thought about going back inside to get some water but instead walked away from the store and headed towards her bus stop. She had just put her sunglasses on when she felt someone grab her arm. She jumped and turned to see Lewis.

"Hey, Bitsy, sorry if I scared you." Bitsy wanted to jump into his arms and hug him, she was so happy to see him.

"Lewis! I'm so happy to see you. I'm sorry about those boys but I wish you had stayed to have lunch with me and Anna." Her cheeks were really hot and she felt sweat run down her back under her new white blouse.

"No need to apologize for them, Bitsy. We just don't get along so I avoid them when I can. It's better that way." Again, the urge to hug and kiss Lewis overwhelmed Bitsy. Instead, she grabbed for his hand and held it in hers. She wasn't sure what she was doing but it felt right and he didn't pull away so she figured it was okay with him, too.

"I know, Lewis. I just wanted you to stay, that's all. I like you." Oh no, what was she saying. She really didn't even know him and she was proclaiming her love for him? Well, she didn't say love, she said like. She did say like, didn't she? She waited for his response.

"I feel the same for you, Bitsy. I really like you, too." Okay, she had said like. She felt immediate relief and continued to hold his hand.

"Can I walk you someplace? Are you going to the bus stop? I take the bus, too. I have a car but I don't take it much. It isn't very dependable otherwise I would give you a ride home."

"Do you ride in the same direction that I ride in, Lewis?"

"I don't know, which direction do you go? Where do you live?"

"Oh, right, you don't know that. I live in Trenton. It's about a twenty-minute ride on the bus and then I walk about fifteen minutes. Where do you live?" They were walking now and Bitsy reluctantly dropped his hand. It started feeling a little awkward, plus his hands were so warm she felt both of their hands sweating.

"I live in a… a not very nice town. There isn't much there to talk about but I can afford the rent. It is a couple towns away."

"What, not Scutton, or scuzzytown as people like to call it?" Bitsy laughed and expected Lewis to laugh, too, but he was quiet. She realized that was exactly where he lived and immediately felt bad that she had tried to make a joke.

"Oh Lewis, I'm sorry…I didn't mean…"

"That's okay, Bitsy. Look, I'm gonna head out. My bus will be here in a few minutes. I'll see you tomorrow." And Lewis ran in the other direction.

Damn! Bitsy was so mad at herself. She should have known when he said it wasn't a very nice town that he was talking about Scutton. She was really on the ball today. She wouldn't be surprised if he never spoke to her again. *What a dope. Oh Lewis, I'm so sorry.*

# Chapter 7

The ride home was long for Bitsy. Her thoughts consumed her and she swallowed the urge to vomit. Twice she almost pulled the cord on the bus but the feeling passed. She took several deep breaths, closing her eyes, focusing on her breath, feeling a calmness flowing through her body. She fought back tears and was happy she wore her sunglasses to hide the few that got away from her. She wished she wasn't so emotional but she knew it came from a deep caring for others. The thought of Lewis living in such a depressed town while she lived in a beautiful home with coordinated linens, rugs, and all of her bedroom accessories in matching shades of purple engulfed her in a new appreciation and gratitude for her life and for all that her parents had provided for her.

She tried to imagine what his apartment must look like. She pictured it dirty with grease-stained walls, refrigerator, and stove together with dishes piled in the sink and left on the table and all around the apartment. The floors, most likely covered in linoleum with gouges showing a painted wood floor underneath. Wallpaper peeling from the walls and dirty, greasy finger-smeared  light switch plates. A mattress thrown on the floor of the bedroom was where he slept with the one set of sheets he owned barely covering the stained mattress underneath – there would be no mattress cover on the bed. Also, no duvet or bedspread to add some color or just a touch of classy ambience to the room. The living room most likely housed another mattress that served as a couch where infrequent guests sat.

Suddenly Bitsy sat up taller in her seat, snapping herself out of this judgmental rant. Something led her on this condemning course and she felt shame and humiliation for these thoughts that she was sure weren't hers. She realized that she couldn't possibly imagine what Lewis' apartment must look like. He always smelled good, like Dial soap, so she knew he was clean. He must have parents who had helped him to furnish his apartment so maybe it wasn't that bad. Maybe it was just in a poor neighborhood. She hated when she thought this way, that just because you are poor you are also dirty or live in a dirty place. She knew that wasn't true, not for all poor people. She started thinking better thoughts about where Lewis lived and pictured his place sparse but clean and neat with just the bare necessities, which is all any of us really need. Her parents taught her to be charitable to those less fortunate, not criticize them for whatever hand they had been dealt in life.  And then a face, Grandma Daniels, flashed before her eyes and with it a memory from when she wasn't more than three years old.

She and Grandma Daniels had been shopping in town, going to all the fancy stores where Grandma shopped. This would be Bitsy's first introduction to class differences between what the wealthy had and what the poor didn't have. Grandma Daniels had always bribed Bitsy with sweets if she was good. On this particular day she would get her favorite dessert, a dish of pistachio ice cream. While walking past all the high-end department stores, a Macy's and then a Bloomingdales, they passed three men, sitting with their backs against the walls of the fancy stores. The management tried their best to keep the men away but they were often too busy inside to worry about the outside of the store. Grandma Daniels rushed Bitsy along, who was fascinated by the men, their grease-stained chino pants revealing sockless feet and sneakers worn through in several places. One man walked on the back of the sneakers that were obviously too small for his much larger feet. A beanie hat sat on the ground in front of their crossed legs, as if they were about to meditate. All three had jackets made of denim with holes showing dirt-smudged elbows and wrists, and missing buttons or zippers in the too-small or too-large clothes they wore. One man smiled at Bitsy who stared back as Grandma Daniels continued to drag the child along.

"See those men, sweetheart? They are poor and dirty. All poor people are dirty just like them. They don't have to be dirty, they choose to be dirty. Stay away from them. They can hurt you or steal you and sell you to the gypsies." Bitsy didn't even know what a gypsy was, had never heard that word. But it was enough to frighten her; and now years later, she was ashamed to pass judgement on people who, often through no fault of their own, were poor.

When she got off the bus, she was thankful she still had the short walk home so that she had time to compose herself and lift up her spirits. She knew her parents would be excited to hear all about her first day at her new job. She certainly didn't want to come home in tears because that wasn't at all the way her day had been. She really had a good day, right up until the end when she had pretty much spit in Lewis' face. She tried to get her head out of that bad place and thought instead about how she would make it up to him. She would give him a hug and let him know she was not judging him and that it didn't matter to her where he lived. On second thought, maybe a hug might be too forward. She didn't want him to think she hugged everyone like that. And then again, she feared that if she did hug him, she might not be able to let him go. She let herself think about hugging him without his shirt on and wondered if he had hair on his chest. She wanted to lay her face on his chest and feel his arms around her.

*Oh Bitsy, you better stop thinking these thoughts! Pizza, think about yummy mushroom pizza.* Food always did the trick. She always thought about some food she really liked when she wanted to distract her thinking and head it in another direction.

And then, within no time at all, Bitsy was home. The walk had seemed shorter than usual. She walked into the house but it was quiet. Both of her parents were home; their cars were in the garage. She walked into the kitchen and the oven was heating up for the pizza that sat in the box on top of the stove. She lifted the cover and inhaled deeply, filling her lungs with the aroma of mushroom pizza. Her stomach growled. Her mom walked into the kitchen in her comfy clothes - which were usually loose sweatpants and a sweatshirt or shorts and a t-shirt, depending on the time of year.

"Hi sweetie, how was your first day on the job? I'm so proud of you, honey."

"It was good mom. This pizza smells so good, I want a piece right now! But I'm going to change my clothes first. Where's Dad?"

"He's putting on his comfy clothes, too."

Bitsy was hungry but needed a little privacy and was happy to get away to her room for just a few minutes before she got involved in telling her parents about her first day on the job. She quickly changed into her knit shorts and a t-shirt and then sat at her desk. She thought she might write Lewis a letter of apology. Too formal. If she's thinking they will be boyfriend and girlfriend, at least that's what she was hoping, then she needed to be honest and open with him right from the start. Again, back to the hug. She really wanted to hug him. Actually, she really wanted to kiss him. She was positive his lips would be soft. She had stared at them enough to know that for sure. She wanted to feel his arms around her, she wanted to press her chest into his. Bitsy had never had sex with a boy before, but now she couldn't stop thinking about Lewis in that way. Her mom had told her all about getting pregnant so she wouldn't do anything until she was ready and either using a diaphragm or on the pill. Bitsy hoped Lewis was thinking the same way about her but she wasn't sure. He had said he liked her. As a friend? Or something more? Maybe she should be sure they are thinking the same way before she throws herself at him!

"Bitsy, pizza time!"

She would have to think more about this later. After all, she barely knew Lewis and was looking forward to learning more about him. She had plenty of time, no need to rush.

For the remainder of the evening, Bitsy decided to forget about work and everything that was bothering her, for a little while anyway. After sharing her day at her new job with her parents while they ate the pizza, they relaxed together and had a competitive game of Scrabble. She would concentrate on looking for a word among her tiles and then Lewis would pop into her head and she would return to her laughing about where he lived. Her mom would remind her that her time was almost up and she'd spell out a simple word with her tiles just to move the game along. Her parents most likely thought she was taking a long time finding a word when she was actually thinking about Lewis and how she would apologize to him. Her parents seemed to have words lined up and when it was their turn, they would plop their tiles down and then it would be Bitsy's turn again.

"You guys are just too good tonight. I must be tired from my first day of work, or something."

"You do seem a bit distracted, honey. Maybe you should go to bed early. It's a routine that takes a bit getting used to having to get up at 6:30 every morning now. I don't want you getting overtired. You need to take care of yourself. Maybe you should take a vitamin C and some zinc, too. You are exposed to a lot of people now, not just the employees but also the customers coming through your register. I hope you are using Wet-Naps, too."

"Yes, I am. I have some in my purse. I can't use them for each person, though."

"Of course not, but just don't touch your face until you can wash your hands."

"Yes, mom, I always do." Sometimes her parents treated her as though she were a five-year-old. Of course, being an only child probably put more pressure on her parents. She was the main focus of the family. Most of the time she loved it but sometimes, especially now that she was getting older and was looking forward to getting her own apartment, she felt irritated, like when you have a piece of fuzz stuck to your eyelash and you just can't get it because it's too fine to even see it. Whenever this happened, it was best to just go to her room and spend some time alone away from the microscope she felt like she was sitting under.

"I think you're right; I think I'll go to bed now. I might read for a little bit first. Good night, mom, dad." Bitsy got up to go to her bedroom.

"Good night, sweetie." Her parents decided to finish the game by themselves. Her mom was winning anyway, as usual.

Bitsy brushed her teeth and put on her PJ's. She picked out her outfit for the next day – she decided to wear her new black straight skirt with a sleeveless yellow blouse. She thought the outfit made her look really grown up and kind of sexy. She hoped Lewis would think so, too.

She climbed into bed with the P.D. James book she had just started reading. She thought she'd get through a chapter or two but after a couple of pages, she couldn't keep her eyes open. She set her alarm and turned her light out.

She  wanted to dream about Lewis. She thought about his eyes, his hypnotic eyes. She thought about his lips, the lips she couldn't wait to kiss. She reached out to touch his arms – they were solid and strong. He had a nice body, a solid body, a manly body. His legs looked strong and Bitsy imagined they had hair on them. She felt them on her own smooth legs, how nice they felt against her naked skin. The hair on his body tickled her bare skin. She touched his legs, his arms. She pushed her face into the curly dark hair that covered his chest. She breathed in the Dial soap smell. He was touching her, gently, lovingly, his fingers running down her arms, up her stomach and up to her breasts, lingering, touching, like a feather, her nipples. She couldn't breathe, she stared into his bold blue eyes, she felt herself melting into him. She kissed his lips, his tongue touched her tongue, and she opened herself to him until something big inside her exploded. They pulsed together, slowly, in perfect sync. They were two puddles that became one, spread out into each other, honey and melted butter. She slipped her hand out of her undies.

Bitsy slept soundly through the night.

# Chapter 8

It seemed that in just one day Bitsy was already into the workday routine. She woke at 6:20am before her alarm went off and showered quickly. She dressed in her black skirt and yellow blouse, tucking the blouse in. She felt different today, she actually felt sexy. She felt like she had lost her virginity and was now a real woman. When she looked in the mirror, she thought she somehow looked older.

Bitsy ran downstairs and found she was the first one up. She poured herself a bowl of Raisin Bran cereal, added sliced banana, and made coffee for her parents. Her mom had made Bitsy's lunch last night so she put it into her paper bag and filled her thermos with water. She grabbed an apple out of the refrigerator and added that to her bag, too. She also put a couple of chocolate chip cookies in a baggie. For some reason she felt really hungry.

After her parents came downstairs the morning routine continued with everyone rushing through breakfast, adding finishing touches to hair, brushing teeth, and running out the door. Bitsy enjoyed her walk to the bus stop and everything seemed brighter and sunnier than usual. She smiled and said hello to the other people waiting for the bus. She found a seat with a window and hummed a song. She wasn't sure what the song was but figured it was something she had heard on the radio. She wanted to sing out loud but decided against it since people were giving her side glances just for humming.

When she got off the bus and as she was walking to the entrance of the A-to-Z Mart, Bitsy realized she didn't know yet how she was going to approach Lewis. She wanted to say something like, "I had a good time last night," but knew he would just give her a strange look since she hadn't actually been with Lewis last night. She didn't know if she could wait for him to ask her out, though. She might have to ask him for a date. That is if he was still interested in her. He might have decided that she was insensitive and cruel and didn't want anything to do with her. Bitsy's sunny mood was suddenly gathering clouds.

She walked into the store and looked for Anna. She didn't see her anywhere and went to retrieve her smock. She put it on and put her lunch bag under the cash register. She would wait a few more minutes and then she would go to the accounting office to get the cash box if Anna didn't show up soon. Since she had arrived a little early and had a few minutes before the store officially opened, she looked around at some of the displays that were near the cash registers – the impulse items. She was just about to put a few items aside for herself to purchase later when a hand touched her shoulder. She knew without turning that it was Lewis. Her body already recognized his touch. Her nose recognized the smell of Dial soap.

"Good morning, Bitsy. How was your night?" She turned to face him. He looked exceptionally attractive this morning and she felt herself blush. She felt like they were lovers who had just spent their first night together. She touched his arm as he pulled it away from her shoulder.

"Oh Lewis, I'm so sorry about what I said. I didn't mean anything by it, really. I'm so sorry."

"I wish you would just forget it, Bitsy. Okay?"

"Okay, I will, if you want me to, Lewis. If it will make you happy."

"Yes, it will. So, Anna is out today. The babysitter couldn't make it so I'll be training you today."

"Oh, you will?" Bitsy remembered her fears of having Lewis train her, how she didn't want to look stupid, figuring she wouldn't get anything right because every time she looked into his eyes, she'd forget everything he'd just said!

"I'm sorry, you sound disappointed. Well, maybe Kathy wouldn't mind teaching you today. Or Kevin might be happy to teach you, I'm sure. Who else? I think they are the only two who are on the registers today besides you. Maybe you should just go to the accounting office and ask them who should train you today." Bitsy couldn't believe she had done it again. She could tell Lewis was hurt. She had to fix this. Right now.

"Lewis, no, I want you, Lewis. I want you to teach me. I just can't think when I, um, you make me nervous, that's all; and I don't want to make any mistakes. I thought maybe it wasn't such a good idea to be, um, with you, all day. At the cash register. You know?" She felt her cheeks heating up. How do you stop your face from turning red? She felt really warm, too, all over. Was the air conditioning even working in this place?

"Is the air conditioning on today? It feels really warm in here. It must be hot out today." Bitsy fanned herself with her hand. Lewis looked at her and gave her the smile that had won Bitsy's heart the very first day she had met him at the A-to-Z Mart.

Lewis reached for the hand that she was using to fan herself with and took it in his hand and led her to the cash register. It was four registers down from the one she was on yesterday. She ran back to get her lunch, thermos, and purse. She remembered that she hadn't seen him yesterday afternoon and wondered out loud where he had been.

"Where were you yesterday afternoon? I didn't see you at the registers."

"Yes, well, sometimes I help in other ways. I bring in the carriages, or I help to unload shipments. Or if a department is short-staffed, I'll help out if they're busy. I wasn't hired to be a cashier, but to work in every department, whoever needs help on any given day. They hired me to fill in a lot of different areas, whatever is needed."

"Sounds like you'll be running the store pretty soon, Lewis." Lewis smiled and looked away.

"Well, I don't know about that."

She wanted to ask him if he had aspirations. Bitsy wanted to know all about Lewis and hoped they could go out sometime soon so that she could find out all about him. But then a customer came up to their register and she had to get to work.

The morning turned out to be pretty busy and Bitsy handled all the sales quite well. She enjoyed talking to people, continued asking them questions or making comments about something they bought.

"This is such a pretty top. I would like this for myself. I'll have to go check it out and see if I can find a purple one. That's my favorite color. I'm thinking your favorite color is blue since you have a blue one. Very pretty, it will look nice with your…um…blue eyes!"

Lewis quietly bagged the customers' items, smiling at Bitsy's over-the-top enthusiasm. When they were alone for a couple of minutes he turned to Bitsy and cleared his throat.

"Bitsy, I have to ask you something."

Bitsy held her breath and stared into those amazing eyes. *This is it, he's going to ask me to marry him, he's going to proclaim his undying love for me, or maybe he's going to at least ask me out.* She felt her cheeks heating up.

"Yes, Lewis?"

"How do you do it? How do you, ah, get so involved with people, ask them such personal questions? How do you give so much of yourself to people? Aren't you a little afraid?"

"I don't know. I guess I don't think I'm 'giving' so much of myself to people. I'm just having fun. I'm curious about people, too. I wonder what makes them tick, why they do what they do, you know? It isn't scary to me at all, Lewis. Is it scary to you?"

He smiled his adorable smile that Bitsy was falling in love with and she just smiled back at him.

"So, I have a question for you, Lewis?"

"Sure, what is it?"

"Are you going to ask me out?" She couldn't believe she had just blurted it out. But somehow she knew that if she didn't ask Lewis, he would've taken forever to ask her out. Or maybe it never would have  happened. Unless, he didn't like her in that way. Maybe he 'liked' her but he didn't like her the way she liked him. She could see herself falling for him, loving him, living with him, spending her life with him. She was head over heels. But maybe he didn't like her in the same way. Now she was regretting asking him, putting him on the spot like that. Maybe he already had a girlfriend, she didn't even think of that. She should take it back, right now.

"I'm sorry Lewis, I was…" But then he cut her off.

"Yes, Bitsy, I would like to go out with you."

"Oh, okay. I just, I'm sorry, I didn't mean to put you on the spot like that. I thought you felt the same way about me… but if you don't… then maybe…"

"How about on Saturday, would that be a good time for you?"

"What, oh yeah, Saturday would be great, Lewis. I would love to go out with you." She thought it might help his confidence to make it seem like he had had the idea to ask her out. But, either way, she was so excited to finally have a date with him. And then she felt nervous thinking about being out with him, no customers, no employees, just Bitsy and Lewis out on a date, talking, holding hands, being alone together. She felt her face getting warm again thinking about kissing Lewis' yummy full lips and looking into those ridiculously beautiful blazingly sapphire blue eyes. She looked up at him and thought the only thing for her to do at that moment was to leave. She somehow had to control her blushing every time he looked at her or smiled. But not right now. Right now, she needed to run away.

"I, um, have to go to the ladies' room. I'll be right back."

Lewis smiled as Bitsy ran off.

Lunchtime was here before she knew it. Lewis invited Bitsy to go outside with him. He had a fairly secluded spot where he usually ate his lunch alone. It was under a big oak tree, shady and much cooler than sitting in the hot sun. Bitsy was really hungry and ate her sandwich before Lewis had even started his. He had what looked like a baloney sandwich on regular white bread, plain with no mustard. She pictured Lewis making his plain baloney sandwich in the morning at his apartment. Bitsy really wanted to see his apartment, where he lived, where he slept, his bathroom where he shaved and showered. She wondered if it was big enough for two people to live there. And then she remembered the 'not very nice town' that he told her he lived in. She probably didn't want to give up the beautiful bedroom in the nice house she lived in with her parents. But for Lewis? She felt like she would give up everything for Lewis. How had he gained such a hold over her in such a short time?

She'd heard people talk about 'soulmates' and figured that this was what they were talking about, this attraction she felt for Lewis. It felt so right to her that she wanted to move it along. But Lewis seemed to want to take his time. Well, she had only been working there for two days now. And she really hadn't had much time to get to know him. She drank some of her water and looked up at Lewis. He had finished his sandwich and was looking at Bitsy. She felt the heat stirring up in her again and really wanted to kiss him. He walked over to her. Standing in front of her, he leaned in, his hand touching her face. This is it, she thought, our first kiss. She was ready, she held her breath and started to close her eyes. No, she wanted them open, to look into his eyes, those beautiful eyes that melted her insides, no close them, no… And then his hand was gone and he backed away.

"You had a crumb on your face. It's gone now."

"Oh, thanks Lewis." She wiped her face with a napkin.

"I guess we should go back in now."

"Already? We really didn't get a chance to talk or anything. But thanks for sharing your place with me, Lewis. I liked having lunch with you."

Lewis smiled.

The afternoon flew by, again. The A-to-Z Mart was busy. This time when they left the store at the end of the day Lewis walked her all the way to her bus stop. They didn't talk much, just small talk mostly. Bitsy thought if she didn't talk so much that Lewis might talk more. But it didn't work that way. She figured he just wasn't much of a talker.

"Well, good night, Bitsy. I'll see you tomorrow."

"Good night, Lewis. Thanks for walking me to my bus stop. Have a good night."

"Okay, you too."

And she watched him walk away.

# Chapter 9

Bitsy was restless at home. She wanted this week to be over. She was enjoying training for her job but she wanted it to be the weekend so she could go on her date with Lewis. She wondered what he was planning so she could prepare what to wear. If he lived in a town that wasn't very nice, and had a crappy apartment, and an undependable car, what would they do on their date? Where would they go, and how would they get there? Would they take the bus? She decided she needed to discuss this with Lewis the next day at work.

She arrived at work on a bus that got her there twenty minutes earlier. She hadn't slept well because all of the unknown details of their first date had kept her awake. She wanted answers. And then of course, as soon as she saw Lewis, she couldn't think of any of the questions. She walked through the front door and he was standing there, almost as if he was waiting for her.

"Good morning, Lewis. You're here early."

"And so are you. I wanted to talk to you about our date on Saturday, if you have a few minutes?"

"Sure, should we go outside?" And they walked back out the front doors.

"So, what is it you wanted to talk about Lewis?"

"Well, I believe I told you that my car was not very dependable. So, I was wondering if we could meet somewhere, or I could take the bus to your house and then we can go from there. How does that sound to you?"

He seemed really nervous about presenting Bitsy with this plan, like she would reject it and call the whole date off. Or maybe that is what he wanted. It seemed crazy for them to be taking buses everywhere on their date. Maybe she could borrow her mom's car for the night. Her parents would probably be home or if they had plans they could just take her dad's car. That seemed like a better solution.

"I think I could probably get my mom's car for the night. And then I could pick you up."

"Oh, I don't think you should come to my place. I wouldn't want you driving around looking for my apartment, it isn't a very good neighborhood. And I think I should meet your parents first, don't you? Or maybe we…"

"Have you changed your mind, Lewis? Do you not want to go out with me now?"

"No, no, I do. I really want to go out with you Bitsy. As I said, I really like you and I want to get to know you better. I just, my place, it isn't anyplace that you would want to be. It isn't in the best of neighborhoods, as I've already mentioned."

Bitsy risked looking into his eyes because she wanted Lewis to know how sincere she was about her feelings for him.

"Lewis, I want to be anywhere that you are. I know we haven't kissed or anything yet but I have this feeling about you and I just know this is right and I really want to get to know you, too…" And suddenly Lewis' lips were touching hers. She closed her eyes, her lips parted just slightly, enjoying the sensation of Lewis' soft full lips touching hers. She pushed back against his lips and followed him as he pulled away. She opened her eyes and they both looked around them to see if anyone was watching. Bitsy's heart was beating so loudly she thought Lewis must hear it, too. She felt her face heating up again and started fanning her face with her hand. Lewis was looking at her, giving her the smile that she couldn't resist. She moved towards him, hoping for another kiss. Lewis just took her hand instead and they walked into the store together.

The rest of that week passed by quickly, but not fast enough for Bitsy. All she could think about at night was Lewis. At dinnertimes, her dad would talk about his day and share some of the jokes the guys at work had told him.  She barely heard what he was saying and would laugh when her mom did. She got into the habit of rolling her eyes like her mom, too, so that they would both think she was listening. But all she was really thinking about was Lewis' kiss. And their upcoming date where they would, hopefully, kiss again. She hadn't really thought much about being with a boy before; not in high school, anyway, where they were just boys. But this was different. And now that was all she could think about with Lewis. She didn't know she could feel this way about anyone. She felt so many things in her coming alive, waking up for the first time. She was happy and she felt like she was finally a real woman. Still a virgin but a woman. A virginal woman. Well, almost a real woman.

She wondered, though, if she should share any of these thoughts with her mom. Bitsy and her mom had always been best friends. Since she graduated from high school, Bitsy hadn't really kept in touch with the couple of girls who were her best friends in school. One of them, Brittany, had gone off to college and was living in a dorm now. They had talked a few times when she first left for college and then they talked less and less until they both just stopped calling. Her other friend, Carrie, was working in the city, taking classes at a local college, and got an apartment there with her boyfriend. They saw each other last Christmas when Carrie had come home and they said they would keep in touch. But, they hadn't. Bitsy didn't even have Carrie's number at her apartment. She felt like she needed to talk to someone about these feelings she was having but her mom just didn't seem like the right person. She wouldn't know how to even begin that conversation. Her mom had been very cool when she told Bitsy about birth control and pregnancy. She wasn't at all embarrassed. Bitsy had blushed the entire time her mom gave her 'the talk' but her mom had just breezed right through it, talking about vaginas and penises like she was giving the weather report, 'Tonight there will be vaginas and a down pouring of penises and tomorrow there will be pregnancy if you forget to take your birth control pills. So, be sure to use protection when you go out tonight!'

Then Bitsy thought about Anna, at work. Maybe she could talk to her. She was out two days this week and so Bitsy got to spend more time with Lewis. But Anna was back on Thursday and Bitsy would be training with her again. Bitsy had only two more days of training this week and then next week she was on her own. Bitsy wasn't sure how to approach the topic with

Anna but figured since she had two kids and was pretty young herself that she would be the perfect person to talk to about the things Bitsy was feeling.

So, on Friday Bitsy suggested she and Anna go outside to eat their lunch. Bitsy hadn't seen Lewis all day – he must have been doing the other jobs he said he sometimes did when he helped out in the other departments in the store. She hoped she would see him before she left though, so they could decide when they would see each other on Saturday.  Bitsy brought Anna to Lewis' spot under the tree. She thought he might be there and then hoped he wouldn't mind her bringing Anna there.

"How are the kids, Anna? I heard your babysitter couldn't take them, that she was sick or something?"

"Oh yeah, she was sick but she's okay now. Two days. She's been really good but I've only had her with the kids for a couple of months now. I hope this doesn't happen too often. I really need a dependable babysitter since my husband and I both work."

Bitsy  really couldn't empathize since she had no idea what it was like to work and raise two kids and have a husband and a house. She thought about her parents but she was grown up and could take care of herself now. She did remember her mom being home when she was a baby and her dad had his hardware store, working long hours.  Then once she started school, her mom went back to work. Anyway, she really wanted to discuss her own concerns so she did what she usually did, she just blurted it out.

"So, there's this boy, or man, that I like and I am having really strong feelings for him and I haven't felt this way before. It is kind of driving me crazy. I can't think of anything but kissing him and feeling his hairy legs on mine and him touching me, naked, you know? And we have a date tomorrow and I don't know, I'm so nervous just thinking about it."

"Wow! You've been busy since I've been gone, and in just two days! Well, aren't you sassy! So, is it Joe?"

"Who? Oh, no, not him. He's cute and everything but no, it isn't him. I don't like his type."

"Hmm, I wonder who else it could be? Let me think…Lewis?"

Bitsy smiled and blushed.

"Anyway, I'm wondering about maybe having, you know, sex with this man and I'm nervous, because you know, I'm…"

"You're a virgin!? How old are you again?"

"I'm nineteen. I'll be twenty in a couple of months. Why? Is that too old to be a virgin? I haven't had many opportunities and I haven't met the right man yet. Until now."

"He doesn't have to be the right man for you to lose your virginity to him, it usually isn't. They always romanticize about 'the first one being the best or the one you never forget' and all that. That's a bunch of crap. My Bobby is the best I've ever had and he was not my first. But anyway, don't worry. Just go with the feelings and it will all work out. Oh, and if you don't want any babies right now, use a diaphragm or at least have him wear a raincoat."

"A raincoat?"

"A condom, make sure he wears a condom. They usually work okay. But being on the pill is the best. I'm on the pill."

"Okay. But we probably won't need one right now. This is just our first date. How many dates should we wait? Do you know is there a right number so that he doesn't think I do this with everyone I go out with? Like maybe six dates?"

"I think if you feel the way you are telling me you feel and he feels only half of what you feel then you better make sure you bring some condoms along with you. Don't depend on the guy to have them, make sure you have your own."

"But won't that make me look kind of like, you know, slutty, to carry my own condoms?"

"It makes you look like a responsible woman.  And don't buy any of his shit about 'oh, I can't feel you when I wear a condom', blah, blah, blah. You make sure he wears a condom. This is your life we're talking about. You have to protect yourself. Who is the one who carries the baby for 9 months and ends up caring for it the rest of its life? You have to have some kind of control here or you'll end up with a baby at 20 years old. I'm thinking you aren't ready for that."

"No, I am not. Thanks for that tip."

"Sure, no problem. You'll do fine. So, are you going to tell me who it is? You didn't say 'no' when I mentioned Lewis so I'm guessing it is him."

Bitsy zipped her lips like she was closing a zipper and they both laughed as they walked back to the store.

It was 5:25pm and Bitsy ran down to the ladies' room before she punched out and left the store. She still hadn't seen Lewis and thought maybe he was going to stand her up. Then she remembered their kiss. He wouldn't have kissed her if he didn't like her and didn't want to go out with her. She was just being paranoid. She hurried back through the store and out the front door. She looked around but did not see Lewis. He didn't have her phone number, and certainly didn't have her address either. So how were they going to get together on Saturday? She suddenly felt sick inside. She had gotten herself all worked up and had fallen for a guy who didn't want to go out with her. *What a dope.* Sometimes she was surprised at how naïve she was. She actually believed people when they told her things like 'I really like you, too.' So much for being a woman. She'd probably be a virgin her entire life and die an old maid, which is what they used to call women who never got married. But that would be Bitsy, the old maid librarian, or schoolmarm. She wasn't sure what 'marm' meant but she remembered hearing the word combined with school teacher or librarian who never married, school marm. One word or two? She'd have to look that one up.

"Bitsy!" Someone was running up behind her and reached out to touch her shoulder. She jumped; she was so focused on planning her wretched empty life that she didn't hear Lewis calling her until he was right beside her.

"Didn't you hear me calling you?" He was a little out of breath and stopped walking, taking Bitsy's hand in his.

"Oh, no, sorry, I was working on a story, in my head. I didn't hear you." She felt such relief that she squeezed his hand and beamed at him. "So, where were you? I thought maybe you decided to cancel our date and couldn't tell me." She wouldn't be able to deal with it if that was what Lewis had to say to her.

"No, why in the world would I cancel my date with you? I'm sorry. I was just helping them unload a shipment and it took a little longer than we thought it would take. I need to get your address, Bitsy, and a phone number."

"I'm still thinking that I can get my mom's car for the night. I haven't asked her yet, but I'm sure she'll let me borrow it. I do use it sometimes when my dad is around so that they have one car between them in case they have to go out. I'm pretty sure they are going to be around this weekend, so I should be able to use her car tomorrow night."

"Well, that would be great. But, I still want to come to meet your parents. If that's okay with you?"

"Okay, sure. Have the big talk with my dad, eh?"

"Well, I think 'the big talk with your dad' is asking for your hand in marriage."

"Oh yeah, right." *Stupid, stupid.* She knew that, too.

"Let's just take it one step at a time. I'd like to meet your parents and let them know their daughter will be well taken care of while she's out with me. That they'll have nothing to worry about."

Bitsy blushed. She knew he meant it and she knew she would be taken care of, too. She held his hand tight. She wanted to kiss it. She wanted to kiss him. She felt their hands sweating together and had a fleeting thought about them, naked, sweating together. She blushed again and looked up into his eyes. He was looking at her with such intensity. Why did he have to have such deep, dark, brilliant blue eyes? Every time she looked up into them she ached all over. The feelings in her body were all so new to her. He was smiling at her. She felt as though he knew the effect he had on her, but he never said a word. She hoped he felt as strongly about her as she felt about him, but she didn't think he did. Maybe, in time.

She didn't want to leave but she knew she had to go. She tore out a piece of paper from the mini notebook she now carried in her purse, wrote down her address and phone number, and also added the bus he needed to take to get to her house. She told Lewis that when he called, she would drive to pick him up so that he didn't have to walk to her house from the bus stop. Since he didn't know exactly where she lived it would be best if she met him there. Bitsy gave him a quick kiss on his cheek and then ran the rest of the way to her bus stop.

On her walk home, all Bitsy could think about was her date with Lewis the next day. It just couldn't get here fast enough. She again thought about what she should wear. She didn't even know what they were going to do. She should have asked Lewis so that she could decide what to wear. But she couldn't think that far ahead, all she could think about was having a real date with him. But now that she had time to think about it, it would help if she knew whether they were going to a movie or maybe bowling. She hoped he didn't want to go to a movie. What she really wanted was just to go out to dinner so that they could talk and really get to know each other better. She thought about calling him but then she realized, she had given him her number but she hadn't asked him for his phone number. She'll remember that for next time. And, hopefully, there will be a next time with Lewis.

When Bitsy got home, she was alone. She went up to her room and started looking through her closet. Maybe she could pick two outfits and when he called to tell her he was leaving to come to her house, she could ask him what they would be doing that night and then she'd decide what to wear before she had to go pick him up. She would have plenty of time to get ready before he got to the bus stop. That sounded like a good plan.

She picked a skirt and a blouse, one of her other new outfits that Lewis hadn't seen yet. And then she picked out a pair of her skinny jeans and a nice sleeveless top and a sweater, in case it got a little chilly at night, although with the temps forecast to be in the 80's all day, she doubted she would need it. But she liked this sweater, in her favorite color - an orchid shade - so thought she would bring it along anyway or just wear it over her shoulders. Plus, it would complement her yellow sleeveless tank top and her white jeans.

As soon as Bitsy heard her mom downstairs, she ran down to ask about borrowing her car. Probably not a good idea to wait until the last minute to ask, but she really didn't think it would be a problem. She figured her parents would be so excited about her having a first real date with a man that they would give her the keys without question. And her dad would be happy that she was driving and not dependent on the man to bring her home or have to take the bus. He always wanted her to be safe and she knew she would be safer with her own vehicle. Of course, Bitsy already felt very safe with Lewis, but she was pretty sure her parents wouldn't feel the same way about a man they just met. They'd have to find out for themselves. Bitsy may have been just a little naïve. That's what her parents would say anyway. Innocent. That was another way her parents often described Bitsy. She had always been really protected. That came with being an only child. They put all of their attention into their one and only child.

Bitsy found her mom in the kitchen.

"Hi honey. How was your first week? Ready for a relaxing weekend with your old mom and dad?"

"Actually, mom, I have a date tomorrow night, with a man I met at work."

"Well, look at you! I hope we're going to get to meet him?"

"Oh, yes, he wants to meet you. So, he's coming here by bus and I thought I'd pick him up at the bus stop and so was wondering, can I use your car tomorrow night?"

"He doesn't have a car?"

"He does, but he said it isn't very dependable. We were just going to go by bus on our date but then I thought it would be better if I had a car, just in case I missed the bus and then I'd have that walk home, at night, unless he came with me and then he would have to get the bus home, if the bus is even still running at night, or he could spend the night here, or..."

"Yes, yes, of course you can use the car, sweetie. So, what's his name? What does he do at the store? Are you going to meet his parents?"

"Mom, this is our first date. I don't know a lot about him, yet. But he does want to meet you and dad after I pick him up at the bus stop, so we'll come back here so you can meet him. But please don't drill him with questions. I'll find out a few things and let you know, okay? He's kind of shy and he might be kind of nervous if you start asking him a ton of questions. Don't scare him off, he's my first real date. Oh, and his name is Lewis."

Her mom laughed and agreed not to be too hard on Lewis.

"And tell dad, too. He can be scary sometimes. I remember when I went to prom. I thought my date was going to leave me at the house and forget the whole thing with all dad's questions!"

"I know. Your dad can be a little tough. But that's only because he knows how guys can be with young girls and he's only thinking of what's best for you. He wants to make sure that whoever takes you out is a good boy and will take care of you and bring you home safely."

"Yeah, I know, mom. But just tell him that Lewis is different. He's not a boy, he's a man, and he'll be really good to me, I just know it."

"Well, sounds like you have a crush."

"I wouldn't exactly call it a crush, mom. I think it is more than that."

"Well, don't rush into anything. You did just meet this boy-sorry, I mean 'man'- a week ago."

# Chapter 10

Friday night went by much slower than Bitsy would have liked. But she enjoyed spending time with her parents and together they watched the show 'Cagney and Lacey' and her mom's favorite, 'Remington Steele.' Half-way through 'Remington Steele' Bitsy decided to go to bed, even though she knew she probably wouldn't get much sleep. She knew she'd spend her time thinking about her date with Lewis. But surprisingly, she fell right to sleep. Having finished her first week at a new job did the trick and Bitsy was more tired than she realized.

Bitsy didn't set her alarm but jumped out of bed at 6am, her new wake-up time, and quickly made her bed.  She threw on a pair of jeans and headed downstairs to make coffee for her parents. She loved the smell of coffee but couldn't stand the taste of it. She made herself a cup of English Breakfast tea with honey and half-and-half. She turned on the TV and watched a morning news program. She didn't know which one it was because she never watched them, but she needed something to distract her so that she would stop thinking and let the day pass by until it was time to get ready for her date with Lewis. And of course, she awaited his phone call when he would tell her what bus he was taking. She was full of excitement about how their date would unfold. Although Bitsy was really enjoying the P.D. James book she was reading, she knew she would not be able to concentrate on a single word and would just re-read the same paragraph again and again.  Yup, watching TV was the best choice. She didn't want to wake her parents so she set the volume down low.

Her dad got up first. It was around 7:30am when he came downstairs in his bathrobe.

"I smell coffee – you aren't drinking coffee, are you Bitsy?"

"No, dad, I made it for you and mom."

"Well, thank you sweetie. That was thoughtful of you." Her dad poured himself a cup and then came into the living room to sit with Bitsy. He watched the TV but, like Bitsy, he seemed to be a little pre-occupied. After about ten minutes, he finally spoke, slowly and carefully.

"So, Bitsy. Mom tells me that you… ah… have a date tonight?"

"Yes, I do, dad. His name is Lewis."

"Yes, your mom did tell me that. What is his last name?"

Bitsy suddenly realized that she did not know Lewis' last name! It kind of surprised her that she didn't and she thought about it, trying to recall a moment in their few conversations when Lewis may have told her his last name. But she could not think of anytime when his last name had been part of their conversations. She blushed, a little annoyed at herself that she didn't have that information.

"I didn't ask him. I work with him, and he's coming here so you'll find out then. Sorry, dad, I should have asked him."

"That's okay, Pumpkin. You know me, I want to know everything about the boy who is going out with my daughter. And it better be only good news."

"Man, dad, he's a man." Bitsy was adamant about this. She was dating a man now, not a boy. And she was a woman. She was surprised that her parents still didn't see her that way. Maybe they would see it once they met Lewis and realized that she was, definitely, dating a man.

"Oh, sorry. So, when do we meet this man that you are dating?"

"I'm not 'dating' him yet, dad, this is my first date. And he'll be here sometime later today. First, he's going to call me to let me know what time he'll be here. So, you'll meet him later today."

"You didn't set a time? What if he calls and says 9? Will you go out then? I know some boys, ah, men that are like that. They just show up whenever they get around to it."

"Lewis is not like that. He is respectful and kind. He will be here at a normal dating time."

"Okay, I can't wait to meet Lewis."

"And you will be nice, right dad? No prying questions. I told mom he is kind of shy so you might make him nervous. Don't make him nervous, please dad?"

"I'll be the perfect dad, Pumpkin, I promise."

Bitsy looked a little doubtful, but hoped her dad would keep his word.

When her mom got up, they all went about making a nice scrambled egg breakfast with bacon and English muffins. The day was actually going by faster than Bitsy thought it would and she was just about to check the time when the phone rang. It was 2:45. She knew it had to be Lewis.

"I'll get it!" Bitsy grabbed the phone and counted to five to calm herself down before answering.

"Hello." She was pleasant and hoped she hid some of the excitement in her voice.

"Hello, is Bitsy there, please?"

"Speaking, is this Lewis?"

"Yes, it is. How are you, Bitsy?"

"I'm fine Lewis, how are you doing today?" Bitsy's heart was tap dancing in her chest and thought surely Lewis could hear it. She took a few deep breaths to calm herself down. She felt her cheeks blushing as she pictured Lewis' lips close to the phone, his penetrating eyes looking deep into hers, causing her to shiver. She felt her knees start to wobble. She was surprised that she didn't even have to look into Lewis' eyes or to be physically close to him in order for him to have the same effect on her that he had when he was standing right in front of her.

"I'm fine, Bitsy. Thanks for asking." Why were they both being so formal and polite? Bitsy felt like she was talking to one of her parents' friends. That was a real mood killer so she decided to spice it up a little.

"I was thinking about you Lewis. I'm really looking forward to our date."

"Well, that's great, Bitsy. So am I, so am I. So, I was wondering when you would like to meet me at the bus stop?"

"Well, it is almost 3 now. I guess it depends on what we are doing tonight." She was still hoping that they would go out to dinner so that they could talk.

"I was thinking about us going to dinner. How does that sound?"

"Sounds perfect, Lewis. How about I pick you up at around 5:30? We can come back here and you can talk to my parents for a little bit and then we can get to the restaurant before it gets crowded. I think there is a bus that will be there around 5:30, I'll get there at around 5, just in case it's a little early."

"Okay, ah, well, I guess I can probably find something to do, or maybe I'll just walk around until you get here in… that would be about two hours, right?"

"Lewis? Are you there at the bus stop now?"

"I am, Bitsy. I hope it's not a problem? If you're busy right now, that's fine, I will just wait until you can pick me up. Don't worry about it. Or you can give me directions to your house and I'll just walk there."

"Lewis! Don't be ridiculous! I'll be right there. It'll only take me about five minutes to get there. See you soon!"

Bitsy was so excited! She ran upstairs, yelling to her parents at the same time.

"He's here, I'm going to pick him up!"

She checked herself in the mirror, put on a nicer top with her jeans, brushed her teeth and ran back downstairs, nearly tripping on the carpet.

"What?! He's here?" Her parents were standing at the bottom of the stairs and caught Bitsy as she nearly fell into their arms.

"Keys, mom, where are your keys?"

"Why is he here now? Is this the time you planned?"

"No, I don't know why he is here. I'll find out."

"You are too excited, why don't I go with you?" Bitsy just looked at her mom. She wanted Lewis all to herself right now. She was not ready to share him with her parents.

"I'm fine mom, I just don't want him to stand there waiting too long. I'm fine, really. We'll be right back." Bitsy took the keys from her mom's outstretched hand and ran out the door.

"Remember, be nice to him! I really like him."

Bitsy felt her heart in her chest and wondered if it was pounding so hard because she had just run up and down the stairs or if because she was just so excited that she was going to see Lewis in just a few minutes, which was hours before she thought she'd see him today.

She drove the speed limit and not a bit over. She didn't want anything to stop her from getting to Lewis on time, least of all a speeding ticket. Even though she continued driving a reasonable speed her heart seemed to be beating faster the closer she got to the bus stop.

And then she saw him. He was staring in her direction as if he knew she would be coming from his left. He raised his hand giving her a short wave while Bitsy pulled up beside him. He got in, turning towards her as soon as he was settled and buckled up.

"Hi Bitsy, nice to see you. You look…beautiful."

Bitsy could not resist and leaned over and kissed Lewis on his soft, sensuous lips.

"Hi Lewis." Breathless, that was the right description for how she spoke his name. She surprised herself a little with her spontaneous show of affection.

"That was a nice greeting. Thank you for that." Lewis turned away, trying to hide his obvious pleasure over the kiss she gave him.

"Was that too forward of me, Lewis? I don't want you to think I'm fast or anything, I mean, I'm not. I think it's you. I feel something… more… I can't explain it. There is just something about you."

Lewis smiled through her explanation, watching the road as she drove. They were both silent for a while.

"This is a nice neighborhood where you live, Bitsy. Have you lived here your whole life?"

Bitsy was lost in her own thoughts and enjoyed the silence for a few minutes. She really didn't want Lewis to think she was like this with every man she dated, not that she ever dated a man before. It was him, only him. She wanted to convey this without scaring him away from her. It was too much too soon. She needed to calm herself and take it slow. She realized he was talking to her but she hadn't heard a word he had said.

"What? I didn't… What did you say?"

"I was just wondering if you've lived here long. This is a beautiful neighborhood, with all the trees and the perfectly landscaped yards."

"Oh, yes, we moved here when I was about four years old. It's my parents' first and only house. They did some renovations, added a sunroom and deck, re-did the carpeting in the living room, put in a new kitchen. And of course, we've painted the rooms, bought new furniture, especially when I outgrew my twin bed from when I was just a kid." She felt better talking with him about these mundane things - it helped her relax. He seemed to know the right thing to say to get her out of her own head. She wanted Lewis so bad she was afraid she would throw herself at him before he was ready. Maybe he had a five-date rule or a ten-date rule, or something like that. And here she was thinking about Lewis in that way before they'd even had one date. That would definitely scare him away. He'd probably quit his job to get away from her. She did not want that to happen so she let him take the lead and bring her into more normal conversation territory.

When they arrived at Bitsy's house, she pulled the car into the garage. She decided she would be a little more detached and not so gaga over Lewis. She felt like that was what he wanted. So, from here on,  she would let Lewis make the first move. She would not kiss him again even if her lips were burning for him to kiss them.

"This way, Lewis." She held the door into the house from the garage open for Lewis and followed behind him.

"Mom, dad? We're here." She called out as they entered the house, looking into the dining room and then heading for the living room where her parents were sitting. They both got up when Bitsy walked in with Lewis.

"Mom, dad, this is Lewis. Lewis, this is my mom and dad."

Dad stuck his hand out and shook Lewis' hand firmly.

"I'm Keith, nice to meet you, Lewis."

"Hello Keith, Lewis Amepurdu."

"Is that French?" Bitsy knew her dad would ask that; he was always interested in a person's ethnicity. A habit he picked up from Grandpa Gordon.

"Yes sir, it is."

"Canadian?"

"No, actually France."

"Oh, interesting."

"And I'm Violet, or Vi. Hi Lewis." Bitsy was grateful her mom didn't let her dad go on any longer about where Lewis' family hailed from or where they settled in the States. She knew it could go on and on if her dad had his way.

"Vi, nice to meet you, also."

"Can I get you something cold to drink? You must be thirsty after riding the bus and then waiting in the hot sun."

"Yes, I could use a cold drink. Thanks... um… Vi."

"Lemonade or iced tea, or I have soda, too. We don't drink a lot of soda, mostly have it for pizza night. Bitsy…Betsy loves her cream soda."

"It's okay, mom, he calls me Bitsy, too."

"Yes, um, lemonade would be great, thanks."

"Here, sit down Lewis." Lewis looked at Bitsy waiting to see where she would sit. She sat in one of the recliners and her dad sat in his recliner. Lewis looked confused and then sat on the couch, alone. Mom came in with a tray of drinks and looked at Bitsy sitting in her recliner. She gave Bitsy a little frown and then put the tray down on the table in front of the sofa. She went around the table and sat at the other end of the sofa. Again, she gave Bitsy a slight frown. Bitsy realized she should have sat on the couch, but Bitsy was trying to be a little cool and not give Lewis the impression that she was clingy. Of course, her mom didn't know this.

"Here you go, Lewis." Mom handed Lewis a glass filled with lemonade and ice.

"Thank you, this is great." Bitsy got up and got herself a glass from the tray and handed one to her dad.

"Are you hungry, Lewis? Can I get you a sandwich? Maybe a snack? We haven't had lunch; we typically have big breakfasts on the weekend days and so sometimes we just skip lunch and have a snack. Or maybe I should make some sandwiches?" Her mom was being very nice, as Bitsy had requested.

"I'm not really that hungry, mom. Maybe just a snack." Bitsy did not want her dinner out with Lewis ruined by her mom filling them up with sandwiches! It was 3:30 now and they would be going out in a couple of hours.

"Oh sure, that's fine. Cheese and crackers, how does that sound? Help me in the kitchen, Bitsy?" Bitsy looked at Lewis and then at her dad. She was hesitant to leave them alone. Lewis looked up at Bitsy, smiled and winked as if to let her know he'd be okay alone with her dad. She gave her dad a look but he didn't look at her. He was enjoying his lemonade and never looked her way as she walked out of the room.

In the kitchen Bitsy grabbed the crackers off the shelf and got the cheese cutter. She was being very quiet, hoping to hear what was being said in the living room. Her mother went about her business, getting the cheese out of the refrigerator. Bitsy got a nice platter to put the cheese and crackers on and some small plates and napkins for each of them. She stood next to her mother at the counter, tapping her fingers in rhythm to her tapping toe.

"Bitsy, will you relax."

"I want to get back in there. Shh… listen… is dad raising his voice?"

"No, he is not. Just give them a few minutes together, will you."

"We have, we've given them a few minutes. We should get back in there. I need to rescue Lewis."

"No, you don't. Here, arrange the cheese with the crackers on the platter."

Bitsy dumped the box of crackers and spread them around with her fingers.

"There, now the cheese."

"Bitsy, arrange those crackers. This isn't a pool hall. We are going to serve your guest some cheese and crackers arranged nicely on the platter."

Bitsy took a deep breath and did as her mother asked. She took a few minutes and arranged the crackers around the outside of the platter and put the slices of cheese, leaning one slice against the other, in the center of the platter. It did look better, Bitsy had to admit.

"There, is that better?"

"Yes, dear. Thank you."

"Can we go back in now. It has been at least 10 minutes, mom."

"Okay, fine. You take the platter. Oh, wait. Bitsy? Why didn't you sit on the couch next to Lewis? I thought it was a little strange that he was sitting over there all by himself and I had to sit next to him. It must have made him feel like a specimen on display with all of us looking at him."

"Oh, yeah. I don't know.  I just sat down on your chair. I didn't really think about it." She didn't like lying to her mother, but she certainly wasn't going to tell her mom that she was giving Lewis some space so that he didn't think she was some fast and loose woman who had to be all over her man, even before he was her man!

Bitsy set the tray on the coffee table and then handed Lewis one of the plates and a napkin. She leaned over the table to hand them to him. She avoided his eyes but she knew his were on her. She handed her dad a plate and napkin and then gave one to her mom, who was now sitting in her recliner. Bitsy took her own plate and napkin and sat on the couch, not all the way at the other end from Lewis, but far enough away that he would have to reach his arm straight out to touch her. She sat sideways on the cushion and grabbed a cracker with a slice of cheese.

"Bitsy, could you pass the platter around?" Again, the stern look from her mom.

"Oh, sure." Bitsy got up and brought the platter to her mother who took a couple of crackers and a couple of pieces of the sliced cheese. Next her dad also took a couple of crackers and some cheese and took the opportunity to whisper to Bitsy.

"It would be nice to serve your guest first."

"Oh, I'm sorry, Lewis.  Here, I should have served you first. Sorry." She felt herself blushing. Just because she  was trying to be a little cooler about her feelings for Lewis, she had no intention of being rude.

"That's fine, Bitsy. There's plenty left for me. Thank you."

She put the platter down on the table in front of Lewis and sat down on the sofa again, this time a little closer to him. He turned to her and smiled. She knew he was aware of her distancing herself and seemed grateful that she was over whatever it was she was going through. He seemed to relax a little more. She finally looked at what he was wearing and thought he looked very sexy in his short-sleeved pink button up shirt and black jeans. She thought he must be hot in the black jeans, though. He wore a pair of bright green sneakers that Bitsy smiled at. He didn't seem like a bright green sneakers kind of guy. She thought that was very bold of him. She also realized she had never seen Lewis wearing these clothes at work. These must be his date clothes. Bitsy wondered how many times he had worn this exact outfit out on a date with another girl… er… woman.  He looked very neat and clean and had that just-washed Dial soap smell she loved so much.

They chatted for a short time. Her dad, of course, brought up sports and asked if Lewis was a football fan. He wasn't. Lewis said he didn't watch sports very much, and apologized. Her mom asked about his parents. He had none. Lewis said they were both dead. Did he like his job at A-to-Z Mart? And how long had he been there? It was okay, better now that Bitsy was working there. He had been there for about four years. Did he have other ambitions, going to college, anything like that? He did have other plans but didn't feel he could really talk about them in much detail since he was still working them out. He did have a degree from NYU majoring in film making and had taken a few other advanced classes in filming documentaries. Although her parents seemed impressed with Lewis' schooling, she could tell they would have preferred if Lewis had a degree in Engineering or Business Management, something more practical than Film Production. But Bitsy realized that she had just learned many things that she didn't know about Lewis.

# Chapter 11

Their conversation ebbed and flowed. The quiet moments were a little uncomfortable, for Bitsy at least. She wanted to fill them with chatter. She wanted Lewis to be so interesting to her parents that they would laugh and joke with him. She wanted them to be asking questions at the same time and talking over each other from their excitement over Lewis. But she knew Lewis just wasn't that guy. He was quiet and mysterious. Yes, he seemed a little shy, but Bitsy preferred to think there was more mystery to Lewis than shyness. He didn't just blurt out his whole life story and his feelings to anyone. He was cautious and a little reserved. It took him time to trust people. Not at all like Bitsy. She told people her life story before she even knew their last name! She was an open book. So opposite to Lewis. Hmm, she'd always heard that opposites attract, but she wasn't sure she really believed that. To her the attraction would only be temporary, more an oddity, like a contortionist in a circus. You are curious and amazed when you first see the person bending and twisting their bodies in unusual and potentially painful poses. But then, after you've seen it a few times, it no longer holds any interest. And you get bored. That was how she felt about opposites attracting. With time, someone would get bored. She hoped it wasn't Lewis getting bored with her. And at this point, she just couldn't imagine being bored with him. Bitsy decided she wouldn't think about it right now. She would just let things happen. There was still so much she didn't know about Lewis. She might find out that they're more alike than she thought.

During one of the quiet times, Bitsy checked the clock. She was surprised to see that more than an hour had passed and it was now 4:40pm. She jumped up and gathered the plates from the side tables and the coffee table and was bringing them, along with the empty platter, back into the kitchen.

"I have to shower and get ready now. Do you need anything Lewis? I won't be long."

"He's fine," said her mom. "Don't worry, we'll take good care of him."

Lewis gave Bitsy his winning smile. She watched his eyes quickly look her up and down. She felt her cheeks turning their usual hot pink color whenever Lewis looked at her like this. But she hadn't seen him do the up-and-down before and liked that he was 'checking her out'! She also thought it was a little risky doing it right in front of her parents. Apparently, they didn't notice; or they pretended like they didn't. Her mom got up from her chair and followed Bitsy into the kitchen. Bitsy noticed her dad watching her mom walk away. Bitsy was pretty sure his eyes looked her up and down.

Bitsy put the dishes in the sink and turned to her mom who was right behind her.

"Well, what do you think? Isn't he wonderful?"

"He seems like a very nice bo… man. He has beautiful eyes, doesn't he?"

"Yes, he does! They just make me melt, I feel all weak-kneed and…" Bitsy stopped because she realized she was talking to her mom. She was so used to telling her parents, especially her mom, everything but she felt just a little uncomfortable talking to her mom about anything that could possibly be related to sex. Her mom, of course, had already had 'the talk' with Bitsy several years ago - before she went to prom. And then, years before that, when Bitsy was about twelve years old her mom had told her a bit about 'the birds and the bees', mostly about menstruating and how she could become pregnant, but she didn't go into details; not until she had 'the talk'. So even though Bitsy was okay with her mom talking to her about sex, she wasn't used to talking to her mom about anything sexual. This was a whole new area that she had never discussed with her mom and thought she should keep it that way. Although Bitsy's mom had told her all about sex, she was quite sure her mom didn't want to hear about Bitsy's experiences with sex. She most likely preferred to believe Bitsy had none. And of course, her dad was completely out of the picture. She would never even say the words, for example, 'sex' and 'Lewis' in the same sentence. Her dad might even kill Lewis right then and there!

Bitsy showered faster than usual and just ran her wet fingers through her hair. She had washed it yesterday and it still felt clean to her. All it needed was just a little fluffing up. She toweled off, sprayed herself with a freesia body spray she loved, and put on her new blue jean pencil skirt and yellow blouse. She applied a little eye liner and mascara followed by a touch of purple shadow. She finished off with a plum mauve lipstick and a pinch to her cheeks and she was almost ready to go. She gave a quick blow dry to her almost dry hair, grabbed her purple sweater, and headed downstairs to begin her much anticipated date with Lewis.

He was still sitting in the same spot on the couch and her dad was talking to him about football. Poor Lewis, he must be so bored was all Bitsy could think. Bitsy's mom was in the kitchen so before Bitsy went into the living room, she stopped in the kitchen to talk with her mom.

"Mom, why are you letting dad bore Lewis with football? He told dad he doesn't watch sports."

"This is your dad's way of bonding. Just let him be. It's only been for about fifteen minutes. I'm sure Lewis will survive. Now, about tonight. You are dropping him off at his place, right?"

"Oh, yes, I will. I mean, I don't think I should drive home and then make him take the bus home.  Do you?"

"No, of course not."

"Okay, great."

"Alright, no later than 11. It is just about 5:10 now so that's plenty of time to be out on a first date. Make sure you leave enough time after you drop Lewis off to be home by 11. And write down his address and phone number for us."

"I don't have his address. I'll have him write it down."

Bitsy was a little nervous about asking Lewis for his address because she knew he lived in a neighborhood that her parents would not want their daughter driving around in at night. All she could do was hope they wouldn't notice until after she and Lewis were on their way. But she had no doubt her dad would know the neighborhood's reputation.

She walked into the living room towards Lewis holding a piece of paper and pen in her hand. Again, she got the once over from Lewis but she was too preoccupied with wondering how her parents might react to where he lived to focus on him checking her out. Lewis stood up.

"Bitsy, you look beautiful." Bitsy held out her hand and Lewis took the paper and pen without removing his eyes from Bitsy.

"Lewis, my mom would like your address and phone number." She said this without looking at Lewis and instead turned her eyes towards the chair where her dad sat.

"Oh, and thank you." She added, acknowledging he had given her a compliment and not wanting Lewis to think she hadn't noticed.

Lewis stood there, holding the paper and pen, still looking at Bitsy. Her dad was looking at Lewis, and Bitsy stood looking at her dad. They all hung in suspended animation until Bitsy's dad stood up.

"That's right. Lewis, we would like your contact information." Her dad stood up, his arms folded in a strong 'dad being tough' pose.

Lewis pulled his gaze from Bitsy.

"Certainly, sir." Lewis wrote on the paper and then handed it to Bitsy's dad.

"Okay, great. What town is this? You just wrote your street address."

"Oh, sorry. It's in Scutton." Lewis turned back to Bitsy.

"Are you ready to go, Bitsy?"

"Scutton, eh? Hmm, how long have you lived there, Lewis?"

Apparently, her dad was not finished questioning Lewis. Bitsy's mom walked into the living room.

"Hey, Vi. Lewis lives in Scutton. You know where that is, right?"

"Oh, yes. I do. How long have you lived there, Lewis?"

"Almost four years now, since I finished college and started working at the Mart."

"Well, I'm concerned about Bitsy driving in that neighborhood." Bitsy noticed that her dad's friendly mood had changed and instead of asking non-threatening questions like he had been all night, he was now giving Lewis the third degree.

"Dad, we aren't going to be walking around there at night. I'll bring Lewis home after our dinner to just drop him off and then head home. I won't be there long at all. We won't even be in Scutton, will we Lewis?"

"No, no sir, we won't be there. I would never let anything happen to Bitsy. She will be fine. But, if you prefer, Bitsy can drop me off before she gets to the bad section of town and I'll walk from there."

"That sounds like a good idea." Bitsy was surprised that her dad would be okay with Lewis having to walk at night in such a bad neighborhood just so she wouldn't have to drive through the town.

"Dad, Lewis is not walking home at night. It will be fine. I'll drop him off and then come right home. I mean, how bad can it be? It's not like there are shootings going on all the time or anything, is there Lewis?"

Lewis dropped his gaze to the floor.

"Lewis, is there?" Bitsy repeated, now completely uncomfortable with her decision to drive Lewis home at night wondering if she would be dodging flying bullets as she drove down his street and out of his neighborhood.

"No, no, nothing like that. There are a lot of unfriendly types hanging around but no, no shootings. I wouldn't let you drive me home if there was any chance of that kind of danger. And I certainly wouldn't live in a place that bad, either." Lewis looked up at Bitsy with his head still down. Bitsy realized that it wasn't because Lewis was afraid for Bitsy to drive into his neighborhood. It was that Lewis was ashamed that he even lived in such a neighborhood and that they were having this conversation.

"Or we could end our date early and Bitsy can drop me off when it is still light out so she isn't in the neighborhood at night. If that would make you feel better, sir, about Bitsy driving in my neighborhood? It would be fine with me if it will make you feel better about this situation." Bitsy stared at Lewis in disbelief. Was he seriously suggesting that they end their date basically right after dinner? That would hardly be a date at all.

"Then we might as well just stay here and not even go out to eat if that's all we'd be doing."

"That's a great idea, honey. Why don't you both just stay here and we'll get Chinese takeout." Bitsy's mom hadn't said anything while they were discussing where Lewis lived and now she thought Bitsy was being serious when she was really just being sarcastic.

"Mom, this is my first date with Lewis. I think I'd rather have him all to myself. I'm not fifteen anymore. I don't need a chaperone."

"You do still live at home though and, if we are concerned about your safety, you are going to do as we ask." Bitsy's dad was still in his Mr. Clean arms folded across his chest tough guy pose.

Bitsy was getting very frustrated. She had no idea what Lewis' neighborhood was like and she had lived a pretty sheltered life. But she didn't like the way her parents seemed to be turning on Lewis as if he had shown up for their first date at 9pm and drunk. He had been a perfect gentleman and Bitsy knew she would be fine the rest of the night until she got home.

"If you promise to drop Lewis off and then head right home from there, I think it will be okay. She can't get lost, can she Lewis? Are you close to a main street that she can get on to head back?"

"Oh yes, she just drives right down my street and it'll take her directly to the main road she'd take to get back home."

Now that the problem of dropping Lewis off seemed resolved, Bitsy was feeling emboldened and offered another suggestion, "Or, we could come back here and Lewis could stay over and then leave in the morning?  I could drive him back then or he could take the bus. We can find out the bus schedule for Sunday."

"Actually, I have plans on Sunday, Bitsy, so I couldn't stay. But that's a nice offer, thank you."

Bitsy turned to Lewis. She expected her parents would object but couldn't believe those words were coming out of Lewis' mouth. She thought it was a great idea and would love to see Lewis first thing in the morning at her house.  Maybe even sneak down to visit him in the middle of the night, maybe squeeze in beside him on the couch. Or, if they let Lewis have the guest bedroom, even better. The more she thought about it the more she thought it was a great idea. But Lewis 'had plans' on Sunday.

"Oh? Well, I guess that's out. Okay, let's go, Lewis. See you guys later." Bitsy kissed her mom and her dad and headed out the front door.

"Very nice meeting you both.  And thanks for the lemonade and the cheese and crackers. Very kind of you. You have a beautiful home." Lewis shook Keith's hand and then took Vi's hand in both of his and rushed out to catch up to Bitsy who was already in the car, waiting.

As soon as Lewis got into the car, Bitsy took off. She was just driving, but she had no idea where they were going. Lewis didn't say a word. He knew Bitsy was upset about something so he waited for her to calm down and ask him how to get to the restaurant they were going to for dinner. It only took a couple of minutes of rage driving before she pulled over.

"Lewis, I don't know where we're going. Do you want to drive?"

"Since it's your mother's car and I'm not on her insurance, that's probably not the best idea. But, are you okay? You seem upset."

Bitsy was happy that Lewis had recognized her mood change. But then again, who wouldn't have?

"Yes, I am, but I'm getting over it now. It's stupid. Sorry. I get upset when my parents treat me like a child. I'm almost 20, and when I'm making enough money, I will get my own apartment and move out. Just because I still live at home, they want to control my every move."

"I think they're just concerned for you and want you to be safe. You're fortunate to have such caring and loving parents."

Bitsy knew he was right. And she decided not to mention his comment about having plans on Sunday. It really was none of her business.

"Well, no need to apologize. So, are you ready to go to dinner then?"

"Yes, I am. So, where am I driving?"

"Well, I want you to head into Trenton. There's a nice little out of the way restaurant that I like. It's called "Geno's". But first, there is something else I really need to do."

"Geno's? Oh Geno's! I love that place, it's a nice restaurant. Good choice. But what do you need to do?"

Lewis leaned over and pushing her hair back behind her ear he pulled her to him and kissed her full on the lips. Even though Bitsy was taken by surprise, she felt her entire body quiver and before she knew it, he was pulling back slightly. The kiss was over. When she opened her eyes, he was still holding the side of her face and then kissed her on the tip of her nose, smiling at her not only with his full lovely lips but with his sky bright blue eyes, too.

"That was nice, Bitsy. I've wanted to do that since you picked me up this afternoon. Well, after you kissed me, that is." Lewis was nodding his head, looking deep into Bitsy's eyes. She felt like he could see her heart and soul and could feel everything that she was feeling right at that moment. She finally understood when people said, 'they were as one.' Time stood still for those few seconds. And her mind went blank. She looked around the car and then remembered that they were on their way to dinner. But first she had to start breathing again. She exhaled and took a deep breath in.

"Lewis, that was… yeah, nice. I agree." He continued smiling and then took his hand from her face and sat back in his seat.

"So, shall we go to dinner now?"

"Oh, yes. I'm starving, what about you?"

◁ 91 ▷

# Chapter 12

Bitsy was impressed with Lewis. They walked into the restaurant and, when Lewis told them his name, they were escorted to a cozy table in a corner, affording them a private spot to enjoy their meal and conversation. Lewis, the perfect gentleman, pulled the chair out for Bitsy, even though the host made a move to do it. After Bitsy was seated and Lewis had sat down across from her, the host handed them each a menu, poured them each a glass of water, and handed Lewis the wine list.

"Well, you can have a drink, Lewis."

"Oh no, that's fine, Bitsy. I don't drink much anyway. I don't really feel like having a drink. But what would you like, maybe a sparkling water, soda?"

"Yes, I'll have a sparkling water, with a lemon?"

"Make that two." And Lewis handed the host back the wine list.

Bitsy was concerned about ordering. She didn't want to choose anything too expensive since she wasn't sure how much money Lewis had. Checking the menu, the shrimp scampi really appealed to her. It was expensive though. She found a baked haddock dish that was also expensive, but less than the shrimp. Maybe she would get the spinach ravioli vegetarian dinner. That was a few dollars less than the baked haddock. She just didn't know. Although she had eaten here only a couple of other times with her parents, she never thought about the cost of any dish because her parents were paying.

"Do you see anything you like, Bitsy?"

"Oh yes, lots of things. I just don't know though, they're all pretty expensive."

"I want you to order whatever you want, Bitsy. Please, I want this to be a dinner you'll never forget."

"Oh, I think it's already a dinner I'll never forget, Lewis!" She laughed a little louder than she meant to and put her hand over her mouth.

"Okay, well, that's great to hear. But I do want you to have a good meal. I've been here a couple of times and the food is excellent. So just order anything you want and don't worry about the price, please."

Bitsy, of course, was distracted now wondering who Lewis had been here with before her. Did he regularly bring his dates here? How many had there been? She couldn't think about ordering. She felt a strange feeling come over her, for the second time that night. She didn't like this feeling and tried to get it out of her head and focus on the menu again.

She decided to just pick, quickly, without thinking.

"Okay, I'll have the shrimp scampi."

Lewis looked up, surprised by her quick selection. It was an extensive menu and he wanted to be sure she had considered all the choices.

"Are you sure?"

Oh no, she thought, I ordered the more expensive dish. I should have ordered a cheaper meal.

"I mean, the baked haddock."

"I wasn't trying to dissuade you, Bitsy, I just wanted to make sure you've looked at all the choices, there really are some wonderful meals here."

"Okay, the spinach ravioli. I want that." She'd had this meal once before when she'd come here with her parents and knew it was delicious.

Lewis just sat and looked at her. She put the menu down and sat with folded hands in her lap.

"Okay, that's what I want, spinach ravioli. How does that sound? Have you tried that meal, Lewis? I've had it, it's really very good."

"No, I haven't tried that, Bitsy. Are you upset, again?"

"No, I just… I was wondering, how many times have you been here Lewis? How many… women…" Bitsy stopped. She did not like this feeling she was having one bit. Even though she had never felt like this before, she suddenly knew it was jealousy. She thought about how it made her feel. She knew Lewis had gone out with other women before her, but she didn't want to think about it. She wanted to think about him being her first and her being his first. But she knew that wasn't the way it was. She felt silly, like a schoolgirl who wanted everything to be the way she wanted it to be. She knew that she was showing her immaturity. Although she was only a little over six years younger than Lewis, she figured it out since he went to college and was working about four years that he was around 25 years old, she felt like it might as well be ten years age difference. She knew nothing about so many things. She had only lived with her parents and was very protected. Lewis had lived on his own for… well, at least four years. Bitsy really didn't know how long he had lived on his own, but she would hopefully find all that out tonight. But she needed to be more mature, act more like a woman and not so much like a young girl. She thought she should explain this to Lewis and hoped he would understand. She didn't want Lewis to think he had made a mistake with Bitsy and that he should be with someone more mature.

"Well, Bitsy, I have been here a couple of times with other women, but it…"

"Lewis, I'm sorry. I don't know what's wrong with me. I'm just… I'm so inexperienced and I feel like you know so much more about so many things. I don't want to disappoint you about anything. I feel like I'm being a silly girl but I want you to see me as a woman. I'm just a woman who doesn't know very much. A woman who hasn't experienced many things." Bitsy said this without looking at Lewis once. She knew looking at him would just distract her and she wouldn't be able to say these things. But now she looked up and he was looking deep into her eyes, a slight, sexy smile on his lips. They sat there quietly for a minute. The waiter had come back with their sparkling water and asked if they had decided on their meals yet.

"I think we need a few more minutes." Lewis turned back to Bitsy.

"Bitsy, I think you need to just enjoy this evening and not think about anyone but you and me having a nice dinner together. The past is past. Let's drink a toast to the future, our future, together."

Bitsy immediately brightened and lifted her glass.

"To us." Lewis said simply and perfectly.

"To us." Bitsy smiled, looked into Lewis' eyes, took a deep breath, and decided she would take Lewis' advice and enjoy their evening together. It was about them and only them. No one else was there with them, so no one else should be in Bitsy's head.

Bitsy put her menu down on top of Lewis' menu. The waiter came over and took their order.

"I'll have the baked haddock with a side salad."

"You get another side dish: you can have the baby carrots, beets, or squash medley."

"I'll have the squash medley."

"And do you want potatoes or rice?"

"No, just the veggies, thanks."

"Very good, Miss. And you, sir?"

"Bitsy you've made a good choice, so I'll have exactly what she's having."

"Very good, sir. I'll bring some bread and your salads directly. Salads have a house dressing, which is a creamy Italian, or you can have another dressing. We have…"

"Creamy Italian is fine with me. Bitsy?" Bitsy nodded agreement.

"I'll bring those right out."

Lewis was so professional sounding. No one would guess that he was a jack-of-all-trades at the A-to-Z Mart. And he was educated, although she wasn't sure what, besides film and making movies, he had learned in his film production classes.

When they had the meal choices out of the way and were sipping their drinks, Bitsy took a deep breath before she started asking Lewis the many questions that she wanted to ask him. Now was her chance to find out about Lewis and hopefully learn about the man behind those beautiful peacock blue eyes.

"So, Lewis. There are so many things that I want to know about you."

"Well, feel free to ask me anything, Bitsy. I'm an open book." Bitsy dove right in.

"Lewis, are your parents really dead? I mean, I'm sure you had parents at one time, so what happened to them? You told my parents that your parents are dead. I'm sorry if this is painful for you and you don't have to answer."

Lewis looked at her. He seemed a little surprised that this was the first question Bitsy asked him. And he didn't answer right away. He seemed to be taking some time to compose his answer.

"I thought that should have been an easy answer, Lewis. It was basically a 'yes' or 'no' question, although I am curious how they died."

"Well, I guess it would seem that way. You're right, it should be. I guess I'm trying to decide if I should tell you the truth about my family. It isn't really as simple an answer as it would seem.  And I didn't think it would be your first question." He was obviously uncomfortable and looked around the restaurant, as if the answer might be out there, waiting for him to find it.

Bitsy gave Lewis some time, not wanting to interfere with whatever Lewis was composing in his head, with whatever he wanted to reveal to Bitsy. But she grew impatient and couldn't wait any longer.

"I really want to know… but only if you really want to tell me. I hope you believe that you can trust me. I know you haven't known me for that long, I can't believe that it's only been one week. I feel like I've known you all my life. And maybe even lives before that, if there is such a thing. I hope it wasn't anything awful that happened to them or to you Lewis, I just…"

"My father left when I was twelve and my mom had early onset Alzheimer's. She had been showing signs of it and, apparently, he just wanted out. Life was very hard for us after that – he married a younger woman and he works for a big company in California making a ton of money but he can't be bothered visiting my mother who lives in a special facility, has been there for nine years now. So, that's my sad story in a nutshell."

"But Lewis, you lied to my parents. They think your parents are dead. How can I tell them that you didn't mean dead, really? I don't know what to think now." Bitsy was shaken and didn't know how she would explain this to her parents. Or maybe it was up to Lewis to explain.

"I think you need to let my parents know the truth. If we are starting a relationship with this lie, how will they ever believe anything you tell them? How can I believe you?"

Lewis looked at Bitsy, stunned at her reaction.

"I'm so sorry Bitsy, I didn't think about it that way. It was just easier for me to say that they were both gone. My father basically is dead to me since I never talk to him. I don't know if I can ever forgive him. And my mom, from what I've read about Alzheimer's, is on borrowed time. I basically lost her several years ago when she started calling me Jason, that's her brother. Sometimes she'd remember that I'm her son, but then she'd call me Jason again. And now, she doesn't know who I am when I visit her and I don't know if she'll even still be alive the next time I visit."

Bitsy didn't know what to say and thought she shouldn't say anything. He really did just spill his guts to her and had obviously decided he could trust Bitsy. Bitsy was suddenly very thankful that Lewis had told her this.

"That was quite a confession, Lewis. I'm sorry your life has been so difficult. How did other, um, people react when you told them about your life?"

"Bitsy, I've never told anyone about my childhood before. I thought it was time I just said it. And I thought you were the right person to tell.  But, you're right, I will tell your parents, too."

Bitsy felt so sad for Lewis and at the same time so privileged that he had confided in her.

Suddenly Lewis got very serious and leaned in closer to Bitsy, taking her hands in both of his. She leaned towards him since it seemed he wanted to say something for her ears only.

"Bitsy, you have to know what you mean to me. I can't tell you how thrilled I am that you feel the same for me that I feel for you. I want you Bitsy, I want to spend the rest of my life with you. I know it sounds crazy, but I've never felt like this for anyone, do you understand, not for anyone else in my life. The few women I've dated can't compare to you. I don't want to frighten you, Bitsy. I want you to know what you mean to me. And yes, it does seem like it has happened very fast, but when you said that you feel like you've known me all your life, and even lives before, I knew at that moment that you felt the same for me. I would do anything for you, to keep you with me, to keep you safe and to take care of you, forever. Do you understand? Anything."

Bitsy felt the energy in his words, in his hands, as he held her hands tightly, not hurting but as he said, safe, like she could fall off a three-story high building and those hands would catch her. If anyone else had heard his words they would think he was, maybe, a little crazy. But Bitsy understood them and felt comforted and protected by them. She felt his love for her, a love she never could have imagined. She was thrilled, excited, and a little afraid all at the same time. She didn't think a forever love would happen to her with the first man she met. But she knew she loved him. That was the only way she could explain her thoughts and all the feelings she had for Lewis. And the way she felt when he kissed her, she knew with their first kiss that he was the one and with each kiss her feelings for him grew stronger. Her desire for Lewis swelled up in her and she squeezed his hands, lifted them up to her mouth, and kissed them. He stood up slightly out of his chair, leaned across the table to Bitsy and took her face in his hands, kissing her full on the lips. She thought she would faint right there in the restaurant. But suddenly Lewis was sitting back in his chair. The waiter was walking towards their table with their salads.

"Would you like any fresh ground pepper?" Bitsy stared at Lewis, her breath not yet back in her body. Breathe, Bitsy, breathe. Lewis was more composed and answered the waiter.

"Sure, I'll have a little pepper. Bitsy, pepper?"

"What, oh, okay, just a little. Thanks." She looked at the waiter who was smiling. Apparently, he had seen them kissing. He quickly walked away, giving them their privacy.

They ate their salads in silence. All the other questions Bitsy had for Lewis didn't seem important anymore. She decided, since they had their lifetimes to get to know each other, that she didn't need to know everything about him right now. She just wanted to enjoy his company and their first date.

Their entire meal was delicious. They split a crème brûlée for dessert. Lewis gave Bitsy a bite and then Bitsy gave Lewis a bite. They laughed and flirted through the entire meal. Bitsy couldn't remember ever having such a good time.

Lewis paid the bill and they left.

They were quiet while Bitsy drove. After driving for a few minutes Bitsy finally realized that she wasn't sure what they were doing. Was she taking him home? Or were they going someplace else?

"Um, Lewis, I don't know where we are going now. Is our date over?"

"Do you want it to be over, Bitsy? I thought we could spend some more time together. It's only 8:25. What would you like to do?"

"Did you have anything else planned?"

"Actually, I'd like to walk through Stewart Park. What do you think? I think we could catch a movie, too, if you'd like."

"No, I don't want to go to a movie. Actually, Lewis, I would really like to see your apartment."

The smile left Lewis' face. He wasn't expecting that. After the conversation with Bitsy's parents, he wasn't sure he'd ever want to bring Bitsy to his apartment.

"Oh, well, I don't know if that's such a good idea, Bitsy. I think maybe we should go someplace else and stick to the plan where you just drop me off later."

"Lewis, unless you're planning on moving out of your apartment anytime soon, I mean, I'm going to eventually see your apartment, right? So, why not tonight?"

"I guess you're right. But we won't stay long. If I had known, I would have done a little cleaning up first, though. It really isn't all that nice, I don't have much. I hope you aren't too disappointed."

"Don't be ridiculous, Lewis. As long as you're there, that's all that matters to me. I don't care what your apartment looks like."

# Chapter 13

Following Lewis' directions, Bitsy drove down Lewis' street until he pointed to a parking place right near his apartment building. A lot of people were sitting out on front steps, walking around in groups, and yelling to each other from porches and hanging out of windows. Everyone in the neighborhood seemed to know everyone else. Bitsy thought it seemed like a friendly neighborhood and wondered what her parents were so concerned about.

As soon as she turned her car off Lewis jumped out of his side of the car and was at Bitsy's side before she had undone her seat belt.

"Come on, Bitsy, lock the car and stay close to me." He put his arm around Bitsy and held her tight against him.

"Hey Lewis, how's it going?" One of the guys on the steps next door called out to Lewis. He was smoking a cigarette and the three other guys he was with all waved to Lewis, too.

Lewis lifted a hand over his head, waving back. Lewis moved along swiftly and within seconds he and Bitsy were up the steps to the second floor of the three-story building and at Lewis' door. He opened the door and guided Bitsy in ahead of him, flipping a light switch on. He locked the door, both the deadbolt and the chain lock.

"You know those guys, Lewis?"

"Oh, sort of, you know, I've lived here for almost four years, so you see the same people every day, you say hi."

Bitsy was feeling a whole new respect for, and was just a little bit in awe of, Lewis for living in such a tough neighborhood and even on a friendly basis with some of his neighbors.

"Would you like something to drink, Bitsy?"

Bitsy stood at the door and scanned the nearly empty room. She had no idea he lived in such dire poverty – it surprised and frightened her. Feeling uncomfortable standing at the door, unable to move for fear she would step on a mouse or a cockroach, Bitsy felt a strong urge to cry for Lewis for the obvious lack of simple comforts that surrounded him.  She wanted to run from this place, she didn't belong here.  She imagined this must be how people feel when they live in a haunted house – uneasy, with some sinister presence living among them, observing them. Only in Lewis' apartment, the sinister presence was lack and shame. It seemed as if the person who lived here said 'no one cares about me and so I certainly don't care about myself. I don't deserve anything nice. I shouldn't even exist.'

It felt contagious, like if Bitsy stayed in this place much longer she would become deathly ill or catch something that she wouldn't ever recover from. She looked at the floor, brown painted wood floors with the paint thicker in some areas, where splinters of wood were missing, trying to even out the floor. She looked for a broom or a mop and saw none. She suddenly realized that Lewis was watching her and she knew that he knew she was judging him.

She forced a smile, and looked back at the floor where Lewis' gaze was also now focused. Her eyes next made a quick sweep of the kitchen. There was a card table and two folding chairs next to the sink and stove area.

She saw a single glass and a plate with a fork and a knife on the counter next to the sink. She knew, without needing to look, that his cabinets weren't filled with plates, cups, and saucers, adorned with pink and yellow flowers or some other pattern, that matched the kitchen décor.  Bitsy wondered if he had more than one glass, one plate, one fork, and a knife. She struggled to find something nice to say but, coming up empty, decided to remain quiet.

"Um, Bitsy, would you like something to drink?"

Bitsy snapped herself out of her increasingly gloomy thoughts as if she'd pinched herself. She blinked and a tear escaped before she could stop it.

"Are you okay?" Lewis' concern made her want to cry even more.

"Uh-huh, I'm good. I think something, dirt or something, flew into my eye when we were outside. I have a Kleenex." She quickly rummaged around in her purse and, finding a loose Kleenex, wiped at her eye and then wiped her nose - once Lewis' back was turned as he moved towards the kitchen.

"Oh, I'm sorry Lewis. What do you have to drink?" It was almost more of a statement than a question. She guessed he didn't do much cooking or shopping.

"Well, I have water and I have Sprite or seltzer in cans and tomato juice." Lewis opened his refrigerator to double check the selections. Bitsy took a peek inside and saw a couple of cans of seltzer, a half-filled bottle of tomato juice, half a loaf of bread, and a couple of condiments that she couldn't make out. Maybe an egg carton, creamer, and a few other items. Maybe some kind of milk, a jar of peanut butter, and an almost empty jar of Ragu spaghetti sauce. There may have been a few other items, but she couldn't see any more from where she stood.

"I'll have some tomato juice."

Lewis went to his cabinet and took out a small glass. Bitsy was able to see that there were about a half dozen glasses along with a few plates and bowls. Certainly not filled cabinets, but at least he had more than just the one plate that sat on the counter.

"Why don't you sit down, Bitsy." Bitsy looked around and saw that up against another wall there was a small gold colored sofa with two more folding chairs in front of the sofa. So, if he and Bitsy sat on the couch and they had company, the company would sit on the folding chairs in front of them so they could all talk. There was a small, no larger than an 18" TV on a TV stand across the room from the sofa. Bitsy walked carefully across the brown floors, hoping there was nothing moving where she stepped. She went to the sofa, checked it for holes, and anything moving on it. The room was dimly lit by a single light bulb in a floor lamp, which looked like an antique. She absent-mindedly swept her hand across the sofa and then sat down on the edge.

"I like your lamp, Lewis. Is it an antique?"

"Yes, it was my mother's. I have a few of her things here, but most of it's in storage."

Bitsy immediately felt a little better, imagining that Lewis had an entire apartment's worth of furniture somewhere in storage that they could use someday. Maybe when he moved from this apartment. Which, of course, made her wonder why he was here in the first place. It must be cheap rent.

Lewis brought her a plain water glass half full of tomato juice. He had another just like it with tomato juice for himself. He sat down next to Bitsy.

"I'm sorry you don't like my apartment, Bitsy. I didn't want you to come here. I know it's not very comfortable for you. You, your parents, have such a beautiful home. It must be difficult for you to be in a place like this."

"No, Lewis, it's okay. I just wanted to see your place, that's all. Don't feel bad. It's, um, nice, you know. It could be really nice. You just need a few pretty things, to brighten it up, that's all."

"Don't worry, Bitsy. When we live together, it won't be here. We'll find a place together, our own place. I want you to have nice things, whatever you want. You deserve nice things and you'll have them. I promise."

"How are you going to do that, Lewis, if this is the kind of place you can afford? I'm only making minimum wage and I don't have any money saved up, yet. So how can we have a nicer apartment?"

"Well, the rent here, as you can imagine, is very cheap. So that's allowed me to save some money from the years I've worked at the Mart. And I do have plans, Bitsy. Don't worry, things will be better for us. I was just waiting for you to come into my life."

Bitsy loved to hear him talk about his future, their future together. She knew they were both young and had a lot of growing to do, that things would get better the more they worked. She knew her parents didn't always have such a beautiful home with new, clean furnishings. They also had started out with nothing when they were young. But Bitsy never lived in poverty and knew that the adjustment would not be easy. But for Lewis, she would do it. She would do anything for

Lewis, as long as he was there with her. And as he said, they wouldn't live here so she really needed to stop focusing on the apartment he lived in now.

"Do you want to see my bedroom? It isn't much, either, but that's the rest of the apartment. Except for the bathroom, which is that door right there next to the bedroom door."

Bitsy walked over and took a look in the bathroom. It was similar to what she had seen so far: a sink, a toilet, and a shower curtain hiding a bathtub. There was a small cabinet with a mirror above the sink, simple and utilitarian, but at least everything was clean.

The bedroom was a little bigger than the kitchen/living room area. A double mattress sat in a bed frame covered with a bottom sheet, one pillow with a pillow case, and a thin blanket. Several books lay on the floor next to the bed – Bitsy could tell they were mostly library books. There was also a stack of notebooks and papers, like he was doing homework or maybe working on a project. The curtain-less single window in the room was covered with a pale-yellow shade with curled edges. The familiar grey duct tape across the left side desperately tried to hide a rip. A small goose-neck desk lamp sat on a small square unfinished wood nightstand next to the bed.  A travel clock also sat on top and a portable AM/FM radio was squeezed in between the two. Another goose-neck lamp was on a 3'x5' table, maybe a little smaller, where a lot of papers, books, and several notebooks were scattered on top. A JVC Camcorder with several tapes sat next to it. A dark brown bureau, that looked like something her grandmother had in her house, was obviously where Lewis kept his underclothes and t-shirts. There was a closet whose closed door she wasn't brave enough to open and look inside. Lewis picked up the Camcorder and tapes and opened the closet door where he had a file cabinet. He took a key from his pocket, unlocked the cabinet, and placed the Camcorder and tapes in one of the drawers.

"I don't usually leave this equipment sitting out. There could be break-ins, you know?"

"You do live simply, Lewis. Don't you want nice things, too?"

"Oh, sure I do. But I don't need things. I have what I need. What I want is you, Bitsy. That is all I really want. I've been waiting for you. And we can buy some nice things together, if that is what you want. But the more things you buy, the more things you have to take care of and then you don't have the time to do anything that you really want to do. I'd rather spend my time with you, living our lives together."

"Oh, Lewis." Bitsy couldn't resist him anymore. She moved towards him and put her arms around his neck, kissing his soft lips. He put his arms around her waist and pulled her close to him. She could feel Lewis responding to her kissing him and feeling a little shy, pulled back.

"I…, I'm not ready for…"

"Oh, Bitsy, no, of course not. I wouldn't ever do… I mean, I want to, but not unless you're ready. But I do love kissing you. You… really excite me… I really want you but I can wait. I'll wait as long as you need me to, until you're ready."

Again, Bitsy had to kiss him. She pressed herself to him and loving how quickly he responded, this time she opened her eyes just a little. He was looking into her eyes and she felt her body go limp in his arms. She wanted him right now, right at this second. He kissed her neck, her mouth, her eyes, her cheeks. She was putty in his hands. She wanted Lewis so bad. She had to stop, she had to wait. It was too soon. This time he pulled back. She almost fell to the floor.

"Ah, maybe we should go back to the living room and sit, or we could go to the park and walk. What do you think, Bitsy? I just think we should get out of my apartment now." That smile, those lips, those eyes. She almost threw herself back at him but somehow composed herself and walked out of his bedroom.

As when they had first arrived, Lewis was extremely protective of Bitsy when they left his apartment, went downstairs, and headed for her car. The neighborhood was still alive but a little quieter. It was now 9:15pm Bitsy was feeling tired but she didn't want to leave Lewis just yet. They decided to go to the park.

They had walked for just a short time when it started to rain. They ran back to the car and sat, listening to the rain.

"Why don't we go into the back seat and I can hold you and we'll listen to the rain?"

"That's a great idea, Lewis. It's kind of hard to get close in bucket seats."

"Okay, one, two, three, go!" They opened their doors, pulled the seats up, and both jumped into the back seat at the same time, slamming their doors shut and pressing the buttons down to lock both doors.

Something about back seats in cars, as soon as they got in their arms reached for each other. Lewis' kisses were warm and the rain had brought out Lewis' Dial soap smell. The windows were steaming up and, once again, they had to unwrap themselves before things went too far.

"I really don't want my first time to be in the back seat of my mother's car." Bitsy realized she had just told Lewis she was a virgin.

"So, yes, I'm a virgin, Lewis. I hope that's okay?"

"I figured you were. And, of course that's fine, why wouldn't it be? It just means I'll be extra gentle with you. I'm honored that you're choosing me to be your first."

Bitsy touched Lewis' face. She kissed his cheek and sliding down in the seat, pressed her face against his chest. He wrapped his arms around her holding her against him in a comforting way. He stroked her hair and they quietly listened to the raindrops falling on the roof of the car. Bitsy had never felt so safe and thought she could lay in Lewis' arms forever.


Suddenly Bitsy jumped up. Lewis also opened his eyes, reached for Bitsy and kissed her neck, touching her hair, her shoulder, and down her arm.

"Lewis, what time is it?"

"It's ah… quarter to 11. We'd better get going. I don't want your parents to be upset with me on our first date."

"And I have to call them as soon as I drop you off."

They got to Lewis' street in no time since there wasn't much traffic on the roads. She pulled up, double parked, and turned off the car.

"So, Bitsy, I had a wonderful night with you, one I will never forget. And I'm looking forward to many more wonderful dates with you. Thank you."

"Well, I was going to say the same thing! I had a wonderful time and I can't wait to see you at work. Thank you for the nice dinner and a really nice time, Lewis."

"Can I call you tomorrow, Bitsy?"

"Oh, I thought you had plans?"

"Well, not the whole day, I'll be available later, like around 6?"

"I don't know, I might go out to dinner with my parents. But you can try."

"Well, I don't think I can wait until Monday to talk to you again. So, I hope you'll be at home. I'll just keep trying until I reach you."

Lewis leaned over and kissed Bitsy, taking her face in his hands. She felt herself relax in his hands and wanted to stay there all night. But she had to get home. Lewis kissed her again on the tip of her nose and ran his hand down her arm taking her hand in both of his and kissed it before letting it go. She sighed and shivered.

"Now, just turn around here and then drive straight and it'll take you right to the highway. You'll be home in about 20 minutes or so. And, I'll call your parents as soon as I get inside and let them know you're on your way."

"Ok, thanks Lewis."

Lewis jumped out of the car and watched Bitsy back the car around and head toward the highway. She waved as she drove past him. He blew her a kiss.

<h1 align="center">Chapter 14</h1>

When Bitsy arrived home, her dad was waiting up.

"Hi dad, you didn't have to wait up for me."

"Well, your mom and I were up watching a movie. Besides, it's only been about 20 minutes since Lewis called and there's always some news or something I can watch on TV. And I wasn't going to go to bed before you came home. Your mom just went to bed and I was assigned wait-up duty."

"Thanks, dad. I know you worry about me. But everything worked out just fine tonight."

"So, did you have a nice night?"

"Yes, I did. It was wonderful, magical even. We went to dinner at Geno's and everything was delicious."

"Geno's, huh? Good choice."

"And we walked in the park a little but it started to rain so we sat in the car and listened to the rain and talked." Bitsy thought it was best not to tell her dad about going to Lewis' apartment.

"Talked, huh? That's good, too."

"Yeah, except the sound of the rain put us to sleep or I would have been home sooner."

"Oh, so you fell asleep. Huh."

"Is everything okay, dad?"

"Sure, yea, everything is fine. I think it's time to go to bed though. So, we'll see you in the morning, Pumpkin."

"Good night, dad."

Bitsy fell asleep almost as soon as her head hit the pillow.

Bitsy woke at 6am, ready to jump out of bed, shower, and head to work. Except it was Sunday. She would have to wait an entire day before she would see Lewis again. She was missing him already. She went downstairs and put the kettle on for tea. She started a pot of coffee for her parents, too. She got her book and tried to read but all she could do was replay the night before in her mind, over and over. She was so happy she thought she might burst. Bitsy never thought she'd meet her soulmate so early in her life. She thought she'd have to kiss a lot of frogs before she met her prince. But still, here he was. She wondered how long they should date before they married. Maybe they should live together before marrying. But she really didn't want to live in Lewis' apartment. She did not like it and didn't like the neighborhood. And she was pretty sure her parents wouldn't allow it, either. But he did say they wouldn't live there, they would find another place to live in a nicer neighborhood. Of course, she was only nineteen and wouldn't be twenty-one for another year and few months. Her parents might forbid her to move in with Lewis. And she would hate to defy them but she wanted to be with him every day. Maybe they'd understand.

After re-reading the same paragraph about a dozen times, Bitsy put her book down and thought about making breakfast. It was only 8 and she was getting hungry. Her mom came out of the bedroom first in her bathrobe.

"Good morning, sweetie. Guess you got in a little later than we thought you would last night. But dad said you had a nice time, right?" That was her mom's subtle way of getting Bitsy to tell all. Of course, she wouldn't pry. She and Bitsy shared everything so it was only natural for her mom to think Bitsy would share all the details of her first date with Lewis, too. Bitsy had already decided that she definitely wasn't sharing or discussing her sexual feelings for Lewis with her mom.

"Yes, we had such a great time, mom. He's so sweet and such a gentleman. I think he's the one."

"Now, honey, you've only had one date with this bo… man, give it some time. Go on a few more dates with him and get to know him."

"I know everything I need to know about him already. He's the man I want. I don't need to look any more."

"Bitsy, seriously honey, you are going way too fast. You haven't had many experiences with men, you really should date a few other men. And if you feel the same way, and he feels the same way, and I'm guessing he does feel the same for you?"

"Yes."

"Well then, he'll still be there waiting for you. And in a couple of years, you can live together or get married, you know, in a few years when you are a little older. There's no need to rush. You have your whole life ahead of you. "

"But why should we wait a couple of years when we know now that we want to spend our lives together." Bitsy felt herself getting upset. Her mom just did not understand how they felt for each other. Her dad must have heard their raised voices and came downstairs with a questioning look on his face.

"What's going on?"

"Your daughter is telling me that after one date with this new… boy… that she is ready for marriage!"

"I didn't say we're getting married now. I said I don't want to be with anyone else, just Lewis. But we will eventually marry, and we'll probably live together first. And as much as you don't want to admit it, mom, he's a man. He's twenty-five years old!"

"Bitsy, you've had one date with Lewis. Why don't you just enjoy dating him for a while without thinking about marriage, or living together, or anything more serious. Who knows, next week you could meet another boy at work and you'll forget all about Lewis." Her dad thought he was being sensible.

That was it. Bitsy had had enough. She should have known her parents wouldn't understand. They'd been married for so long they forgot what real love felt like. Bitsy grabbed her book, her cup of tea, and walked out of the room.

"Sweetie, aren't you going to have some breakfast?"

"I've lost my appetite." Bitsy didn't particularly like this change in her relationship with her parents. They'd always gotten along so well and had a good time together. Bitsy should have guessed they wouldn't be happy about a man coming between them. But they should have expected this would happen one day, that a man would come along and take Bitsy to be his wife. Bitsy thought she might be partly to blame; her parents had depended on Bitsy always being there with them for too long. Bitsy hadn't done much with other friends, she always had such a good time with her parents that she usually preferred to be with them. She didn't like drinking or hanging out at the mall or hanging out at the beach in the summertime with a group of kids. She'd done these things a few times but it had always felt like a waste of time. She much preferred to read a book or watch a movie with her parents or go to a museum. Or do almost anything else.

She sat on her bed trying to decide what to do. She opened her book but couldn't focus; all she could think about now were the things her parents had said and how unreasonable they were being.  And she really was hungry. But she wouldn't apologize, she didn't do anything wrong. Bitsy knew how she felt, she knew how Lewis felt. Even if her parents didn't want them to feel this way it didn't matter, this is how they felt about each other. Her parents just needed to accept it. Maybe Bitsy needed to cool it with her parents now that she realized how they felt. From now on, Bitsy would keep her feelings about Lewis to herself. This felt like the best way to keep peace in the house. Bitsy didn't have to wait long before there was a knock on her door.

"Bitsy? It's mom. May I come in?"

"Sure."

Her mom gave her a big smile and sat on the bed beside her.

"Sweetie, you know that your father and I are just concerned about you, always only you. We want the best for you. We want you to find a man who will love you and make a good husband. And, if you decide to have children, who'll be a good father, too. We always want the best for you. You know that, right?"

"Yes, I do. I just want you to give Lewis a chance, get to know him more."

"Absolutely. And you'll do the same, too, okay?"

"Okay."

Bitsy and her mom hugged. Her mom stood up and started to walk out of Bitsy's room. She turned and with a big smile asked, "Pancakes?"

"Yes, I'm starving!"

Like every day without Lewis, it went by slower than she wanted. Bitsy was waiting for Lewis to call. It was a rainy day so her parents decided to cook in rather than go out to dinner and then they were going to watch a movie together. Bitsy hoped it was something that kept her attention so she could get into it and not think about Lewis, which is what she had done for most of the day already. Her mom made portabella mushrooms and baked scallops and Bitsy made a salad.  Everything was delicious and Bitsy offered to take care of the clean-up. She was putting the dishes in the dishwasher when the phone rang. It was 6:10pm and it was Lewis.

"Hi Bitsy, how are you doing?"

"Lewis, hi, I'm good, how was your day?"

"Well, I was pretty busy but I'm better now that I'm talking to you. Just hearing your voice relaxes me." Bitsy smiled the whole time he was talking.

"I miss you, Lewis. I wish I could see you. The day is dragging, and of course, it's rainy and cloudy so the day seems even longer. I can't wait to see you tomorrow."

"Well, it'll be here before you know it. I have to get something to eat now and then I have a few more things to take care of so I'll see you tomorrow at work, okay?" Bitsy was surprised. She'd just barely said hello to Lewis and he was already saying good-bye.

"Oh, well, okay. I guess."

"Don't be upset, Bitsy. Like I said, I've had a busy day and I still have more to do and I have to eat, too, but I wanted to call you and tell you how much I miss you."

It was hard for Bitsy to be mad at Lewis after he'd just told her that he missed her.

"Okay, Lewis. I'll try to understand. I really wanted to talk to you though. Can we find some time tomorrow at work?"

"Sure, why don't we take our lunch and go somewhere."

"Well, we only have a half hour.  That's not much time to go anywhere."

"I know a place, it's very close by, that will give us some privacy and we can talk and eat our lunch, okay? Can you wait until then?"

"I suppose."

"Okay, then, I'll see you tomorrow. I'll be dreaming about you, Bitsy."

"Good-night, Lewis."

"Good-night, my sweet Bitsy."

Bitsy was sure the rest of the night would drag, but her dad found an old movie on TV from the 1940s, The Maltese Falcon, that kept them all up and watching until the end.

Chapter 15

The next morning Bitsy got up before her alarm went off and left for work earlier than usual. She caught the early bus, arriving at work before the store opened. She sat outside the A-to-Z Mart and continued reading the book she had brought to read on the bus. Even though it had only been one week, she was looking forward to getting her own car. Of course, she hadn't even gotten her first paycheck, so she knew it would be a while before she'd be able to buy a car. It was going to be a long summer. But Bitsy remembered that her dad did mention getting her a car in the fall, before the time and weather changes, so that wasn't too long to wait.

She was enjoying her book, another spy mystery by Rita May Brown, featuring her favorite character, Sneaky Pie Brown, when someone whispered in her ear, "Are you waiting for me?" She smiled and put her book down, ready to wrap her arms around Lewis. But it wasn't Lewis. It was Joe.

"Oh, it's you." She sat back down and picked up her book.

"Oh, it's you? What does that mean? What have I ever done to you? I think you'd really like me if you got to know me. Just give me a chance. How about we go on a date, you and me and my mattress. It's very comfy, all the girls tell me it is. Of course, I don't think it's just my mattress they find so appealing."

"No thanks!"

"Then how about just you and me go out to dinner. And if you want to try out my mattress later, we can do that, too. Or we can just talk and get to know each other. You're very cute, you know. I've been fantasizing about you a little. You have that cute, innocent look that I just can't resist."

Joe was sitting beside her on the bench, pushing up against her, taking her hand and pulling it into his lap so she could feel how much he turned himself on. She felt like she didn't even have to be there, all he needed was to look in a mirror and that was all the company he needed. She pulled her hand away and stood up.

"Stop it, Joe. Just leave me alone."

"Why, what's wrong? Do you have a boyfriend or something?"

"As a matter of fact, I do."

"Oh, yeah? Anyone I know?"

"Lewis."

"Lewis? Ha, really! Well, that's interesting." Bitsy remembered what Anna had told her about Joe, that he had stolen Lewis' last girlfriend. Well, it wasn't going to happen with her. Definitely not.

"You don't know anything about Lewis, or me. So, just leave me alone, Joe."

"You're right, I don't know anything about you. But I sure would like to get to know you better. Come on, I'm just kidding around. Go on a date with me. I'll make you forget all about Lewis."

"No, Joe. I'm not interested. Really."

"Hmm, playing hard to get. Okay, I'm up for the challenge. I'm not gonna give up until you say yes. I'll beg until you do." And Joe dropped to his knees with his hands folded as if he was praying. Bitsy had to laugh.

"Yes, good. I got a laugh out of you. That's a start." He took her hand and kissed it.

"What's going on?" It was Lewis who saw Bitsy and Joe laughing and Joe kissing Bitsy's hand.

"Hey Lewis. I was asking Betsy out for a date."

"Oh, and what did Betsy say?"

"I said no, Lewis." Joe stood behind Lewis, his hands in prayer. Bitsy could read his lips saying 'please'. Bitsy couldn't help but smile. Lewis walked away and into the store, which was open now. Bitsy wondered if it had been open all along and if she just didn't try opening the right door.  She ran after Lewis with Joe calling after her, "Please, just one date, give me a chance."

"Lewis, wait."

"What do you want, Bitsy?"

"Lewis, don't talk to me like that. Please. It will kill me."
She grabbed his arm and felt how strong he was. She pulled as
hard as she could to get him to stop. He finally did and turned
to look deep into her eyes.

"Lewis, you know I just turn to butter when you look into
my eyes like that."

"Well, where do you want me to look, Bitsy?"

"Okay, just look at me, I'll just… Okay, listen, I was
hoping you would be here early. I couldn't wait to get here to
see you. Joe came up behind me and he was rude and then he
was trying to be nice and trying to get me to go out with him.
But he was funny, too, so I laughed. But I'm not at all interested
in him, Lewis. You have to believe me. I want you, just you, and
only you. How could you possibly think that's changed since
our date on Saturday? If anything, I feel even stronger about my
feelings for you, Lewis."

She kept her eyes focused on the second button on Lewis'
shirt but she could feel Lewis' gorgeous eyes on her. She looked
up and saw his lips slightly parted as if waiting for Bitsy to kiss
them. She wanted him to wrap his arms around her and to kiss
her right there in the middle of the store and she didn't care
who might see them. His slowly growing smile stretched his
dark mustache out to the dimples in his cheeks and made her
shiver. His soft eyes smiled down at her and he touched her hair
with his fingers, pushing one side behind her ear. He kissed his
finger and touched her nose. She took his hand and they walked
into the back office together to get their timecards.

The morning went by quickly. Bitsy, having had a week of
training, was on her own register now. Anna was at the next
register, so if Bitsy had any questions, she could just ask Anna.

By the time it was lunch, Bitsy was pretty hungry. She
looked around for Lewis but didn't see him anywhere.

"Ready for lunch?" Anna asked as she got her purse and
started walking away from her register.

"Oh, um, I'm going out today. How about tomorrow?"

"Oh, okay, sure. I'll see you after lunch." Anna walked away, heading towards the break room.

Bitsy continued working since a couple of people had come into her checkout lane.  As she was ringing them out, Lewis appeared and put the sign up that told customers her register was closed behind the last person so Bitsy could go to lunch. Bitsy handed the last customer their change saying, "Thank you and come again."  And then she turned to Lewis, who had been waiting patiently.

"I still have to punch out."

"Already done – let's go."

Bitsy followed Lewis out the front doors, letting Lewis go first since she had no idea where they were heading. If they were walking, she figured they would spend most of their time talking while walking since, wherever it was Lewis was heading, they would most likely get there and then just have to turn around and come back to work. A half-hour lunch break goes by fast.

Lewis took a left out the front door and proceeded around to the back of the store to the employee parking lot. He walked over to a blue Honda Accord and, opening the passenger door for Bitsy said, "Your chariot awaits, my love."

"What? Is this yours Lewis? I thought your car was undependable."

"Which is why I got rid of it. What do you think of this one?"

"Well, it looks pretty nice."

"It's three years old and only has 45,000 miles on it, give or take a few. And you know Hondas, they are very dependable. I figured, if we are going to keep seeing each other, and I'm pretty sure we are, then I needed to upgrade my wheels. I need a dependable vehicle so that I can pick you up and I can take you home. Now we can have our own vehicle to go out in instead of always having to use your mother's car.  I did this for us, Bitsy, for you. I actually decided on the bus ride over to your house for our first date. It was time. I had just been putting it off, until I met you."

"Wow, Lewis, this is fantastic. It looks brand new, and very clean, too. The carpets look new. And it has air conditioning?  I like it, Lewis, I really like it."

"I'm glad you approve. Now, let's go for a ride."

Lewis drove out of the parking lot and went just a few miles down the street, taking a left and then a right. At the end of the street, a dead end, he stopped. A pond was right in front of them and Bitsy got out, bringing her lunch with her.

"This is great, Lewis." She jumped up on the hood of the car.

"Is this okay?"

"Of course." Lewis jumped up beside her.

They ate their sandwiches; Bitsy's from home, Lewis' from the snack bar.

"So, when did you get the car?"

"I picked it up yesterday. I told you I had a busy day. This was one of the things I had to do. You know, make the down payment, signing papers and all that stuff. I pick up my plates next week and I have to register it with the town and get it inspected, too. But, I'm sure none of this is what you wanted to talk to me about."

"No, it wasn't.  I just, um, I talked to my parents about us. I told them how I feel about you and, um, they weren't really happy with me, with us. They think I should date other people and take a few years and if I, we, still feel the same way then we can live together or do whatever we want to do. And I'll be 21 in just over a year so can do what I want, legally."

Lewis wasn't smiling and stopped eating his sandwich.

"Is that what you want, Bitsy?"

"No, it isn't. I want you, that's all. I don't want anyone else and I don't want to date anyone else. I don't think they understand how we feel about each other. I just want what we have, Lewis. We're so lucky, we found each other without having to kiss any ugly frogs. Or, well, I didn't have to kiss any frogs. I get to kiss you. I don't know who you may have kissed, though. You've had more experiences than I've had." Okay, she needed to shut up now. She wasn't making any sense. But hopefully Lewis knew what she meant.

"So, what they were saying upset you?"

"Yes, it did."

"It's okay. We know how we feel about each other. You could date other people if you wanted, Bitsy, I mean, if that's what your parents want. If you don't want to upset them, maybe you should do what they ask."

Bitsy was surprised that Lewis was suggesting she date other guys. It didn't matter one bit to Bitsy what her parents wanted. She had to do what was best for her, and being with Lewis was all she wanted.

"So, should I go out with Joe, then?" Bitsy could barely say this without shivering, thinking about how crass and vulgar he could be. She would never go out with him but she wanted to make her point.

She saw Lewis clench his jaw. He didn't answer her but just looked out at the pond.

"If that's what you want, Bitsy, I won't stand in your way."

Again, Bitsy couldn't believe what Lewis was saying. She knew his history with Joe, about the woman Lewis had been dating who Joe had stolen from him. Why would he just let Bitsy go if he really cared for her the way he said he did?

"Maybe I should Lewis, if it doesn't matter to you." Bitsy wanted to cry. What was happening? She thought they were stronger than this, than anything. Bitsy had just told him that her parents wanted her to date other men and Lewis was ready to let her go. Just like that. She didn't want to think about this anymore.

"I think we should go back to work, Lewis."

Lewis got off the hood of the car and got into the driver's seat and Bitsy got into the passenger side of the car. The drive back to the store was quiet. Bitsy was so upset she ran back into the store ahead of Lewis. She went right to her register and didn't look to see where Lewis went.

Bitsy was busy with customers all afternoon and before she realized it, it was time to punch out. She saw Lewis' card – he hadn't punched out yet. She walked to the front of the store and out the door. She got on her bus and although she tried to read her book on the ride home, she couldn't get past the first sentence in the chapter. She fought back tears and couldn't wait for her stop to get off. On the walk home, she didn't want to think about what had just happened but she couldn't think of anything else. Bitsy started to cry, unable to hold back the tears that had been on the brink of overflowing since she had gotten back from lunch with Lewis. She looked through her purse and, finding a Kleenex, wiped at her eyes. Just as she was about to blow her nose, someone called her name.

"Bitsy." It was Lewis. He pulled up to the curb. Bitsy stopped and just looked at him, sitting in his car.

"Bitsy, please get in the car."

"I don't think so Lewis. I think I want to walk."

"Well, then, can I walk with you?"

"Maybe you should go home, Lewis. I'll see you tomorrow."

"I can't wait until tomorrow. I have something to tell you."

"I'm sure you can tell me tomorrow, whatever it is."

"I love you, Bitsy. That's what I want to tell you. I love you."

Bitsy stopped and looked right into Lewis' dark stunningly sky-blue eyes. Lewis got out of his car and was walking over to where Bitsy stood on the sidewalk, unsure of what Lewis had just said but at the same time knowing full well what he had said. Still, just to be sure, she wanted to hear it again.

"What did you say?" He was standing right in front of her now.

"I said, 'I love you, Bitsy.' Do you want me to say it again?" He was smiling as he leaned in and kissed her on the mouth.

"Yes, say it again." And this time Bitsy kissed Lewis. They wrapped their arms around each other and Bitsy felt her knees buckle under her. How could she ever want to be with anyone else when Lewis had this effect on her? She *didn't* want to be with anyone else, she only wanted to be kissed by Lewis for the rest of her life.

"I love you, I love you, I love you." With each 'I love you' Lewis kissed Bitsy on her face, her neck, her arms, and taking her hands from around his neck, he held them both in his and kissed them all over. Then she realized, she had not said it back to him. She stopped Lewis from kissing her and looked into his eyes, at his mouth that she wanted to continue kissing, and took a deep breath. She had never told a man this before. But she felt so much love for Lewis right now that she had to say it; she was overwhelmed by her love for Lewis.

"Lewis?"

"Yes, Bitsy?" There's that smile.

"I love you, Lewis. I love you so much. Please believe me. And please let's never argue about whether or not I love you ever again. Please let's just love each other more and more. I don't want to go out with anyone else. I just want you, only you. Promise me, okay?"

The entire time Bitsy was talking, Lewis continued to gently kiss her face, her mouth, her hair, and her arms. Lewis looked around the neighborhood and, seeing someone peeking from behind a curtain in the house they were standing in front of, thought they should get into his car. He walked with his arm around Bitsy, opened the car door, and helped her get in. He went around to his side and got into the driver's seat. He reached over and took Bitsy's hand.

"I promise."

Bitsy smiled, turned Lewis' hand over, and kissed his palm.

# Chapter 16

Weeks turned into months and time did what it always does, what it's best known for; it flew by. She had lunch with Lewis and sometimes with Anna and Lewis would give her a ride home after work. Sometimes they'd stop for an ice cream before he'd drive her home. They couldn't stand being apart from each other and every night he dropped her off in front of her house they had a difficult time saying good-bye to one another. Sometimes Bitsy would invite Lewis in to have dinner with her parents, but only after she had called her mom and asked first. Other times they'd stop at a take-out place, drive to a park or the pond, and eat dinner together. They enjoyed their time together and were feeling more and more comfortable with each other.

When the weekends came, they'd spend most of Saturday together. Bitsy's parents were still uncomfortable with Bitsy spending so much time with Lewis and hoped it would soon fizzle out and she would be on to the next young man who hopefully had more ambition and a more responsible degree than film making. They knew it would upset Bitsy if they mentioned this, so they didn't say anything to her but decided to just wait it out instead. If too much time went by, they would intervene and start fixing her up with who they considered to be more appropriate men.

After Bitsy had deposited a couple of paychecks, she wanted to take Lewis out to dinner. He protested, at first, but thought it would be best if he went along with her and let her take him to dinner. Bitsy chose her favorite Asian Restaurant, Peking Gardens, that was in Trenton. They were seated in a cozy corner, giving them lots of privacy. Bitsy figured they must look like a couple in love and that explained why everyone always sat them in cozy corners with lots of privacy. The seating worked out perfectly, though, because Bitsy wanted to talk to Lewis about something private and wasn't sure how he might react to some of her questions.

After they had ordered a few of Bitsy's favorite dishes, Shrimp Egg Foo Young and Vegetable Fried Rice, and Lewis ordered Beef Chow Mein and Dumplings, Bitsy got very serious.

"Lewis, I feel like I know you so well now, but I don't know, maybe I really don't know you? But I feel so close to you and feel like I can trust you completely. I hope you trust me, too. Do you?"

"Yes, Bitsy, I do, of course I do."

"Okay, good." This wasn't as easy as she thought it would be.

"Well, I was wondering Lewis. I was wondering, if you'd tell me, um, what you do on Sundays? We never get together on Sundays and, I know we do spend a lot of time together and if you need your private life too, well, that's okay, but I was wondering if you would tell me, um, what… where you go, or what you do on Sundays?"

Lewis smiled as Bitsy stumbled over her words. She felt a little self-conscious since he hadn't stopped her even though he seemed to know what she was going to ask him. When she stopped talking, he continued smiling at Bitsy, then took a deep breath before he answered her.

"Do you remember what I told you about my father leaving us when I was about twelve?"

"Yes, of course I do. I've wanted to know more about that, but you just seem so private, Lewis, and I don't want to pry…"

"That's okay, Bitsy. I want to tell you. I've never told anyone about my parents. Anyway, my mom is in a special facility, I think I already told you that, right?"

"Yes, you did, I remember that." Bitsy remembered every single thing about their first date but didn't think she needed to tell Lewis that.

"Well, I visit my mom on Sundays for a couple of hours. Every Sunday. She doesn't, ah, she doesn't know who I am, anymore, but I feel better visiting her. I just feel so sad seeing her there, having no one, and if she does remember anything, I want her to know she isn't alone. And my father… he… I can't ever forgive him… for leaving."

"Oh Lewis, I'm so sorry." Now Bitsy felt embarrassed for having asked. She should have guessed, but how could she have known. She felt like she knew hardly anything about Lewis, but she really wanted to know everything about the man she was falling so deeply in love with.

Their food had come so they busied themselves filling their plates. Lewis quietly picked at his food. He seemed to be thinking about something else he wanted to say. Bitsy was patient, giving him the opportunity to talk if he wanted to, even though she was bursting to ask more questions. They both continued eating in silence.

"There's more that I want to tell you, Bitsy. More about me, about why I live where I live, what it means to me."

Bitsy put her fork down and gave Lewis her complete attention. She felt like this was one of those moments in life when you need to empty your mind of all distractions and absorb everything that was happening around you, especially if it was what someone was saying. She held her breath waiting for Lewis' next words.

"I'm making a documentary. I went to NYU because I want to make film documentaries. It has taken me the past five years to get a lot of people to trust me, to let me into their homes, to share their lives with me. So many of them are on drugs, their babies are on drugs, their kids… they steal. They're just little kids. Their lives are just… not worth living, for some of them. So, they do drugs and buy drugs instead of buying food. And their babies die. Their lives are just, well, something that needs to be told. It's something that I need to do. And that's why I live there, Bitsy. Can you understand what I'm saying?"

Bitsy was speechless. She had no idea. She'd hoped, really hoped, that he had career goals that went beyond the A-to-Z Mart. And not because her parents weren't happy with Lewis working as a cashier and the other odd jobs he did at the A-to-Z Mart, but because she felt like he had so much more to offer the world.  But this, she never could have imagined. Tears came to her eyes and she reached for Lewis' hands.

"Oh Lewis, I'm so proud of you. That's just, amazing. You are amazing."

Lewis smiled and took a deep breath.

"I wasn't sure what you'd think, Bitsy. I don't want you to worry about me going into the homes of some of the people that I'm interviewing, you know."

"Wait, what? What do you mean, Lewis?" Bitsy's naivety was showing. She couldn't understand why she should be worried, until Lewis had brought it up. Lewis had also forgotten how much of a sheltered life Bitsy had lived until now. He wondered if he'd made a mistake by telling Bitsy the truth about his life and some of the dangerous situations he had gotten into – was still getting into –by going into the apartments of drug addicts.

"I think maybe we should talk about something else now, Bitsy."

"No, Lewis, I want to know what you mean.  What is it about the people, or the homes that you go into? Why would I worry, Lewis? Please tell me." Bitsy's stomach was twisting into knots and she wanted to know why she would worry about Lewis. What kind of dangerous situations was he putting himself into? She felt so naive, like she knew nothing at all about life.

"Like I said, Bitsy, I don't want you to worry. But please, for now, let's just eat our dinner and forget about everything else. Maybe I shouldn't have shared this with you. I don't know what I was thinking." Lewis seemed upset with himself for maybe having said those last thoughts out loud. Bitsy realized she had to reassure him right now that he hadn't made a mistake by telling her or he may never open up to her again.

"Okay, Lewis. I'm really glad you told me. I'm sorry, but I love you and I will worry about you, no matter what kind of work you do. Everything that happens to you, everything, is important to me now. I want you to be safe, always. Okay?

That's it, I just want you to be safe. And I want you to tell me everything, too. Okay?"

Lewis nodded but kept his head down while he ate. She could tell he was still upset.

They finished eating their meals in silence. Bitsy wanted to talk more about Lewis' documentary. She had questions, she wanted to know more about it. She decided it could wait for another time. She wished she had reacted differently. But she couldn't stop herself from worrying and knew she probably never would.  They drove back to Bitsy's, both keeping their eyes on the road, not speaking. When Lewis walked Bitsy to her door, he pulled her to him, wrapped her in his arms, and held her tightly for several minutes. She felt his strong body against hers. She relaxed and held Lewis tightly. She was floating in his arms, safe and warm. He kissed the top of her head. She kissed his chest. He kissed her cheek and with one hand, lifted her face to his. He touched his lips to hers and she pressed her lips to his. There was nothing and no one else around, just the two of them, only them at that moment.

The porch light came on. Bitsy pulled away from Lewis since they were now standing under a spot light. This was her parents' subtle hint that their evening together had come to its end. Even though Bitsy considered herself a full-grown woman, she knew her parents still saw her as their little Bitsy. She wondered exactly how old she'd have to be before they'd see her as an adult.

# Chapter 17

Bitsy usually spent her lunch or breaktime with Lewis or Anna, but on this particular day she found herself alone in the Employees' Lounge. Eating and reading, but reading more than eating because she was so involved with the characters and the story in another P.D. James book she had taken out of the library, she didn't hear someone come up behind her and was startled when they put their hands around her eyes so she couldn't see who it was. Her first thought, of course, was Lewis. She giggled and, taking his hands away, he ran his hands down her arms, giving her shivers. But something about his touch felt different to her. She thought she was imagining it and started to turn around for a kiss when Joe jumped out from behind her. She nearly fell off her chair, surprised that she had thought, even for a second, that this had been her Lewis.

"So, it seems I got your motor running, Bitsy." Joe was smiling so big but Bitsy felt slimy now that Joe had put his hands on her.

"No, Joe, you just tried to fool me, that's all."

"Oh, so you wanted it to be Lewis, is that it?"

"Yes, yes I did."

"What is it about him, anyway? I have so much more to offer you than Lewis does. And if you saw me naked… well, let's just say, all your dreams would come true, you know what I'm saying?"

"Well, I don't really care what you have to offer… me… or anyone, Joe. I'm just not interested." Bitsy turned her back to Joe, in essence saying that their conversation was finished. But instead, Joe sat down beside her.

"So, when are we going out, beautiful?"

Bitsy felt the color rush into her cheeks. She was too embarrassed to say anything so she opened her book and, pretending to read, hoped Joe would leave.

"I think we'd have a lot of fun together. You know, I kid a lot but mostly because you make me a little nervous, you're so pretty. A lot of girls will go out with me, sure; they say I'm so good-looking, but they really aren't that pretty and I don't feel a lot for them."

Bitsy gave him a shocked looked. Of course, she was thinking what a creep for saying these things to her, like she'd have any sympathy for poor Joe who has to go out with all these unattractive women. And she was sure these were just lines he was using on her – she also had no doubt many of the other girls he went out with were attractive.

"But you, Bitsy, you are really beautiful. Truly. And I would be honored to go out with you. Just one date. I would be the perfect gentleman, I promise."

Now he was annoying her again. She had no interest in going out with Joe and the sooner he figured that out, the better.

"Joe, I really don't think..." He grabbed her hand and started to kiss it, holding it between both of his hands.

The door to the Employees' Lounge opened and they both looked up. Lewis walked in, stopping when he saw them. Bitsy was turned to Joe who was still holding her hand in both of his. Bitsy pulled her hand out of Joe's hands and, standing up, went over to Lewis.

"Hi, I was looking for you. I didn't know if you were busy or if you could have lunch with me?" Joe got up from the table and headed for the door. Lewis glared at him but Joe just kept walking. He turned, looked at Bitsy and winked, and then smiled at Lewis as he pulled the door open and went out. Lewis continued staring at the door after it had closed.

"He keeps asking me out, Lewis. And I keep telling him to leave me alone. I don't know why he won't."

"Don't you, Bitsy? Don't you see what he is doing? He is doing exactly what he did before. He is trying to get you to go out with him and then you will be just like Ginny and he'll sweep you off your feet with his charm, and all his... everything."

"No, Lewis. He won't. You have nothing to worry about. I am not like Ginny at all, even though I didn't know her. But you know me, you know how I feel about you." Bitsy stood on her tippy toes and kissed Lewis on the nose. He smiled and wrapped his arms around her, kissing her on the neck. She pulled away, reluctantly.

"I have to get back to work. I'll see you later?" Bitsy picked up her book and lunch bag.

"Sure, want a ride home?"

"Of course."

Lewis was out front waiting after work when Bitsy came out. She ran to his car and jumped in. He leaned over to her and gave her a kiss, his smile peeking out from under his mustache.

"Why are you smiling at me like that?" She felt herself blushing. He always made her blush; she just couldn't help herself.

"Because you make me happy; don't you know that?"

Bitsy, still blushing, smiled and nodded.

They stopped for an ice cream on the way home and Bitsy sat in the car, more quiet than usual. She was thinking, thinking it was time. She was ready. She wondered how to approach the topic. She didn't want to just blurt it out. She felt herself blushing and turned away.  Lewis, picking up on her mood, asked "A penny for your thoughts?"

"Oh, ah, yeah." Bitsy felt her face getting even hotter and knew the color must be very bright now. Thanks to her reddish blonde hair she couldn't hide any of her emotions.

Lewis looked at her questioningly.

Bitsy laughed a little, more uncomfortable than ever.

"Bitsy my love, what is it?" He stopped eating his ice cream and turned to Bitsy, that adorable half-smile on his face.

Bitsy looked around and saw people waiting in line for their ice cream. She hit the automatic button to roll up her window and looked to Lewis to do the same. He took his cue and raised his window, also.

"Okay, love, it's going to get really hot in here really fast since it's around 80 degrees out today."

Bitsy laughed again.

"You have no idea!"

Again, the questioning look from Lewis.

Bitsy knew she had to just blurt it out or she would be too embarrassed to say anything.

"I'm ready, Lewis. I want us to have sex now."

Lewis didn't say anything but just continued to look at Bitsy, as if she hadn't said anything yet and he was still waiting.

"Lewis, did you hear what I said, I want to have…"

"Yes, yes, Bitsy, I heard you. I'm thinking about what you said, that's all."

Bitsy suddenly felt completely unsure of herself and her stomach was feeling like she was going to puke her half-eaten pistachio ice cream all over Lewis' new used car. She wondered what he had to think about. Didn't he want to have sex with her? Did he decide they would just be really, really close friends, without the sex? She wanted him to say something and because he didn't say anything, she needed to talk. She couldn't stand the quiet.

"I didn't know how to say this, Lewis, but I've been thinking about having sex with you for a long, long time, and I just wanted you to know that I didn't want to just keep dating you and not have sex with you because I really, really do and since you haven't said anything and I thought you were maybe waiting for me, I thought I should tell you that I really, really want to… and that now… now… I'm ready, Lewis."

Lewis leaned over and kissed Bitsy on the mouth. They both put down their ice cream dishes and reached for each other over the stick shift between the bucket seats.

Lewis looked into Bitsy's eyes and smiled at her innocence, so obvious in her clear blue eyes, her face so full of love for him.

"Your wish is my command."

# Chapter 18

Bitsy and Lewis had been together just a little more than three months. But they spent so much time together that to Bitsy it felt more like a year. And Bitsy knew it was time to take their relationship to the next level, as she had heard people say on TV. She figured this usually meant they were going to either have sex or, if they had already had sex, they were going to live together. It meant their relationship was progressing, just like her love for Lewis was progressing. She was so excited that she had finally made this decision and, now that she had shared it with Lewis, it was all she could think about - even though she had no idea what to do.  Every time she saw Lewis, she tried to picture him naked and felt strong urges that caused her to blush. She figured the rest, meaning, them actually getting naked together, wouldn't be anything too scary for her even though this would be her first time. She thought it might just be a natural instinct and she would know what to do and how to react. Like the way dogs just naturally know how to take care of their puppies, without anyone ever teaching them.

She, of course, had seen movies with love scenes but these didn't really go into much detail or tell her the things she needed to know. Like does she take off her clothes or does he take them off and also take off his own?  Does she let him do things to her and then she does things to him? And what kind of things should she do to him? She wished she had some experience but, of course, Lewis would probably be the best person for her to have her first sexual experience with since he was so sweet and she knew he would be gentle. She thought that perhaps she should rent a porn video. But she didn't really want to rent one and didn't know where or when she could watch it if she did.  She had heard they could be pretty explicit which is exactly what she wanted to know. In most of the romance movies she had seen on TV or cable the actors were kissing and then it showed them when 'it' was all over and you didn't actually get to see what happened in-between. She wanted to know the in-between parts. And, although she had seen a few R-rated movies, she preferred romantic movies, which had some love scenes but not the kind with the information she was looking for. She also really liked comedies, but they typically didn't have any sex scenes since they were almost always rated PG for the whole family.

Although her mom had told her the basics of getting pregnant, she had never gone into any kind of detail. So, Bitsy could only imagine, and try to recall what she had seen on TV or at the movies.

Of course, she did know enough to make sure Lewis had something for protection. Her mom did at least tell her that much. Or maybe, like Anna had suggested, she should have protection with her and not leave it up to Lewis? That meant going to the A-to-Z Mart and buying condoms and then checking out at the employee register.  That would be an embarrassing moment! She should probably just get on birth control – but how could she go to a doctor without her parents finding out? She needed to talk to Lewis about all of this.

The whole ordeal was beginning to feel less romantic and more like a business arrangement.  Did you bring the condoms? Check. Are you on birth control? Check. Better to be safe than sorry. Yes, sir! But she knew this was the best for both of them. She was not going to start a new relationship with Lewis as a pregnant woman that he felt obligated to marry. Bitsy would not ruin his life or her own life that way. He had important things to do and she had some plans of her own, too. Part of her plan was to get to know Lewis, to become his friend, his life partner. And you can't really get to know someone else when you have a baby who needs care 24/7. That becomes your entire focus, your life every day. She wasn't even sure if she wanted any babies. That was something they needed to discuss, too. They both needed to take responsibility for making sure no babies were conceived during their first sexual experience together.

Lewis pulled up to the Holiday Inn and ran inside to check in. Bitsy thought it best if she remained in the car since she'd feel too self-conscious if the person at the front desk looked at her. She didn't want to give it away that they were not married and so obviously were only staying here long enough to have sex. Lewis had called ahead and reserved a room for them on the top floor. The hotel did have a nice view of the river and they were about an hour's drive away from where either of them lived so it was less likely they'd run into anyone either of them knew. These had all been requests from Bitsy.

The clock on the dashboard said 1:12. That gave them at least nine hours before they would have to drive back to Bitsy's house. She managed to put a few items together in a beach bag that doubled as an overnight bag so that she could bring a change of clothes. She told her parents they were going to the beach to walk and get away from everything, just to be alone, and then they were going out to dinner so she needed to have a large bag to carry clothes and other necessities.

Lying to her parents bothered Bitsy more than she realized it would. But she didn't see any other way to plan this day with Lewis without her parents getting suspicious. It was just a few weeks before she turned twenty so she figured her parents thought that she'd probably already had sex with Lewis. Of course, this was just her way of alleviating the guilt she was feeling over lying to them. Most likely they still thought she was a virgin and would remain one until she married, whenever that might happen. Or so, she imagined, they hoped.

Lewis came out the front door and hopped back in the driver's side. He smiled at Bitsy and she blushed. He drove around to the back of the hotel and parked. Bitsy grabbed her beach bag and purse and followed Lewis through the back door and then over to the elevators. Lewis pulled Bitsy to him as they stood waiting for the elevator doors to open. He kissed the top of her head and hugged her to him. Bitsy tried to calm the butterflies that were flitting around in her stomach. The elevator doors opened and they got on. Neither spoke a word.

Lewis took Bitsy's beach bag and his own canvas bag that he had brought in one hand and took Bitsy's hand in his other as they walked down the corridor together. They passed door after door until they came to #422. Lewis took the key from his pocket, slipped the key into the lock, and opened the door, allowing Bitsy to walk inside.

The chilly A/C hit her and she wrapped her sweater around her, hugging herself with folded arms.

"Are you cold?" Lewis walked over to the air conditioning unit and turned it off.  He checked the temperature in the room; it read 68.

"It's a little warm out today so they had it set to be a comfortable temp in here. But I turned it off so it will warm up now, okay?" He put their bags down and walked over to Bitsy who stood about three steps into the room where she had stopped when she saw the king bed. She surveyed the room which had the usual furnishings: two nightstands and two lamps, a chair in the corner next to the window and facing the bed, a set of drawers with a TV on top across from the foot of the bed. The room appeared to be clean and the bed had a pale, yellow floral comforter. There was a digital clock on one nightstand and a phone on the other nightstand. She peeked into the bathroom, pushing the door open. She flipped the light switch and went into the bathroom.

"I'll be right out." She shut the door, put the cover down on the toilet, and sat down. Her stomach was a wreck, nervous and jittery. Her hands were cold and sweaty. She wondered if she stayed in here long enough, maybe Lewis would fall asleep. Then she realized, it was only 1:30 in the afternoon. She was sure he was wide awake in anticipation of the afternoon activities. Her stomach jumped again.

"Are you okay, Bitsy?"

"Oh, yeah, sure. Um, I'll be right out." She checked her face in the mirror. She wanted to brush her teeth and went out to get her bag.

"I'll just be another minute." Lewis was sitting in the chair in the corner. He smiled at Bitsy.

"That's okay, take your time."

Back in the bathroom, she decided she needed to just relax and enjoy this special time with Lewis. She would either love what was about to happen or hate it. She hoped she would love it. She was sure she would but she was still nervous about the whole thing. Losing her virginity. That's a big thing. But she knew she waited for the right man and that he would do everything to make it a beautiful experience for Bitsy.

She brushed her teeth, combed her hair, and put a tiny bit of lipstick on. She took a deep breath and opened the bathroom door.

Lewis was standing a few steps away.

"Bitsy, are you having second thoughts, because if you are, I understand. We don't have to do this now, don't feel…"

Bitsy walked over to him and put her arms around his neck and kissed his mouth. His tongue slipped into her mouth and he pulled her closer to him. They held each other tight, kissing and touching, their hands finding each other's clothes and making the effort to unbutton and unzip. Lewis stepped back and held Bitsy by the shoulders.

"I want to do this right, okay?"

Bitsy had no idea what that meant but since she was unsure of everything, except how turned on by Lewis she was right now, she'd let him lead the way. All of this was new to her so she took her role as the student seriously and nodded her assent.

Lewis unzipped his pants and took them off, tossing them onto the chair. He unbuttoned his shirt and tossed it over with his pants. He stood in his boxer shorts. She let her eyes do a quick body scan, admiring his muscles built by a life of lifting heavy items and hard work, not from pumping iron in a gym. His chest was covered with a thick coating of curly dark hair that matched the hair on his head. His arms and legs had a layer of dark hair, too, just enough to complement his masculine physique. She shyly glanced at his briefs, where his excitement from their kissing was plainly visible. She looked at his eyes and after he took his glasses off, he slipped Bitsy's sweater off her shoulders and tossed it over to the chair with his clothes. He unzipped her jeans and bending down on one knee, slid them slowly down her body. She put her hand on his shoulder and stepped out of them, one leg at a time. Lewis stood back up and unbuttoned Bitsy's blouse, slipping it over her arms. He reached around her back and unclasped her bra. She put her arms down and let it fall to the floor. Again, he dropped down on one knee and putting his hands behind her and into her panties, he slid them down her legs and lifted each leg to take them off. He slid both hands, slowly, up her legs and kissed her down there, softly, once, twice. When she felt his tongue, she jumped a little.

Bitsy stood there, naked, shaking a little.

"Are you still cold?" Lewis stood up and pulled her to him.

"No, it tickled a little." She giggled but didn't want to break the mood.

Lewis smiled and with one swift and tender movement, he lifted Bitsy up and carried her to the bed. He had already pulled the comforter and sheets back. He gently laid her down in the middle of the bed, a pillow behind her head.

"Are you okay?" He slipped his briefs off and leaned over her and kissed her forehead, her cheeks, the tip of her nose, her chin, and her neck.

Bitsy was really shaking now.

"I'm just nervous, I think."

Lewis looked up from kissing her neck.

"Do you want a blanket?"

"No, I'm not cold, just a little scared."

"There is nothing to be scared of. You know I would never hurt you. And if anything does hurt you, I want you to tell me right away, okay?"

"Okay." Bitsy relaxed a little after he told her that. She closed her eyes and took a deep breath.

"What should I do, Lewis?"

"I want you to relax and enjoy. That's all you have to do."

He continued kissing her neck. He climbed onto the bed and was lying beside her, kissing down one arm and each of her fingers. He pulled himself up and over Bitsy, lightly touching his body to hers, brushing his erection across her stomach. She jumped.

"Oh! Sorry!"

"That's okay, I didn't mean to surprise you. Just relax."

She could feel his body over hers, holding himself over her with his strong arms, kissing her chest, her breasts, first one, then the other, then back to the first one, kissing and licking and teasing.

Bitsy felt her body rising up, wanting to feel Lewis closer to her, wanting to rub her face in his chest.

She felt her heart pumping, racing, in her chest. She wondered if she could have a heart attack. She heard about some men having them, mostly when they are older, and wondered if there were any cases where a woman her age, and having sex for the first time, ever had a heart attack. She shook her head to get those silly thoughts out and focus on the sensations she was feeling.

Lewis was still giving his undivided attention to her breasts. She was getting very excited by his tongue. Then she wondered if she could have an orgasm just from this. She certainly felt like she was going to explode. Suddenly she felt his leg between her legs, trying to push them apart. She held them tightly together.

"Lewis, I have condoms."

"We won't need them, Bitsy, not tonight. Just relax."

She felt a little tension wondering what he was thinking, that they didn't need the condoms. She certainly wasn't interested in the possibility of getting pregnant on the same night she lost her virginity. But Lewis soon put that idea to rest as he worked his way down to her stomach, kissing and gently nipping her skin with his teeth. He continued to move down her body, kissing her thighs, moving over to her pubic area. She felt his hardness moving down her leg as he slowly worked his way in and the excitement built up in her even more. He settled his face between her legs, spreading them so that he could move in and kiss her down there. She resisted at first, keeping her legs tightly clasped together but slowly, as he continued to kiss and coax her legs open, she felt herself relax. At this moment, she trusted Lewis completely.

Once between her legs, he pulled her closer to his mouth by putting his hands under her buttocks, slightly lifting her to him. His tongue worked its way around and she felt pleasure like she had never imagined. She shut her mind off and let Lewis have her completely, body, mind, and soul.

"Oh, Lewis!" She raised her body up closer to him, feeling all her muscles tighten, and then an explosion, throughout her entire body, she pulsed, she thrashed, she lunged, tears ran from her eyes, she screamed, "Lewis!" And then softly, "Lewis, oh Lewis."

She lay on the bed, spent, her heart, which she was once again concerned about since it was beating so fast, was racing inside her chest. She opened her eyes. Lewis was lying beside her, touching her breasts, running his fingertips down her legs and up her stomach, down her arms, taking her hand and kissing each finger. She tingled all over. She couldn't remember ever feeling so relaxed, so satisfied.

She looked into Lewis' eyes.

"Wow!" That was all she could manage to say.

Lewis continued kissing her face, her hands, and her arm. He raised himself up and straddled her, kissing her chest and her breasts, lingering playfully over each one.

"Lewis, are you trying to drive me crazy." She pulled him up to her, kissing his face and moving her tongue into his mouth. They kissed long and she felt herself getting excited all over again.

"Wait, I want to do something for you now. But I'm not experienced so you'll have to help me. What can I do for you?"

"You're already doing it, just being here, being you, letting me love you and enjoy your body."

"No, Lewis, you know what I mean. I want to pleasure you, too."

Lewis lay back down beside her bending his elbow and resting his head on his hand.

"I would love to come inside you Bitsy, if you really want to know. But I know this is your first time. I want to be gentle with you but you have to know it might hurt."

"It's going to happen sooner or later, right, so it might as well be now."

Lewis got up from the bed and went into the bathroom. He came back with a condom which he removed from the package.

"I'll try to be as gentle as I can Bitsy and let me know if you want me to stop, okay?"

"Oh Lewis, I can't imagine loving you any more than I do right now."

She pulled his face to hers, kissing him with her entire body, melting into him. She slowly opened her legs to him, waiting for him to come inside her. He took the condom and with one hand, rolled the condom on. He helped Bitsy relax by kissing her, slowly, down her chest, teasing her breasts, down her stomach and below, kissing and exploring. He opened her legs a little wider and moving back up towards Bitsy's face, kissed her on her lips, gently, while he moved in front of her, slowly pushing into her. She jumped when she felt the pressure of him and tried to relax.

"I'm sorry."

"No need to apologize. Just let me know if it is too painful."

"I want this, I want you, and I want to feel you inside me."

Lewis was inside her, slow and gentle, tender in his love-making. Slower and deeper he went until he felt the life drain out of him. Lewis held her closer to him, her arms around his neck as they melted into each other, his other arm holding them up off the bed.

They clung to each other, hugging, kissing, smothering each other in their love and satisfying love-making, content in their mutual orgasm, cementing their love, their obsession, their fate.

They relaxed in each other's arms, enjoying this special moment together. Lewis kissed her head, her face and Bitsy felt him getting aroused again.

"You'd better be careful, you might break me." She smiled at him while they lay together on their sides, facing each other.

She rubbed her face in his chest feeling his hairs tickle her cheeks and her nose. She sneezed and giggled. Lewis kissed the top of her head. She sighed contentedly.

"I think you've cast a spell on me, Bitsy."

Again, she giggled.

"No, you have a spell on me! I feel so fortunate that you have so much experience now. Before I was jealous, but now I feel lucky. I mean, if I had my first experience with someone who didn't know anything, just like me, it probably would have been awful instead of having this beautiful experience that I'll remember for my entire life. I'm so glad I had you as my first."

Lewis just smiled and kissed her again, hugging her tighter.

"So, I have to ask you Lewis, I have to know. I'm sure you didn't learn everything you know from someone like me who doesn't know anything."

"Who didn't know anything."

Bitsy laughed. "Right, I'm so knowledgeable now! A regular sexpert!"

"Well, you know more than you did coming into this room!"

"That is true! But I would like to know, how did you get so good at this and know exactly what to do to get me so excited?"

Lewis took a deep breath and took his time answering, like he was looking for the exact words to use to explain to Bitsy. That was something she loved about Lewis, he never just started blabbing. He took his time and really thought about what he wanted to say and always seemed to express himself so that you never had to question what he meant.

"Okay, so you know my mother had early onset Alzheimer's."

"Yes, I do, and you visit her every week even though she doesn't know who you are anymore."

"That's right. Well, I was trying to finish high school, I was 16, 17 years old, and I really couldn't leave her and I was missing a lot of school. I, uh, I had a neighbor, a woman, her husband was in the military and was shipped overseas and she stayed home all day. She didn't work. She had hobbies, like making cards for people or she would sell them and she did a little painting that she sold locally to a gift shop. And she made a few other things. But she was home mostly. Well, I got to know her and she was great. She knew I was missing school and so she started bringing some of her work to my mom's and would sit with her while I went to school. It was a big help. I appreciated her help so much. She was really quite wonderful and special."

Lewis stopped here. Bitsy looked up at him. She could tell he was remembering the pain and emotion that he was going through with his mom getting worse every day. She waited for him to continue.

"Then one day, a black sedan drove up and two official looking military officers got out and rang her doorbell. When she opened the door, she knew what it was and fell apart, right there in front of them. She and her husband were very much in love. And now he was gone. They gave her an American flag and he was awarded a purple heart. He had died when the jeep he was in was blown up."

"Oh no, how horrible for her."

"Yes, it was. And I was glad that I could be there for her the way she was there for me and my mom."

"A few weeks went by and she continued to come to my mom's house and watch her. I thought she would want to take some time but she said she had to keep busy and not dwell on the sadness. Mom slept a lot so there were times when I would visit Rachel and…"

"Rachel, that was your neighbor's name?"

"Yes, Rachel. Anyway, sometimes I would take a little time when mom was sleeping and visit her. She would give me a beer and she would have a glass of wine and she would talk about her husband and how they met. She needed to talk and I listened."

"Then one night, we were both laughing about something, some movie we both had seen or something funny and she started to cry. I wanted to hold her and comfort her but I didn't know if that was appropriate or if she would be more upset. So,

I went over and sat next to her and touched her arm, trying to comfort her. She looked at me and our eyes met and then we grabbed each other and started kissing. I was like you were, a little awkward, you know, that 'first time' thing. She took me by the hand and led me into her bedroom. And the rest, as they say, is history."

"So, she taught you everything she knew?"

"Pretty much. She taught me how to pleasure her, she guided and directed me. It was awesome, really. Not many guys get that kind of guidance. I was pretty lucky."

"But Lewis, a lot of people would call that rape, you know. You were under-age. How old was she?"

"She was 27, 28, something like that. Our love-making had nothing to do with rape. Rape is unwanted forced sex. It was definitely mutual for both of us. It wasn't at all about our age differences, it was about two people who needed and felt a kind of love for each other. She was so lonely and missed her husband so much and she was a beautiful woman that I had always had a crush on, even before we got involved. I was happy I was there for her. Some other creep might have taken advantage of her vulnerability but I knew she was hurting."

"So, why didn't you stay with her, get married or something."

"That would never happen. I was there and what she needed at that time, the most painful time in her life. She stayed there another six months and we continued making love for those six months and then I moved my mom into the facility she is in now and I started college. Within a month Rachel had sold her house and moved away. I never saw her again."

"Wow, just like that she left you."

"She was never mine to begin with. But she knew I was falling in love with her. She knew I needed to live my life and she needed to start hers over again."

"That's quite a story, Lewis. Have you ever tried to find her?"

"No, it was a moment in our lives. We didn't need to go anywhere else with it. I only hope she found someone she deserved and is happy."

They were both so comfortable in each other's arms that Bitsy could have stayed there forever. And then her stomach growled. They both laughed.

"Would you like to go get some dinner?" Lewis smiled and kissed her face all over. "Or I could just eat you up and you'll go hungry." And he started nibbling on her arms and down her stomach, stopping for a moment to kiss her breasts.

"We won't go anywhere if you start doing that again!" Bitsy love-tapped him on his head, grabbed a hunk of his hair and pulled him up to her. They kissed and she pulled away, making a sour face.

"What's that for?" Lewis was surprised at her expression.

"I think I need to brush my teeth." She jumped out of bed and ran to the bathroom, with Lewis close behind.

"I'll wash your back if you wash mine." Lewis smiled and she felt herself weakening. She couldn't tell if it was from the thought of making love with him again or from lack of food. She went with her instinct.

"Deal."

The shower scene was one for Hollywood, soaping and touching each other, kissing and laughing. Another new experience for Bitsy, orgasms while standing up in the shower, using their hands, ending in laughter and contentment. They found a Weathervane restaurant close by. Bitsy couldn't remember fish and chips ever tasting so good.

Chapter 19

Upon waking, Bitsy knew this day was going to be anything but routine. It was her 20th birthday. She and Lewis took the day off – she had earned at least one vacation day from her more than 4 months of working at the A-to-Z Mart. This was going to be a birthday like no other because now she had Lewis in her life. Whenever she'd asked him what they were going to do he had just smiled. He was definitely good at keeping secrets. She hoped she could stay awake for the entire day though because she'd had a restless night's sleep. This wasn't an unusual occurrence for Bitsy. Whenever an exciting event was coming up such as: starting her new job, going to the Mart after the weekend when she would see Lewis, her 20th birthday, Bitsy's sleep tended to be disturbed. It was something she'd experienced since her childhood when, after 3 months off for summer, she was starting school in a new grade.  She couldn't turn her brain off as she created scenario after scenario of the coming day's events. And that is exactly what had happened last night. She thought about all of the things she loved to do and wondered which one Lewis had planned. Or if he had come up with a list of different ones himself and it would be a complete surprise. Either way, the excitement was more than she could bear and at 6am she got up having barely slept. She put on her bathrobe and went downstairs. It was a Friday. Her parents were just getting up and showering as it was a regular work day for them. Bitsy made coffee for them and put the water on for tea for herself. She was just sitting down to have her tea, trying to decide what she wanted for breakfast, when the front door bell rang. It was 6:40am.

Looking out the front window, she didn't see anyone or anything out of the ordinary. Going to the front door and, standing on tippy-toes and looking out of the three small windows at the top of the door, Bitsy saw the thick dark head of hair that had become so familiar to her. Opening the door, there stood Lewis, holding a tray with two tea cups and a bakery box in one hand. In the other hand, he held a mixed bouquet of freesia, roses, tulips, baby's breath, and a few other wild flowers that Bitsy, at one time or another, had mentioned were her favorites. Lewis had obviously hand-selected the entire bouquet. Bitsy's face held the biggest smile it could possibly hold. Quickly opening the storm door, which her parents kept on year-round, she held it wide so Lewis, with his hands full, could enter.

"Was that the door?" Her mom yelled down the stairs.

"Yes, it's Lewis, with gifts!" Bitsy was beaming, her face flushed.

"Oh, isn't that sweet! We'll be right down."

Bitsy took Lewis' arm and led him into the kitchen where she took the box and two cups in the tray out of his hand. The bouquet of flowers he then presented to Bitsy.

"Oh, they are just beautiful, Lewis. All my favorites!"

"I know. I remembered." Lewis leaned over and kissed her cheek.

Her mom came downstairs and, exclaiming over the beautiful bouquet, reached up to a top shelf in a cabinet for a clear glass vase. She put water in the vase and handed Bitsy a pair of scissors to cut the stems and package of floral preservative to put into the water.

"Now, you need to cut each one before you put it in the water, just a little, so it can drink the water."

"Okay, I will." Bitsy had received flowers only one other time, from her parents for her high school graduation.

"I'm sorry I didn't bring coffees for you and Keith." Lewis apologized to Violet.

"That's okay, Lewis. I made coffee for them." Bitsy spoke before her mom got a chance.

"Oh, no problem, Lewis. This is Bitsy's day. But thank you for thinking of us. And thank you, sweetie, for making coffee for your dad and me." Her mom put her hand on Bitsy's shoulder and gave a squeeze.

Bitsy was grateful that Lewis had thought about getting coffee for her parents. She knew that both of her parents were warming up to Lewis. He was always the perfect gentleman and they could see how much he cared for Bitsy.

Bitsy's dad came into the kitchen at that moment.

"So, what's this? Flowers? Why, is today a special day or something?"

Bitsy smiled at her dad. Lewis extended his hand.

"Keith, good to see you again." Bitsy's dad shook Lewis' hand.

"It looks to me like you're spoiling my daughter."

"Yes, sir, I'm trying my best."

Bitsy beamed as Lewis and her dad joked. But she also knew it was true – about the spoiling.

They all sat down at the kitchen table, her parents with their coffee, and Bitsy handed Lewis one of the cups of tea he had brought, taking the other one for herself.

"I think we need to open this` box. A special day deserves some special treats." Lewis took the scissors Bitsy had used for her flowers and cut the string. The large box was full of Boston crème and jelly doughnuts, two of Bitsy's favorites, crullers for Keith, and an apple cinnamon for Violet. There were also a couple of bagels and a corn and a blueberry muffin.

"That one has my name on it." Keith took a cruller and dunked it into his coffee.

"And I think this is an apple cinnamon?" Violet took the one that Lewis had bought for her and returned the cereal box she had taken down back up on the shelf.

"Which do you want, Bitsy?" Lewis waited for her to pick.

"I don't know, there are so many that I like. I think I'll have the blueberry muffin."

Lewis took one of the Boston crème donuts. They all smiled contentedly at the simple breakfast pleasures.

"I think you need to shower and dress, Bitsy." Her mom gave her a look. She obviously was uncomfortable leaving Lewis with Bitsy still in her bathrobe while she and Keith went to work.

"Heading right up. I'll be done in a few minutes. Lewis, why don't you watch TV while I shower. Oh, and what should I wear? What are we doing?" Bitsy asked walking into the living room and turning on the TV.

"Casual is fine for now, jeans, you know."

Violet got sandwiches out of the refrigerator for her and Keith and followed Bitsy upstairs to finish getting ready for work. She came down just a few minutes later and joined Lewis and Keith in the living room.

"Lewis, I wanted to talk to you about Bitsy's birthday. I know you have plans for dinner out, but we also have a birthday cake and some gifts for her. So, maybe we could have the cake before you go out, in case you are a little late coming home? And we can give her our presents?"

"That sounds fine. We have dinner reservations at 7, so how about we come back here around 5:30 or so. Bitsy will want to change, I brought a change of clothes with me, and we'll have time to spend with you and Keith before we go to dinner."

"Perfect! Thank you, Lewis." And, having settled that, Violet kissed Keith and left for work.

Keith also got up and, after saying good-bye to Lewis, went to the foot of the stairs and called up to Bitsy.

"Bitsy, your mom just left and I have to go now. Are you almost ready?"

Bitsy came downstairs dressed, her hair still damp.

"Almost done, just have to make myself beautiful for Lewis."

"Pumpkin, if he doesn't already know you're beautiful, then there's no hope for him."

Bitsy kissed her dad good-bye and he headed to the door, turning before he went out.

"Happy Birthday, Pumpkin."

"Thanks, dad." Bitsy ran back upstairs to finish getting ready.

When Bitsy came back downstairs Lewis, standing at the bottom of the stairs, wrapped his arms around her, kissing her on the mouth.

"I've wanted to do that since I saw you at the door in your bathrobe. And then I wanted to take that bathrobe off and kiss you all over and…"

"You better stop now or we'll never leave the house. And, that's exactly why my parents didn't want to leave us alone. Plus, now I have to redo my lipstick!"

Lewis kissed her again, smearing her lipstick even more.


Getting onto the highway, Lewis drove for about an hour. When they got close to their destination, he said to Bitsy, "Close your eyes now and no peeking."

He drove into a parking garage and, having parked the car, guided her through the garage to the elevator, making sure she kept her eyes closed. Finally, getting off the elevator and, after walking just a few steps, he said, "Okay, open."

Bitsy looked around someplace she was completely unfamiliar with until she saw something she recognized; a poster for La Cage aux Folles. Her face lit up and, wrapping her arms around Lewis' neck, hugged and kissed him.

"Thank you, thank you, thank you! This is so amazing, I've always wanted to see this show!"

"I know, and now you will. Let's go inside, I already have our tickets."

"Oh Lewis, you are awesome. I love you!" Lewis stopped and turned to face Bitsy. He took her face in his hands and kissed her.

"And I love you."

The show was over before they realized it. It was everything Bitsy had imagined and so much more than the highlights in the few commercials she had seen. She was so happy and squeezed Lewis' hand as they walked out of the theater.

After they had returned to his car and were exiting the parking garage, Lewis turned right and headed out of the city.

"How about some lunch?"

"Or how about just some snacks because we'll be going to dinner and I don't want to be too full." Bitsy realized she was assuming they'd be going to dinner. Maybe her parents had something planned.

"Oh, I'm sorry, I don't even know if we're going to dinner."

"Yes, we are, of course. But don't worry, we have a few more hours. It is only 2:30, so I think we can get a bite to eat."

He brought her to a sushi restaurant where they had a few California rolls, unagi, ebi, and each a bowl of miso soup.

"This is just about right, Lewis. You are the best."

"I aim to please, only you, Bitsy."

The time flew by and suddenly it was 4:45pm. Lewis paid the bill and they left. They had about an hour's drive home and arrived at almost 10 of 6. Bitsy's parents were both home. Lewis grabbed his dinner clothes out of the back seat, something from his glove box, and followed Bitsy into the house.

Bitsy's parents were in the kitchen, just finishing up their dinner.

"Hi! You're just in time! Happy Birthday, birthday girl! How has your birthday been so far?" Violet hugged Bitsy and smiled at Lewis.

"Oh guys, we've had the best time. Lewis took me to see La Cage aux Folles! It was fantastic. You have to go see it!"

"That sounds wonderful. But why don't we go into the dining room, before you get changed for dinner."

Keith, beer in hand, motioned to Lewis if he wanted one. Lewis declined.

He put his clothes down on the sofa in the living room and followed them into the dining room. A cake that said "Happy 20th Birthday, Bitsy" was on the table along with four plates and silverware. Keith brought in vanilla ice cream. There were three wrapped boxes on the table, too.

"Oh, mom, dad, this is so nice."

"Well, I always wish we could do more. But I hope you like everything."

"Well, I know one thing she will love," Keith blurted out.

"Keith!" Violet gave him a look that said 'not another word'.

Violet lit the candles and they all sang "Happy Birthday" to Bitsy. She stood for a minute and, looking right at Lewis, made her wish while blowing the candles out. Violet exchanged a worried look with Keith.

"Okay, let's open the presents." For some reason Keith wanted to move things along.

"Keith, relax. First the cake."

Bitsy cut pieces of cake for everyone and her mom put a scoop of ice cream on each piece. After they finished their cake, Keith got up and put an envelope in front of Bitsy.

"Hmm, what could this be?" Inside she found a gift certificate for $50 to JC Penney.

"Thank you so much!" Bitsy said, giving each of her parents a kiss.

"And next." Her dad seemed ready to burst as he handed her a small box.

Bitsy shook the box lightly, carefully took off the frilly bow, unwrapped the birthday paper that was decorated with colorful balloons, and opened it to find a beautiful gold watch. She had pointed it out to her mother the last time they had gone shopping together. It was exactly the one she wanted.

"Oh mom, I love it! This is the one they had at Karol's Jewelers!"

"The exact one. I knew I couldn't go wrong since you had picked it out!"

"I love it!" She quickly took her Timex off and put her new watch on. It was a little big, so she took it off and, at her mom's suggestion, they'd have some links taken out so she could wear it.

"Okay, okay, and now this one." Her dad was nearly jumping up and down. It was the biggest box and Bitsy couldn't imagine what her parents got her that would be in such a big box. And it was heavy, too. She carefully unwrapped the box and when she took the cover off, it was full of magazines.

Keith started laughing. Bitsy looked at him like he had two heads and Violet shook her head and rolled her eyes. Then Bitsy saw a smaller box in the corner of the big one she'd just opened. She picked it up, took off the cover, and inside was a set of keys.

"Dad? Mom? Did you get me…?" She couldn't make herself say the words. She was so excited and when she turned to her dad, he actually was jumping up and down a little.

"So, let's go see… your new car!"

"Oh my God! Dad! Mom!" Bitsy was so excited. She ran to Lewis and, wrapping her arms around his neck, kissed him. Lewis was always a little hesitant to show too much affection in front of her parents, especially since he knew the effect Bitsy had on him, and glanced at them while kissing her.

"Why don't you go see your car, Bitsy?" Lewis coughed, composing himself. Her parents each took her by the hand and brought her to the back of the house where her red Honda civic sat.

"It's two years old, very clean, and only has 22K miles on it. Never been in an accident. Has A/C which you could definitely use this summer. I couldn't believe it, the person who had traded it in got a new car from them every two years. It had just come in when I was looking that week. But remember, Pumpkin, you have to pay the insurance."

Bitsy ran around to the driver's side and opened the passenger side for Lewis, who got in.

"I love it! Isn't it great, Lewis? This is the best birthday ever." She leaned over and kissed him hard on the lips. Again, he was aware of her parents watching. Bitsy didn't seem to care at all.

"Maybe you should thank your parents, Bitsy. And we should probably get ready for dinner. We have about 20 minutes before we have to leave."

"Oh, yes, right! Okay, let's go." They both got out of the car. Bitsy hugged and kissed her mom and dad and they all walked back into the house together.

"I think I'm going to have to sleep in it tonight!" Bitsy was about ready to head upstairs when Lewis called her back.

"Bitsy wait, can I talk to you a minute?"

"Sure, oh, you can change in the bathroom down here and if you need to wash up, there are towels and washcloths in the closet."

"Okay, thank you." Bitsy's parents stood by, Violet poured herself a glass of wine and Keith got himself another beer. They were about to walk into the living room when they saw Lewis pull a small box out of his jacket pocket and then bend down on one knee as he handed the box to Bitsy.

Bitsy stared at the little box and looked down at Lewis. He looked deep into her eyes and smiled. She felt herself shaking. She didn't notice her mom looking up at her dad with a look of surprise, her mouth stern, her eyes wide. This certainly was not the kind of birthday surprise they wanted for Bitsy. Keith started to say something but Lewis turned to him and held up his hand.

"Let Bitsy open her gift. We let her open your gifts. Please let her open my gift now." Her parents were a little shocked by Lewis' terse yet polite request and decided to see exactly what was in the little box. It could, after all, be earrings. But of course, bending on one knee was not the usual stance for giving earrings.

Bitsy was so nervous. Could it be? It was way too soon, although she knew they'd someday marry and be together forever. But it did seem really soon to be engaged. She tried as carefully as she could with shaking hands to remove the bow and paper from the box. She was pretty sure someone else had wrapped the gift. She slowly opened the box. Then she started to think 'earrings'. Her mother leaned in to see what was in the little box. It was a brilliant blue sapphire ring encircled with diamonds. It took her breath away. Her mother had a similar reaction.

"Will you be… my best friend, Bitsy?"

"Oh my God, Lewis, this is the most beautiful ring I have ever seen! I don't know what to say? Is it an engage…?" Then she realized what he had said and said, "Oh, yes, of course I will." And jumped into his arms as he stood up.

"It's a friendship ring because you are my best friend and I want to celebrate that with you."

Bitsy's head was spinning. She knew how expensive sapphires and diamonds were and she couldn't imagine for a second how much this ring must have cost.

"I took a guess on the size, so if it doesn't fit, we'll have it resized for you." Lewis took the ring out of the box and Bitsy held out her left hand.

"Since this is a friendship ring, I think we should keep your engagement finger available, don't you?" Bitsy, understanding, gave him her right hand and he slipped the ring on her finger next to her pinky. It fit perfectly. Bitsy continued staring at the ring, fascinated by its beauty. Her mom and dad both came over and stared at it with her. They looked up at Lewis and then back at the ring.  Bitsy's mom spoke first.

"How could you aff…"

"How could I afford it, working at the Mart? Well, I guess that's a story for another time. But I think right now that Bitsy and I both need to get ready to go to dinner."

Bitsy pulled herself away from gazing at her ring and started to run off to get ready for dinner, but she stopped and running back to Lewis, she wrapped her arms around his neck giving him another big kiss. Again, Lewis looked uncomfortably at her parents.

"Thank you just doesn't seem like enough, but thank you so much for my beautiful ring and for everything you've done for me today, Lewis. You've made this day so special, so magical. I feel like I'm dreaming."

"Well, you better wake up or we'll be late for dinner. Remember, wear something kind of dressy."

And with that Bitsy ran upstairs to her bedroom.

Lewis nodded to her parents without saying anything and, taking his change of clothes, walked to the downstairs bathroom.

About 10 minutes later Bitsy was ready. Lewis was waiting in the living room.

Bitsy wore the nicest dress she owned, one that she had bought for a friend's wedding that had been canceled.  Since she loved the dress and had gotten it on sale, she had decided to keep it. And now, she was glad she had. A silky dark mauve sheath, it fit Bitsy like a glove, accentuating the slight curves in her slim body. She wore it with black suede 1" heels. Lewis stood up when Bitsy walked into the room.

"Wow! Look at my girl!" Her dad was always good at compliments. Her mom came over and kissed her on the cheek.

"You look beautiful, hon."

Lewis walked up to her, took her hand, and kissed it.

"Your carriage awaits, m'lady."

The dinner was, of course, magical. How could it be anything else after the perfect day Lewis had planned for Bitsy? They each had lobster with shrimp cocktail for an appetizer. Bitsy was stuffed after their meal and, since they had already had a piece of her birthday cake, they both skipped having dessert. Bitsy had seltzer and Lewis, surprisingly, had a glass of white wine. This was the first time Lewis had any alcohol while out with Bitsy.

"So, how is your birthday so far, Bitsy? Are you having a nice time?"

"Oh Lewis, words can't express how perfect it's been. I can't imagine a more perfect birthday. Maybe you shouldn't have been so extravagant. I mean, how will you ever top this one?" Bitsy giggled, turning the color of her dress.

"I guess I'll have to get creative, that's all. I certainly never want to disappoint you, Bitsy."

"Lewis, I can't imagine you ever disappointing me, about anything."

"Well, I hope not. I hope I can always satisfy your every need." He winked which pushed an even darker shade of mauve into Bitsy's cheeks.

The ride home was quiet, Bitsy holding Lewis' hand the entire way and nodding off to sleep. It was just a little after 10pm, but it had been a long day full of surprises for Bitsy and she was definitely winding down, especially after having that decadent lobster dinner. Lewis pulled into the driveway and the automatic porch light came on. Bitsy jumped, squeezing Lewis' hand.

"Oh, we're home. I'm sorry, I guess I dozed off. Do you want to come in?"

"No, I think you should maybe spend a little time with your parents today. They haven't seen you much today on your special day. I see a light on in the living room, so I think they've probably been waiting for you. But I'll see you tomorrow, ok, since it's Saturday. Unless you have other plans.

"Yes, I would love that. Maybe we can just relax together, or spend part of the day with my parents."

"That sounds good to me."

"Thank you again so much for a beautiful birthday!" She smiled and looked at her ring.  And then she wrapped her arms around Lewis' neck, kissing him ever so lightly on the mouth. He responded back pressing a little harder. Bitsy pressed back moving closer to him and then Lewis backed away.

"You'll never get in the house if we don't stop now. Besides, I think we're being watched."

Bitsy kissed the top of his nose and each cheek and then jumped out of the car. Lewis opened his car door to get out and walk her to her door, but she was already inside. He stood next to his car, took a deep breath and, looking up at the stars, smiled, got back into his car, and drove to his apartment.

# Chapter 20

Before Lewis, Bitsy had always looked forward to Sundays and doing something fun either with her parents or her two best high school friends - before they had both moved out of town. Now, she couldn't wait for Mondays so she could be with Lewis again. Her favorite part of her job was meeting the customers, but she was also getting to know the other people who worked at the A-to-Z Mart. She met most of them while she was either taking a break or at lunch. Lewis wasn't always available to take his lunch break with Bitsy, so on those days, Bitsy would have lunch with Anna or she'd have a quick lunch and then walk around the building outside, just to get some exercise and a little fresh air. And sometimes she sat in the Employees' Lounge reading while eating her lunch. On those days, sometimes someone she didn't know would show up and she'd immediately engage them in conversation. And, just like that, she'd make another friend. Or, if it was someone she already knew, she'd find out a little more about them. And, of course, the longer she worked at the A-to-Z Mart, the more friends she made. Soon nearly everyone who entered the Employee Lounge was someone she knew, either from meeting them during her lunch breaks or when a group of them had gotten together at Gini's. Gini, the Front Desk Manager, was like the store's matriarch and kept everyone in line, watching out for the younger employees and keeping some of the older ones from over-indulging, especially when they came to her house.

Some of the people she talked to had interesting hobbies, too. Like Carl, in Housewares, who was a really good bowler and had played in championship games across the country. And Bridget, who worked in the cosmetics department, was a talented seamstress and redesigned wedding dresses for many young women who brought her their mother's wedding dress to tailor for them to wear at their own weddings. Once, she brought in a binder full of before and after photographs that she had taken of these wedding dresses. Bridget got teary-eyed showing these pictures to Bitsy. She said she was one of those people who always cried at weddings, even if she didn't know the people. Bridget was married to the love of her life for 27 years.

So many stories and so many talented people. Bitsy decided to keep her paintings and her sand terrariums to herself. It certainly wasn't anything she would get teary-eyed talking about with anyone. Maybe she could look for more meaningful hobbies. Of course, she loved reading and sometimes shared the latest book she was reading with others.

But Bitsy couldn't be happier at her job. In just a few months her life had changed dramatically. She had met the love of her life, she had a job that she enjoyed going to every day, and she'd made several new friends. It was the start of what she hoped would be her beautiful new life.

There were so many people at her job that she was becoming good friends with and most of them were around her age, just a year or two out of high school. They just seemed like genuinely good people. Sure, she was young, but she also knew that they weren't all nice, and she had met some of them already. For one, Joe was too aggressive for her. She had never met anyone like him before and sometimes he scared her. Then there was Kathy, another cashier who flirted with all the guys. Even though, Bitsy was sure someone had mentioned, she was married. She wondered why people got married to people they didn't really love.

There were a few people who were always nice to her and went out of their way to smile, say hi, and ask how she was settling in. She knew her naivety was showing because she felt herself blushing when they spoke to her. Mostly it was a couple of the more experienced men who worked in the store; she found herself intimidated by them, like Nick in Sporting Goods. He was such a big, powerful guy, like a wrestler or a body-builder. Guys that big scared her. But he was always so pleasant to her and had a smile when she said 'hi' back to him. He certainly would be a good person to have as a body guard. A few times he had shown up at Gini's and, if Micky wasn't there to protect her, Nick always seemed to find his way beside her without being too obvious. Joe, on the other hand, was always trying to get a kiss or would squeeze in between Bitsy and whoever else was sitting beside her on the couch. One time when Joe was getting too close to Bitsy, she got up off the couch and headed towards the bathroom to get away from him. Joe took this as a sign that she was encouraging him to follow. She glanced back over her shoulder and saw Nick blocking Joe's way. She didn't know what he'd said, but not only did Joe not follow her, he didn't bother her again the rest of that night. Bitsy felt safe when Nick was around. He didn't always come to the parties, but if he wasn't there, Micky usually was.

Micky was one of Bitsy's favorite people. They had connected right away and she was sure Micky had a crush on her. But Micky knew she and Lewis were tight so he never asked her out. Bitsy thought of Micky as the little brother she'd never had, but she was sure he didn't want to know this was how she felt about him. When they went to Gini's after work, Micky would sit near Bitsy and make sure that if Joe showed up, he didn't bother her. There were other women for Joe to bother, like Kathy who always seemed available. A couple of times she'd seen Kathy and Joe kissing in a dark corner at Gini's. Or they'd go into the bathroom together and lock the door until someone banged on the door for them to come out. When they finally did come out, Joe was usually zipping up his pants and Kathy was buttoning up her blouse.

Bitsy also liked Mandy, who had started dating Ed. Mandy and Ed got together for the first time at Gini's and they were becoming like Bitsy and Lewis, inseparable. Chrissy was another sweet girl who Bitsy sometimes took her breaks with, even though she didn't say much. Of course, Bitsy was never at a loss for words; maybe that was why Chrissy liked Bitsy. Chrissy was so shy and quiet, and she had eyes like a homeless puppy. Bitsy didn't want to pry, but she thought maybe Chrissy was in an abusive home. Bitsy mentioned this to Anna and she confirmed that she had talked to Chrissy and the poor sweet girl almost started to cry when she shared some stories about her neglectful parents. It really upset Anna who obviously loved her children and couldn't understand how anyone could hurt them. Chrissy started coming to Gini's place with Jack and Bitsy had overheard someone say they were moving in together. But Mandy had told Bitsy that Jack was married with three kids. Mandy knew this because Ed worked for Jack. Bitsy hoped Chrissy wouldn't get hurt; it seemed as if she'd already suffered enough at her young age.

Then there was Diane. Bitsy thought she and Diane could probably become good friends. She was so down-to-earth, just a genuinely good person. Diane was interested in Kyle, in the Shoe Department, and Diane wondered if he'd ever ask her out, even though she usually spent her break pretending like she was looking for a pair of shoes.

Although Bitsy had not had a lot of life experiences and knew that even though she wanted to believe everyone was honest and good, mostly, she had already, in her short time at the A-to-Z Mart, met some people who she knew instinctively could not be trusted. Kathy was one person who Bitsy found out early was not to be trusted and was not her friend.

Employees brought their purchases through a special register specifically for them. When Bitsy had gotten her first few paychecks, she couldn't help but spend the money on a couple of new outfits. Kathy happened to be on the employee's register and Bitsy noticed that she had only rung up 3 of the 4 items that Bitsy was buying; 2 blouses, a pair of pants, and a skirt. Bitsy looked at Kathy who winked at her and told her the total she owed. Bitsy was surprised that Kathy was trying to set Bitsy up to steal one of the blouses she was buying and thought Bitsy would go along with her. Bitsy knew right at that moment that if they got caught, she could lose her job. Plus, stealing was something Bitsy would never consider, ever. She felt like Kathy was trying to trap her.

"You forgot this blouse." Bitsy said as she pulled it out of the bag.

Kathy sighed, rolled her eyes, and played dumb.

"Oh, sorry." Kathy rang up the purchase, shoving it into the bag.

From that moment on, Bitsy avoided Kathy, understanding quickly that Kathy was a person she could never trust.

There was so much drama and romance going on in the store, it was sometimes hard trying to keep it all straight. But again, so many people were genuinely nice and Bitsy was happy she had gotten the job, or she never would have met Lewis.

Chapter 21

It was late afternoon and things were a little slow at the cash registers. There were four cashiers on that day and Bitsy was getting antsy. She and Lewis had a date that night and she wanted to leave so that they could be together. She was looking for something to do and asked Anna, who was at the register next to her, if there was anything she could do to pass the time. Sometimes the cashiers helped out in the departments if they got a new shipment in and the floor needed restocking. And when the registers were busy, the various departments sent some of their clerks to help with bagging the purchases. It was a good system and worked out for everyone.

"Well, we are getting low on cash register tapes. You could go down to the stock room and get a few boxes."

"Perfect, I'll be right back."

Bitsy didn't know exactly where to look but she figured one of the stock guys would know. And she might even see Lewis who sometimes helped out in different departments, especially unloading trucks, which he welcomed as a way of getting in a work out.

Bitsy went through the swinging doors at the back of the store that led to the stock area for all departments. There were huge metal shelves full of unopened boxes. She had no idea where to go and didn't see anyone around.

"Hello?" She called out. And then a little louder, "Is anyone here?"

She walked down the aisles, looking but finding no one. It seemed strange to her that no one would be around. It wasn't yet quitting time. Then she thought that maybe they were all at the loading dock, unloading a shipment that had recently come in.

She walked down one row of shelving and up another, searching for what looked like a back door to the unloading area. Suddenly, someone came up behind her and put their arms around her. Her first thought was Lewis, but there was no Dial soap smell, only some overpowering man's cologne mixed with body odor. She tried to pull away but was held tight.

"Joe, let me go." She demanded, her voice quivering slightly. He was very strong but she did not want him to know she was afraid.

"Hey baby, I thought you were looking for me."

"No, I was looking for someone to help me find the register tapes. We need some." He wasn't loosening his grip. And then with one quick move he turned her around to face him, not loosening his hold even the slightest.

"Hi beautiful, how about a kiss?"

"Joe, let me go!" She felt her face turning red and her body stiffening from a combination of fear and anger. She tried to lift her leg to kick him but couldn't move at all.

"What are you trying to do, kick me? You know, you are such a dick-tease. You have been flirting with me since I first met you and I know you want it from me so why don't I just give it to you right now!"

He held Bitsy with one arm and she struggled to get away while he reached down to unzip his pants.

"Lucky for you I didn't wear underwear today, and look at you wearing a skirt. So convenient. I'll bet you were thinking the same thing."

He started kissing her neck and pulling her skirt up.

Bitsy was terrified and could barely move, waiting for an opportunity to kick or at least get her arms away to gouge his eyes or punch him in the throat. She desperately tried to remember everything she had learned at a couple of self-defense classes she had taken at the Y. Never thinking she would have to remember the moves, they all came flooding back to her now.

She tried to scream but his mouth was on hers, his tongue pushing down her throat. She felt his hardness against her stomach as Joe tried lifting her up. At that moment, his grip relaxed slightly and she took off running, leaving him with his jeans around his ankles. She ran like she had never run before, back the way she had come in, out the swinging doors onto the store floor. She was shaking and nearly ran into a woman pushing a shopping cart, who gave her a stunned look.

"I'm sorry," Bitsy mumbled and walked quickly back to the front of the store, searching for Lewis.

She got back to her register and stood there, not putting her light on but composing herself, fluffing her hair, wiping her eyes, trying to stop the tears that were running down them.

A hand was on her shoulder. She spun around, ready to fight. It was Lewis.

"Hey, what's up? Are you okay?"

She wanted to burst into tears right there and fall into Lewis' arms but she knew she had to keep it together for a little bit longer, at least until they left the store.

"Joe... he..."

She didn't need to say anymore. The smile she loved so much quickly left Lewis' face and he turned away, looking toward the back of the store.

"Lewis, no, just stay with me. It's almost time to go home. Please."

She saw the look in his eyes, a look she had never seen before but knew it meant Joe would somehow regret ever having touched Bitsy. But she also feared for Lewis. Joe was strong and she was worried he could hurt Lewis if they got into a fight. For now, though, she wanted Lewis close to her. That was the only way she felt safe.

"Let's go, Bitsy. Sign out of your register and let's go." Someone had just come into Bitsy's lane but Lewis put her closed sign at the end.

She took out her money drawer and went to the office.

"Just stay here and I'll go punch you out."

Bitsy thought that was not such a good idea and that Lewis was so fired up that he would go looking for Joe. She had to keep him with her.

"No, Lewis, we'll go down together, please."

Bitsy explained to Elaine, head cashier in the office, that she wasn't feeling well and held her stomach. Elaine nodded understanding and gave Bitsy a sad face.

Bitsy held Lewis' arm as he punched out for both of them and they walked back through the store and out the door.

Outside, Bitsy turned to Lewis and wrapped her arms around his neck, mascara-stained tears running down her face. Lewis held her tightly while at the same time leading her to his car. Once inside, she could no longer control herself and wept loudly.

Lewis held her, waiting for her to get it all out before he asked any questions. But he was pretty sure he knew what had happened.

After a few minutes, Bitsy calmed down a little, wiping her eyes and face. Lewis couldn't wait for her to speak.

"I'm taking you to the police." He started his car and started to put it into gear when Bitsy grabbed his arm. Lewis stopped the car and put it back in park.

"No, Lewis. You can't."

"Do you want to tell me what he did to you?"

Tears were filling Bitsy's eyes again and she dabbed them away with a tissue.

"Did he…"

"He didn't rape me. He tried to rape me. I got away."

Lewis grabbed the steering wheel, tightening his grip, his jaw.  His whole body seemed to tighten and his face turned the color of pure anger.

"We should go to the police, Bitsy."

"If we go to the police they'll probably just slap his wrist and then he'll be back at work and I don't want…"

"Then I'll kill him."

Bitsy knew he was serious. He wouldn't joke about something like this. She really didn't know what to do but she felt, unless she was actually raped, that the police would do nothing.

"We need to tell your parents."

"No, please Lewis. Not my parents."

"Why, Bitsy. They should know what kind of…"

"Because they'll make me quit my job and then I won't see you every day, Lewis, and I like it here."

"It's just a job, Bitsy, you can get another job, we'll both get other jobs. Your life is far more important than this job. You aren't giving me any help here and I need to fix this. Now."

"Just give me a little time, Lewis, let me figure this out."

"Three days. I'll give you three days and then I'll take care of this."

"Lewis, I know you said you'd kill him but I hope you weren't serious, you can't be serious. I wouldn't be able to live without you if you went to jail. You have to think about this seriously. They'll know it was you. And since it wasn't rape but attempted rape, you know he'd probably get off and that would just anger you more. "

Every time Bitsy mentioned 'rape' Lewis' whole body visibly tensed.

"Three days." Lewis pulled her close to him, holding her so tightly he was slowly squeezing the air out of her and, for just a second, she could barely breathe.

# Chapter 22

Bitsy couldn't wait to get home and shower, to wash off the feeling of Joe's hands on her body. Her car was still in the parking lot at the A-to-Z Mart but she knew Lewis would pick her up and drive her back to get her car the next day. She was sure it would be fine overnight. As they were driving to her house, she tried to fabricate a story that would sound believable and true enough so that her parents wouldn't ask a lot of questions. She thought role-playing with Lewis might help.

"Okay, you have to pretend to be my parents and ask me questions they might ask. And then I'll decide if they'd believe my responses or not. If there's any chance they might not buy it, then I'll change my answers."

Lewis was gripping the steering wheel so tightly Bitsy thought he might either bruise his hands or rip the steering wheel right out of the dashboard.

"Please, you've got to help me with this, Lewis."

"I think you should tell them, just tell them the truth. Don't lie to them Bitsy, I don't want you to start lying to them now. They'll think I had something to do with it."

"No, they won't. You're right, they trust me, they'll believe me. But it has to be something that won't cause them to jump into their car and take me to the hospital. Like, I can't say I tripped over boxes and hit my head. They would definitely rush me to the hospital, so I can't say that."

"I don't know, Bitsy, I can't think right now."

"Please Lewis, help me with this." She knew she had to get his mind off of killing Joe and not show up at her parents' house with this intense look on his face. They would know something was going on and wouldn't even listen to Bitsy at that point. She thought Lewis should know this, that he was giving off a vibe that would cause them to be suspicious.

"Okay, you're right. I'll get through this. But I don't want to leave you." Lewis reached for her hand.

"But we can't look suspicious. If you stay too long, they'll know something more happened. I'm going to tell them I was having bad cramps, that time of the month, and I didn't feel like driving. I was feeling a little dizzy so asked you to drive me home."

"Do you get cramps that bad?"

"Not usually but I have had them a few times. And I'm sure they'll believe it. Especially my mom.  And if she believes it, then so will my dad."

"And then tomorrow I'll pick you up. Or maybe you should stay home. I would feel much better if you stayed home."

"I'm not staying home. I'm not going to let him win this no matter what. I've decided this is the best course of action. I'm going to pretend, for now, that nothing happened."

"That is NOT happening. But you're right about one thing, he isn't getting away with this. You aren't giving me many options, Bitsy." She knew Lewis was right. She really had no idea what a just punishment would be, only that killing Joe wasn't it. There had to be another solution. But Bitsy truly believed that if she went to the police, they would simply slap Joe's hands for attempted rape, and that's if they even believed her. And that meant that he might get away with it. If that happened, then she'd always feel uncomfortable working at the A-to-Z Mart, knowing that at any time she could be in a similar situation and that Joe might actually rape her the next time. Her life at the A-to-Z Mart would never be the same again. She sighed and looked out the window, hiding the tears that were now streaming down her face, the rest of her mascara blending with her tears. Lewis handed her a Kleenex. She took his hand in both of hers and kissed it. His face transformed back to the one she loved so much. But for only a second.

Her parents believed Bitsy's story and after about twenty minutes, Lewis left, telling Bitsy he would be there to pick her up early the next morning. After he left, Bitsy told her parents she was tired and wanted to shower and she was going to bed early.

"How about a little dinner, sweetie? I can bring you some soup, or a grilled cheese, something light? You should eat something."

"I'm not hungry but thanks, mom. I'm just tired and want to get some sleep. I'm sure I'll feel better in the morning."

Her parents watched her walk upstairs, her mother standing with her arms folded across her chest, her dad with his hands on his hips. For the first time they felt helpless and catching each other's eyes, Violet walked into Keith's open arms.

Bitsy couldn't wait to go upstairs and get into the shower so she could get all the anxious thoughts and feelings out of her body, along with the touch of Joe's hands off of it. She thought that if she could just wash it all off then it might feel like it had never happened. But no amount of soap or hot water could change the fact that it had. She could still feel his hard-on pressed against her stomach as he tried to pull down her panties. She was trying to erase this memory, to find a safe place inside her where things like rape couldn't happen to her. Her parents had done their best to protect her all these years and now she was out in public, meeting new people, having new experiences, and finding out about the evil in the world. Overwhelmed by her feelings of helplessness, she slid to the bottom of the tub, as the tears mixed with the warm water that poured over her head, rushing towards the drain, off her body and out of her forever-altered life.

The three days passed quickly. Lewis stayed as close to Bitsy as he could while still doing his job. She never saw Joe in those three days. She didn't think he was the kind of guy who felt remorse for his actions so decided he was just busy with his own work. Or maybe he wasn't even at work. She didn't know and didn't care. All she knew for sure was that she didn't want to run into him. Lewis always clocked her in and out for the day now. And he was always there to go outside to eat lunch with her. It was getting a little cooler out now that it was September and Bitsy wondered what they would do when it got even colder out. Maybe they could eat in her or Lewis' car. She was fine with eating lunch in either just to get out of the store. She used to like eating in the Employees' Lounge with Anna, or even Diane or Mandy who were both sometimes taking their lunch break when she was. But now she worried too much that Joe might show up and she was terrified of being around Joe without having Lewis close by.

She ran up to Lewis' car and he was already inside. He was half-finished with his sandwich. She jumped into his car, leaned over giving him a kiss on his cheek, and took her peanut butter and jelly sandwich out of her bag, along with a bottle of milk. She smiled as he turned to her, swallowing his last bite.

"Am I late? Sorry, I had a customer and I was trying to get out of there."

"So, you were working on your lunch break. I clocked you out 10 minutes ago, Bitsy."

"Sorry, I said I was sorry."

"Yes, okay, I'm not mad at you. I have other issues on my mind."

"Oh? What is it, Lewis?"

"It's been three days, Bitsy. I said I would give you three days to figure out what you wanted to do about Joe. After three days, if you didn't come up with any kind of plan that I agreed with, then I was going to handle this problem myself. You do remember this, right?"

"Yes, of course I do."

"So, do you have any ideas? I'm listening."

She bit into her sandwich, suddenly not feeling very hungry and put the other half back into her bag. The truth was, she hadn't thought about it at all. She had tried to keep herself busy, disappearing into a novel or a movie that she watched with her parents. She didn't have any solution to the problem and had resigned herself to moving forward with her life. She saw no other option but didn't want to share that with Lewis. She had to tell him something.

"Well, I was thinking we'll just avoid him. Maybe he'll get fired. Or maybe he'll quit. Someone said he gambles. Maybe he'll hit it big and won't have to work anymore and he'll leave and be out of our lives forever."

Lewis listened, not speaking for what seemed to Bitsy like twenty minutes.

"Lewis, I…"

"Doing nothing isn't an option, Bitsy, which is what you're suggesting. This is something that has to work for both of us and doing NOTHING, doesn't work for me, at all!" Lewis had never raised his voice to Bitsy and she felt herself shaking. She didn't know how to respond; his anger was frightening. She witnessed his intensity before, that first time in the restaurant, but this was something else. This was an anger that seemed to come right up out of his soul, something primal, almost animal-like. It scared her so much she thought she might throw up. But she was quiet, waiting for him to come back to her, the loving, supportive, caring man she had grown to love more than she could ever imagine. The windows in the car were steaming up as Lewis deeply inhaled and exhaled out. She knew he was trying to calm himself down. He turned to her and reaching for her hand, brought it to his mouth and kissed it.

"Oh Lewis, you frightened me." She fought back tears that were forming at the corners of her eyes.

"You never have to fear me, Bitsy. Ever. I will always look out for you and do what I need to do to care for and protect you. If that's too much for you, just tell me to leave. But I would never, ever hurt you in any way. I'm sorry. I let my anger take over sometimes. Just know that any anger I feel is never directed at you. I don't care what you say or do, I will never turn my anger on you. But right now, I need to take care of this 'problem'. This is my problem now. You no longer need to worry about Joe or whether or not you'll run into him. I won't let you live like this. And if you won't leave this job…" Lewis didn't have to finish his sentence. Bitsy knew she had more to worry about now. She had to worry about what Lewis was going to do.  And, whatever he did, what it might mean for them and their relationship. She didn't want to speak the words but sooner or later the words would be spoken.

"Lewis, I'm afraid. I'm afraid of what you'll do and what might happen to us. I couldn't bear to live without you. What if...?"

"Nothing is going to happen to us, Bitsy. I would never jeopardize our relationship, you know that, right?" All she could manage was to nod her head. He continued holding her hand. He brought it up to his lips again and held it against his face. He closed his eyes and she let the tears spill out of her eyes and onto his jacket sleeve. He opened his eyes, reached for her and pulled her as close to him as he could, holding her tightly as he kissed the top of her head.

"Okay, wipe those eyes." Lewis took a tissue from the box and dabbed at her face, making sure not to smear her eye make-up. She started to laugh because he was so careful until she took the tissue from him, dabbing under her eyes while looking in the mirror, removing the mascara that had washed off.

"Good, smiling and laughing, that's what I want to see." Again, Lewis reached over and kissed her on the lips.

"And now I have to put on my lipstick." She smiled as she took her lipstick out of her purse.

"Well, okay, I guess I won't do that again." Bitsy leaned over and kissed him on the lips, leaving her re-applied lipstick behind. They both laughed as he wiped the lipstick off as she once again re-applied hers, and then they walked back into the store, holding hands.

# Chapter 23

Walking through the automatic doors of the A-to-Z Mart, Bitsy immediately felt something was different. There was something in the air, something that wasn't quite right. She looked around to see if other employees were around but saw no one. She had been running a little late this morning and, since the store would be opening in ten minutes, by this time the cashiers should be at the front and other employees should be buzzing around. She saw nobody. She began to wonder if the store was closed today, but then she remembered the store was open every day of the week, except from 11pm until when they re-opened the following morning at 9am. So, what was going on? Her usual morning ritual consisted of her and Lewis sharing a tea in the lounge and so, because she was late, she rushed to the back of the store to the Employees' Lounge hoping to find Lewis there. She had spotted his car in the lot so knew he was already here.  She walked through the "Employees Only" door and found wall-to-wall people who were overflowing from the Employees' Lounge.

"What's going on?" Bitsy asked the first person who looked at her. It was Cindy.

"Joe is dead."

"Wha… What?" Bitsy's heart stopped beating and she couldn't catch her breath. She thought she was going to have a heart attack right there on the spot. She felt sick to her stomach and thought about running to the ladies' room but she didn't want to bring attention to herself and she didn't want to miss a thing. Lewis. Where was Lewis? That was all she could think about now. She didn't think about Joe, she didn't think about her job, she thought about Lewis. She pushed through the crowd and saw Lewis in the lunch room, back in a corner. The store manager was talking.

"So, when the police show up, please cooperate with them and answer all their questions as best as you can."

Bitsy stared at Lewis. He was looking at the store manager, Mr. Roldark. Bitsy had only seen him once before. He was usually in his office meeting with the various department managers and didn't walk around the store very often. He was a tall, thin man with thinning light brown hair and thick black-rimmed glasses. His white long-sleeved shirt was threatening to push out from under his belt and he kept tucking it back in. His right hand moved from tucking to straightening his glasses, like he was trying to focus. Maybe he thought if he adjusted his glasses just right, he could see who the killer was. He walked around in a circle as if in a slow dance without a partner scanning all the faces in the crowd, watching their reactions.

"Any questions?"

Lewis raised his hand. Bitsy stared at him. He still hadn't looked at her.

"Lewis?"

"Mr. Roldark, do you know what time this happened?"

"Ah, no, not quite. What we do know is that Joe was here until about 7:30 last night. At least, that is when he punched out his time card. So, it was sometime after that."

Again, Lewis raised his hand.

"Yes, Lewis."

"So, he had punched out his timecard but stayed here and was murdered in the store?"

"Apparently. Unless the killer punched out Joe's timecard to make it look as if Joe had already left the store. Joe's body was found on the loading dock, so either he was killed here in the store or he was killed somewhere else and for some reason the killer brought his body back here. But again, the police will figure this out, I don't have all the facts." There was a lot of buzz from the crowd.

Someone else asked, "How was he killed?"

"With a knife – stabbed right in the heart."

"Isn't that gangland style?" Someone in the crowd yelled out.

"We don't know but the police might know."

At that moment Bitsy felt movement behind her and turned to see a couple of policemen making their way over to Mr. Roldark.

The two policemen, dressed in plainclothes, were tall and similarly built. One had a full head of light brown hair while the other tried to hide the shiny scalp that was revealing itself under the few thin hairs that stretched across the top of his head. A guess would put them both somewhere in their mid-30's to early-40's.

They both shook hands with Mr. Roldark and then Mr. Roldark turned the meeting over to them.

"Yes, good morning. I'm Detective Billings and this is Detective MacDougall. We have been assigned to this case and are asking for your full cooperation in our investigation. We'll be asking certain individuals questions first, but we'll eventually need to speak to each of you. If any of you have any information you think might help us quickly solve this murder and bring the guilty party to justice, we would greatly appreciate your sharing that information. But, for now, it's important that no one shares any information with the public or the media until the case has been resolved and the guilty party has been found.

"For a short time, Detective MacDougall and myself will have an office set up here, just off the Employees' Lounge, where our door is always open should you have any knowledge that you believe may help us with this case. Thank you for your cooperation."

"Oh, one last thing. Mr. Roldark has given us a list of the employees' names who we'll be talking to first. Don't be concerned if we're talking to you that you may be a suspect. We'll be talking to any of you who've had any kind of direct interaction or relationship with the victim during the time that he's worked here. That'll be all for now and, again, thank you for your time and cooperation."

Bitsy kept her eyes on Lewis the entire time Detective Billings was speaking. He never looked at her but instead kept his eyes on Detective Billings, taking in every word he said, paying the closest attention to what they wanted and expected of every employee at the A-to-Z Mart.

Detective Billings turned to Mr. Roldark and Mr. Roldark stepped forward, hands on his hips, ignoring the shirt that was now hanging partly out of the top of the waist of his pants.

"Okay, you all heard the detective. They need your full cooperation to solve this murder and I expect each and every one of you to fully cooperate with them. So, for now, go back to work and hopefully we'll get this murder solved quickly."

It was surprising to Bitsy how Mr. Roldark seemed to change right before her eyes, as if he was trying to impress the detectives. Or as if he was one of them and being a tough guy or wanted them to know he was a tough guy just like them. Maybe he always wanted to be a detective but somehow ended up in retail. She wondered if anyone else had noticed.

The crowd dispersed and everyone went back to their departments. Bitsy left the room with everyone else but waited outside the "Employees Only" door until Lewis came out. He was almost the last person out and seemed surprised to see her waiting for him.

"Bitsy, what are you doing here? Shouldn't you be at your register?" She got the feeling he didn't want to see her at that moment.

"Lewis, of course I waited for you and I'm sure you know why. I wanted to talk to you about Joe." She whispered and turned to make sure no one was near them when she said Joe's name.

"What did you want to ask me?"

"You know what I want to ask you! You know exactly what I want to ask you, Lewis."

"Bitsy, I think we should talk about this later, okay. Now you should just concentrate on your job and I'll see you at lunch, okay?"

He kissed her on her forehead and headed off towards the loading dock. Bitsy stood there, unsure of where she should go or what she should do as she watched Lewis walk away. When he was no longer in view, she turned and walked towards the front of the store to her register.

The morning seemed to drag on, you could feel the tension in the air with everyone waiting to be called in to talk to the detectives. Bitsy was unable to concentrate on her job all morning, even making a couple of mistakes giving people back their change, which rarely happened. She was worried because she knew there were at least a few people who'd seen Joe flirting with her.  She waited, knowing for sure she'd be called in. When it was finally lunchtime Lewis came up to her and, without stopping to talk, merely said "Let's go" as he passed by and continued walking out the door.

Bitsy called over to one of the other cashiers, a new lady about her mom's age, that she was going to lunch. She called, "Beverly?" but wasn't sure if that was her name. The woman turned and said "Okay" so Bitsy figured that was right. She grabbed her purse from under the counter and ran after Lewis.

He was sitting in his car a little beyond the front door and Bitsy ran over and got in.

"Oh my God, Lewis! What is going on?" She was close to hysterical and choked back tears. She'd never known someone who was murdered. It frightened her and she was shaking all over.  Nerves overtook her and she didn't know if she wanted to laugh or cry.  No matter how bad Joe was and what he had almost done to her, she didn't think he deserved to die. She wondered if he'd done this before and maybe he succeeded. Maybe he'd raped a girl and he'd told her that if she told anyone he'd kill her, or her family. Even though he hadn't said any of those things to Bitsy, she wondered if that was just an unwritten rule with a rapist, particularly if the victim was underage, like a teacher with a student. She knew he'd come after her, though, just to piss off Lewis. Lewis. Had he done this? She didn't want to let herself think about it. He couldn't have. But he'd given her three days and then he was going to do something about it. That's what he'd told her, wasn't it? So, did that make her an accessory to murder? And would she be withholding evidence if she didn't tell the detectives what Lewis had said to her? But she was getting way ahead of herself. She was thinking the absolute worst about Lewis. She was thinking that he'd killed Joe.

Lewis' foot lay heavy on the accelerator as he drove to the place he'd brought her when they'd first started dating. As soon as he parked, Bitsy jumped out of the car.

"Lewis, talk to me! Tell me the truth."

Lewis slowly, calmly, got out of the driver's side and walked over to Bitsy. He took her by the shoulders and pulling her close to him, she burst into tears.

"Oh my God, oh my God! This is so horrible! I can't believe it. What is going on, Lewis? Please, tell me." She pulled away from him and looked into his face. It was blank, she couldn't read him. She often couldn't read him. He went inside and stayed there, like a machine with no emotions. Shut off, unplugged, empty and dead inside. She knew none of these things were true about Lewis, she knew he was a passionate, loving man and loved her more than she could ever imagine being loved. But right now, she didn't know who he was. And his passivity frightened her.

"Lewis, talk to me, please."

Lewis looked at the ground, staring at the patterns made by the stones pushed into the dirt, deep inside his own thoughts. Finally, he looked up.

"I want you to be safe, Bitsy. Always. The less we talk about this the better it will be. Okay?"

Bitsy started to cry. This, to her, was an admittance of guilt. He was telling her he'd done it and wanted to keep her out of it. He wanted her to be safe. He was also saying he didn't want her to have to lie for him. If he told her he did it, and she didn't tell the cops, she would be an accessory to murder. He was right when he said he wanted her to be safe. She was always in his thoughts, every move he made. She wiped her eyes and went to Lewis, knowing now that he was going to carry this burden himself. But then as she held him, she continued to cry. She was going to lose him. They would find out and he would go to prison.

"Lewis, I can't lose you. I can't go on without you. This can't be happening."

"It's okay, Bitsy. Everything will be fine. Please don't cry. We have to head back to work soon. I want to talk to you now, okay? Let's go sit in the car." And they walked back, his arm around her shoulders, closing the door when she was inside.

"We don't know what happened to Joe, okay? You have to believe we. I don't know what happened. They might arrest me because we've had problems over the years but that doesn't mean I killed him. So, please, you have to stop thinking that I did. I know I said 3 days and I would take care of it. But that doesn't mean I did it."

"So, you're saying it was just a coincidence that he happened to be killed right when you were going to do something to him, to get back at him for what he did to me?"

"That's right, that's exactly what I'm saying. I'm as clueless about his death as you or anyone else in the store." Bitsy stared at him, trying to see the lies in his eyes. But she couldn't see them. She had to believe what he was saying.

"Okay, Lewis. I believe you. But what are you going to say if they arrest you? Or what should I say if they question me?"

"What can you say? Do you know anything about Joe's death? Can you help them in any way? You certainly aren't going to tell them that he tried to rape you, right? I doubt if that information would help them now."

"No, of course not. You're right, Lewis. I have nothing to tell them. But what about you. Do you have an alibi for last night? Do you want me to tell them you were at my house?"

"Now why would you tell them that? I wasn't at your house. So that would be a lie. You don't know where I was. You know they can often figure out lies, they can break you down on the stand. All you have to do is tell the truth. Okay? It's much easier than lying. And never volunteer more information than what they ask for. That's really all you have to remember."

"You're right. I know you're right. But I'm still afraid, Lewis." Lewis reached over and wrapped his arms around her.

"Everything will work out, please don't worry."

# Chapter 24

As it turned out, telling the truth was exactly the right thing to do. She knew nothing and so had nothing to share. When she was called into the room where the detectives were conducting the business of interviewing employees in private, they asked her questions that she couldn't even answer. Except one. And she decided that even though she knew someone who would kill Joe, she wasn't about to share his name.

"Ms. Gordon, Betsy Gordon, is that correct?"

"Yes, that's my name." She wanted to go on about how long she'd worked at the A-to-Z Mart and where she lived but as Lewis had instructed, she only needed to provide them with the information they'd asked for.

"And how long have you worked here now, Ms. Gordon?"

"Just under six months."

"Did you know Joe Bendetti?"

"Only as another employee. I really didn't have anything to do with him; we work… worked in different departments."

"We heard he was a ladies' man. Did he flirt with you Ms. Gordon or try to make any moves that you didn't want?"

Bitsy felt herself shaking inside and she was sure her face was glowing red. She couldn't believe how close to the truth they were. How could they possibly know? She had to keep her cool for Lewis.

"Am I a suspect?" She stared right into Detective Billings and then Detective MacDougall's eyes, challenging them to come right out and tell her yes, she was a suspect. She was sure they wouldn't say that and they held her stare, possibly hoping to find the answer in her eyes. They looked at each other and suddenly each in his own way began to squirm. She almost started to laugh but knew she had to keep her cool.

"Ah, no, Ms. Gordon. You are not. We are just trying to figure out if he was well-liked and who might have wanted him dead." Detective Billings seemed to be in charge.

"As I said, I didn't have much to do with him. I'm a cashier and he worked in receiving or unloading shipments or whatever it is they do at the back of the store."

The two detectives looked at paperwork in front of them while slowly nodding their heads.

"Did you know if he was dating anyone in the store? Or maybe there was a jealous husband involved?"

"As I've already told you, I didn't know much about him so I certainly wouldn't know if he was cheating with another man's wife."

Again, the two slowly nodding, looking like a pair of bobble-head dolls that you sometimes see sitting in the rear window of a car. For the second time Bitsy had to suppress a smile.

A few minutes went by as they checked their notes, with Detective Billings scribbling a few more notes on his pad and then looking up, briefly, to address Bitsy.

"Okay, Ms. Gordon, you may go now. Thank you for your time."

Bitsy got up, fearing her legs would buckle under her, and walked to the door.

"Oh, Ms. Gordon." Bitsy had her hand on the door and without turning, replied.

"Yes."

"Could you please send in Mr. Amepurdu, ah, Lewis Amepurdu?"

"Certainly."

She left the room and rushed to find Lewis. She thought she would have time to talk to him. She wanted to update him on her conversation with the detectives. But now there wasn't time. She walked quickly to the snack bar and found him talking to Jack Donato, the manager of the Hardware Dept.

"Lewis, please, come with me. Hi Jack. They want you now, the detectives. I need to talk to you."

Lewis took another swallow of his lemonade and then left with Bitsy.

While they walked toward the "Employees Only" door, she quickly updated him on everything she'd said to the detectives.

"I didn't say anything about you. They just asked me if Joe flirted with me or put any moves on me that I didn't want. They know something Lewis. I'm frightened."

"What did you tell them?"

"I didn't really answer them – I asked them if I was a suspect." Lewis couldn't help laughing and put his arm around Bitsy, kissing her on the top of her head.

"That was perfect. Good for you. They try to intimidate. But not my Bitsy." And he kissed her again, this time on her cheek. She smiled and kissed his cheek.

"Oh yes, one more thing. They asked if I knew anyone Joe was dating or if there was a jealous husband. I'm telling you, Lewis, they know something."

Lewis gave her a half-smile and then headed off to the "Employees Only" door while Bitsy walked back to her register at the front of the store.

Of course, once Lewis was in talking to the detectives, Bitsy could barely concentrate on what she was doing. He seemed to be in there a long time, certainly much longer than Bitsy had been. She thought she saw him but it wasn't him. She tried to relax and waited for 5:30pm so she could leave and hopefully the detectives would be finished asking Lewis their questions. If Lewis was in there that long, they must consider him a suspect. They must know something; she was sure of it.

Bitsy busied herself cleaning up around her register, glancing towards the back of the store, hoping to see Lewis walking towards her. But he wasn't. At about twenty past five she was gathering up her lunch bag and bringing her cash drawer to the cashiers' office when Lewis came up behind her.

"Hey."

"Lewis, you scared me. I've been looking for you. Is everything alright?"

"We'll talk on our way back to your place."

"But I have my car. Why don't we meet someplace and talk. I don't want to leave my car here."

"Okay, I'll take you to dinner."

"Or maybe just for a cup of tea and a cookie, something like that."

"Whatever you want, my love. Follow me."

Lewis drove about 5 miles away to a bakery that had a small seating area. Bitsy didn't think it was private enough but there wasn't anyone else inside so it turned out to be a perfect spot to talk for a few minutes.

Bitsy could barely contain herself and ran up to Lewis as soon as she had parked. She hugged him hard and kissed him on the neck.

"Are you okay?" He held her back, looking into her eyes.

"I'm fine. I was so worried about you."

"Remember they don't know anything. They like to think they do and start by making assumptions but they're just basing everything on past experiences they've had. It has nothing to do with us." They walked inside and Bitsy found a seat as far from the front of the bakery as she could get and sat down. Lewis ordered 2 macadamia nut cookies and two cups of Earl Gray tea.  They each sat dunking their tea bags, lost in their own thoughts for a few minutes. Lewis put the packet of honey on the table next to Bitsy's cup and when she looked up, she had tears in her eyes. He took her hand in his, squeezing gently but firmly.

"Oh Lewis. I'm so afraid. I don't know what I'll do if they find out it was you."

"Why do you still think it was me, Bitsy? I never said I did it." She realized he was right. He never admitted to it. He didn't want her to know anything, to keep her safe. So, she'd just assumed it was him. Still.

"You're right. I'm sorry Lewis. It's just that, you did say you would take care of it. And then he was… dead." She whispered the last word, not wanting anyone to hear the word even though the person behind the counter had gone into the back room. She came out a few minutes later with a tray of cookies, adding them to the ones in the display case, and went out back again. Bitsy followed her moves and when she went through the door to the back room, she spoke again.

"I don't want to think it was you Lewis but I guess I'll never know. I think I'm okay with not knowing, too."

"Well, good. So now you have to stop thinking it was me who killed Joe, okay?"

"Okay. So, what did they say to you, Lewis? What kind of questions did they ask?"

"Similar to yours. They asked me if Joe was having an affair with my wife or girlfriend and maybe I wanted to get even." Bitsy stared hard at him, waiting for a smile. But none came and she knew Lewis wasn't joking.

"What did you say?"

"I told them I wasn't married."

"What did they say to that?"

"They wanted to know where I was on the night he was killed, of course."

"What did you tell them?"

"I told them I was home. I went home after work."

"But you were with me."

"Yes, we went to dinner but then we went our separate ways and I went home."

"And what did they say after that? You have no proof, right? Did you talk to any of your neighbors?"

"No, I didn't see anyone. People usually don't have proof of their whereabouts. So, unless someone saw me at the Mart, they would have nothing on me."

"What about cameras? Did they see anyone in the parking lot at the Mart besides Joe?"

"They told me there were a few cars but they haven't been able to make out license plates yet. The store didn't spend a lot on cameras. They installed them mostly because insurance requires it, in case someone sues the store because their car was broken into. I doubt if they'll be able to know for sure who was there and who wasn't."

"Were there that many people there, though?"

"Some departments come in, besides the cleaning personnel, to stock shelves instead of taking time during the day. So, there were probably a few cars there, maybe a dozen. Anyway, that's what the detectives told me."

"Why did they tell you that?"

"Because I asked them if they'd looked at footage on the cameras and whether they could tell who was there that night. That's when they told me it was lousy footage and they couldn't really make out much, certainly not the makes of any of the cars and forget about trying to read license plates. They probably shouldn't have told me that though. I mean, I could be a suspect."

They finished their tea and left the bakery.

"I have some work to do tonight so I'll see you tomorrow at work, okay?" Bitsy was disappointed but didn't want Lewis to know since she was sure his work was about the documentary he was creating. She would never get in the way of something that was a passion for him.

"Okay. I'll miss you." They magnetically reached for each other and their hugging turned to kissing until a car driving by beeped and the occupants whooping out the windows pulled them apart. They got into their separate cars and drove away in opposite directions.

# Chapter 25

The following day was unusually quiet at work. There weren't many customers and the employees seemed to be on high alert. Bitsy knew it was because Detectives Billings and MacDougall were still around interviewing employees. She wondered when they'd be done and work could get back to normal. A low but persistent tension filled the store while they were around, making it impossible for anyone to relax. Everyone seemed to be looking over their shoulder, wondering if they were going to be accused of the crime. Even if you had nothing to do with it, and the majority of the employees did not, you still felt some guilt and thought maybe the detectives could read minds and would know that one time when Joe grabbed your ass or made a sexist comment you wished him dead or at least wished he would lose his job. Maybe you even envisioned yourself kicking him hard in the groin or hitting him with a baseball bat. Bitsy realized that she was probably the only one having those thoughts about Joe. And maybe Lewis was, too. But she also knew it was ridiculous to think they could read her mind about anything. She tried to relax and focus on her job.

The day wore on and late in the afternoon, as she was ringing through a few customers, there was a commotion at the back of the store. All the cashiers tried to see what was going on, even a few customers stopped to look toward the noise, but no one could see anything. Several minutes later a group of men, Detectives Billings and MacDougall with Store Manager Jim Roldark leading the way, were walking towards the front of the store. There was another person with the group but Bitsy couldn't see who it was. The cashiers nervously huddled together as the parade of men walked up to the front of the store, passing in front of the cashiers while several customers stopped to stare, heading for the front entrance doors. The man in the middle of the group could now be clearly seen. It was Lewis. Bitsy stepped away from the group and toward Lewis, who was walking between the two detectives, his hands cuffed.

He turned briefly to look at Bitsy. Bitsy could only mouth his name "Lewis", soundlessly. Anna came up behind Bitsy and putting her hand on her back squeezed her shoulder.

"Oh Bitsy, I'm so sorry."

"He didn't do it. They have the wrong man."

"I'm sure you're right."

They all watched while the group walked out the front door. The cashiers slowly went back to their registers. A couple of customers came into Bitsy's line but Anna waved them over to her register and put up a closed sign on Bitsy's register. Bitsy was unable to move, as if she was waiting for them to walk back into the store, Lewis with them, laughing together at the joke they'd played on everyone. And, for just a second, Bitsy was hopeful when Jim Roldark walked back into the store. Bitsy tried to see around him but there was no Lewis, no detectives. Jim saw Bitsy standing there and obviously knew she and Lewis were a couple because he came up to Bitsy, touched her shoulder, and whispered, "Everything will be okay. Don't worry." He whispered something to Anna and putting the closed sign at the end of Anna's register, directed the customers to the next register. And then he was gone.

Bitsy continued staring at the front doors. She felt helpless. She'd never felt this helpless before. Even when Joe had attacked her, she somehow knew it wouldn't end in rape. She'd known she would get away from him. She was a fighter and, especially after having learned basic self-defense at the Y, was confident that no man would ever take advantage of her. If he was able to overpower her, it may well end in her death because she would go down fighting. The element of surprise would be on her side and that meant for most situations, she would survive. But right now, she had nothing. She had no direction, no plan, no hope. Her future had just been taken away from her. How could she go on? She needed to sit down and looked for a chair. She wanted to leave the store. Anna was closing up, took Bitsy's cash drawer with her own, instructed Bitsy to take her purse and together they walked to the cashiers' office. Anna punched out for both of them and then led Bitsy from the store. Fortunately, Anna knew Bitsy's car and brought her to it. Unlocking her door, she sat Bitsy in the driver's seat but didn't give her the keys.

"Now you're going to sit here for a while until you come out of this, Betsy. I know this is a shock for you but you need to be able to drive home. I have to pick up my son from school but I need you to be okay before I leave you."

Bitsy turned her attention to Anna, trying her best to comprehend what she'd been saying.

"Okay, I hear you. Thank you, Anna, for this. But aren't we leaving early? I mean, it is only 4 something, isn't it?" She brought her watch up to her face to read the time.

"It's okay. Jim told me to pack up and get you out of there. Since the boss gave the okay, I'd guess we're good to go."

"Oh, that was nice of him. And you, too, Anna. Thank you for helping me. I'm okay now. I need to go home.  I'll talk to my parents. My parents!" Bitsy realized she hadn't told them anything about Joe, that had been her choice when she and Lewis discussed it. But now she'd have to explain about Lewis being arrested. How was she going to do that? After trying so hard to keep the attempted rape from them she was going to have to start at the beginning and confess to her parents what she'd avoided telling them. They'll be so disappointed in her. They always taught Bitsy to tell the truth and they were right. Not telling them had just set her up for a series of lies. But now she'd have to start from the beginning. She knew they'd probably demand that she quit her job. But now that Joe was dead, he was no longer a threat. Next, they'll tell her to leave Lewis. Of course, she had no intention of leaving him. He said he didn't do it and she believed him.  But, even if he did, he did it for her. How could she walk away from him after that? Besides her parents had to consider how much they loved each other. But they couldn't possibly know or understand that kind of love. They were older and settled, comfortable with each other. They didn't have the passion she and Lewis had together. She knew what she had to do, what she would do, and that was to stand by Lewis no matter what happened. She realized, suddenly, that Anna was still standing there, talking to her. She hadn't heard a word she said.

"I'm sorry Anna, I didn't hear what you said."

"That's okay, sweetie. I need to leave but I'll stay if you aren't ready to drive home yet. I can call my son's school and have him stay with his teacher. He sometimes does that when I can't get out of work a little early."

"Oh no, you go now. I'm fine. I have to think about this. And I need to talk to my parents. I'll be fine. Thank you for bringing me to my car. Thank you, Anna."

"If you're sure? I don't want to leave you if you aren't ready to drive. Really, I can just call, it will only take a sec…"

"No, no. Thank you. I'm okay now," and she put out a hand for her keys, which Anna dropped them into. Betsy grabbed the door handle and Anna stepped back to let her close it, watching as Betsy started the car, put it in gear and, waving, drove off. Anna continued to stand there, hoping she was doing the right thing by letting Betsy drive.

"Poor kid."

Bitsy took her time going home, driving just under the speed limit, working on a plan of how to approach her parents with the news of the attempted rape and then of the death of the man who'd tried to rape her and finally of Lewis being arrested for committing the crime of murdering her attempted rapist. When she got onto her road she pulled the car over, put it in park, and let the tears pour out of her. How could her life, nearly perfect in every way, so suddenly go to hell? She dropped her head against the steering wheel and let the pain of what she may lose, Lewis and their life together, come out like a roaring lion, screaming until her throat hurt, banging her hands on the steering wheel again and again, wanting to feel some other pain besides the breaking of her heart. She cried until she couldn't anymore and wiped the mascara running from under her eyes and onto her cheeks. She sat for a few more minutes, taking deep breaths, focusing on her breath until a calmness came over her, easing some of the pain away. She touched up her lipstick and checked her eyes again; it was obvious she had been crying, but she was sure that wasn't over, not once she told her parents the whole story. And now she felt as prepared as she could be for the conversation that lay ahead. There was nothing left to do. She needed them now, more than ever.

<h1 style="text-align:center">Chapter 26</h1>

Bitsy wasn't quite sure how she'd made it, but she found herself sitting in her car in the driveway of the only home she'd ever known, where she still lived with her parents, for all of her twenty years. She looked around and suddenly recalled one of her earliest memories, from when she was just a toddler, her mother pushing her in a baby carriage up their tree-lined street. The hood of the carriage blocking the sun from her eyes, but her mother had also put netting over the carriage so that the bees, mosquitos, and other flying insects couldn't potentially bite her baby. She wasn't quite sure if this was an actual memory or if she'd seen this in a photo, but she was absolutely certain of this: she had been protected from day one and now, more than ever, she appreciated all the love and care her parents had showered on her. She knew her parents had wanted another child, but it wasn't possible since, due to complications after Bitsy's birth, her mother had to have an emergency hysterectomy. Although Bitsy thought she may have liked having a younger sister or brother, a playmate through her younger years, and a partner in crime as she reached her early teens, she also loved having her parents all to herself, whatever she needed, whenever she needed them. She felt a little selfish but also incredibly grateful for the privileged life she lived. And now, at 20 years old, she couldn't imagine how she would get through her life if she didn't have them as her parents. She thought about Lewis, alone, with no parents to talk to, to love and support him, and help him through his arrest, to bail him out, to stand by him in the court and do their best to convince the jury that he was innocent. That their son, who was a model son that any parent would be proud of, could be charged with such a heinous crime. Bitsy felt so fortunate to be a part of Lewis' life now, to be there for him, to support and love him now when he needed her, needed someone, to be there for him. She knew she was all he had.

She steeled herself for how she'd tell her parents the story of Joe and his eventual murder and Lewis' arrest. They needed to know everything. They needed to know about Joe's attempted rape of Bitsy. They needed to know about her conversation with Lewis when he'd said he would take care of this. And they needed to know, to understand, that she was going to be there, completely, in support of Lewis. She was prepared to move out if they insisted that she leave him. And she would move out, she was that serious about her position on how much she loved and supported Lewis. If they didn't know that by now, they would soon find out.

Her confidence building as she finished her pep talk, she got out of her car and walked into the house. Her dad was in the living room, watching the news. Her mom was in the kitchen, about to prepare dinner. They both looked up and greeted her with a friendly "Hi" when Bitsy walked through the door. She stood looking at one and then the other, suddenly wavering, thinking this wasn't the right time to tell them, trying to come up with an excuse to go to her room and not explain all the drama that has happened in her life these past few months. But she knew she had to tell them. And now was the best time to do it. Her mom even gave her a cue to start.

"What's up, sweetie? Everything okay?" Her dad continued working on his crossword puzzle, occasionally glancing up at the TV when a news reporter said something of interest.

"I need to speak to both of you, now."

"Well, I was just going to start supper. Do you want to help? Dad is going to peel potatoes and I was going to start cooking chicken and you could…"

"Now, mom. I need to speak to you both now." Bitsy didn't let her mom finish but interrupted her, which she never did. Bitsy knew she was being disrespectful but needed to let her mom know how serious she was.

"I'm sorry, mom, but I really need to talk to you both, right now."

Her dad looked over the top of his reading glasses, first at Bitsy, then at his wife. He tried to suppress a cough and went into the kitchen for a large glass of water. Her mom took her glass of Chardonnay and walked into the living room where Bitsy was standing. When her dad walked back into the room with his water, he exchanged a look with his wife that said, if you were good at reading faces, 'oh no, this can't be good news'. Once her parents were both seated, Bitsy paced in front of them, waiting for a push, like a car with an almost dead battery, to get her started.

"Honey, we can wait until after dinner if you don't…"

"No, I've got this. I need to tell you this. I've been putting it off but I need to explain everything to you. And please, please, let me finish before you say anything. This is going to be hard."

Again, her parents exchanged that worried look and her mom grabbed her dad's hand, expecting the absolute worst.

"I see the look on your faces and let me just tell you right now, I'm not pregnant." Her mom and dad visibly relaxed and her mom took a big sip of her Chardonnay. Her dad rubbed his face and smiling at his wife, jumped up from his chair.

"Well, that is something to celebrate. I think I'll have a glass of wine myself." He went to the liquor cart and poured half of a wine glass with Merlot. Bitsy waited until he sat down again.

"Okay, Pumpkin, anything else you tell us can't be anywhere near as bad as what your mom and I were imagining. So, go ahead and tell us your news."

"Well, it isn't really news. But it is something that I think is much, much worse than being pregnant."

The worried looks returned to her parent's faces as Bitsy began the story that had started just a few months ago when Joe was flirting with her, touching her inappropriately, and then when he'd got her alone in the back of the store, when he'd tried to rape her. She then explained what Lewis had said when she'd told him what had happened.

"He said he would kill him. He gave me three days to decide what I wanted to do about this. And then he would take care of it. And now Joe is dead and Lewis was arrested this afternoon."

Saying these words out loud hit Bitsy like a slap across the face and she fell to the floor, crying tears that came right out of her heart. Her mom was right next to her, holding her child who was obviously in so much pain, her own tears falling into her daughter's hair.

"Oh, my sweet Bitsy, I'm so sorry all this happened to you. You should have gone to the police."

"Lewis suggested the police, too, but you know mom, nothing would happen to him for attempted rape. And then he would be back working in the store and maybe he'd try it again and maybe the next time…" Bitsy watched her dad, his face resembling Lewis' when she'd told him that Joe had tried to rape her. He paced up and down in the living room, unable to expel the anger welling up inside him.

"Dad, please sit down, you're making me nervous. There isn't anything you can do, unless you can help Lewis. I need to be there for him. I need to find out where he is. Please, can you do that for me?"

Her dad knelt down on the floor next to Bitsy and her mom, putting his arms around both of them.

"Of course, Pumpkin. Whatever you need. But I have one question; do you think Lewis did it?"

"I don't know, dad. He wouldn't tell me. He wanted me to stay out of this; the less I knew the better, that's what he said."

"You know, he's right. I think maybe you should just step back, maybe not see Lewis for a while, wait and see what happens. He'll likely go to court if he has been accused of murder. I mean, if he doesn't have a rock-solid alibi, he could spend years in prison."

Bitsy couldn't believe her father was even suggesting she desert Lewis right when he needed her most. Her mother was nodding agreement to her dad's suggestions. For all the good upbringing she'd had by these two people, she was ashamed at this moment to call them her parents. She would not even for one second consider this as a solution. She jumped up from the floor, facing the enemy.

"How can you even think for a minute that I would consider deserting Lewis. If he did it, you do realize, he did it for me. And if he didn't do it, he's innocent. I will not desert him when he needs me most. He has no one!!! At least I have both of you. Or I thought I did." Bitsy stormed out of the room and ran upstairs, crying so hard her mom thought her own heart was going to break. She walked into her husband's always open arms and cried for her only child.

# Chapter 27

Bitsy sat at her desk and started thinking of all the places they might have brought Lewis. He was most likely wondering where Bitsy was and why he hadn't heard from her, his only real advocate.  Her first thought was that he'd been taken directly to the local police station and started her search by calling the one in Trenton, although she was positive he wouldn't be there. And he wasn't. She looked up the number for the police station in Campton, where the A-to-Z Mart was, and when she asked if Lewis Amepurdu was there, she was put on hold. A man's voice came on the line.

"This is officer Delany, how can I help you?"

"Yes, hello officer Delany, is that right?" Bitsy wanted to document every conversation she had with the police.

"Yes."

"Okay, I'm looking for Lewis Amepurdu and I was wondering if he was at your police station."

"What's this in reference to, ma'am?"

Bitsy had this sick feeling in the pit of her stomach, a combination of fear with a strong dose of anxiety, anger, and distress mixed in for the man she loved. She stood up, feeling this position would give her more authority.

"Yes, officer Delany, I'm looking for Mr. Amepurdu because I'm worried about him. I'm his girlfriend."

She sat back down in her chair, feeling like she was ten years old and about to be told no, she can't have a boy come to her house. Fiancée, wife, almost anything else would have more influence than 'girlfriend'. She was positive she heard a smile in officer Delany's voice when he spoke.

"I'm sorry, um, ma'am, but I can't give you any information about the case."

"I'm not asking for information, I simply want to know if Mr. Amepurdu is at your police station. Can you tell me that?" She stood up again, finding her strength that was there all along and not allowing this bully, officer Delany, to laugh about Lewis' girlfriend looking for him.

"Sorry ma'am, yes, Mr. Amepurdu is at our station. But you can't speak to him and he's not allowed any visitors at this time. He had one phone call and he's already made that call, so there is nothing I can do for you. Is that all?"

"Yes, thank you officer Delany." And she slammed her phone down and paced her room, trying to figure out her next move. She just knew she had to see him; but she couldn't speak to him and he wasn't allowed visitors, so she didn't know exactly what to do next. And then she remembered, he'd already made his one phone call. If not Bitsy, who else would he have called? She was lost in this thought when there was a soft knocking at her bedroom door.

"Come in." It was her mom.

"Oh Bitsy, darling, I'm so sorry. I know you have strong feelings for Lewis and I don't want you to think we're deserting him. We care about him, too."

Bitsy felt angry that her mother used words like 'strong feelings' and 'care', as if those even compared to how Bitsy felt about Lewis. As if they felt the same about Lewis as she did.

"Mom, I love Lewis. I don't just have 'strong feelings' or just 'care' about him, I love him. Do you love him, too?"

"Well, no, but…"

"Then we don't feel the same way about Lewis, so please don't compare my feelings to your feelings and dad's feelings because they are not even close to being the same. Is there anything else you wanted to say because I need to figure out how I can see Lewis now?"

Bitsy's dad appeared at the door to her bedroom.

"Did you come to tell me how much you care about Lewis, too?"

"Well, yes, I do."

"Save it, dad, I don't want to hear it. The fact that you and mom both agree that I should desert Lewis, right when he needs me most, I mean, what kind of a foundation is that for a long-term relationship? If one little thing goes wrong, I should just run away from our relationship?"

"This is more than 'one little thing', Pumpkin." Her dad was trying to be rational. That was his usual stance on an issue, pointing out the obvious.

"Yes, of course it is, but I thought you raised me to stand by those you love and support them when they need it most. Well, that's what I'm doing. I understand you don't feel the same way about Lewis that I do, of course you don't, but don't expect me to make the same decisions you'd make about this situation. I'm going to be with Lewis and that means standing by him no matter what the outcome. If you want me to move out, I'll do that, too. I'll understand."

"Oh no, sweetheart, we don't want that. We want you to live here as long as you want to. Please don't think we're deserting you. That will never happen." Her mom couldn't hold back her tears any longer and sat on the corner of Bitsy's bed, wiping her eyes with a Kleenex. Bitsy handed her a fresh one and took one herself. It was difficult seeing her mom cry. She thought of her parents as both being so strong and always being there for her. But this was different. And she knew they needed her as much as she needed them. She sat next to her mom and they both hugged, tears falling onto each other's shoulders.

Her dad did what he often did in these situations, he paced, rubbing his forehead as if hoping that would help conjure up the right decision to make. This was beyond anything either of her parents could have imagined even though they knew a man coming into Bitsy's life was going to happen one day. They just thought they had more time. And that it would be less complicated. But they raised a strong girl and even though they would have preferred she fall in love with 'the boy next door', they knew she would only choose the man who was right for her. And there was no doubt in either of their minds that Lewis would do whatever he had to do to protect Bitsy. They both believed he would, in fact, give his life for her.

Her mom, grabbing Bitsy by the shoulders and looking directly into her eyes so that Bitsy would know, for sure, that she'd be there for her no matter what, said; "What do you want us to do?"

Bitsy hugged her mom and her dad, without hesitation, wrapped his arms around the two of them. They fell over onto the bed, laughing, which finally lightened the mood.

Bitsy's dad turned out to be a great resource, as Bitsy knew he would be. He called people he knew on the local police force and called a lawyer friend to see if he could represent Lewis. Bitsy and her mom held their breath, waiting to see if the lawyer could represent Lewis and how much it would cost. They were both surprised that the lawyer had already heard about the case and also that he couldn't take the case.

"Why, why couldn't he take the case? Fine, we'll just have to find someone else. There has to be a really good lawyer out there that we can find for Lewis." Bitsy's thoughts ran wild as they were facing their first stumbling block already. Her dad quickly put an end to her concern.

"Bitsy! Relax, please! He said he can't represent Lewis because he already has a lawyer. He has Matthew Norwich, and he's the best defense lawyer around. He lives on the west coast but surprisingly, is taking Lewis' case. You really couldn't hope to get anyone better."

"What? How? I mean, Lewis can't afford him."

"Apparently, he can, because this man does not work for free. I read about him in Time magazine, there was a big article on him a while ago. And rarely does he take a pro bono case. He proved himself years ago and now he charges big bucks for his time. The thing is, he never loses. Even, I've heard, if the person he represents is guilty, which isn't always a good thing."

Bitsy's dad looked at Bitsy with real concern in his eyes.

"What? Dad! Do you think Lewis is guilty? He's not, I know he isn't. He told me he didn't do it. But, even if he did, he was defending me, your daughter! From a man who tried to rape me, and might possibly have tried it again!"

Her dad got up from his chair, wrapping his arms around his daughter who was shaking, possibly re-living the frightening incident.

"I'm sorry, Pumpkin. There are other ways to deal with monsters like that. You don't have to kill them. Getting them off the streets is one way to do it; to be sure they never try this with any other woman again."

"And sometimes they get off, too. Sometimes they go free and sometimes they rape and maybe even kill other women. I was lucky. And I never have to worry about him trying to rape me or any other woman again."

"She's right. I heard of a case the other night where a woman was raped and killed by a man who'd been previously arrested for rape. Sometimes the women don't testify because they're too afraid that if the man gets off, he'll come after them." Bitsy's mom readily backed Bitsy up; she also worried about the same situation for herself as well as her daughter, which was why she never stayed late at work. The world wasn't always safe for women. To not be prepared was just naïve and her mom was glad Bitsy was being realistic about protecting herself.

Her dad shook his head. He had no idea what the two women he loved more than life itself had to put up with every day. He wished he could just hold onto them and protect them forever, never letting them out of his sight. But since he knew that was unrealistic, he was sure the next best thing was to do what he could to help the man who had saved his daughter from possibly more abuse or worse.

"Okay, let's do whatever we can to help get Lewis out of jail."

That definitely called for a group hug!

# Chapter 28

The subpoena came by certified mail. It was hand-delivered to her home in an official-looking envelope from the District Court and she had to sign for it. Bitsy shook as she signed for the envelope. She opened it and stood staring at the information that was written, including the date and time when she was to appear in court. She was shaken up and wasn't sure why she had to appear in court. She brought the letter into the living room where her parents sat watching the evening news.

"Why do I have to go to court?" Her parents both jumped up and read the subpoena she held. Her mom slipped an arm around her shoulders and led her to the couch, where they sat down while her dad read through the short and direct document.

"Sorry, Pumpkin, that's what it says. You have to go to court. We'll talk to Lewis' lawyer and find out why they want you to appear as a witness, okay? Don't worry. He's a good guy, well, as far as lawyers go, but he's smart and remember, he's the best. He'll brief you on all of this. I'll call him right now."

Bitsy and her parents had met with Matthew Norwich just a few days before. At Lewis' request, Mr. Norwich had contacted them. They'd talked about Lewis and how good they thought his chances were of going free and of finding out who had actually killed Joe instead of Lewis going to jail for the crime. Mr. Norwich was very confident about the case and, more importantly, convinced of Lewis' innocence.

"I have multiple witnesses I'll be putting on the stand so there really isn't anything to worry about. This is pretty much an open-and-shut case in my opinion. I'm sure the judge will throw it out of court. Judges really do hate people wasting their time and I'm familiar with Judge Costos who'll be hearing the case. He's a tough bird, looking forward to retirement in just a few years, and doesn't put up with any bullshit. You have nothing to worry about."

Bitsy remembered that day and now here she was receiving a subpoena.

"He didn't say anything about me having to go to court. What do they want from me? I'm so afraid I'll screw up and then Lewis might be in more trouble because of me."

"Sweetheart, that isn't possible. There's nothing you can say that'd make anything worse. Just tell the truth." Her mom was always there with the perfect answer. Her dad came out of his office and gave them a thumbs-up.

"Okay, let's go. We're meeting with Mr. Norwich in an hour. He's staying at the Hyatt so we'll meet him in their restaurant. He said there's nothing to worry about – he'll tell you what to expect and give you some tips."

Bitsy's stomach flip-flopped so many times on the ride to the meeting she thought she was going to lose everything she'd eaten that day. Fortunately, it hadn't been much. She was too upset since she'd received the subpoena to even think about putting food in her stomach. It was late afternoon and not many people were in the restaurant since the staff was preparing for dinner. Her dad checked with the front desk and the manager called up to Mr. Norwich's room. Her dad had just settled into his chair, ordered a beer, while her mom and Bitsy each got a seltzer with lime, when Mr. Norwich walked into the restaurant.

He shook hands with each of them before sitting down. One of the waiters brought him a cup of coffee with creamer as soon as he sat and as he stirred in the cream, he looked at each one in turn, ending on Bitsy whose face was blushing red.

"What seems to be the problem, Ms. Gordon? Something about a subpoena?" Bitsy swallowed before answering and looked up at the striking face of the man who was going to save her Lewis. His lightly gray streaked hair was perfectly coifed, thick and every hair in place. He had the slightest hint of 5 o'clock shadow that framed his angular face, causing his emerald green eyes to stand out like he had x-ray vision. Bitsy caught her mom admiring the extremely handsome man who was a cross between Cary Grant and Sean Connery. Bitsy smiled at her mom, which  helped her to relax.

"Yes, I was surprised to receive this. I didn't know I'd have to testify. I didn't know anyone even knew about me."

"Of course they know about you. You're Lewis' fiancée, correct?"

"Well, no, not fiancée. But we have been dating for about seven months now, almost."

"Well, then, I'm sure everyone where you work also knows that. Which means the people who want to throw Lewis in prison know it, too. There really is nothing to worry about. All you have to do is tell the truth." Bitsy exchanged smiles with her mom.

"You have nothing to hide. You've already told me that Lewis wouldn't tell you anything, so you have nothing to offer. I'm sure you will only be asked a couple of questions. Since they won't get anything out of you, because you have no information, they'll ask their questions and then you can go. I won't even cross examine you. Okay?" Mr. Norwich looked at his watch.

"Do you have to leave?" Bitsy was hoping to have more time with the lawyer.

"I'm trying another case right after Mr. Amepurdu's and I need to meet with the client in 5 minutes, so if there is nothing else, I'll see you in court? Are you okay now?" Bitsy smiled and felt her face brightening again. Mr. Norwich got up to leave when Bitsy remembered something she wanted to ask him.

"Mr. Norwich, I was wondering, how can Lewis afford you? I mean, I know he doesn't make a lot of money at his job and you're so expensive, I'm guessing since you are so famous. But I was wondering, how? And you flew here from the west coast just for this case?"

Mr. Norwich smiled at her question and answered as briefly as he could.

"Well, I did set up a couple of other interviews for potential cases while I'm here, as well. And yes, I do live on the west coast. But the simple answer is, I golf with Lewis' dad." And then Mr. Norwich turned and left the restaurant.

"Great answer!" Bitsy's dad was impressed and, folding his arms across his chest while nodding, smiled and then took a big swig of his beer.

# Chapter 29

Bitsy asked her mom to shop with her for a new outfit to wear to court. She wanted, more than anything, to appear professional and mature. Her mother didn't quite get what Bitsy was looking for and had picked out, again and again, something in pastel; pale lilac, baby pink, or an off-white. Although the white did appeal to her most out of the three outfits her mom had suggested, Bitsy was looking to make a bolder statement and chose a dark eggplant purple colored suit for her day in court. This was the look she was going for. Her mom frowned at the dark color and tried to change Bitsy's mind.

"You look like you're going to a funeral, sweetie."

Bitsy gasped and looked at herself in the store's full-length mirror. She almost took the suit off right then, but stared at her reflection just a little bit longer. And decided she liked what she saw; a confident, sophisticated woman who would be taken seriously. This was the look she was going for, this was who she was now.

"I'm getting it." Her mind made up, she took the suit off and brought it up to the register.

"I can wear my black heels with it." Even though her mother preferred the softer pastel colors she'd chosen for Bitsy, she couldn't help but admire the strong, determined woman her only daughter was becoming right before her eyes.

The stairs to the courthouse were long and Bitsy found herself counting them as she climbed the length to the large double-doors. She hadn't spoken to Lewis since his arrest; it seems he didn't want to take any calls with anyone other than his lawyer and his lawyer had said that seeing him was out of the question. That sounded unusual to Bitsy and when she'd asked her parents about it, they'd only shrugged and told her it might have been at the lawyer's request. What Bitsy had no way of knowing was that it had been at Lewis' request; he wanted to keep Bitsy out of it as much as he possibly could. He feared that if he talked with her, he might give her some information that she'd be forced to reveal on the stand. Lawyers could be really persuasive. He wanted her innocence in that courtroom and that was all.

Once inside, Bitsy was escorted to an area at the back. There were only a few people in the courtroom since it had been decided that this would be a closed court case. She wasn't quite sure what that meant, but Mr. Norwich had suggested that Joe's relatives were the kind of people 'who were more interested in how they could profit than in seeking justice.' He feared they might swarm the courtroom and create a lot of unnecessary chaos. This was also the reason why he wanted his witnesses to testify and then leave the courtroom when they were finished. Apparently, he had worked this out with the judge.

She only had to wait a few minutes before she was called to the witness stand. After swearing that she would tell the truth, the whole truth, and nothing but the truth, she was asked to state her name by the prosecuting attorney the state had assigned to the case. He was a bit overweight and wore a jacket that was a tad wrinkled. His tie, Bitsy noticed, had a stain right in the middle that he'd obviously tried to clean himself since it still had remnants of paper towel stuck to it. His pants were about a half inch too short.

"Elizabeth Daniels Gordon."

"Do you know the man, Lewis Amepurdu, sitting right here and who is being charged with the crime of murder?" Bitsy looked over at Lewis and saw him staring back at her, those intense deep blue eyes seeing right through to her soul. She felt tears forming at the corner of her eyes and fought to keep them from spilling. One of them escaped and she brushed at her cheek. She felt more love than she could ever express for him and sat up straighter in the chair.

"I do."

"And will you state for the court your special relationship to Mr. Amepurdu."

"Objection. Vague."

"I'm simply trying to establish the kind of relationship that exists between the defendant and the witness."

"Overruled. You may continue."

Bitsy listened to this back-and-forth of the lawyers but never took her eyes off Lewis and he stared intently back at her. They were together and that was all that mattered. That was all that would ever matter.

"Please answer the question. Ms. Gordon."

Bitsy tried to think of the right thing to say. Mr. Norwich didn't prompt her about what she should say about her relationship with Lewis.

"We have been dating."

"You have been dating. Are you serious? Are you exclusive? Would you say you are engaged?"

"No, we are not."

"You are not what? Serious, exclusive, engaged?"

"We are not engaged." Bitsy was beginning to see what Mr. Norwich had said about the other lawyer trying to confuse her.

"But you are… serious?"

"Yes."

"Exclusive?"

"Yes."

"And you would say just about anything to save your boyfriend from jail, isn't that right Ms. Gordon?"

"What? Yes. I mean no. I mean I wouldn't lie." She looked over at Lewis who now had his head down looking at papers on the table in front of him. She felt more tears forming but swallowed hard to stay in control. She would not let this man rattle her.

"Objection. Leading."

"I withdraw my last question."

"Where were you on the night of the murder, Ms. Gordon?"

"I was home."

"All night? Right after work you went straight home?"

"Well, no. First Lewis and I went to dinner." When she said his name Lewis looked up and she had to force herself to stay in her seat. She knew how horribly inappropriate it would be to run to him in the courtroom. She just wanted him to hold her and she wanted them to walk out of this place and get back to their lives together.

"So, then, after dinner, you went straight home?"

"Yes, after dinner I went home."

"Did Mr. Amepurdu go to your home with you?"

"No, he did not."

"Do you know where he went?"

"No, I do not know. I thought he went home, too." She stopped because she was doing what she was told not to do. She was volunteering information.

"So, he could have gone back to work?"

"I don't know." She barely whispered it. Bitsy was so afraid she would say something wrong. She felt herself going inwards, not wanting to speak anymore, hoping this would all be over soon. And then Lewis' lawyer spoke up.

"Objection, your honor. Mr. Cumming's question calls for speculation. The witness obviously has no idea where Mr. Amepurdu went after they left the restaurant and she has stated as such. Can we move on from here, Mr. Cummings?"

"Objection sustained." Judge Costos nodded in agreement.

"Mr. Cummings, if there are no further questions for this witness, please move on to your next witness."

"I do have one other question, if I may."

The judge looked impatient but waved Mr. Cummings on.

"What was your relationship with the deceased, Ms. Gordon?"

"We were co-workers." Bitsy kept her hands in her lap and could feel them starting to sweat so she put them face up in her lap, hoping the sweat would dry up.

Mr. Cummings smiled, nodding his head, as he moved in closer to Bitsy.

"Co-workers, you say? Just co-workers? Then can you explain to the court the how some of your co-workers saw you and the deceased laughing together and how he seemed to have quite an attraction to you. I wonder how a pretty young girl could resist such a good-looking young man like Mr. Bendetti; or maybe you couldn't and you aren't telling us? And perhaps your 'boyfriend' here, Mr. Amepurdu, found out and killed him out of jealousy."

"Objection, your honor. Argumentative. Mr. Cummings has created this scenario in his own warped mind based on hearsay. I request the last question be stricken from the record."

There was clamoring among the few people in the courtroom and judge Costos, banging his gavel said, "There will be order in my court. Objection sustained. You do not need to answer, Ms. Gordon. Strike that question from the record. Mr. Cummings, perhaps you can stick to facts?"

Bitsy, who sat through this last question in disbelief, could only stare at Lewis. Lewis kept his head down. Bitsy felt impelled to yell out the truth about Joe, that he had attempted to rape her, but she knew that could spell the end for Lewis as this could definitely be seen as potential motive for him killing Joe. She tried her best to keep her cool, wringing her hands, fighting back tears. Mr. Cummings was staring at Bitsy, watching her reaction. When she saw him looking at her, she turned her attention back to him and stared right back. She would not let him see how much he had upset her.

"No further questions, your honor."

"Mr. Norwich?"

"I have no questions."

"You may step down Ms. Gordon." The judge seemed as frustrated by Mr. Cummings as Mr. Norwich had been.

"You may call your next witness, Mr. Cummings."

"The court calls Ms. Katherine Donovan to the stand."

That was the last thing Bitsy heard as she was escorted from the courtroom. She looked over at Lewis but he never looked her way. He was in conference with his lawyer as she went out the door and down the steps of the court house. She couldn't imagine what Kathy would have to say about Lewis but Bitsy knew Kathy didn't like Lewis. Bitsy also knew that Kathy and Joe had a thing and she wondered if that would come out in the trial. She had no idea how she was going to sleep that night if she couldn't talk to Lewis. Mr. Norwich had made it clear he had other cases to try while he was here on the east coast, which was only for a few days. Which must mean Lewis' trial would be over soon. One way or the other, Lewis would either be free to go or he would be thrown in jail. He was innocent or he was guilty. She needed to talk to Lewis. She knew court would be in session until 5pm. She would wait until then and then call Mr. Norwich and keep on calling until he picked up his phone. She wouldn't be able to wait any longer. She even considered waiting outside the courthouse until today's session was over. She'd been one of the first to be called as a witness today. Mr. Norwich had been close-mouthed about the other witnesses he had; she knew this was at Lewis' request. But it was frustrating for her not knowing what was coming up and who else would be taking the stand as a witness for Lewis.

As she sat in the courthouse parking lot mulling all of this over, she spotted Nick from the A-to-Z Mart get out of his car and head for the courthouse stairs.

*Nick? Why would Nick be here? What could Nick add to the information they already had?* She knew he was not a fan of Joe, so she was sure he must be there for Lewis. She didn't even know they were friends. Bitsy was realizing there was a lot she didn't know. And she knew it was Lewis' way of protecting her. Again.

About 10 minutes later Nick came out. She slouched down in her car so that he couldn't see her. A few minutes later Micky walked out of the parking lot and up the stairs to the courthouse.

"Okay, this is getting really weird. Why is Micky here?" Again, she knew Micky and Joe were not friends. But what could he possibly say to help Lewis out?  Micky was in the courthouse for even less time than Nick had been. When Micky left, Bitsy was ready to go home to change and write down the questions she had for Mr. Norwich when a suspicious-looking man, who kept looking over his shoulder as if he expected someone to be following him, slinked out of the parking lot and up the courthouse stairs. He was in the courthouse the longest. Bitsy waited for him to come out and when she checked her watch, she realized she'd been sitting there for over three hours. She had to go to the bathroom, but she didn't want to go back into the courthouse.

The slinking man came out the same way he'd gone in and within a few minutes, the doors of the courthouse burst open and the few people who had been allowed in the courtroom, mostly relatives of Joe, came out and hurried to their vehicles. Bitsy flattened out, laying across her seat, as they seemed to be heading her way. She heard them start their vehicles and several of them burnt rubber as they flew out of the parking lot. After a few minutes, Bitsy decided it was safe to sit up. She looked towards the courthouse stairs and saw two people standing just outside the courthouse doors. She was positive one of them was Lewis. She got out of her car and walked towards the stairs where she stood looking up at Lewis and his lawyer. Mr. Norwich spotted her first and after just a few seconds, Lewis turned towards Bitsy and, after shaking Mr. Norwich's hand, ran down the stairs towards Bitsy, who was running up to meet him. She stopped two steps below him and he stopped at the same moment.

"Are you free to go?" Bitsy could no longer stop the tears and felt them run down her face, no longer concerned with the mascara that must be leaving black streaks on her cheeks.

"I'm free." Lewis jumped the two steps to Bitsy and wrapping his arms around her, picked her up and swung her around, laughing together as they kissed, holding each other as if they would never let go.

Bitsy looked up at Mr. Norwich, who was coming down the stairs towards them and stopped when he reached them.

"I don't want to break this up, I just want to say, you did just fine in there Ms. Gordon. And the very best of luck to both of you. Lewis, we'll talk soon." And he patted Lewis on his back as he descended the stairs, leaving them in their full embrace.

"I don't want to let you go Lewis. I've missed you so much these past couple of weeks. It has been so awful without you."

"I agree. I've missed you, too." And Lewis stopped to give Bitsy a proper kiss, which immediately relaxed her and caused her to hold on to him even tighter.

"But right now, we need to get off these steps. So, what do you want to do, my love? Out to dinner? Or back to my place?" Lewis pushed her hair back and kissed her neck.

"Oh Lewis. I would love to lie naked with you. I can't think of anything I'd rather do. But I have so many questions. And I think, now, you can answer them. So, I would like to go to my parent's house where I'm sure they are also waiting to hear the verdict."

"Your wish is my command, my love." Bringing her hand to his mouth and kissing it, they walked to the parking lot.

Bitsy, still shaking from the excitement, knew she wouldn't be able to focus on driving.

"Would you mind driving back to my parents' house?"

"Of course not." Lewis opened the passenger side for Bitsy and, getting into the driver's seat, drove them away from the courthouse.

# Chapter 30

Arriving at Bitsy's house, her parents greeted them both with open arms. Obviously, since Lewis was there, they knew instantly that he'd been found 'not guilty'. Her dad was on drinks and checked with Lewis before pouring.

"Lewis, scotch?"

"Oh, no thank you, sir. I'm not a big drinker."

"You at least have to have a celebratory shot, maybe just a short one?"

Not wanting to disappoint, Lewis nodded.

"Okay, dad, if Lewis doesn't want to drink, let's not force him, okay?"

"It's okay, Bitsy. I think your dad is right. One shot is called for on this occasion. I mean, I was accused of murder. It isn't every day that you are accused of murder and they end up throwing the case out."

Bitsy, of course, not having heard any of the details of Lewis' trial yet, looked shocked when Lewis made this statement.

"The judge threw the case out?"

"He did. Norwich had all the perfect witnesses and you could see the judge was getting frustrated with Cummings. And then, when they brought in Norwich's final witness, a guy who knew Joe had a serious debt, well, Judge Costos was done at that point. Norwich knew that the police had said it looked like a mafioso killing, so that final guy just confirmed everything and it was over."

Bitsy's mom came back into the room with a platter of cheese and crackers for them.

Bitsy was anxious to have Lewis answer her questions. She wanted everyone to sit down and waited patiently while her dad held up his glass to Lewis' shot glass and toasted to his freedom. Then they all sat down, Lewis reaching for Bitsy's hand as they sat close to each other on the sofa, and Bitsy, after taking a few deep breaths, turned to face Lewis.

"Why were Nick and Micky there?"

"Well, I'm surprised that this is your first question. And how did you know Nick and Micky were there?"

"I waited in the parking lot for more than 3 hours. I just couldn't leave. I had a feeling it was coming to the end and I just needed to see you."

"Okay, so, yes, Nick and Micky. We are all good friends, actually. And we all have your welfare in mind. I told them what had happened to you, my love, and they both promised me they'd watch out for you whenever I wasn't around. They are good friends. Very good. They testified on my character and work ethic, that sort of thing."

"Oh, okay. That's good to know. Why was Kathy Donovan there?"

"So, a couple of different reasons. First, right after you left, they called Kathy Donovan as a witness. Well, she told them she saw my car at the A-to-Z Mart the night that Joe was murdered. I was arrested based on that information that she'd given to the two detectives, Billings and MacDougall. But Norwich had a witness who knew that Kathy and Joe had had an affair, actually were still in an on-going sexual relationship, so her testimony was thrown out. She admitted that she'd loved him and would do anything for him. She tried to cry but only alligator tears came out. The judge didn't buy it and excused her and threw out her testimony.

"Okay, so who was this final witness?"

"I don't know where Norwich found this guy, he must have an amazing group of researchers, but this shady-looking guy knew, and he had facts to back it up, that Joe was deep in debt to the mafia. He was a serious gambler and owed them a ton of money. They don't mess around with people who don't pay. He was absolutely sure that's what got Joe bumped off. It was that final witness who sealed the deal. And, as I mentioned, the police backed up what this guy said. And then, I was free to go." Lewis let out a huge sigh and squeezed Bitsy's hand.

Bitsy's parents were all smiles and after a few minutes her mom jumped up and announced she was making a special dinner of baked chicken, green beans, and mashed red-skin potatoes. The chicken was already in the oven and she just had a few things to do to prepare the potatoes and green beans. Supper would be ready in about half an hour and they wanted Lewis and Bitsy to relax. Bitsy's dad went into the kitchen to help her mom with the cooking, leaving Bitsy and Lewis alone in the living room.

"I need to change into something comfortable. I'll be right back. But I hate to leave you here."

"Then I'll come with you."

"You can't come up to my bedroom, my parents are right here." Mischief spread across her lips.

"Well, what do you think we'll do in half an hour." Lewis' eyes told her everything she needed to know and he pulled her to him as he kissed her on the lips.

"Mom, I'm going upstairs to change. I'll be right down." Lewis tiptoed up the stairs behind her and into Bitsy's room. Bitsy slipped into her bathroom where she took off her new suit and slipped on a pair of jeans and a sweatshirt. When she came out Lewis was sitting on her bed, looking down at his hands folded on his knees. He looked up and gave her his most winning smile and stood up. She hugged him and wished she never had to let him go. A sigh, one that filled her lungs with all the frustration, anger, and fear that she'd been holding in for weeks now, pushed out of her and she felt tears running down her cheeks.

"Babe, are you ok?" Lewis held her tight. She nodded and pulling back from Lewis, searched one eye and then the other, hoping to find the answer to the question she had to ask. He wiped the tears from her cheeks.

"Lewis, I still have one question."

"What is it, my love?"

She had thought about this for weeks now, how she would put the question. And if he would tell her the truth. The trial was over now. Lewis was free, there was no reason for him to not be completely honest with her. He no longer needed to protect her from Joe. But she had to know. She moved back to her bed and pulled Lewis over with her and they sat together, holding hands.

"Lewis, I have to know. Did you do it? Did you kill Joe?" She held her breath as she waited for Lewis to look up and into her eyes. He seemed to be searching for the right words, the ones he thought she wanted to hear. But she only wanted to hear the truth. She was prepared whether he said yes or no. Lewis looked up and put his hands on her shoulders, rubbing them, squeezing them lightly. Bitsy felt his strength and knew at that instant that he certainly was capable of killing Joe. She knew he never would've been able to let it go, wouldn't have been able to let Joe get away with his attempted rape of her. She knew Lewis would do what he had to do even if that meant killing somebody.

"The man is gone and he won't hurt you or anyone else ever again. That's really all you need to know. Do you want to know if your future husband is capable of murder? I don't think anyone would want to know that. But if the situation ever arises, just know that I wouldn't hesitate to do whatever's needed to keep you safe. I hope that answers your question?"

That really was all Bitsy needed to know. They hugged and walked out of the bedroom together.

# Friends, Lovers, and Other Strangers

# What's in it for Me

A young man, probably in his mid- 20's, tall and slim with jet black hair and pale skin, walked into the A-to-Z Mart and right into the front cashiers' office. The cashiers, who were setting up their registers for the day and had been chatting about their previous night's activities, all turned and watched him walk into the cashiers' office like he had been doing this every day for the past five years.

"Who is that?" asked Kathy, the first to speak. She didn't miss a thing that happened at the Mart, particularly when it had something to do with a man.

"Wouldn't you like to know!" Ginger, the cashier right beside her, laughed.

"Ha, you know me too well!" Kathy replied as she continued to stare at the cashiers' office door, waiting for him to come back out.

Betsy didn't say anything but felt herself blushing and busied herself at her register.

In a few minutes the man came out and, walking past them, smiled at each of the women, knowing he was causing a bit of a scene. He winked at Betsy. Of course, her blush turned a shade redder.

"Ooh, looks like someone has his eye on Betsy. Better not let Lewis find out." Ginger giggled.  Everyone knew Betsy and Lewis were inseparable so they joked with Betsy every chance they got. Betsy could take the joking, even though she turned several more shades of red. No one really joked much with Lewis.

Colin walked through the store until he came to the Domestics department. Little did the cashiers know that he was the new manager of the department that stocked linens, bed sheets, pillows, tablecloths, and every other item associated with kitchen, bathroom, and bedroom covers. He walked into his stock room where his clerks, Jason and Cassie, were hanging out chatting and laughing. They looked up and stopped talking when he walked in.

"Can I help you?" Jason spoke first, obviously the older of the two.

"Yeah, I was looking for the men's room." Colin thought he would have a little fun with his new employees.

"Oh, um, I don't think the store is open yet and you really shouldn't be back here." Cassie, a petite girl with mousy brown hair, took a step behind Jason who stood strong with his arms folded across his chest.

"Okay, relax, just kidding. I'm your new boss." Not the best way to introduce himself to his employees but he didn't always do the right thing and wasn't always politically correct. He was a joker and that was usually his first priority; trying to get a laugh, often at the expense of someone's feelings.

Jason and Cassie visibly relaxed and Cassie stepped out from behind Jason.

"Hi, I'm Cassie." Cassie waved at Colin.

"And I'm your boss. Mr. McDonough. But you can call me Colin."

"I'm Jason." Colin extended his hand and when Jason went to shake it Colin pulled his back and ran it through his hair.

Jason and Cassie both laughed nervously.

"Okay, so, where's my office?"

The two employees genuinely laughed.

"No, I'm serious. I don't have a big office with a big desk?"

More laughing from Cassie and Jason who, by now, were a little more relaxed.

"Man, that's disappointing. My brother, one of the assistant managers of the store, you know him as Mr. McDonough, and please don't ever call me that, has led me astray. I thought this was going to lead to one of those big shot jobs, you know like at a Fortune 500 company where eventually I'd be the CEO. Hmmm, that is so disappointing!"

They were all laughing now.

"Okay, well, why don't you fill me in on what you guys do and then I can figure out what I'm supposed to do. What is it, almost 9, store is open now, right?  So, let's take a break at the snack bar and talk about this. I think the store can get along without us in the department for a few minutes, don't you?"

Jason and Cassie exchanged a look and a smile that said, this guy's going to be a great boss!

Colin did fit in just fine at his new job and his brother was thrilled. Typically a screw-up and someone who just didn't give a damn about anything, Colin had been given this job and had also been warned by his big brother that this was his last chance. If he screwed up this time, Colin was on his own. He now had a record and his brother, Darren, had vouched for him and said he would take responsibility for Colin. Since their parents were both dead, Darren was really the only one Colin had.  Although just five years older, Darren had let Colin live with him for a short time but it cramped his style having his younger brother hanging out in his bachelor apartment so he set him up with the A-to-Z Mart job and his own studio apartment.

Colin was a player and felt stifled by his big brother always breathing down his neck. But he knew he couldn't risk screwing up again and he even found a young girl at the Mart to date – thinking that might show Darren that he was committed to living a more responsible life. Linda had worked there about 6 months before Colin showed up. Recently graduated from high school, Linda didn't really have any future plans and, like most girls her age without a college degree and no clear career goals, thought she would follow in her mom's footsteps and marry and then start a family. She liked Colin and was impressed by his experience and seemingly worldliness.

Colin liked Linda but she was just another girl, nothing really special to him. They went to the beach with another couple, friends of Colin. Sometimes they went to see a movie or got takeout pizza and watched a movie at his friend's apartment. Fun for everyone except Colin who was bored. He just wasn't ready to settle down.

An old friend, Benny, one of his "druggie" friends as Darren referred to them, called Colin and invited him to come for a visit to 'talk about old times and have a few beers'. Colin declined and after they hung up, Colin called Linda and invited her to his apartment. Linda didn't think it was a good idea; she still lived with her parents and, after four months, she and Colin still hadn't had sex. Colin was getting frustrated and wasn't sure how much longer he could date the virgin; they hardly even necked. He thought about Benny, the drugs, the beer, and free love that was always available at his place, and decided he'd take Benny up on his offer. Although Colin had a girlfriend now, it never hurt to look; plus, they weren't married and as far as he was concerned it wasn't even that serious. Also, there was nothing wrong with having a couple of beers and maybe a joint or two with some old friends. It would be fun and just what Colin needed after months of boredom and celibacy.

Although it had been almost a year since the accident that put Benny's then girlfriend in the hospital, Colin figured he was just lucky and that he would be lucky again. He didn't remember much about it even though he had been driving the vehicle. He was so high he didn't even know what had happened and just got out of the car that he had smashed into a tree and started walking down the road. The cops had picked him up and the ambulance took Benny's girlfriend, the name still escaped him, to the hospital. She was in bad shape but lived; she didn't press charges since she was as high as he was so she figured she was equally to blame.

But this was different, it was just going to be a few beers, maybe a little pot. He would bring Linda. They would take the subway so no driving; no one would get hurt. Suddenly he was really excited about it and called Benny back and said they would see him on Saturday.

It was a long subway ride and a short walk to the triple-decker house. Colin stood out front and all the good times, mostly while high, came rushing back to him. He'd had almost as much sex in this apartment as he'd had drugs and alcohol. He felt himself getting excited just thinking about it. He walked up the stairs to the front porch.

"Is this the place?" Linda hesitated at the bottom of the stairs.

Colin seemed surprised to hear someone's voice behind him and turned around to see Linda looking at him with a fearful look on her face.  He grabbed her hand and gently pulled her up the stairs.

"Yes, yes, this is it. It's fine. You'll love Benny, he's a fun guy."

They walked into the hallway and knocked on the first-floor apartment door. The door was flung open by a tall guy with a bushy curly head and a full beard. His face was full of surprise, his eyes wide open with a smile to match. Benny outweighed Colin by about 50 pounds and grabbing Colin's hand, yanked him into his chest, patting him on the back as if trying to dislodge a hunk of steak that was stuck in Colin's throat.

"Hey, hey, hey, buddy, long time. How's it going?" He pulled Colin indoors and was about to shut the door when Colin remembered that Linda was with him.

"This is Linda, a friend. We work together, she's a friend." Linda was a little surprised at how detached he was from her and how much he down-played their relationship.

"Hey, I'm Benny." Benny gave her about as much attention as Colin did. Benny quickly turned all his attention back to Colin. He dragged him away and into the kitchen behind a closed door. Linda looked around the room that was full of plants and a couple of odd pieces of furniture. There was another guy and two women in the room and they all looked at Linda standing there.

"Why don't you sit. I'm Jerry, this is Candy and the other woman walking around is Barb." Candy, sitting a little awkwardly on Jerry's lap, waved and said 'Hey' then gave her attention back to Jerry and they continued talking quietly while they shared a joint. Barb was watering the many plants and gave Linda a quick smile. She was wearing short shorts and Linda could tell she wasn't wearing any underwear, no panty lines. She was well-endowed and had a tight sleeveless t-shirt on that pulled on her breasts and showed her nipples that Linda couldn't help noticing. She gave a little shiver and looked away.

"Would you like a beer or a Coke or something to drink." Barb was being nice.

"No, thanks, I'm fine. I don't think we're going to be here long."

"Oh, really?" Barb seemed to know something that Linda didn't.

Just then Colin and Benny came back into the room, laughing. Colin had a joint in his hand and he was rubbing his nose.

"Wow, that is good stuff, where did you get it?" He took a drag on his joint and handed it to Linda. She refused and Barb stepped in and took it.

"Hey, Barb, how are you?" Colin turned his attention to Barb who took a deep drag on the joint and blew it into Colin's face as he breathed it in deeply. She put her hand on his chest and pressed her body up against his, pulling his face to her as she whispered something in his ear. Linda couldn't hear but she thought she heard the words, 'missed you.' She wondered what kind of relationship they had once had. Colin ran his hand up her leg, letting it rest on her ass, and then as if remembering that Linda was there, let his hand fall. He walked over to Linda and sat next to her on the couch.

"So, how are you doing?"

"Are we ready to go?" Linda was very uncomfortable, especially seeing Barb rubbing herself all over her boyfriend and him rubbing her back.

"Go? No, I'm not ready to go, we just got here. I thought we'd stay a few hours, hang out, have a couple of beers, you know?

"I'm not comfortable, I want to go."

"Well then go, who's stopping you."

Linda was hurt and felt herself tear up. Colin knew he had hurt her, but she was being a bore and it really was better if she just left.

"Why don't I walk you back to the trolley stop and you can go home."

"Okay."

No one seemed too upset that Linda was leaving and Barb gave a little wave and pursed her lips in a kiss while looking at Colin. Linda saw Colin give her a wink back.

"I'll be right back."

The walk to the trolley stop was quiet. When they got to the spot where, according to Colin, the trolley was supposed to stop to pick people up, they waited. No one else was there.

"Okay, so just wait right here and the trolley should be here any minute. Then the trolley will take you all the way to the subway and I'm sure you know your way from there." And he turned around and left.

Linda stood there, upset and hurt that Colin was so inconsiderate and uncaring that he would just leave her here to wait by herself in the middle of a city where she felt so lost and had no idea where she was or even what town they were in. She was a little afraid and started shaking. She wasn't sure if it was from fear or anger. She stood there another 10 minutes and when there was no sign of a trolley, she walked back to the apartment.

She stood in the hallway outside the apartment, listening at the door. It was quiet inside as if everyone had left. She went out the door to make sure she was at the right house even though she knew it was. She went back inside and again waited, listening at the door. Then she heard the sounds of heavy breathing, moaning, kissing. And then Colin said, 'that feels so good, baby.'

"I'm just going to go slip into something comfier."

"Okay, hurry back, Barb. I can't tell you how much I've missed you." She heard more kissing and heavy breathing and giggling and a door closing.

She knocked, loudly.

"Who is it?"

"Linda."

The door swung open and Colin stood there, his shirt off, his pants unbuckled. All the other people who were in the room had disappeared.

"What are you doing here, Linda?" He seemed angry, which made her angry.

"I'm not waiting there by myself. I don't know where I am, I just want to go home." She felt herself getting upset and once more fought back tears.

Colin took a deep breath, laced with frustration and anger, and let it out.

"Yeah, okay. Let me call you a taxi."

Barb, thankfully, didn't come back into the room. They waited silently for the taxi which arrived about five minutes later but seemed to take much longer. The taxi's horn roused them out of their thoughts and Linda got up off the couch.

"Bye Colin."

"Yeah."

# Raised This Way

The hand hit her face before she could move out of the
way. But then, she never knew when it was coming.  Like a
missile programmed to hit its target, the hand never missed. She
blinked her eyes and wiped her face with the back of her hand.
It wasn't that she didn't want him to see her wipe away the
tears, but more that she wanted to wipe his smell off of her
face; his cologne, the same one he wore when he fucked her
once a week, thinking it attracted her to him, clung to his body
and now her face. He smiled, satisfied, superior in his brutality,
knowing she was there, would be there, whenever he felt the
need to assert his strength, his dominance over her. He was
repelled by her weakness, but he also depended upon it to
disguise his own. And then, puffing himself up like a cock, he
left the house. Slamming the door, the hinge pins lifted up and
settled back down, the vibration shaking the walls around the
frame. She slid to the floor and sobbed the tears only a trapped
woman could cry.

He got into his Honda Civic and drove the nearly ten miles
to the A-to-Z Mart. Art walked into the store like he owned it.
He knew he was cut out for store management and wondered
why he hadn't yet been promoted to the position. He had filled
out all the paperwork, but still he remained the manager of the
shoe department for going on two years. He should be running
the place by now. Things would change for the better, he was
certain. Whenever Art approached the District Manager, who
visited about every other month, he had to chase the guy down
to ask about moving up the chain. There were A-to-Z Marts all

over and he was okay with moving anywhere in the country if there was nothing local for him. He hadn't yet bought a house so it would be easy to up and move out of their apartment. Darlene could pack while he worked - he wouldn't even have to take off much time and could start immediately. He'd probably have to take some kind of store manager training, though. He was tired of feeling stuck in this dead-end job and was more than ready to take the next step. He knew they were just putting him off and now he wanted an answer. He remembered the last time the District Manager, Paul Young, had visited.

"Mr. Young, can I have a minute of your time, sir?" Art hated calling a guy who had half as much knowledge about the business as he had 'Mr.' and 'sir'. He should be calling Art 'sir'. He was superior to this prick in every way. He knew it and Art was pretty sure "Mr. Young" knew it, too. Obviously, the guy had friends in high places. How else could he have gotten the job?

Mr. Young turned to see who had called out to him. When he saw Art, he sighed and held out his hand to Art. Art knew Paul didn't like him either.

"Arty, how's it going?" He kept walking and Art had to walk behind Paul, talking as they went. Arty. Paul always gave Art one more thing to dislike about him. Art hadn't been called 'Arty' since he was about 13, when he started high school and decided it was time to have a more grown-up name. Of course, people who knew Art when he was younger, like aunts and uncles, still called him Arty. But that was family, it was different. But here was Paul now calling him by his childhood name. He knew it was Paul's way of putting himself above Art, by calling him by a child's name. Art clenched his teeth, ignoring the implication.

"I was wondering, did you get a chance to look at my application for store manager? I'll travel anywhere you need me. I'm ready to go any time. Sir." He nearly coughed the last word out but thought it was to his benefit to show respect, even if it was fake.

"Application, huh? Um, I don't remember seeing... oh, yes, right. I do remember your, um, application." He stopped short, turning to face Art, nearly causing a collision between the two men. Paul held his arm out to brace Art so he wouldn't actually fall into him.

"The problem is, buddy, you are doing such a fine job in the shoe department, it would be really hard to replace you. You know what I'm saying? It is so hard to find good people. We get the kids right out of high school and then they are either off to college or on to better jobs." Paul had started to walk again so Art stayed close to hear what he was saying. He knew he was just being blown off. He had heard it all before. Each time was a little different but it was pretty much the same tune. 'We need you, we can't replace you, you are doing such a fine job,' etc., etc. Bullshit.

"But hey, who am I to stop you from reaching your goals, huh? I'll read through your application and then send it on to corporate. See what I can do, okay?"

"Hey, Tom, I need to talk to you." And that was the end of their conversation as Paul walked off with Tom Chesley, manager of the men's department.  Art stood there, watching them walk away. Paul whispered something to Tom, Tom glanced over his shoulder toward Art, and they both had a good laugh. Art knew they were laughing at him. Assholes.

Art had so many good ideas and implemented as many as he could without the store manager, Jim Roldark, having a fit. Now there was a man with no vision. Jim liked keeping things going the way they were without change and Art knew that was going to drive the store into the ground. There were new department stores opening up every day around the country. Why would people keep coming to the A-to-Z Mart? Everything was starting to look old and outdated. And Jim seemed okay with that. If Art could take over his job, that would be perfect. Art could see himself in that job. He would bring class back to the store. That dick, Paul, couldn't see past his own nose. He had as much vision as, as a…, as a bat! Art thought that was pretty funny and walked into his department with a smile on his face.

A bit of a neat freak, Art ran the shoe department like a drill sergeant; which was ironic since he had never been in the military. He only knew what he had seen on TV where they always portrayed drill sergeants as being strict about cleanliness and neatness. Art believed he would have been an asset to the military. His three employees, Kyle, his assistant manager, and Dave and Shawn, were similar to him in their appearance; neat, clean-shaven, white shirt and tie. He never had to discipline them for looking wrinkled or dirty. Of course, Art wore a suit jacket but, knowing that they didn't make much over minimum wage, wasn't too upset that Dave and Shawn didn't wear suit jackets. Of course, this made Art stand out when three of them occasionally went to lunch - it was obvious that he was the boss. He tried to mix it up so that one time Dave went and the next time Shawn joined him and Kyle as he wasn't comfortable leaving his department without a sales associate available to help the customers. He was a professional and he demanded the same of his workers, too. Art enjoyed these lunches because he got a chance to share some of his ideas with his staff.

"So, what do you think of this? We'll give a coupon for 10% off the next pair of shoes they buy. How about that?"

Kyle frowned. "Will the store honor this coupon?"

"Of course they will, they'll have to. We'll make up the coupons and when they buy the shoes, the cashiers will stamp it at the register and the customers will bring it with them the next time they shop. I think it's a terrific idea."

Again, Kyle shook his head. "I don't know, sounds like it might get complicated. Can they use the coupon with a pair of shoes that are on sale? And can they use it with the shoes they already bought? Or what about this - they return a pair of shoes they got with the discount and the store, that maybe doesn't know they got the discount, refunds them the full price. That would not be good."

Art was getting impatient with Kyle's questions. Sometimes he was so negative and didn't appreciate Art's creativity.

"I don't know, Kyle. I'm still working on the idea. I don't have all the bugs worked out yet."

They only traded small talk after that and finished lunch quickly.

It was important to Art that he be home for dinner with Darlene every night, except department meeting nights, of course. He did work Saturdays, too, so he made sure he promptly left work at 6pm. Darlene was told to have dinner on the table by 6:30 every night. Art liked to relax a little when he got home and expected either a cold beer or a martini when he walked in the door. Darlene never knew which so she was supposed to have both ready and waiting to pour into a glass. Sometimes, to keep Darlene on her toes, Art would tell her to pour him a glass of scotch with ice and a twist of lemon. He would count the seconds it took her to have it ready. If she took more time than he thought was reasonable to pour a shot or two of scotch into a glass and add ice and the twist, he would have to punish her. One backhand to the face was usually enough to get the message across. Home was a man's castle and she was fortunate to have a man to feed, clothe, and take care of all her needs. If she did anything that disrupted his life after working hard all day, she deserved to be punished. She had to know this was not a free ride. She had to earn her way, as he did. He had to put up with people like Paul. She had to do what Art said, follow his rules, and keep him satisfied. This was the way with his people and had been for generations. The man ruled the house, always. He wasn't about to change that. He strongly believed that a woman needed to be controlled and her spirit broken, just like a wild horse. Otherwise, she would rule the house, or try to. He vowed that would never happen in his house.

He thought, often, about having a son. Darlene would be a good mother, would care for her son, breast-feeding, changing diapers, bathing the boy. Art would teach him the ways of the world as Art himself was taught by his father. Having a son would be the ultimate show of his manhood. After five years of marriage, Art was ready to impregnate Darlene with his high-quality sperm that he knew would bring him a strong, virile son. All the Pedarkian men were extremely masculine. Of course, there was Art's second cousin, Tomas, who lived in East Village, NY with another man. The family tried to say he was Tomas' roommate and even said the roommate had a girlfriend. But Art knew Tomas and his roommate were sharing a bed. The thought of it made him ill and to Art, Tomas was dead. He never told anyone about this cousin, he was too embarrassed by Tomas' chosen lifestyle.

Art knew Darlene had been taking birth control but he informed her that it was time to have a son and he would no longer purchase her birth control pills. That was more than six months ago and he was surprised that Darlene was not yet pregnant. It would be just his luck to have married an infertile woman. In his culture, that was reason for a man to divorce his wife. He thought about having an affair and staying with Darlene but he didn't want to bring a bastard into the world. No, divorce would be better. He thought about taking her to the doctor to find out what was going on but instead decided to give it another month or two. If by the end of a year she was still not pregnant, he would bring her to the doctor. Of course, he knew it had nothing to do with him. He knew he was perfectly healthy and his sperm were strong and powerful and could impregnate any woman. There had to be something wrong with her.

After dinner on Saturday night was usually the time when Art was ready to have sex with his wife. She would change into her sheer nightgown that Art bought her for the purpose of seducing him. It was understood that this was the only time she would wear the outfit. It didn't take much for Art to get aroused; he considered himself to be a very sexual man and knew any woman would be thrilled to have him fuck her.

Darlene had a beautiful body so seeing it through the sheer gown added excitement to his arousal.

His wife was sitting on the bed when Art came into the bedroom. She stood up because as he said, an obedient wife never sits; she should always be attending to her man, finding ways to excite him so that he wants to have sex with her. Sitting was never allowed. Art quickly took off his clothes and lay naked on his bed. He directed her to walk around the room with her sheer gown on, letting it flow away from her body and then fall back on it, accentuating the curves of her breasts, slowly turning to reveal the curve of her ass and the outline of her shape. The lighting made all the difference; a red light sitting on top of the bureau gave the room a glow that allowed him to see her body clearly through the gown without showing any details of her face. The idea of fucking a stranger gave Art an instant erection. He spent almost as much time looking at his erection as he did looking at her body. The combination of the two was sure to have him come within seconds after entering her. When he was that close, he called her to him. She slid the gown off her shoulders and laying back on the bed, he would climb on top of her in time to enter and come inside her in one hard, brutal movement. Quickly now he slammed into her, harder each time, until he was done. At that moment he would pull himself out and lay next to her, panting. Soon after he would fall asleep. She would lay there, feeling nothing, her face turned away from him, a mascara-smeared tear escaping from the corner of her eye and onto her pillow, wetting the corner of the case with the only fluids she wanted to keep inside her. She'd stealthily crawl off the bed and deposit his sperm into the toilet bowl. Showering with the hottest water her skin could tolerate, she wanted his smell and his sperm off of and out of her as quickly as possible. After drying herself off, she put on her regular nightgown and reaching up under the claw-foot tub, pulled out a small bag that she had hidden there. She'd quickly open the package of birth control pills, take one, and place the bag back under the tub. She'd check to make sure it was secure with the duct tape, leave the bathroom on tiptoes, and slip back into bed.

Mornings after sex always started out the same. Art was loving as they dressed for church, helping her with her necklace, smiling often at Darlene, and opening the door to the car for her. A curious neighbor looking through their blinds at the young couple might think they were so in love. But it wouldn't be long before Art was upset about something that Darlene did or that he imagined she was doing and the hand would once again fly across her face. This particular morning it happened at church. A tall, good-looking young man sitting in the pew just in front of Art and Darlene, seemed more interested in Darlene than Art liked. At the Stand and Greet your neighbor time, when he turned to greet Art and Darlene, not only did he stare into Darlene's eyes but when he shook her hand, he put his other hand on top of hers and said, "Very nice to meet you." Darlene dropped her eyes, whispered "Nice to meet you, too" and an ever so slight smile curled the corners of her lips.

Art could barely contain himself until the service was over. He grabbed Darlene by the arm and pulling her along, cursed through his teeth the thoughts that had been building up inside him.

"You whore! What do you think you were doing, embarrassing me like that? Flirting with that man right in front of me, your husband. How dare you! You no-good whore. You aren't a lady, you are a common slut. I should rent you out to other men and make some money on you instead of all the money I spend on you. But what man would want such a slut? Maybe there are some in prison who haven't had a woman for years, or some poor bum in the street, those are the men who want whores like you."

Darlene shook with fear and anger over what awaited her at home. She wanted to pull away from Art and run, run into the arms of the kind man in church. His hand was strong but gentle, she could still feel his skin on her skin. She put her hand to her face, not to wipe away tears but to smell the man, so masculine, so pleasant like a clean soap. Not overpowering like Giorgio Armani, Art's cologne. She tried to turn to see if the man was there, watching. But Art pulled her harder and soon they were at his car.

He continued to berate her, quietly at first. Then, as he got louder, spit flew from his lips as he banged his hand on the dashboard, resisting his overwhelming urge to let his hand fly across her face. He was always the perfect gentleman in public and, even though they were in his car, he knew people could see. This is how he was taught; do not display anger in public. His wife flirting with another man was a private matter and would be dealt with on his terms, in his home.

When they got to their apartment, he quickly jumped out of the car and walked in long strides over to her side of the car. He flung open the door and she did not jump out as he expected. She couldn't possibly be toying with his emotions this way and he reached in and pulled her by the arm. She nearly fell on the ground as her upper body moved but her legs stayed in the car.

"Get out now!" Art looked around the neighborhood, up at the windows. He suddenly realized that they were still out in public and quickly bent over to help her sit back in the car.

"Get out of the car, now." He said forcefully but a bit more gently.

"I'm afraid." Darlene had never spoken those words before. She refused to let him see her fear. She kept all emotions inside, guarded, protected. But she couldn't bear to be hit anymore. She knew the women in her family just dealt with the beatings and didn't speak of them, ever. But she had had enough. She wanted to run away. She wanted to run into the arms of a man who would love and protect her and who would never even think of hitting her. She had met women who didn't fear men but were loved and protected by them. She knew all men did not beat their wives. But Art was not one of those men who cherished and loved their wives, who protected and cared for them. He was a wife-beater, a monster.

"Good, you should be afraid. What kind of a man would I be if you didn't fear me? I'll tell you what kind of a man, the kind whose wife flirts with other men, the kind of man who is embarrassed by his wife and humiliated when she doesn't respect him and they don't show their respect when they hold hands with other men, they fuck other men, they cheat and lie and steal from their husbands!"

She could feel the anger building up in him as he spoke and then he grabbed her by her hair and pulled her out of the car, carefully but forcefully, until she was standing on the curb next to him. He slammed the door, carefully looking around for sneaky, nosy neighbors peeking behind window blinds. He took his wife's hand and firmly placed it on his arm, only to give the appearance that he was guiding his wife towards the front door. That he was a gentleman. That he took care of his wife.

Darlene held the tears in. She would take what he gave her. She would not let him see her cry. She knew what she had to do, now, finally.

Once in the house, Art changed from his suit and tie into his jeans and Darlene remained seated on the sofa, where he had led her. He walked back into the room holding his belt, slapping it across the chair, the seat of the couch next to where she sat, the floor beneath her feet. She jumped when the belt touched her foot.

"Oh, did I touch you? Maybe you want a little more, that was more like a caress, wasn't it?" He lifted the belt and slapped it across her calves. She jumped again.

"What, another caress?" He lifted the belt again and whipped it harder across her thighs. She let a small yelp escape from her mouth and closed it tighter, keeping her eyes away from his face.

He lifted his arm again and as he brought it down towards her face, she reached her arm up and grabbed the belt, staring hard into his eyes. He froze, unable to believe what he was witnessing.

"How dare you!" He pulled the belt from her grasp and beat her harder than she had ever been beaten before.

"You will never do that again! Do you hear me? Never! I will break your fuckin' arm if you ever try that again. You bitch!" He turned and left the room, leaving her in a lump on the floor like a pile of dirty laundry.

The next morning Art left for work. There was no mention of the previous day's punishment, there never was. He felt he didn't need to go there again, that she had learned her lesson and that they would go on from there, as before. He gave her a kiss on her bruised cheek and left for work.

Darlene watched out the window as he drove away. She quickly showered, dressed, and taking a small packed suitcase from the closet, she took her purse and left the apartment.

It was a long ride to the shelter.

# It's a Shame

A fastidious man, Kyle Williams arrived at work without a single hair out of place. Of course, keeping it short proved to be the secret that made it easier to control.  His tie deftly knotted, his belt buckle centered at his navel, his pocket handkerchief with the point perfectly centered above his jacket's pocket identified Kyle as a man who was familiar with and had a close, personal relationship with detail.  Never late, he punched in at 3 minutes to 9, which gave him time to hang his suit jacket on the wooden hanger he brought from home. His boss, Art, who was nearly as neat and orderly as Kyle, provided them with a rack to hang their jackets on. Although the back stock room was filled mostly with boxes of shoes, they did have a small desk area where Art could sit to place his weekly shoe order. Or, occasionally, one of the clerks would take a 5-minute break, particularly right before school started and there were non-stop customers to help. And then there were the weekly meetings when the neatly stacked folding chairs would come out to seat the clerks for Art's 15-minute department update.  Art had transformed their stockroom so that everything in it was placed in the most efficient and orderly way. Kyle approved.

Kyle was a simple man, happy with his job and with his life. Although he didn't really have anything except his job to occupy his time, still he was content. He had turned 31 just three months ago and felt this was a perfect time in his life. He really didn't want for anything. Sometimes he thought about dating, but his shy demeanor kept him from asking a woman for a date. Relationships always complicated life, too. He'd had one girlfriend, back in his mid- 20's, but that had only lasted 6 months. Kyle had felt pressured to take things farther, but he wasn't ready to let someone into his life on a full-time basis back then. He needed his privacy and enjoyed living alone.

Sometimes when he was checking in new inventory and stacking the shoes out back, he thought about Kelly. It wasn't that he missed her so much as that he sometimes wondered what happened to her. He hoped she found someone else, someone more suited to her.

"We belong together Kyle - Kelly and Kyle - K&K? See? We're perfect for each other."

Sharing the letter K for their first names wasn't enough to convince Kyle that they should be together. He would smile when she said this and then he called her less and less. Until one day he decided that was it, it was over. He knew she wanted more than he was able to give her. He needed order in his life and she wanted babies. She talked about it a lot.

"You with your blonde hair and me with my reddish-blonde hair, our babies would be so beautiful. Can't you just see it?  It will be so perfect! Oh, I can't wait, Kyle!"

But Kyle couldn't see it, didn't want to see it. He thought his life was perfect as it was. Marrying Kelly, marrying anyone would change his life in a way he wasn't prepared to change. He needed to get away from Kelly and the day he decided not to call her anymore was the day he took this job. He was back in control of his life, living it the way he wanted, on his terms only. Now everything was perfect.

On the weekends, after he finished his cleaning and laundry, he would try a new recipe from The Joy of Cooking. Many times, he discovered something wonderful but had no one to share it with and at these times he would also think about Kelly. Once he even almost called her. But he was living several towns away now and imagined she must have moved on with her life, too.  He thought about getting a cat, but pets weren't allowed in his building. Probably not a good idea anyway. Cleaning up after himself was all he wanted to do.  Cats are pretty clean, he had heard, but he would have to have a litter box and sometimes they scratch furniture and might pee on a carpet. He couldn't risk that happening. No, this was best for him, living alone. He felt better having this much control over every aspect of his life.

Kyle usually did his food shopping on his way home from work. That way, he could avoid the weekend crowds. Most weekends he spent reading or watching a movie on TV. He didn't like going to the cinema, although sometimes there was a movie that he really wanted to see.  He couldn't bear to sit in the seats at the movie theaters. They were so close together, like sitting on an airplane with the next person leaning on your arm rest. A small man, Kyle never sweated, but the thought of someone big and sweaty touching him was enough to make him gag. He just couldn't do it.

He thought about finding a hobby that suited him but every hobby seemed to involve creating messes more than anything else. He did enjoy reading, usually a good murder mystery that he would try to figure out before he got to the end. Some of his favorite authors were Agatha Christie and Frederick Forsyth, and he had read a few Michener's, too.  He also liked doing crossword puzzles, often not moving from his kitchen table on Sundays until he finished the entire puzzle. He rarely had to look up words in the crossword puzzle dictionary and mostly filled out the puzzles without any help. It upset him too much to look up a word - it felt like cheating and when he was just a boy, anything his father considered cheating was severely punished. Not knowing the correct word was certainly reason for punishment according to his father's rules. More times than Kyle could count his pants had been pulled down and his bottom reddened with his father's belt until he couldn't sit down. Too many years went by without any chance of being rescued from these severe beatings. Not even his mother could rescue him because she worked two jobs to keep Kyle and his younger brother Teddy fed and clothed while his father lay on the couch suffering from a back injury he got on his construction job. But Kyle saw his father lifting weights in their basement, so even at 9 and 10 years old, he understood that his father, who couldn't stand anyone cheating, was a bigger cheater than anyone else he knew.

The beatings continued until he was almost 12 years old. By this time, he no longer cried which only incensed his father more and caused him to beat Kyle even harder. Until the time Kyle saw blood fly off the belt and land on his bare foot. He stared at it, partly in surprise, but mostly curiosity, wondering what his bottom must look like where the blood had come from. Did it blister first or did the belt just rip the skin off his body, exposing flesh and maybe bone underneath? Kyle's thoughts were interrupted by his mother, standing in the doorway of the room he and Teddy shared, screaming. His father dropped the belt and turned to Kyle's mother while lies poured out of his mouth.

"He hit Teddy and then he made a mess in the kitchen spilling his glass of milk. I've been cleaning up after him all day." His mother looked over at Teddy, cringing on the bed, shaking his head 'no'. The look of terror on his face was heartbreaking.

"I've never hit him before, I swear, it's just that this time was more than I could take." Again, Teddy told the truth without opening his mouth.

"Get out of my house, now! You monster! How can you do this to your son, my son. I want you out of this house and never come back. We are officially divorced, you sick bastard!"

In the past his father had come home drunk on money he took from his mother's purse or took out of the boys' piggy banks, and she would threaten to kick him out. Then his father would cook a nice meal and all was forgiven. But this time it was different. Kyle's mother couldn't apologize to Kyle and Teddy enough and couldn't stop crying when they told her the truth of what happened in the house when she wasn't home. She spent the rest of her life trying to make up for the severe punishments they had both endured at the hands of their father.

But it was too late. Teddy committed suicide when he was 18 years old. Drug overdose. And for Kyle, something died inside him like a fallen leaf from a tree curling up when it lay on the ground too long.  If he ever let himself go back to that place and think about it, he would know that this was partly responsible for his split up with Kelly. He had no idea how to trust.

And then he met Diane. She was confident and relaxed in a charmingly goofy way that drew Kyle to her like he had never been drawn to anyone before. He referred to her, in his own private thoughts, as his honey and he was the bee. He was a little nervous about this because he feared he might one day call her 'honey'. Her short, light brown bob haircut fit her slim face the way petals cling to a rose before they open to reveal the beauty inside. And then the over-sized, brown-framed glasses accentuated the goofy look with her slightly larger than normal front teeth. If you didn't look closely, you might miss the penetratingly deep hazel eyes that smiled right along with her perfectly shaped bow mouth.

Kyle was mesmerized by Diane and her comfortable laugh. He stopped whatever he was doing whenever she came by to say hello. He was a little envious of, and at the same time admired, her easy-going manner. She charmed him in a way he never thought possible.  He felt all of these things without even being aware of the effect she had on him. So insecure about his own stiff manners, he found it impossible to look her in the eyes and would stare instead at a pair of shoes on display or a particular tile in the floor, or even sometimes something off in the distance. Anywhere but in her eyes.

Diane liked Kyle. He certainly wasn't anyone she ever imagined she would get involved with but there was something about him that drew her to him. When she was ready to take a break from her job in the women's department, she often found herself heading to the shoe department. She convinced herself it was because she liked shoes and she was always looking for her next pair. But she really didn't own that many pairs of shoes and whenever she went to the shoe department she spent the entire 15 minutes of her break talking to Kyle. What it was about him she couldn't say. He never went out with the crowd or went to Gini's where they all often ended up. She knew he wasn't married but thought he might have a girlfriend or he might even be engaged - she wanted to find that out but wasn't sure who to ask. He seemed more mature than most of the other employees in the store and she guessed he was probably in his late 20's. He seemed stiff and conservative, almost as if he couldn't relax. He certainly was neat and polished – like a new doll just taken out of the box and put up on a shelf for display, but don't touch. She knew he would treat her like a lady, she definitely felt that just based on how polite he was whenever she stopped by. He had a habit, though, that annoyed her - he never looked her in the eyes. She hadn't brought it up, fearful she would scare him away. He looked at the floor, off in the distance, and even at the button on her sweater.  Sometimes she thought he would take a quick peek; but mostly his conversation, although directed to her, was spoken to the floor or a spot just beyond her shoulder. And because of this, and his apparent nervousness around her, she was almost positive he didn't have a girlfriend. But there was something else, and she wasn't sure if this was also what attracted her to Kyle. There was a sadness about him. Even though he didn't look into her eyes, she stared into his and imagined that even though he was talking to her and physically present, he was really somewhere back in his past and that was where his eyes were looking. And that was where she saw the sadness. She wanted to know what it was he was looking at, she wanted to help him get out of there and look into her eyes and see how loving she could be for him. She blushed when she had these thoughts because she had no idea if she was right about any of this or if she was creating a romantic scenario in her mind where she saved the boy in the man and they lived happily ever after.

If he wasn't dating anyone, she wondered what it would take to get him to ask her on a date. She thought about asking him, but wasn't sure if he would be turned off by a woman who was too forward. At least she could find out if he was involved with anyone. So, one day when she took her break and walked to the shoe department, she decided, without much preparation, to just ask him. When to bring it up during their usual conversation was another problem she needed to solve.

Their topics of conversation were expanding and becoming more in-depth. Diane was trying to figure out when to jump in when Kyle brought up, again, about all the leftovers he had when he tried out these new recipes for himself. Diane took that as a hint, but also wondered why he didn't ask her at that point. It was coming to the end of her break and she decided it was now or never.

"Maybe next time you make too much food you can invite me over to help you eat it."

Kyle stopped talking and stared at the floor. He had thought so many times about asking Diane out but couldn't make his mouth say the words. What if she said 'no?' And then just like that she had asked him. She was so much braver than he was. He was focused only on these thoughts when he realized Diane was starting to move away from him. She put her heart out there and he never answered her. He was sure she must see his lack of response as rejection and he quickly snapped out of his head.

"Well, I should be getting back." And Diane turned to leave.

"Tonight." The word forced its way out between Kyle's closed lips.

"Excuse me?" Diane turned back to Kyle, waiting for confirmation on what she thought Kyle had said.

He thought about Diane, again, how brave she was and pushed forward.

"I'll make you dinner tonight." Not really a question but he hoped she would take it that way.

"Oh, okay." Diane moved back toward Kyle, smiling.

Kyle smiled and, for just a second, looked into Diane's eyes. It was there he knew he would be brave, where he would move forward with confidence, finally let go of his past, and stop it from controlling his future. Through her eyes he would finally become the man he so wanted to be.

# Settle Down

Mandy had no plans for her future. Having just graduated from high school she found herself applying for a job at the A-to-Z Mart. It didn't really matter what job she took, but being a clerk in some department sounded like it would be okay. Cashiers were too busy. She thought anyone who worked at the front desk was crazy; there was always a line with someone complaining about something. And returns were the same, maybe even worse. But a clerk, that suited her ambition; to stand around and fold or refold clothes, maybe pick something up off the floor that fell off a hanger, occasionally run up to the registers with a price check or, when it was really busy, to help bag items for the cashiers. That was as close as she wanted to get to the registers. Making some money for smokes, beer, and some new clothes was her priority. She didn't need much.

Living at home helped. She was thinking about looking for an apartment, but with two younger brothers, Jason, 7 and Kevin, 10 and Denise, her 15-year-old sister, she needed to stay around the house to occasionally babysit. Denise was old enough and she usually did the babysitting, but sometimes Mandy had to help out. She was happy when she could pass the babysitting off to her younger sister since she had been in charge for so many years. And now that she was looking for a job at the A-to-Z Mart, she would be working full-time and wouldn't be available to babysit her younger brothers. An apartment, if she couldn't find someone to share it, would be too expensive. So, for now, living at home worked, but she knew she would be restless to get her own place. She wished someday she could afford to buy her mom, brothers, and sister a house and get them the hell out of the projects. But she knew that was a pipedream. It took more ambition than she had to get things like that. Getting herself out of the projects was one thing and probably doable. But buying a house was way out of her reach. People who lived in the projects usually never made it out and ended up dying there after spending their whole lives in one of the crowded apartments. This wasn't something she thought of as depressing, it was just the way it was, what she was born into, and what she accepted as her fate. All she wanted to think about was where the next pack of cigarettes was going to come from. And right now, having this job would satisfy all her simple needs.

A week after she applied at the A-to-Z Mart, she got the call and started working the following Monday. The job was a clerk in the Men's department. Perfect. It paid minimum, what she expected, and she worked every day with Tuesdays and Sundays off. Which meant she worked a full day Saturday. She wasn't too happy about that but she knew how these things worked. Once she got a little seniority, she could ask for Saturdays off. That was the only time she really needed to help out at home with her brothers.

Denise, who was still in school, babysat on Saturdays for a couple who had two boys, ages 5 and 7. The Marvins owned a dry-cleaning business and they both needed to be there on Saturdays. Since there wasn't school on Saturday and not even a day-care that was open, there was nothing else to do but find a babysitter. Since Denise had two younger brothers that she babysat a lot, the Marvins knew she was the right person for the job. And it gave Denise a little money, too. Their mom worked six, and sometimes seven, days a week at Jimbo's Bowling Alley. Jimbo, the owner, was mom's brother-in-law so she was pretty secure, as long as her sister stayed married to Jimbo. She ran the register and handed out the bowling shoes for people needing to rent them. It was a pretty cushy job but she had to work a lot. Jimbo made sure she had insurance, too, which was a definite bonus, especially with four kids.

Mandy quickly made a few friends at the Mart. She liked Betsy, who worked as a cashier, and tried to get her register whenever the cashiers needed help bagging. They sometimes took their breaks together, too, along with Micky who worked in automotive. And occasionally Diane, who worked in the Women's department, joined them, too. They were forming a nice little clique. And they even started going out after work, mostly on weekends. Since none of them were old enough to drink and no one had a fake ID, they often went to visit Gini, the front desk supervisor. She was a lot of fun and loved having the kids hang out at her house. Her own kids were grown and out of the house and her husband, who Gini called 'the bum', she had kicked out of the house a few years back. After 18 years of his womanizing and hard drinking, and with her kids out of the house, she knew she had had enough and it was time to end it with him. She was much happier once he was gone. She heard he had died in a car accident but no one ever contacted her about it so she wasn't sure about that.  But, at that point, Gini had lost all feeling for the man even though he was the father of her children only in that he had donated the sperm. And, according to Gini, her son and daughter didn't miss the guy either.

Gini didn't have a problem giving the kids from the Mart a beer or two. Her only stipulation was that they would either have to sleep on her couch or take the subway or a taxi home. No one was driving, not on her watch. And if you threw up, you cleaned it up. But she loved having the young people around and was happy they liked hanging out with her. Her own kids were both living out of state, married and settled. She was happy for them but missed them. So, the kids at the Mart were a nice substitute and she took to her role of 'mom' to them naturally. Sometimes there were three or four, other times there were seven or eight. And the group changed when a few of them hooked up with others and started dating, like Betsy who was dating Lewis. But it was a good group, good kids. Any fights and you were thrown out and never invited back.

Mandy usually went to Gini's with Micky. Sometimes it was just the two of them. Other times it was just Mandy and she'd meet some older people, friends of Gini's who were closer to Gini's age. But she never felt unwelcome. She might have a beer or a Coke. Micky would always go if Betsy was going. Everyone knew Micky had a crush on Betsy, but he kept a safe distance once she started dating Lewis. A quiet boy, Micky always seemed to have a good time at Gini's. Mandy figured that, like most kids who lived in the projects, he was bearing more responsibility than a teenager should have to carry. But she really didn't know his story.

One Friday night they all seemed to need a break and five of them went to Gini's together; a new girl, Chrissy, who had just started in the children's department, joined Micky, Diane, and Mandy along with Jack who drove them. When they arrived a couple of other people from the Mart were already there. Mandy spotted a guy who worked for Jack, she was pretty sure his name was Ed, and felt her face flush. Unusual for Mandy who rarely blushed and appeared much older than her 18 years, she looked away and went to the kitchen to get a beer. Jack had stopped at the liquor store and got a 12-pack of Budweiser. He had one out of the package before they entered Gini's house. When he spotted Ed, he greeted him with a slap on the back. When Mandy returned, Jack and Ed seemed to be sharing a joke and Mandy saw Ed look in her direction while taking a long swig from his beer. Again, the face blush.

Although she hadn't spoken to Ed since she started working at the Mart, they'd nodded at each other a few times when passing and Ed gave her a big smile, which unnerved Mandy since she was usually cool around guys and sure of herself. There was something about Ed that attracted her to him more than anyone she had ever met. She could tell he was a little older than her, she guessed maybe 22 or 23, and he was ruggedly handsome. One of those guys who was not only a man's man but also a ladies' man without even trying. He was like a movie star or a sports figure who was completely unaware of his good looks. Mandy tried her best to ignore the stares he gave her from time to time and wondered what kind of a guy he really was. Little did he know that his good looks would not be enough to keep her interest. Although she didn't consider herself a beauty, she usually did give off an air of confidence or some might call it conceit.

The night was unusually loud with lots of laughing and a little dancing. Gini kept her eye on the drinking and shut off a couple of the younger ones, confirming rides home for them with one of the more responsible adults in the group. Mandy couldn't believe that Ed didn't come over and talk to her even though she had returned some of his looks complemented with smiles. She decided he was being stubborn and so it was up to her to make the first move. He got up to stretch and was walking towards the kitchen to get another beer. She watched him walk, skin-tight sharkskin pants that clung to his thighs, his calves, following his every move like they couldn't wait to see where he went next. His short-sleeved collared pullover pressed against well-defined abs and accented his biceps that were most likely home-grown, not pumped up at a gym. Mandy didn't really care too much about fashion and mostly went for comfort. She liked skirts that showed off her legs. At 5'6" she was tall enough to carry a short skirt and usually paired it with a blouse or pullover that showed just enough skin to make you want to see more. But she knew her eyes were what usually drew men to her, the deep blue azure color and thick black lashes often signaled an availability and willingness to go all the way, even though she considered herself mostly inexperienced and not at all an easy lay. She decided now was the time to make her move and walked right in front of Ed, almost causing him to trip over her.

"So, do you have a cigarette?" She really was out of butts at this point and since she saw him lighting up, thought he probably had another one to share.

Without saying a word Ed grabbed the pack out of his pocket, never taking his eyes off Mandy, and after putting the cigarette in her mouth, leaned in and lit her cigarette with the end of the one in his mouth. His face was very close to hers and she felt her face heating up again. She reached up and took the cigarette out of her mouth, exhaling.

"Thanks."

Ed nodded and walked towards the kitchen, leaving her with his big smile.

"Well, what the fuck?" Mandy said under her breath and turned to walk away when she felt a hand reach for hers and pull her back. She was standing face to face with Ed. He leaned in and, pulling her close to him, kissed her tenderly on the lips. She kissed him back and found herself more receptive than she thought she would be. His kiss couldn't have been more perfect, just the right pressure and right amount of time. He pulled away but she wanted more.

"Do you always kiss a girl before you know her name?"

"I know your name, it's Mandy. Jack told me." That sexy, sheepish half-grin and running his hands through his thick curly brown hair brought a smile to Mandy's lips, thinking about running her hands through his hair.

"Oh, so you were talking about me. What else did you talk about?"

"Nothing."

"Okay, sure."

"Because that's all Jack knew about you. But I'd like to find out more."

"Well, it so happens I'm available right now, so ask away."

"What department do you work in?" She was sure he knew and was just making small talk with her but she decided to go along.

"I'm in Men's. Yeah, fun stuff."

Ed snickered and took a swig of his beer.

"Oh, and since you didn't ask, I'm Ed."

"Yeah, I know. I heard Jack say your name."

They were quiet for a while and Mandy was afraid he'd walk away and quickly thought of something else to say. Ed didn't seem to be much of a conversationalist.

"How long have you worked at the Mart?"

"Oh, ah, about a year, year and a half. Yeah, it's okay. Jack is a great boss, no hassles, you know? And Billy, Billy McConnell, have you met him yet, over there on the couch, trying to kiss that girl he's sitting next to?  He's a great guy, a little crazy though. We've got a good thing going working for Jack." Ed laughed as he took another swig.

"No, I haven't met Billy yet. Still feel pretty brand new, you know."

"Yeah, I get that." Quiet set in around them, a little too long, and Mandy burst out the first thing that came into her head.

"So, Ed, what are your plans? Are you going to work at the Mart forever or do you plan on running the place someday or go to college or anything?"

"Wow, you ask a lot of questions."

"Sorry, just making conversation. I didn't mean to be nosy or anything."

"Yeah, well, I kind of felt like I was getting the third degree. You kind of sounded like my mother, 'What are you gonna do with your life, Ed?'" He spoke in a higher voice, his attempt at imitating his mother.

Mandy laughed. That was exactly how everyone imitated their moms, but it sounded so much funnier when guys did it.

"Well, at least I made you laugh." At that moment, Ed reached over and pushed a piece of her hair that had fallen on her face back behind her ear. His hand caressed her face and ran down her arm before pulling away. Then he leaned in and blew lightly into her ear. Mandy giggled and couldn't suppress a shiver.

"Are you cold?"

Mandy smiled nervously and shook her head. She was sure Ed already had an ego the size of a house and didn't want him to know what kind of an effect he had on her.

They walked back into the living room together where the party was heating up. Mandy suddenly wasn't feeling in the party mood but instead wanted to be alone with Ed. Ed seemed to have the same idea.

"Do you have a ride home?"

"Well, I came with Jack and a few others but I don't think they'll be leaving for quite some time. Why, are you offering?"

"I was thinking we could leave now."

"I'm not ready to go home. It's only 8:30, isn't it?" Mandy wasn't picking up on Ed's hint so he spoke a little more bluntly.

"I wasn't planning on taking you home right now. I thought maybe we could go somewhere and be alone, you know? Maybe get a bite to eat."

"Oh, yeah sure, okay, that's fine. We could leave now. I'll just let Jack know."

Ed caught Jack's eye and gave him a nod and a wink. Jack nodded back and smiled at Mandy. She was heading towards him when Ed grabbed her hand and led her to the door.

"We're cool."

Ed had an older model red Chevy Impala convertible with a white top. It was a little chilly tonight so he had the top up. Mandy loved the long front seat and scooted over closer to where Ed sat. He slid in next to her and put his hand on her leg, sliding it up under her skirt.

"Whoa cowboy, not so fast." She slid back over to the passenger side of the front seat and put her seat belt on.

"Okay, okay, you can't be mad at me for trying. You never know."

"What, how easy someone is? I'm not that easy."

Ed felt sheepish and nodding his head, lit another cigarette.

"Gotcha."

Mandy loved how quickly she was able to put him in his place and couldn't help smiling. Fortunately, it was dark out so Ed couldn't see her smile. She couldn't resist teasing him, just a little.

"You can at least buy me dinner first."

Ed smiled and looking over at Mandy, laughed out loud. Mandy laughed along with him, thrilled that they were hitting it off so well. If he only knew; dinner or not, he was getting laid.

They stopped and got take out from McDonalds. Mandy was starving and ordered a Big Mac, fries, and a vanilla shake. Ed ordered two Big Macs, fries, and a coke. Neither wanted to eat in the McDonald's parking lot so Ed drove to Sunset Lake that had lights along the beach area. Even though it was dark out, Mandy preferred the scenic spot to the yellow glow of the McDonald's sign, lighting up the cars in the lot enough to see what everyone was eating. "You really know how to show a girl a nice time." Mandy laughed but then realized it really was perfect.

"But seriously, this is nice. I would prefer this to going to a fancy restaurant. It's really nice here."

"Yeah, I like it here, too. Sometimes I come here when I take a lunch break from work. Kind of restores my soul to look out at the water. It's nicer in late fall, or like this at night, when there aren't many people around. So, glad you like it. And now you know my secret spot."

They were both hungry and finished their sandwiches quickly.  Out of the blue, Ed returned to their conversation at the party and answered some of the questions that were left open. He had been thinking about them and wanted Mandy to know he wasn't just another loser working at the Mart.

"Anyway, I started taking a few classes at Bristol Hill Community College and I'm thinking of transferring them to UNH and getting my Bachelor's degree. I almost have my Associate's degree right now. I have to take about 2 or 3 more classes. In Engineering. So, just wanted you to know that."

Mandy was surprised that he remembered the third degree she was giving him at the party and felt so close to him right at that moment. She resisted the urge to climb onto his lap and kiss him and instead kept her composure, nodding agreement.

"That's great, Ed. You should be proud."

"Yeah, well, I'll be proud when I have that degree. No one in my family has ever gone to college. I'll be the first."

That was it, Mandy couldn't resist. She moved closer to Ed and without warning, wrapped her arms around his neck and kissed him. He responded immediately and, soon enough, they were in the back seat. Most of their clothes came off and within minutes they had consummated the relationship. Mandy was a little disappointed in herself because she had told him she wasn't that easy, and then she was. She also knew that even though they had just met, he was probably already hooked on her and would be back for more. At least she hoped.

She hadn't been the shyest girl in her senior high school class but she also wasn't as experienced as many believed. She just had that grown up look that living in the projects gives most girls. You had to grow up fast or you would be destroyed by the other girls. Like a pack of wolves, they singled out the weak ones and relentlessly abused them until they broke. Breaking them came in many forms; some left school while others cried or walked the other way when they saw any of the in-girls coming their way. Or they befriended someone with some clout, mostly dorky smart guys or one of the jocks, who promised to stand by them. The smart guys were the saviors of the in-girls when they needed to pass a grade so the in-girls left them alone. But that was a rarer situation. Mandy didn't hang with the in-girls; she had that tough girl look about her that said 'don't mess with me' so they left her alone. Over the years she developed a sense of confidence that people often misinterpreted as maturity or thought she was older than her actual age. Only Mandy knew there was a scared child inside, waiting to be rescued.

Ed lit up a cigarette and passed it to Mandy. She took it and then he lit one for himself.

"So, are you working tomorrow? Maybe we can have an encore?" Ed knew he was pushing his luck but he also knew that Mandy had said she wasn't that easy.

"I have to work. What time is it?"

"Yeah, I have to work, too; but we could meet up tomorrow night."

"Look, this was great, but I'm not going to be your fuck buddy. I want something more. I want to go on dates, you know?

"Okay, we can do that. What would you like to do?" He was hoping it was just dinner at McDonald's and then sex in the car. Since they both still lived at home, there wasn't much of a chance that they could get together any place else.

"I don't know, something fun, like going to a museum, or the opera, you know, something classy like that."

Ed looked at her in disbelief. He didn't take her for the classy type who liked to do boring things like go to a museum. And then Mandy burst out laughing.

"You should see the look on your face! You looked positively terrified!" Ed grabbed her and started tickling her which quickly turned into kissing. He felt himself getting turned on again but she pushed him back, and slipping her clothes back on, jumped out of the car and into the front seat.

"I really have to go home now. Come on, put your clothes on."

"Man, oh man, you are a ball buster! Okay, okay, let's go. But think about what I said, about tomorrow."

"Oh, no, I can't. I have my book club." Again, Mandy couldn't keep a straight face and started laughing. This time Ed laughed along with her.

The weeks passed with Ed and Mandy spending more and more time together. Ed started looking for an apartment that he and Mandy could live in. The only requirement for Mandy was, anywhere but the projects. She was hoping for a nice apartment, even in a triple-decker, that had a yard. Someplace where she could plant some flowers. She was sick of the cement walls, stairs, and sidewalks in the projects. Nothing grew in those places, even the residents all seemed lifeless and pale. Mandy needed a new start and a new life to go with her new job.

Six months into their relationship, Mandy was still living at home. They couldn't seem to find a place they could afford and the apartments they could afford were already rented before the people moved out. Ed seemed to be dragging his ass, too, and Mandy was getting impatient with him. They had a few fights, even at work, and got some looks from the customers and other employees. Jack finally pulled them both into the back room and let them know this had to stop.

"You can't hang your dirty laundry out at work. If you want to yell at each other, you have to take it outside. But while you're here, just get along, okay, even if you have to fake it."

Ed and Mandy hung their heads while Jack scolded them. They looked at each other and smiled, knowing that nothing was important except being together. They hugged. Ed slapped Jack's hand on his way back to the floor.

"Thanks, man. We needed that."

"No problem, glad I could help." Jack liked playing the father figure, even though he was only about five years older than Ed.

To make it up to Mandy, Ed rented them a motel room. They had the best sex they had ever had. Ed promised Mandy things were going to get better. He had registered at UMass to get his Bachelor's degree in Engineering and he got in. They celebrated by having an endless night of love-making.

Ed kept his word and found them an apartment in a triple-decker. There was a small yard but also a back porch where Mandy could have planters for flowers. They would be moving in at the end of the month. Mandy was thrilled to be moving out of the apartment she shared with her mom, brothers, and sister. She knew this would cause some tension since she helped out with the boys sometimes. But she had to do what was best for her. And Ed was what she wanted more than anything in the world. It would all work out, she knew it would.

Mandy was never good about breakfast but when she started waking up feeling nauseous, she thought she needed to eat something. That only made her feel worse. She thought it was just nerves since so much was happening with Ed and moving and all these changes happening in her life. She didn't want to worry anyone so decided to go to the clinic to find out why she felt so sick. The news was unexpected but when she thought about it, it couldn't be anything else. She didn't want to tell Ed and kept it to herself for another couple of weeks. She and Ed moved into their apartment, furnishing it with his double bed, a couple of bureaus, a table, and a few chairs from the Goodwill store, and some sheets and towels he took from his parents' home. Mandy didn't have much but her clothes - she had to leave the furniture for Denise. There wasn't a spare anything at her mom's apartment.

One morning as Mandy and Ed were getting ready for work, Ed walked into the bathroom when Mandy was vomiting. He had only ever seen anyone vomit from a hangover and stood looking at Mandy, not sure what to do.

"Are you okay?" He put a hand on her back and handed her a washcloth.

"I'm pregnant." She blurted it out before she could stop herself.

"You're what?" He wasn't sure he heard her correctly. He always used a condom and they had been okay for more than eight months. He wondered how she could be pregnant.

"Pregnant, Ed, I'm pregnant." She stood up, wiping her face with the damp cloth.

"But we used condoms. How is that possible?"

"Because they aren't 100% safe, you know. And then there was that time, remember, in the motel room. How many times did we do it? I don't remember you changing your condom every time."

"Jesus. Jesus, you're right. Fuck, goddamn it. What the fuck! Man, this is going to ruin everything! What am I gonna do? I'm taking classes to get my degree in another month. What am I gonna do with a kid?"

"No, Ed, what are we gonna do. It will be our kid, together? I didn't do this alone!"

"Yeah, no, right baby, I know. I'm sorry. Shit, shit!" He hugged her but she wasn't feeling the love. She gently but firmly pushed him away.

"I'm not giving it up so you better figure out what you want to do, Ed."

"How many months?"

"About three, three and a half now."

"How long have you known?"

"I went to the clinic about a month ago. I couldn't tell you. We were just moving in here. Everything was perfect. I didn't want to ruin anything." Mandy couldn't stop the tears that filled the corners of her eyes and ran down her cheeks. She sat in one of the two kitchen chairs they owned and put her head down on the table. Ed, trying to comfort her, rubbed her back.

"Look, it's okay, we'll work it out. You know, we'll think of something. I don't know, maybe we can get married, you know. How about that? We can get married."

Mandy looked up, her red and tear-smeared face beaming at Ed.

"Is that a proposal?"

"Yeah, sure, that's a proposal." To prove his point Ed dropped on one knee, looked around for something that could substitute for a ring, ripped a ring off an empty beer can sitting on the table and slipped it onto Mandy's finger.

"Will you marry me?"

"Yes!" Mandy laughed, stood up, and hugged Ed, while he laughed and kissed her face and neck all over.

Although they were starting to get their apartment together, they needed everything for a baby now, too. They could go to Goodwill to hopefully find a crib but they needed so much more for the baby from crib sheets to blankets to clothes, it was overwhelming to think about. At least she would breast-feed so the baby food was taken care of, for now. She remembered what her mom went through when her younger brothers were born but it is so much more real when it is your baby.

By the time they had the wedding Mandy was a little over six months pregnant. The wedding was a small one with friends and close family invited. It was held at a Knights of Columbus Hall. Mandy and Ed asked for household items for wedding presents and also baby diapers, clothes, and other nursery items. About 30 people attended the wedding. Denise was her Maid of Honor and Jack was Ed's Best Man. It was a small ceremony but fun. Someone brought a boom box and played a lot of dance music. Mandy was happy to see Betsy and Lewis and was sure they would be the next to marry.  And of course, Chrissy was with Jack. She walked around to all the tables, thanking them for coming and for their gifts. With a baby coming in a couple of months, she didn't know if she would have time to write thank you cards. The wedding invitations had been verbal since they were saving money for the baby.

Mandy was sitting at a table, watching others dance, when she realized she hadn't seen Ed for a while. She looked around the room and then, with the baby pushing on her bladder, headed for the ladies' room. She heard voices in a room next to the ladies' room. She was sure she would find someone in an awkward position and quietly pushed the door open to peek in.

She saw Ginger, a new cashier from the Mart, and standing in front of her with barely room to fit a sheet between them was Ed. He was reaching over to push a piece of hair that had fallen on her face back behind her ear. His hand caressed her face and ran down her arm before pulling away. Then he leaned in and blew in her ear. Ginger blushed and giggled.

# Into the Fire

Chrissy hoped she would get the job at the A-to-Z Mart. She didn't even care what position she got. She had to get out of the house. A senior at English High School, she would only be working nights and weekends, at first. But that would be enough for now. In about a month she would be graduating and working full time and with any luck, she could find a friend at the A-to-Z Mart, they could get an apartment together, and she could move out of the hell hole in the projects that she shared with her parents. Parents. Chrissy was sure they didn't know the first thing about parenting. Her two older brothers had moved out as soon as they had turned sixteen. They both lied about their age and joined the army. Guys could do that and escape whatever prison they grew up in. Tim, who was now 23, lived in Germany. As he once joked, 'the farther away from this dump the better.' Her other brother, Donnie, was 20 and stationed at Fort Dix and was hoping to go to France but was pretty sure he was going to get Korea.

"Commie bastards; the army'll send me where they want. They say, yeah, tell us the top three places you want to go and then they send you where they want. They don't care what you want." Chrissy realized the 'commie bastards' he was talking about were the ones who made the decisions over here as to where he would be stationed.

Both brothers did feel bad about leaving her under the care of their parents. Care. More often it was Chrissy picking her dad up off the floor where he passed out on his way to the bedroom where her mom was also passed out, sometimes on the bed, sometimes on the floor next to the bed. The worst was when one of them headed for the bathroom and after missing the toilet, lay down in their own puke on the floor and slept there. Several times that was the scene that greeted Chrissy first thing in the morning on her way to shower before leaving for school. She was late more times than she could count. She knew her teachers didn't believe her. Or maybe they did since that was the life for many who lived in the projects. Other kids might have covered up for their alcoholic or drug-addicted parents. Chrissy refused to do that. Even though she never talked about her parents and what her life was like, if someone asked, she would tell them the truth. And then change the subject. She didn't want anyone feeling sorry for her. She knew she would be leaving soon. And now that she was sure she would get the job at the A-to-Z Mart, she was more hopeful than ever.

One day after school, on a Thursday afternoon, Chrissy was in her bedroom working on a math problem when the phone rang. She didn't know where her parents were or if either were even home so she went into the kitchen to the wall phone.

"Hello?"

"Hello, is Christine Murphy there?"

"Speaking."

"Yes, Miss Murphy, I'm calling from the A-to-Z Mart. We almost gave up on you. We've called twice already and you have not gotten back to us."

"I'm sorry. I never got the message."

"Oh, I see. Well, fine. This is Ms. Johanna, Accounting Manager, and I'm happy to tell you that you got the job. You will report to me on Saturday, that is in two days, and I will give you your schedule. You can start Saturday, correct?"

"Oh, yes, I can. Thank you."

"Great. I understand here that you can only work evenings and weekends?"

"Yes, I graduate from high school in May and then I can work full time."

"Oh, good. So, come in Saturday to see me and we'll get you set up and you can start working then. Be here a little before 9am, okay?"

"Thank you. Oh, where will I be working?"

"Oh, sure. You will be working for Mr. Highfield in the children's department. Mr. Highfield is the children's department manager."

"Oh, okay, good."

"Okay then, we'll see you Saturday.  Have a nice day now, bye."

Chrissy was so happy. She was beginning to wonder if she didn't get the job since she hadn't heard from them. But, the A-to-Z Mart had called, twice, she just never got the messages. No surprise. If either of her parents wrote it down, they probably were drunk or just forgot they ever even answered the phone. But now, more than ever, she had reason to stay hopeful. She got the job and her next step was to move out in just a few short months.

Chrissy showed up early for her meeting with Ms. Johanna. She filled out all the paper work and then Ms. Johanna brought her over to meet Mr. Highfield. A pleasant man with a round face, a mostly balding head with short, neatly trimmed sides and a few stray hairs on top that looked like a baby's head, and a belly that spilled over the top of his belt. Mr. Highfield had a kind, happy look about him. Chrissy imagined he was a glass half-full kind of person, even if he had a streak of bad luck. She liked him immediately.

"Bill, this is Christine Murphy, your new employee. Christine is starting today so she's all yours. You have any questions, Miss Murphy, I'm sure Bill, um, Mr. Highfield can answer them. Or you can come see me, okay? You have a great day, now, and don't forget to punch out when you leave today."

"Thank you."

"Well, Christine, welcome to the department. Why don't we get you started. Now every day we straighten the shelves and the racks where the clothes are. Just make sure everything looks nice. If packages are opened, put them in the back, you'll see a bin that has opened packages. Once a month we take inventory. And if you ever have any questions, please just ask. Oh, and you can call me Bill."

"Okay, and please, call me Chrissy."

"Chrissy it is."

Bill was very thorough and Chrissy could tell he was proud of his department. For some managers, it was just a job. But for Bill, it was something he was responsible for and he took that responsibility seriously.

Chrissy hoped that getting into this department would also help her come out of her shell. She was always known in high school as 'the quiet one' and 'sweet'. She was okay with that; it was who she was. She really didn't know how to be anything else and was attracted to people who were outgoing and bold.

The first day passed by quickly for Chrissy. She met several people who dropped by just to say 'Hi.' She really liked Betsy, who worked as a cashier. Although Betsy seemed like she was kind of shy herself, her shyness didn't stop her from speaking to Chrissy. Chrissy met her at the snack bar with Micky. She thought they were a couple but then another guy, Lewis, came up behind Betsy and it was clear that he was her boyfriend.  All the employees wore a smock, except the managers, so you mostly knew who was an employee and who was a customer. The bosses wore shirts and ties, usually. Most of the people around the snack bar wore smocks.

Chrissy didn't want to take more than her fifteen minutes and kept checking her watch. After checking for the third time, a guy standing a little away from her and drinking a cup of coffee finally spoke up.

"So, do you have to be somewhere? You've checked your watch about three times since you got here. "

"This is my first week and I don't want to be late from my break."

"Are you afraid they'll fire you your first week here?"

Chrissy smiled. The man smiled back. He had a nice smile. He tapped his fingers on the counter. He probably drank too much coffee. His eyes wandered around the counter as he sipped from his paper cup, always coming back to Chrissy. She smiled again and felt her face warming up.

"No, but I want to make a good first impression."

"Well, you've made one on me, if that counts."

Again, she blushed and looked away, hoping he wouldn't see her red cheeks. When she looked back at him, he had slid over and was standing right beside her. She jumped back.

"Don't worry I won't bite. So, what's your name?" His smile was contagious and Chrissy almost giggled from nervousness. He was so close she could smell him, a clean soap smell, like Irish Spring or maybe Ivory. She liked it.

"Um, Chrissy, my name is um, Chrissy. What's yours?"

"Jack. Jack Donato. If you need anything, Um Chrissy, just come and see me and I'll try to help you.  I manage the hardware department." Another smile, a wink, and then he walked away.

Chrissy couldn't stop smiling as she walked back to the children's department.

Chrissy loved working at the Mart and couldn't believe how nice the people were. There were a few who were grouchy but she stayed clear of them. Jack filled her in on who was friendly and who was not – he had worked there for about three years. But most of them, like Jack, Ed, Bill, Betsy, Micky, Anna, Nick, Lewis and many others, whose names she didn't know yet, were so nice to her. Always a shy girl, Chrissy felt like she was coming out of her shell and knew it was with the help of the friendly people at the Mart.

Graduation was just a few days away and she wondered if there would be anyone there to support her. She could never depend on her parents to be there for her since they were usually both in some state of intoxication. She decided to ask Betsy, who she was becoming good friends with, if she would come to her graduation. Betsy was more than happy to go and said she would borrow her mom's car and pick Chrissy up at her apartment and they could drive there together. But as word got out more people decided they wanted to go, too. Chrissy, despite her shyness or maybe because of it, had made a lot of friends in a short time. If you asked any one of them, they would have said there was a vulnerability about Chrissy that made them want to protect her. Small and waiflike, she also had a heart of gold and didn't have a mean bone in her body. She was kind and friendly to everyone, thankful for her job and for all the kindnesses that were bestowed upon her, never realizing that it was her own personality that was responsible for people behaving in such a caring way towards her.

When Betsy arrived at the apartment where Chrissy lived with her parents, the door was open. She knocked and called for Chrissy but when no one answered, she walked into what she assumed was the living room where a small color TV with a flickering picture sat on a wood crate. She looked around quickly and noticed the shabby furniture in what was probably the living room; a few cigarette burns on the mustard yellow and brown sofa, the recliner that was leaning to the left with either a broken spring or damaged leg, and a kitchen chair with its ripped seat cushion exposing the foam under the red and gray plastic cover. There were papers and cigarette packages balled up on the floor and a number of random pieces of paper on the orange shag rug. Betsy stepped carefully through the room afraid that she might step on something that shouldn't be on the floor and didn't want to be responsible for breaking it. She tiptoed down a short hall briefly thinking that she was illegally entering the apartment, when she started to walk past a room where she heard something that sounded like crying. Betsy opened the door just enough to see inside, and found Chrissy sitting on a bed, tears running down her face. She was dressed in a simple pink shift and beige flats.

"Chrissy, what's wrong?"

"It's my parents. My mother is at the kitchen table, drunk. She doesn't even remember that it's my graduation day. And my dad, he can't even get out of the taxi because he's so drunk."

This was foreign territory to Betsy. Her parents were so loving and she was such an important part of their lives, she couldn't imagine what it must be like to have parents who were drunk all the time and didn't care about you at all. Her heart broke for Chrissy.

"It's okay, Chrissy. You'll have lots of people who love you and care about you at the graduation. Why don't we go now, okay?"

Betsy suddenly and somewhat guiltily realized that she didn't want to spend a moment longer than she had to in this sad apartment. And she wanted Chrissy to be in a better place, too, among friends at her high school graduation. Although Betsy was an only child, she always wanted a little sister and her protective instincts came out when she was around Chrissy.

Chrissy wiped her eyes and got up from the bed. She excused herself and went to the bathroom. When she came out, she had a jacket on and Betsy could see she had reapplied her makeup.

"Let's get out of here."

Chrissy's graduation was typical of all graduations; long and drawn out. You wait while all the names are called until the one name you are waiting for is announced. When Christine Murphy's name was announced, the entire A-to-Z Mart gang stood up and cheered.

"Yeah, Chrissy! Way to go!!" They clapped and whistled loudly causing Chrissy to blush, using her hair to cover her face as she walked up on the stage to receive her high school diploma. But her smile revealed how she really felt about all of her new friends.

She was happy for more than one reason; now she could work full-time and get an apartment. She wanted to move as far away from her parents as she could. She had asked Betsy but she still lived at home with her loving parents. Besides, she was most likely going to move in with Lewis since they were inseparable. She talked to Jack about it since he was a little older. She thought he might know someone at the Mart who was looking for a roommate. She was feeling a strong connection to him but wasn't sure if he was married; he didn't wear a wedding band. Not all guys did which made it difficult to know if you should go out with them or not. She really liked him though and was hoping he would ask her out.

Almost as if he could read her mind, the next time she was on a break at the snack bar with Betsy, Jack came up behind her and whispering in her ear so that she nearly jumped out of her seat, he asked "Can I talk to you for a minute?"

She felt her face heat up and turning to face him, she said "Sure" and got up, waving to Betsy as she walked away.

Chrissy was nervous. She thought he might be asking her out but wasn't sure. Her nervousness turned into a giggle and she let her hair fall from behind her ear, covering half her face.

Jack took her by the hand and led her to the back room in the hardware department. He turned to face Chrissy, holding both of her hands. He reached up and pushed the hair that had fallen onto her face behind her ear. Chrissy shivered when his hand touched her face.

"Okay, now we have a little privacy. So, Chrissy, now that you have graduated and are a real adult, whaddya say we have a date?"

She felt herself blush even brighter than she most likely already was and smiled as large as she could without showing teeth.

"Sure."

"Well, don't be too excited," Jack joked.

"I mean, yes, I would really like that."

"Okay, that's a little better." He laughed. She loved his laugh; it was a little too loud but so real. And happy, he seemed really happy. She wondered why he wasn't married since he was such a catch. Thin and kind of wiry, he was about an average man's height, maybe a little shorter. But Chrissy was only about 5'3" so most people were taller than her. But despite his small size, she liked the way he made her feel: protected and special. She pulled her head out of the clouds and remembered the apartment.

"Oh, yeah, I wanted to ask you if you found anyone who was looking for a roommate? I don't have a car so it has to be near a bus stop or the train."

"I could use a roommate," he said laughing. She wasn't quite sure why he found that funny, but she smiled anyway.

"No, but I'll ask around, okay?" Chrissy nodded and they left the back room.

As she started to walk away, he grabbed her hand and pulled her back. She bumped into him and he put his arm around her waist. She looked up into his deep brown eyes and felt her stomach do a kind of over-easy flop. She knew her face was beet red and she stepped back.

"Wait, we didn't set a date for our date. Are you busy tonight?"

Chrissy was never busy, and almost said that, but she wanted him to think she actually had a social life so she hesitated for a brief moment.

"Oh, um, no, I don't think so. I work until 6."

"Well, so do I. So, how about we leave from here together. We can go to dinner. How does that sound?"

Butterflies took over her insides and she nearly jumped up and down with joy but tried to remain sophisticated or give the appearance of someone who goes on dates all the time. Except for the one or two boys she went out with in high school, and all they wanted to do was find a dark corner at a McDonald's or get into the back seat of the wrecks they called their cars and neck, she hadn't been on a real date.

"Sounds good."

"Ok, I'll come get you when I'm ready to leave."

The three hours seemed to drag until the work day ended. Chrissy took her time punching out and went to the ladies' room to freshen up. But she didn't want to stay in there too long in case Jack went looking for her and couldn't find her. She walked out the door and nearly walked right into him.

"Oh, hi!" Jack grabbed her hand and they went out the back door, through the loading dock area, to the employee parking lot. He didn't speak until they got into his car.

"I have to do something I've wanted to do for a long time." And he leaned over to her side and kissed her hard on the lips. She thought she was going to faint right there in his arms and when he pulled away, she followed.

He smiled and then leaned in and kissed her again.

This time she pulled back.

"Sorry, I couldn't leave you hanging there. It seemed like you wanted more."

Chrissy smiled. "I did."

Jack took that as an invitation and pulled Chrissy to him, kissing her for what seemed like ten minutes. Chrissy started thinking about those boys in the back seats of their cars and quickly pulled away.

Jack picked up on her cue and apologized.

"I'm sorry, it's just that I've wanted to do that since the first time I met you almost three months ago now. I'll try to control myself."

Chrissy was happy he apologized - he sounded so sincere that she wanted to kiss him again. She also decided not to tell him that she felt the same way. This wasn't high school; this was so much better.

They had a nice dinner at Leone's, a little Italian restaurant not too far from where they worked. They were seated in a nice dark corner but they just talked. The only thing that bothered her was that he checked his watch a couple of times. She finally asked him if he was supposed to be somewhere.

Jack laughed. "Well, yeah, I told a friend... anyway, not important."

He seemed a little mysterious and Chrissy waited for more. But Jack wasn't talking anymore and changed the subject. They finished dinner and left.

"So, I'll give you a ride home, okay? Unless there's something else you want to do?" Chrissy was inexperienced in this area but she was pretty sure he was asking her if she wanted to have sex. He was leaving it completely up to her. She really didn't want to go home, she never wanted to go home. And now that she was no longer in school, she had no homework to do and could do what she wanted with her time. She just didn't want to go home.

"I really don't want to go home." She thought she was saying it to herself but then realized she had said it out loud.

"Okay. Where would you like to go?"

They stood outside Jack's car, leaning up against the passenger door. She made a bold move and put her arms around his waist holding him close to her. He wrapped his arms around her and kissed the top of her head.

"Anywhere you want."


It was the kind of place that rented rooms by the hour. Chrissy knew this wasn't a good idea, but for some reason she felt a trust for Jack that she had never felt before. Plus, they worked together and she wasn't leaving her job and she was pretty sure since he had been there a few years that he wasn't going anyplace either. So, if he was a good man, like she was sure he was, he wouldn't just have a one-night stand with her and then risk having to see her at work every day. It would be too uncomfortable for both of them.

He was a tender, caring lover and she wanted to stay in his arms forever. Lying together in the bed she felt his fingers drumming on the mattress, like a nervous habit. He reached over to the nightstand and checked his watch.

"Do you have to be somewhere, Jack?" She was feeling uncomfortable with his nervousness and wanted him to just relax so they could enjoy being together. He let out a sigh and kissed her cheek.

"Yeah, I have a sick cat. I need to take care of him. I've had him a long time and he needs some, ah, medicine and stuff."

She wanted to believe him, but this sure sounded like a fake excuse.

"Well, that is about the worst excuse I've ever heard." She was surprised at her own boldness and giggled.

Jack sat up in bed and started putting his clothes on. Chrissy did the same since it was obvious it was time to leave. She started feeling sick to her stomach, wondering if she had just made a huge mistake by having sex with Jack, which was beginning to feel more and more like a one-night stand.

"Yeah, it is a bad excuse, isn't it. That's because it's a lie. I'm married, Chrissy."

Chrissy stopped dressing and stared at the back of Jack's head. He couldn't even tell her to her face. But then he turned to face her and repeated what he had said. She quickly put the rest of her clothes on and stood at the door, ready to leave. She didn't know what to say. She felt sad and angry at the same time. So, it was like high school, he just wanted to get into her pants. How could she think it was any different? How could she think that just because Jack was a little older that he would be more honest, that he would be different from the boys she had known in high school. She was so naive. She felt so much younger than 18 to fall for all his lies and bullshit. Jack was just better at doing what they did; he was smoother, more polished. He had more experience and everything he said or did to Chrissy, who was so innocent and gullible, was said in such a way to convince her he was sincere. She just wanted to leave, now. And the worst part was, she was going to have to get a new job.

"Can we just go..."

"I'm in love with you, Chrissy."

"What?" Chrissy wasn't sure she had heard him right and sat in the chair next to the door.

"I said, I'm in love with you, Chrissy. I am. Maybe I should have started with that." He smiled weakly.

Tears spilled out of Chrissy's eyes and down her face. She kept her head down, thinking about the words that Jack just spoke to her. She had never heard anyone say those words to her before.

"But your wife, what about your wife?" Of all the people on earth to fall in love with, why did she have to fall for a married guy. She shook her head trying to make sense of what was happening in her life right now. She had just graduated from high school; how could she now be in love with a married man? It seemed like it was happening to someone else. She couldn't believe this was her life now. She just had sex with a married man. She had only had sex one other time and it was awful; the boy was awkward and inexperienced, grabbing and hurting her, in a hurry to get in and get out. This was so much better. Jack was gentle and loving.  She started to feel sick to her stomach. But he said he loved her. She wondered if she should even believe him. He did just have an orgasm – wasn't that what all guys said after they came in you? She also wondered what other secrets he was keeping from her.

"So, what other secrets do you have? Do you have kids?" 'Please say no, please say no' kept running through her head.

"Well, since you asked…"

Chrissy looked at Jack and her mouth dropped open. She searched his face for answers to the many questions filling her head. There were none. How could he? Why would he? And mostly, how many?

"How many?" She continued to look into his eyes that would not look back into hers. Despite her few young years, she knew that meant he was lying. Anyone who was afraid to look into your eyes was avoiding confrontation and didn't want to see the hurt in yours. They were saying what they needed to say to get you off their back. But they couldn't face the hurt they were inflicting on you so looked away and lied.

But Chrissy persisted. She had to know the truth.

"How many, Jack?"

Jack felt the sweat pushing out along his hairline. He wasn't expecting this to all come out at once. He thought he'd have time to slowly fill Chrissy in on the life he lived away from the Mart. He thought he could tell her he loved her and she would wallow in those words for a while. And now he was sweating, he was uncomfortable, and he couldn't look her in the eyes. Now he wanted to run, away from his responsibilities, away from his life. He did care for Chrissy and was pretty sure he loved her. He knew that would soften the blow when he told her he was married. Why the hell he told her, he wasn't sure. Something about her innocence, her shyness. He felt like she had already been hurt too often and he didn't want to be the one hurting her again. He wasn't a monster. He knew innocence when he saw it and also knew about her home life. A part of him just wanted to protect her, to take care of her. And now it was all out. His life was spread out before him and he had to come clean about it. Not only to himself but mostly to Chrissy.

He let out a deep sigh and finally looked into her eyes.

"I have three."

"Three! Oh my God, Jack! Three kids!!! What the hell! How could I get involved with a man who not only is married but also has three kids?! I can't believe it." She sat down in the chair near the door again. Jack knelt on the floor in front of her and took her hands in his.

"Remember what I said. I said I'm in love with you, Chrissy. There really is nothing between Brenda and me anymore. It's over, it's been over for a long time. We've been staying together for the kids, that's all."

Through tears, which ran down her face like a faucet that you can't shut off, Chrissy pulled her hands from Jack's hands and stood up from the chair.

"Isn't that what every guy who cheats on his wife says? 'She doesn't understand me, we don't love each other anymore, it's over.' I thought you were different Jack. But you're not, you're just like every other guy out there."

Chrissy grabbed her purse off the bed and ran out the door. But where would she go and how would she get there? She hadn't thought this out, she just needed to get away. She started to walk. But to where? She didn't want to go back to the apartment from hell where her parents lived. She didn't know what to do. Maybe she could go to a shelter. She needed a friend to share an apartment. She thought of Betsy, maybe she would ask her to share an apartment. All these thoughts ran through her head as she walked, not sure in what direction she was going.

Jack's car pulled up beside her and Jack leaned over and opened the door.

"Come on, Chrissy, get in the car. You can't walk. You don't even know where you are. I'll take you home."

"Home, I don't have a home." Chrissy burst out crying, covering her face with her hands. Jack turned off the car, got out, and pulled her close to him, holding her head against his chest.

"Look, I know you must think I'm scum right now, but I'll make this right. I promise. I'll leave Brenda and you can move in with me. Just give me a little time to get things straightened out. I have to get a few things from home and I'll file for divorce. She can have everything, I don't care. I've been looking for an apartment and I think I've found one. You could move in but it won't be for about a month. Do you think you can wait that long?"

Chrissy started to feel a little hopeful. It sounded like he really was planning to leave his wife if he was looking for an apartment. She was sure he had to be telling the truth.  She raised her head up and looked into Jack's eyes. He looked directly at her, didn't look away, so she knew he was telling the truth.

"Whaddya say? One month?"

She smiled and nodded her head. He kissed her face all over and when his tongue went in her mouth, she felt herself melting into him. All the tension left her body and she wanted him again. He pulled away.

"Oh, man, you drive me crazy. But we really have to go."

The weeks dragged by and Chrissy saw Jack as much as she could, knowing that he also had to spend time at home with his wife and kids as he made plans to move out. Jack got the apartment he had been looking at but couldn't move in for several more weeks. Chrissy spent as little time as possible in the apartment where her parents lived. She dreamed of living with Jack, just the two of them in the apartment, sharing everything, driving to work together, she'd learn how to cook and make him some wonderful Italian meals. She'd buy a cookbook. And they'd buy some new furniture. She knew he didn't make a lot of money and he would probably have child support to pay. But they would do alright now that she was working full-time.

It was about five weeks since the night at the motel when Jack had told Chrissy everything. Chrissy always got to work a little early, mostly to get out of the apartment with her parents but also to get in to see Jack before she had to start work. He was usually in the back office in his department but when she walked in, no one was there. She waited for about ten minutes but he never showed up. It was time to punch in so she left and busied herself with work. Around ten o'clock Betsy came by.

"Want to take a break?"

"Oh, okay, sure." Chrissy truly liked Betsy. She was a genuinely nice person, not like some of the other cashiers who you couldn't trust. They seemed nice to your face but then they would say things behind your back. Some of them gossiped about Betsy since she and Lewis were so tight but she didn't listen to them. She knew Betsy was nice and Lewis, who she didn't know much about, was crazy about Betsy and very protective of her.

They were the only ones at the snack bar and then Ed showed up with Billy. Since Chrissy knew they worked for Jack, she was sure they would know where Jack was.

"Hey, is Jack in yet?"

"No, he's not coming in. Yeah, he called and said he was going to be out for a few days. He didn't say why."

"Do you think he's sick?" Chrissy hoped that was it but was sure it wasn't. She also wished she could be there for him to support him. She couldn't imagine what he was going through with his wife and kids, telling them he was leaving them, that he wanted a divorce. It must be so hard. She wished she could call him.

"It didn't sound like it. I didn't talk to him, the front office let us know, that's all."

"Okay, thanks, Ed."

Chrissy didn't say anything to anyone but her period was a week late. Even though she was the closest to Betsy, she didn't want to say anything to her yet, either. It was probably just stress from everything that was going on with Jack and his leaving his family. It had to be. She wouldn't let herself think of anything else.

Chrissy kept herself busy at work and went out with some people after work whenever anyone asked. She didn't want to go home and didn't want to think about Jack and what he was doing with his family. A few times, when she let her imagination go, she was sure Jack was dumping her, that he left the job and wasn't coming back. That he wasn't leaving his wife and kids and he was just like all the other guys who just wanted a free lay. Then she would snap out of it and remember how he said he loved her and he'd found an apartment and knew she was wrong to think such awful things about him and she would be overwhelmed with love for him.

The weekend came and went and now Chrissy's period was two weeks overdue. She thought she should take a pregnancy test, just to rule that out. She bought one and that night at home, she took the test. The color was faint but it was definitely blue. She sat on the floor in the bathroom and feeling more alone than she had ever felt in her life, she cried. All the dreams she had of living a perfect life with Jack were over. No driving into work together, no buying nice furniture. Nothing. Between his child support and her new baby there would be nothing left. And then she would only be able to work for a short time and then she'd have the baby. It would work out, it had to. She knew Jack would take care of everything even though he now had four kids but he would just have to take care of her and their baby. They could still have a wonderful life together, just the three of them. Anything would be better than the life she'd had with her parents.

On Wednesday of the next week Chrissy was walking into the A-to-Z Mart when Jack drove up to the front door and caught her before she went inside.

"Hey Chrissy, come here. Get in the car, I need to talk to you."

She didn't like the way he said that he needed to talk to her and a feeling of dread came over her. She sat in the front seat and he drove to the far end of the parking lot and turned off the car.

"First, I need to do this." He pulled her to him and kissed her. She started to giggle and kissed him back.

"I missed you." Chrissy sighed when he said that and everything was instantly better.

"I missed you, too. So much. Jack, what's going on? Why were you out so many days? Were you sick?"

"No, no, not sick. Just...working on things, you know. Lot of stuff to take care of and divorce is kind of a big deal. Things change, lots of things change. Lots of things."

"Jack what are you saying?" Chrissy giggled, mostly because Jack was still talking about divorce, he did still love her and she was happier than she could possibly imagine ever being. But also, because he wasn't really saying anything. She smiled at him, waiting for more details.

Jack looked back at her, not smiling, not laughing. He looked serious and not happy. Chrissy's heart sank. She couldn't imagine what might have happened.

"Did you get the apartment; can we move in now?"

"Yes, yes, we've got the apartment. We can move in this weekend. Or we don't take the apartment. You move into my house." He looked into her eyes. She knew he was waiting for a reaction. But she didn't know what he meant. Did he think she would move in with his wife and kids? That was what it sounded like. That was plain crazy and never going to happen.

"Jack, what are you saying? Move into your house? What do you mean? I'm not living with you, your wife, and kids. Who do you think I am? I can only imagine that she hates you for asking for a divorce and leaving her with three kids. But how can I fit into this? This is sounding crazy to me!"

"She left me, Chrissy."

"Oh, well, that's okay then, right? So, you have a house? Then we can live there, that's even better."

"No, you don't understand. Brenda left me... with the kids."

Jack was right. Chrissy didn't understand what he was saying. How could a mother leave her kids? And then she thought about her own mother, who at that moment was probably passed out on the kitchen floor, drunk, possibly choking on her own vomit. She didn't know where Chrissy was and she didn't care. Her mother didn't even know that Chrissy had a job, that she'd had sex with a married man, and that she was now pregnant, at 18, with that man's baby. Her mother didn't know any of this about her and Chrissy was positive her mother didn't care. Suddenly Brenda leaving her three kids behind and moving on to a different life wasn't a surprise to Chrissy. You never know what a mother will do if she believes she has nothing to live for.  For some women, if the man they thought they'd grow old with doesn't love them anymore and leaves them for another woman, that's the end of their world. Chrissy could understand how Brenda probably just wanted to run away and thought she might do the same thing.

"Chrissy, did you hear what I said?"

"Yes, I heard you. What does that mean, Jack, for us? Is there still an 'us'?"

"Yes, of course, of course there is. Like I said, you can come live in my house now. You don't have to work if you don't want to, you can stay home now. But if you still want to work here, you can work here. That's okay, too. I'm sure we can use the money. But it will be great Chrissy. You'll love my kids, they're good kids, most of the time. The oldest, Jack Jr., is 11 but very mature for his age. And the next is Terri, she's 9. Then there is the youngest, another girl, Mindy, she's 4 1/2. Great kids."  Chrissy knew he was going for the hard sell. He stopped talking and watched Chrissy closely. She felt the color draining from her face and her vision started to blur. She wanted to lie down. Instead, she opened the car door just in time and threw up.

"Jesus, Chrissy, are you okay? Did you eat yet? Why don't we go inside and get you something to eat." Jack pulled the car into a parking place closer to the front door. Jack opened his car door and got out, going over to Chrissy's side of the car, but Chrissy didn't move. Instead, she sat in the seat, all her thoughts of the wonderful life they would have together were melting away. How could her life change so fast and go from wonderful to the worst possible situation? The tears welled up in the corners of her eyes and one by one, ran down her cheeks, into her mouth, falling from her chin and into her hands that were folded on her lap. She sat motionless, not sobbing, but still with the tears flowing out of her. Jack crouched down to Chrissy's level and took her hands in his. He brought them to his mouth and kissed them.

"Look, Babe, I know this isn't how you imagined we would start our lives together, but it will get better, I promise. And the kids, the kids are great. They won't be a problem. They'll love you, I just…"

"I'm pregnant, Jack."

The next words Jack planned to say got stuck in his throat. He wasn't even sure he heard her correctly. He needed to hear what she said again.

"You're what?"

"I'm pregnant, Jack! pregnant!!! That will make 4, 4 kids under the age of 11!"

"Well, actually, Jack Jr. is 11 and will …"

"Jack! What the fuck, Jack! I'm 18 and I'm going to have 4 kids to take care of? I can't do this. I can't!!"

She wanted to go running and screaming down the street. But where would she go? She would have to end up somewhere. And right now, she felt like she didn't have a home, not with her parents, not with Jack. She had no place to go. No one else who cared about her. She had always felt alone but now, this was a different kind of alone. She felt it deep inside her. And then she remembered the baby. This baby would be hers. She would finally have someone, someone who cared about her and someone she cared about more than anyone else in the world. Finally.

The tears stopped, she sat up straight, and took Jack's hand as she got out of his car and walked towards the doors of the A-to-Z Mart.

# Hard Knocks

From day one, Nick knew this was the perfect cover. It was someplace where he could come and go and no one would question his moves. No one cared. There was so much day-to-day drama, so many people; between the employees and the customers, no one would pay any attention to him. It was the ideal situation. He actually enjoyed getting up for work every day - it was one place where he could relax without any concern that he might get a visit from the police, or worse. And Nick knew first-hand how much worse it could be. He rubbed his left side where a scar, left over from a bullet that had gone right through his body, served as a daily reminder of the many close calls he had survived over the years. But Nick wasn't the type to dwell on the past. He lived one day at a time. A survivor, he had no expectations of his fellow man. No one he would rely on. No one he could call about a job that had gone bad, if he ever had one of those. But so far, they all went exactly to plan so he had no need to call anyone. Nick was a loner and he liked his solitary life. It suited him. Or, was it what his life had become? He couldn't remember which came first.

There were times he would think about his life before he enlisted with the Marines. He had a girl, Stephanie. He was pretty sure he loved her. Or it was the closest he ever came to feeling love. She said she would wait, but she didn't. And by the time he got out of the Marines, he didn't care. He was a military man - or at least some semblance of one - after living the life of a Marine for six years.

So many memories he wished he could erase. Like the time he had hit that dog that ran out in front of his car. Nick swerved to miss it but it seemed to run right into the direction he swerved. The dog was dead before he jumped out of his car. And then there was the little girl who came running over to see her dog, Toby, lying there, blood splattered all over Toby, the road, and the front of Nick's car. He'll never forget her scream, how she dropped to her knees and put her head on Toby's still-warm chest, wrapping her arms around him, never caring about the blood that covered Toby and now covered her. The girl's mother came running over and looked at her daughter hugging her dog and then looked at Nick. Nick couldn't apologize enough and felt his own tears spill out and down his cheeks. The woman saw this and touched Nick's hand that covered his face, letting him know she understood and didn't blame him. She saw that his pain was genuine. He never knew when this memory would find its way to his consciousness and pull his heart up into his throat, nearly choking him. He loved dogs and he always pictured Grover, his dog and his best friend from the time he was seven until he was seventeen, lying there in the street.

Now Nick just lived day-to-day. And he was fine with that. Sometimes a pretty girl would give him a look or a smile but he wanted to keep his life as simple as possible. It was for the best. He wouldn't have to lie to anyone about anything. It was all his secret.

Nick walked through the front door and headed to the back left corner of the store. The Sporting Goods sign hung above the aisles so you could see it, and the other department signs, from wherever you were in the store. Nick had to smile every time he looked at the sign. 'Sporting Goods' meant so many different things to people. For some it was where they went to buy supplies for baseball, football, or golf. Some came looking for weights and workout equipment. And then there were others who wanted to buy a gun or a rifle. What was their sport? Hunting animals, mostly. For Nick it was hunting men. Of course, not just any men. Nick hunted bad men, really bad men. At least that was what he let himself believe. Although a couple of contracts had initially been for the government, it didn't take him long to realize he wasn't always killing the bad guy. He was just killing the guy the government couldn't control and so they wanted him dead. They believed that was easier than trying to negotiate or reason with their targets. But they didn't want to let Nick go because he was an expert shot, never missed his target, and left no traces behind. A true professional. So, one day Nick just left and tried his best to disappear into an ordinary, everyday, nobody kind of existence working a variety of different jobs, like this one. He knew they were trying to find him and would send local cops looking for him whenever they thought they'd tracked him down living in a certain area of the country. But he always got out because they couldn't hold him. They never had anything on him. It was all part of the game the government was playing to try to get him back.

But he needed to eat and the pay these minimum wage jobs afforded was barely enough to cover his rent. People living the seedier side of life needed favors. It was all very neat and clean. They advertised in the Want Ads looking for 'the Pole'. He had plenty of time to research the target he was supposed to eliminate and he could decide if he wanted the job or not. If it looked to him like the target didn't deserve to die, that it was just a grudge killing, he was out. He didn't respond to the ad and as far as he was concerned, that was the end of it.

Not the kind of life most people would choose, but he wasn't most people. Nick knew his special skill, that of an assassin, was a rare gift and he never took it for granted or misused it. His fists usually stopped the common meathead in a bar who saw Nick's muscles and wanted to impress a date or prove to himself he was a man by starting a fight with Nick. Nick did his best not to hurt these poor dumb slobs and would only break one finger when he could easily have broken their entire hand or arm. That was usually enough to discourage even the most dull-witted among them. But other than for business, he never used any of his tools-of-the-trade on a regular citizen. There were too many people who would be able to identify him and that would be playing right into the government's hands. He wasn't that naive. Nick was even pretty sure they set up these bastards to challenge him just to see if he would use his tools and then they could arrest him and force him back into his role of government assassin.

Nick whistled while he straightened the boxing gloves and weight belts. He needed to order more large and x-large belts. He made a mental note. He also noticed the shelves were getting low on Top Flite golf balls. It was a great buy; 15 for $15, a buck a ball. He never played golf but he knew a few guys who played and they said Top Flite was one of the best, cheap golf balls around.

"Hi Nick. What's new?" It was one of the cashiers, Kathy. He turned to wave. She was trouble.  Nick could spot them a mile away. He knew she was married but she flirted with all the guys in the store. It didn't matter to her if they were married or not. He was pretty sure she and Joe, the jock who had worked in the warehouse, screwed around.  Nick was a one-woman guy and didn't respect others who didn't respect marriage. Especially if kids were involved; the innocent ones always got hurt. It wasn't their fault they were born to asshole parents.

Nick stopped when he saw Betsy walk by with Kathy. He liked Betsy; she was sweet and innocent, that was his type. He had seen her with Lewis so figured she wasn't available but he could hope. Although deep down he knew he was better off living the life of a loner – it was better for all involved.

"Hi Betsy." He smiled. She blushed and waved, smiling back at Nick. He sighed and then returned to straightening the shelves. He felt a hand move up his back and fingers tickled the back of his neck. Betsy? He hoped but turning he saw Kathy inches from his face.

"What's up, Kathy?"

"You, I hope. Ha! Hey Nick, a few of us are going to a party tomorrow night. Thought you might like to join us? I could use a ride, too, if you can make it."

She rubbed her hand down his chest and was working her way down when he grabbed her hand.

"I don't know, I might be busy. Where is it?"

Her eyes continued to roam all over his chest and down his arms. He hated the fact that she could turn him on. He turned to Betsy who was obviously embarrassed by Kathy's blatant sexual touching.  She was looking towards the back of the store.

"I'm going to take my break, Kathy.  I'll meet you at the snack bar." Betsy looked quickly at Nick, smiled briefly, and walked away.

"Yeah, yeah, okay. Miss perfectly politically correct. Whaddya say, Nick? Can you give me a ride?" He knew what she meant by ride and wasn't falling for it.

"Like I said, I might be busy. Just tell me where it is and I might go. But I can't commit right now so you'll have to get a ride from someone else. Maybe your husband will take you, why don't you bring him, Kathy?"

Kathy pouted and stuck her tongue out at Nick.

"The party is at Jack's. He just got a new apartment, with Chrissy, I think. I'll let you know the address before I leave. Or you can just ask Jack."

"Wait, Jack, with Chrissy? Isn't Jack married?"

"You don't know anything. He's been bopping her for a while, well, a few weeks anyway. And I think he's leaving his wife, too."

Nick shook his head. Kathy started to walk away.

"Wait, is Betsy going?"

"You really don't know anything, do you. You go near her and Lewis will kill you. But if you want to take your chances, go right ahead. You know, I don't get you. You go for the ice princess who is so tight with Lewis you can't get a stick of gum between them. Me? I'm a sure thing, but you turn me down."

"What can I say, you aren't my type, Kathy. I'm a one-woman kinda guy."

"Well, I'm one woman, but probably more woman than you can handle." She laughed and walked away.

"Yup, you're probably right." And Nick went back to taking inventory.

Jack walked up behind Nick, who was sipping a coffee at the snack bar, and gave him a whack on the back. Nick turned towards Jack and nodded.

"So, what's this I hear you're having a party tomorrow night? And you're living in a new apartment?" He decided not to add 'with Chrissy' and would let Jack fill in that blank if he cared to share that tidbit. Nick knew marriage was tough and it didn't always work out between people, but he thought people should be fair to each other and instead of making each other miserable, just call it quits. He also knew it had to be a lot tougher with kids and he was pretty sure Jack had a kid or two. He hoped Jack had told Chrissy about the kids, not that any of this was her fault since she had just graduated high school and was the picture of innocence. Jack was a player and if he got Chrissy into bed, which if they were living together it was obvious that he had, he was the one in charge and she was just following along like a lamb to the slaughter.

"Yeah, I am. Can you make it?"

"I might be able to, I have to check a few things first." He recently saw an ad in the paper for 'the Pole' but didn't have the details on this latest potential target.

"Cool, yeah, it's a small place but it has a porch on the back, a couple of 20-somethings live downstairs so they shouldn't have a problem with the new guy having a party. And I have no idea who lives on the first floor, it might be empty." He wrote down the address on a piece of napkin and slid it over to Nick.

"So, you living there alone?" Jack wasn't volunteering any information so Nick decided to dive right in. It was unlike him since he didn't like to get involved in anyone's business. But something about this place, about the anonymity of working here with people who had so many problems, the dysfunctional makeup of the employees got through to him and he could feel something bordering on love developing for many of them. Most of the time he either wanted to laugh or cry at their situations and the choices they had made in their lives.

Jack laughed a little.

"Well, not really."

"You're married, right? Got kids?"

"Yup, married, for now. That probably won't last much longer, though. So, see you tomorrow night, maybe?" And Jack quickly walked away.

Nick wasn't sure why Jack was trying to keep so quiet since everyone would find out tomorrow that he was living with Chrissy.

The day passed as it usually did, helping customers and stocking shelves. He also spent a lot of time chatting with customers. Jim, the store manager liked to hang out with Nick, too. Nick wasn't sure why but the guy told him everything. There were a couple of assistant managers, also, but they weren't as friendly. One in particular stayed clear of him and would just occasionally look in Nick's direction. Nick thought the guy might be afraid of him.

When the day ended, Nick punched out and stopped at Millie's Diner for a bite to eat. Sometimes he cooked something for himself, but mostly he just had a burger or meatloaf from the diner. The food was pretty good and he felt like he was having a home-cooked meal. He picked up the paper and looked at the want ads section. He had researched the current client and decided he was worthy of a bullet to the head. He had responded to the ad and the next step was receiving the money; he didn't do anything until the money was in his hands. When his fee was paid in full, which he required, he was good to go. Living within driving distance of a major city afforded him endless customers. And when he felt like the feds were closing in, he packed up and left the area, blending into a new town with another new low-paying job. He really hoped that didn't happen here for a while; he kind of liked this place.

The next morning, having checked out the target and having received payment in full from his latest client, he decided he would pay a visit to the target, do the job, then go to the party at Jack's that night. He liked having an alibi even though he usually didn't need one. No one was looking for him, yet.

The party at Jack's new place was typical - everyone was drinking. If they were a rowdy crowd, any one of these guys could find a reason to swing a left hook at the guy beside him. That usually brought the cops. For some reason this party made Nick think of the joke about hockey games: there was a fight and a hockey game broke out.

Nick looked around and saw that the party was mostly A-to-Z Mart people. He saw a few of the girls sitting on the couch, Betsy among them. He got a beer and walked over to the couch.

"Hi Betsy, how are you? Nice to see you here." He looked around and was surprised not to see Lewis nearby.

Betsy gave a little nod and blushed. Adorable, thought Nick.

"So, are Jack's kids here, too?"

"No, I think I heard Chrissy say something about them staying with their grandmother for a few days."

Suddenly he felt someone rubbing his back. He was looking at Betsy and couldn't help but feel himself getting turned on. The hands moved down his arms and pulling herself around and pressing into him, was Kathy. Nick backed away.

"Kathy, what's up?"

"I'd say you were!" Kathy laughed and took a swig of her beer. Nick realized she would always respond that way so he made a mental note to use a different line. Although he was pretty sure Kathy could turn the most innocent comment into something sexual.

"So, did you bring your husband tonight?"

"Don't be ridiculous. Why would I bring him?"

"Because he's your husband. You need another reason?"

"Yeah, I do. Let's talk about something else. Or we could do something else. You don't want that hard on to go to waste, do you Nick?" Kathy laughed; a drunken, high-pitched, almost hysterical laugh.

Nick shook his head, smiled at Betsy, who was blushing a bright shade of red, and walked away.

He found Jack talking to someone who, as far as Nick knew, was not from the Mart. He decided to join their conversation. Jack seemed to be getting a little over-excited and, if anything, maybe Nick could calm him down. But Nick had no idea how many beers Jack had finished by the time he had arrived at just after 10pm.

"The Marines, they're the guys. They do all the hard fighting. That's why they have to be the toughest. No one trains like the Marines do." Jack was adamant in his conviction. Nick was pretty sure Jack had never seen combat.

"No way man, the combat guys are the army. They fight harder than anybody. The Marines are a bunch of sissies." The guy took a swig of his beer and spit it out in Jack's face.

Something went off in Nick's brain like a rocket and everything went red. He didn't know what happened until after it was over and Jack was pulling him to the front door. He turned to see the guy who had been talking to Jack lying on the floor, blood smeared all over his face.

"Come on Nick, just get out of here. We'll take care of this. It'll be okay. Just go."

Nick looked at Betsy standing with the other girls watching Jack lead Nick out the door. Her face was full of horror as she put her hand to her mouth.

"We'll see you at work tomorrow, okay? Don't worry, everything will be fine." Jack shut the door behind Nick and shouted for Chrissy to bring him a wet towel.

Nick stood on the sidewalk in front of the triple-decker of Jack's new apartment. He couldn't have been there 10 minutes. The words 'what happened' kept playing in his head, over and over. It was as if he had blacked out. Not the first time that this had happened but it came on him so fast. He sat down on the steps but then decided he should just leave in case the cops showed up. He sat in his car, thinking about the look on Betsy's face, wondering what she must think of him now. A monster would be one word she might use. She looked terrified. He was a scary guy to a lot of people, he knew that. But he never wanted to scare Betsy.

The next day at the A-to-Z Mart was quiet. Nick went to his department without seeing anyone. He kept busy the entire day not even taking a break. No one stopped by to say hello and he was fine with that. He looked for Betsy a couple of times and saw her once but she was walking so close to Lewis it was difficult to tell there was more than one person.

The next day Jack came by and gave him an update about the guy he had hit at the party.

"Hey Nick, so the guy is still in the hospital but he should be getting out tomorrow, that's what we heard. There's no brain damage. The story is, the guy was so drunk he fell down and hit his head. Fortunately, he had a lot of alcohol in him so they're buying it. The only thing is, I'll be seeing him because he's one of my new neighbors, the guy lives on the first floor. Brian, I think his name is, or Dylan, I don't remember. Hopefully he won't remember anything and our story will stick. Anyway, just lay low for a while, okay?" And he walked away.

"Yeah, okay, thanks Jack."

He had put the guy in the hospital! What the fuck! He couldn't believe it. He knew his punches could be deadly but he had never really hit a regular guy before. Something in him snapped and it frightened him a little to think about it. He felt out of control. Nick was always in control and wondered how this could have happened. He had put himself in a dangerous position. The cops were involved and they might be looking for him, especially if the guy, Brian or Dylan, remembered what had really happened. He didn't want to leave but he knew it was time. He couldn't let this one stupid incident put him in jail.

Nick was planning his exit and how to tie up any loose ends when the store manager, Jim Roldark, came around the corner followed by two plainclothes cops. No badges were visible but Nick could spot them a mile away.

"Nick, these two gentlemen would like to have a few words with you." Jim wished he could have warned Nick they were coming but the guys had walked into his office and didn't give him a minute to catch his breath and then they had escorted Mr. Roldark down to Nick's department.

"You're welcome to use my office to talk with Nick." Jim was hoping to find out a little about what was going on. The two men turned to Jim and made it clear they were done with him.

"We're all set, thank you Mr. Roldark but we won't be needing your services any longer." Nick came out from behind the counter and fell in line between the two men.

Nick was put in the back seat of a black sedan. The two guys got into the front seat. One of the guys, the older of the two, turned in his seat and faced Nick.

"Are you familiar with someone known as 'The Pole'?"

Nick didn't blink an eye and stared back at the cop.

"The Pole? No sir, I am not."

Nick knew how these interrogations worked. He kept his cool and only answered the questions, not volunteering any information that might incriminate him.

The older guy looked at the younger one in the driver's seat. They seemed to exchange a look. Nick kept his eyes on the older one who was obviously in charge. They were quiet while the older cop took some notes then he turned back to Nick, as if remembering that he was still in the back seat.

"Okay, you can go."

As Betsy and Kathy and a few others watched him walk back to his department, Nick smiled.

"Mistaken identity," was all he said. He and Jim exchanged a nod.

The next day Nick packed up his few belongings and drove south.

# Wrong Place

The day started early for Micky. At sixteen, he was the self-appointed head of the household.

"Don't take on that burden, Micky. You need to finish school." His mom tried her best to reason with the boy. But he wouldn't hear it.

"Who'll take care of you and the kids? I'm the oldest, it has to be me. I'm fine. I make good money. We'll be fine. I don't need the diploma. I have a job."

"A mechanic? That's good money? You'll make better money if you stay in school. We can get by on just my salary."

"No, we can't. I know what you make, ma. You work for shit. I'm not talking about this anymore. I'm done. This is what I'm doing. This is what I have to do. I'm taking care of my family."

It always ended the same way with Micky walking out and slamming the door behind him. Everyone slammed doors in the projects because everyone was angry when they left their apartment. Angry because they couldn't pay the rent, couldn't buy new clothes, couldn't afford enough food to feed their families. The hallway's yellow-tiled walls, scarred with paint-smeared graffiti, vomit, indistinguishable particles that were most likely a combination of skin and blood from dirt-smeared hands, blurred whatever clean spots remained. Old newspapers, store flyers, and cigarette butts lined the floors and scrambled along behind you, looking for a way out.

Micky reached into his shirt pocket and took out a pack of Marlboros. He stopped for a second to light the cigarette, throwing the match to the ground. He sucked in the smoke, long and hard. That first drag, that first precious drag and suddenly everything was right with the world. It was a simple action but sometimes that was all you needed to make things right, something simple.

He hopped into his Chevy and drove the couple of miles to the Mart. He was early, but he always got there early, putting in extra hours whenever he could. And they let him. He was becoming a skilled mechanic at a young age.

"You're a natural, Micky". His boss, Carl, let him know he was doing a good job. Carl had taught Micky everything he knew. He watched out for the kid, too. He knew Micky didn't have a dad and tried to steer him in the right direction. Micky sometimes hung out with a couple of bad seeds who stole parts off of parked cars. Carl warned him that he was looking for trouble; but like a lot of kids Micky's age, he thought he was immortal and above the law.

"What's the worst that could happen", Micky asked. "What, they send me to reform school or something? You know me Carl, I'm good. I won't get caught. I promise."

Carl would just shake his head at the stupidity and naivety of youth. "I hope you're right, Micky."

Micky knew Carl was concerned about him and appreciated these 'dad' talks. Micky missed having a dad since his walked out on his mom and the family three years ago. It was hard but living in the projects is hard no matter what. His dad leaving didn't change their living situation. Money just became a little tighter but they were still managing, barely. Plus, with his dad out of the picture none of the money was being pissed away on the booze his dad always managed to have around. Sure, he brought in a paycheck, as insignificant as it was, but his dad would often take something for himself at the expense of buying the basics for the three little ones. Micky didn't care so much about himself having to do with less, but he hated seeing his two sisters and baby brother crying because they were hungry.

Micky let himself into the automotive department and changed into his work clothes. It was 7:20am and the store didn't officially open until 9am. Micky found this time to be his most productive with no customers nagging him to fix their car first, they had to get to work, what is taking so long, you said it would take only half a day, etc., etc. But they forgot to mention that along with the new water pump they also needed their brakes done, both front and rear, because their car wouldn't pass inspection otherwise.

Micky was just finishing up replacing a busted muffler when Carl showed up.

"Hey, kid, how's it going?"

"Oh, it's going."

"Is that the muffler job?"

"Yep, almost done. What's on for today?"

"We got a couple inspections that set up appointments for this afternoon, should take about ten minutes. And we have two pickups coming in for new tires, 4 all-weather radials each, top of the line."

"Wow, must be nice. Anything else? I could use a challenge."

"Hmm, let me see. You wouldn't be interested in rebuilding an engine, would you?"

Micky stopped what he was doing and looked up at Carl.

"Are you serious?"

"I'm serious. But nah, I didn't think you'd be interested so I told them we'd have to think about it. Or maybe ask someone else, you know I have a buddy who could use the work..." Micky wouldn't let him finish.

"Come on, don't fuck with me. You know I would love that job."

Carl couldn't keep from laughing, but he tried and held it in as long as he could.

"Man, you should see your face."

"Very funny, so do I have the job or are you gonna keep fucking with me?"

"Yup, yup, you got the job. But you'll need some help. And this isn't a regular job, this is on the side. It's for a buddy of mine. We'll have to do it after hours. We can use the equipment here and the tools but it's strictly under the table so don't talk to anyone about it. Okay? If the boss finds out we're screwed."

"You got it."

Micky didn't get out of the garage much but when he did, mostly to buy another pack of cigarettes or a soda, he would stop by to talk to one of the newer cashiers, Betsy. He knew she'd started dating Lewis but he felt a big brother-like responsibility to her. He'd rescued her a couple of times from Joe, who had been a slime ball and couldn't be trusted. Micky thought she was pretty and sweet and had an innocence about her that made her attractive that she didn't even realize. Micky knew she wasn't interested in him 'in that way' but he would settle for what he could get, and the big brother role suited him just fine. More than anything, he just felt protective of her. And she seemed to gravitate towards him when several of them went out after work. He was pretty sure she felt safe with him and that pleased him.

He found her at her register, ringing out a few people. It was a slow morning on the floor. Coming to the end of summer was a strange time at the Mart. Sometimes it was like a ghost town in the place, other times it was booming and you'd think it was the week before Christmas. Of course, August and September were times when people were looking for the back-to-school sales so business picked up for everyone.

"Hey Betsy, wanna take a break?"

"Oh, hi Micky." She started searching the floor and he knew she was looking for Lewis. Micky wasn't sure if their relationship was healthy – it seemed as if she was becoming completely dependent on him and was unable to do anything without first checking with Lewis. He pretended to search the floor, too.

"What are you doing, silly?"

"I'm helping you look for Lewis. Do you think he will let you take a break with me?"

Betsy smoothed her hand over her hair, flipping it over her shoulder. She stood a little taller and pretended like she didn't know what he was talking about.

"I was looking for customers, but okay, we can go now." She locked her cash drawer, turned off her light, and walked around her register to join Micky. Two other cashiers were available and Betsy waved to one of them signaling she was taking a break.

They walked to the Snack Bar at the back of the store and sat on a couple of stools. Betsy ordered a seltzer with lime and Micky got a Coke. They chit-chatted and in a few short minutes, Lewis came up behind them and, putting his hands on Betsy's shoulders, kissed the top of her head. She jumped and tensed for a second. When she turned and saw Lewis, she gave him a wide smile and visibly relaxed. Micky also noticed that her face turned a full shade of dark pink.

"You taking care of my girl, Micky?"

"Hey Lewis, I'm trying. But I don't think she needs me to take care of her. She's got you." Lewis extended a hand to Micky and stared into Micky's eyes like a dog challenging a rival, until Micky started to turn away, without taking Lewis' hand. Lewis gave Micky a swift slap on the back instead, just his way of saying 'back off'.

"Just kidding Lewis. Relax." And he continued to drink his Coke.

Lewis turned his attention back to Betsy.

"I just saw you sitting here and had to stop by to say hi. Are we going to dinner tonight or do you want to try my pitiful cooking?"

"Oh, we've been invited to dine with my parents tonight. Is that okay?"

"Sure, as long as I don't have to cook. So, I'll see you at your house then? Right after work? I have an errand to run. And you have your car, right?"

"Yup, I'm all set. I'll see you at my house, around 6."

Lewis gave Micky a wink and walked away. Micky liked Lewis and didn't really feel like he was a threat but there was something about him that made Micky a little uneasy. He knew Lewis was crazy about Betsy and didn't think he would ever hurt her. That wasn't it. There was something else. Something animal, instinctive, like a wildcat that will kill to protect its cubs.

Micky walked Betsy back to her register and then back to the automotive department. He was feeling an uneasiness about a job he was in on. It was supposed to be an easy job, a quick get-in-and-get-out, but he wasn't entirely sure about the guys he would be pulling the job with since he didn't know if he could trust them or if they would have his back. The job was tonight and Micky hadn't told Carl about this one. He knew Carl wouldn't approve and Micky just wanted to get it done. He wasn't even sure if he would tell Carl about it tomorrow. He just wanted it to be over. But it would bring him some big bucks, which Micky needed right now. He knew the rent was coming up and his mom was having a tough time making ends meet. Plus, the kids needed shoes and his sisters some new dresses, his brother some pants, and maybe a nice dress for his mom. He grabbed a hammer and hit the already dented fender that he was replacing on a Buick. The car had just come in, the result of driving too close to the car in front of it, and the Buick's owner was a big deal, a friend of some politician. Somehow, he got the state to pay for it. Micky didn't care, it was a job and he got paid. What burned him was that the people who already had everything seemed to be the ones who always got more while the ones who were struggling just seemed to dig themselves deeper and deeper into debt. He was happy to have a fender to smash up and hit it harder each time until the piece fell to the floor.

Carl, who was talking to a customer, turned to watch Micky as he lifted the hammer again and again bringing it down on the fender. He didn't say anything, but when Micky was done, Carl glared at him for a few seconds and then went back to talking to the customer. Micky threw the hammer back into the tool box and set about replacing the now severely dented fender with the new one.

Micky felt some of the tension leave his body.

On his way home, Micky couldn't think of anything but this job he was going to pull off. He had that uneasy feeling again, but he thought it was probably just brought on by the nagging thought of never having enough money that had consumed him while he was making scrap metal out of the Buick's fender. He thought he had gotten it all out but the feeling lingered.

He stopped at McDonald's for a quick bite. He knew he should have gone home to check on his mom but he didn't want to face her and then have to lie about where he was going when he went out after dinner. This was easier. He took his time eating, reading the newspaper and working on the crossword puzzle while he killed some time. At ten to eight, he left McDonald's and drove to the warehouse where he was meeting the other two guys doing the job with him. He had worked on only one other job with Tony and had never met the other guy. Tony told him the guy's name and he tried to remember it. Bugsy, Dougy, Lumpy? Something like that. A name like his, with an 'e' sound on the end. Like when you are a little kid before you drop the 'e' sound and after when you are now officially a grown-up. Like he might change his name to Mick someday. So, Bugsy would be Bug or Bugs?

Micky pulled around to the back of the warehouse. It was in a mostly deserted neighborhood where the houses all had broken windows. He figured they were probably occupied by heroin addicts - the state left them alone in their misery since the landlords didn't care about the houses and no one who was actually working lived in them. The landlords were just letting them fall apart. Probably waiting to tear them down to build some fancy apartments where they would charge beaucoup bucks for rent. Micky got out of his car and threw his cigarette to the ground. Two dark shadows moved out from behind the building and walked towards him.

"Hey, Tony."

"Hey. So, this is Beany. He's doing the job with us."

Micky nodded and Beany nodded back. A little short guy with stocky legs. Micky hoped Beany could run fast if they had to make a quick get-away. Then he thought about the name, Beany. So, he would be Bean? Micky smiled.

"You all set Micky?"

"Yeah, I'm good. We taking your car or what?"

"No, no cars. We're on foot for this one. Just follow me, I know all the back alleys. The place we're going to is just five minutes from here. Leave your car, mine's over there, and we'll run back here and go our separate ways."

"Wait...wait a minute. No cars? Are you nuts? How are we gonna carry the stuff and run?"

"That's why we have Beany. He's a good runner and can carry stuff, heavy stuff, too."

Beany did a muscle man pose to prove Tony's point.

"I don't know. I'm not liking this."

"So, what, you out now?" Micky had that uneasy feeling again. He needed some reassurance this was going to be a profitable job for him since it was sounding like a job where he might get caught.

"Now, how do you know there are going to be high-end cars there?"

"I told you Micky, these pimps and big spenders visit this whore house and they all drive these big-ass luxury cars. They'll all be busy inside, if you know what I mean, and no one will even know what happened. We're just taking the hub caps. That's it, nothing else. They'll go buy some new ones tomorrow. Did you bring your crowbar and other stuff?"

"Yeah, yeah, I'm all set. I have what I need. This isn't my first rodeo."

"Okay then, let's go."

They walked for several blocks, trying their best to stick to the shadows, to the street with the house that Tony had marked as their target. They casually walked down the opposite side of the street checking out the cars. Tony was right: Mercedes, Lincolns, and Cadillacs lined the street. There were even a couple of Jags and a BMW. Micky felt his heart pounding in his chest. He thought it would pop right through his shirt.

"You set?" Tony whispered as they checked up and down the street looking for anyone. A lot of laughing and music poured out of the house but no one was on the street. The three thieves got down low and going from car to car, started popping off the hub caps as quickly and quietly as possible. Beany's job, Micky found out, was to collect the hub caps. That's all he did. He went back and forth from Micky to Tony, stuffing hub caps into the two big canvas bags he had brought with him. He definitely had a system and it seemed to work just fine.

Micky was finishing up his third car when someone yelled. He wasn't sure if it was Tony and he stood up to look around.

"What are you doing there? Hey! Get away from that car!" Micky ducked back down behind the car. He didn't know what to do. Neither Tony nor Beany were anywhere to be seen. One of Beany's bags was sitting on the ground next to him with the hub caps from just two cars. Micky decided to pick it up and run for it. He grabbed the bag and as he ran, trying to stay low, Tony and Beany came out from behind the BMW and ran in front of him.

They heard shots.

"What the fuck!" Tony ran faster. Beany, right behind Tony, picked up his pace. Micky tried to keep up but two more shots rang out and Micky heard as much as felt a dull thud in his back. The bag slipped off his shoulder as he fell to the ground, the hub caps spilling out and circling around his head.

# Special Acknowledgements

First and foremost, I must always thank and be forever grateful to my extremely talented and always loving husband, Jim Fontaine. He is always there to help and support me in whatever endeavor I choose to pursue. Fortunately, he is as well-read as I am and I trust his reviews and edits to my work as much as I would trust any other professional.

Thank you to the people who took time to read through my novel and give me valuable feedback. Valerie Cooper and John Perron were particularly helpful. I am forever indebted to the time and effort you both took to help make this novel the best that it can be.

I also need to thank and acknowledge all the people who inspired each story in this book. Of course, many of them are created from my own endlessly deep well of characters. Although much of the writing has been enhanced with my own prosaic style, many people that I knew, as it is with most authors, were the impetus for me to even begin thinking about a story. Whether good or bad, each story needed to be told. And I hope they're seen as accurate portrayals of the lives many are living in this diverse and often unfair world in which we find ourselves.

# About the Author

DJ Geribo, self-published author and fine artist, lives in rural New Hampshire near Lake Winnipesaukee. After pursuing fine art for many years, she decided to focus on her writing and has completed several children's books, 'Eddie Easel and the Case of the Missing Green', 'Mouse Bound', and a middle-grade book, 'The House at the Top of the Trees'. She has also written a non-fiction book about one of her dogs that contracted a life-threatening disease, 'The Miracle Dog'. Her more recent books include a collection of literary short stories in 'Seven Storied Houses', and a collection of memories compiled from childhood events in 'Me and Them'. 'The Mart' is her seventh book.

Besides writing, which keeps DJ very busy, she also enjoys reading, of course, painting, exercise in many forms from lifting weights, e-bike riding, golfing in the summer with her husband, snowshoeing in the winter months, and walking any time of year. She also loves just hanging out with her Pomeranian and her Cockatoo.

DJ's books can be purchased at any of the following:  the author's website at www.DJGeribo.com,  BBD Publishing's website at www.BBDPublishing.com and from Amazon where you can also purchase a few select titles in Kindle format.

To learn about her latest and forthcoming books, visit her website and join her e-mail list or visit BBD Publishing's website.

# Other Books by DJ Geribo

*Me & Them*: A memoir like none you've ever read before.
If you grew up during the 50's and 60's, you'll feel right at home
in this collection of daily life events. Some will make you laugh
while others may make you cry. But you won't leave this
collection without reminiscing about your own childhood
memories.
Softcover - $15.95


*Seven Storied Houses*: A house isn't always a good indication
of the kind of life that is lived by the people who occupy it. A
mansion doesn't mean a happy family, nor is a much-in-need-
of-repair home indication of a life of misery. Both are full of
memories and only the occupants can decide if they will be
good or bad.
Softcover - $15.95


*The Miracle Dog*: When the author's dog, Kameko,
collapsed into her arms one summer morning, she knew
something was very wrong. A trip to the vet confirmed a life-
threatening diagnosis with DJ's precious Pomeranian spending
nearly a week in an ICU at an emergency vet hospital that
included four blood transfusions. After many almost daily trips
back to the hospital, finally a combination of medicine saw DJ's
beloved Pom back on the road to recovery.
Softcover - $16.95


*Mouse Bound*: A story that came about after a mouse set up
residence in the author's studio. After live-catching and driving
the mouse to another location, she imagined the adventures
he'd have experienced in returning to the best and only home
he'd ever known, back in her studio.
Softcover - $10.95

*Eddie Easel and the Case of the Missing Green*: A creative children's story that teaches a child the basics of art and painting all through an engaging mystery. A story any child will love and one that may even start your child on an artistic career path.
Hardcover - $17.95 – Exclusively through BBD Publishing

*The House at the Top of the Trees*: While riding their bikes, Nat and Devon spot a house that appears to be sitting at the top of a tree. Curiously, they find a way to get there and discover a world unlike anything they've ever known before, a place where all of their dreams come true. Is it safe to stay or should they return home to their hard-working single mom who does her best to support her children who mean the world to her?
Softcover – $16.95

**Coming Soon!**

*Useful Things*: Seth and Jill move into the rental cottage owned by the older couple who occupy the mansion that dwarfs their modest guest house. While Seth and Jill each pursue their own artistic interests, a series of unusual events occur causing the young couple to question the motives of their landlords. Are they friends? Foes? Or, is something else the root cause of the strange happenings?

*Deep Lake House*: A unique collection of stories as told by a most unusual narrator, the House. Told over the life of the House, the stories highlight some of the most memorable people who stayed at Deep Lake House.

All of DJ's book can be purchased at www.BBDPublishing.com

Selected titles can be purchased on www.amazon.com in either paperback or Kindle editions.

# Leave Us a Review

Did you like "The Mart"?  BBD Publishing would love to hear your thoughts on this and any of the other books by author DJ Geribo you've read.

Visit www.BBDPublishing.com and on the home page, click on the 'Submit Comment' button in the right-hand column under the Readers' Comments.  This will take you to the 'Submit Your Reader's Comments' form where you can share your comments about this or other books by DJ Geribo.

If you purchased this book on Amazon, please leave an Amazon Review to help other readers find and enjoy DJ's books.

Thank you for your interest in DJ Geribo's books.

www.ingramcontent.com/pod-product-compliance
Lightning Source LLC
Chambersburg PA
CBHW020327120726
47904CB00002B/310